Alex Shaw spent the second half of the 1990s in Kyiv, Ukraine, teaching Drama and running his own business consultancy before being headhunted for a division of Siemens. The next few years saw him doing business for the company across the former USSR, the Middle East, and Africa.

Cold Blood, *Cold Black* and *Cold East* are commercially published by HarperCollins (HQ Digital) in English and Luzifer Verlag in German.

Alex, his wife and their two sons divide their time between homes in Kyiv, Ukraine, Worthing, England and Doha, Qatar. Follow Alex on twitter: @alexshawhetman or find him on Facebook.

Also by Alex Shaw

Cold Black
Cold East

Cold Blood

ALEX SHAW

ONE PLACE. MANY STORIES

HQ
An imprint of HarperCollins*Publishers* Ltd
1 London Bridge Street
London SE1 9GF

This paperback edition 2018

First published in Great Britain by
HQ, an imprint of HarperCollins*Publishers* Ltd 2018

Copyright © Alex Shaw 2018

Alex Shaw asserts the moral right to be
identified as the author of this work.
A catalogue record for this book is
available from the British Library.

ISBN: 9780008310172

Hetman – the title of the highest military commander, after the monarch, in fifteenth- to eighteenth-century Poland, Ukraine and the Grand Duchy of Lithuania.

Prologue

20th September 1996. SchreinerBank, Poznan, Poland

He set his watch, pulled down the black balaclava and stepped out of the van. As one, the men stormed the bank. '*Na Podloge Natychmiast!*' On the floor now – the Polish was precise, clipped and accented. With a swift bark from a Kalashnikov, the sole SchreinerBank guard was neutralised.

Shocked customers screamed and threw themselves down as two men in black coveralls pointed their automatic weapons; the dead guard was evidence they weren't afraid to use them. Two other assaulters wearing empty backpacks vaulted over the counter and headed towards the safe. A fifth and sixth sat across the street in two high-powered BMW saloons. Parked facing down cobbled side streets, the cars were poised for a speedy exfiltration. At either end of the main street identical Opel vans stood, packed with Russian-made plastic explosives. No further words were exchanged as each member of the assault team took up their prearranged positions.

Bull had watched and waited for months for this shipment to arrive, had persuaded an 'eager' government employee to give him the building's schematics, and was now ready to collect his four million Deutsche Marks. A stunned silence took hold of the banking hall, broken only by the whimpering of a youth. Bull looked down at him in disgust. Seven years ago, such a boy would have been his to command in Afghanistan.

Police Training Area, Poznan, Poland

Aidan Snow sat on the wooden bench and stirred his tea. If it hadn't been for the sound of gunfire and smell of cordite, the training camp would have been idyllic. As part of a four-man training team, Snow had been in Poland for over two months advising the Polish Police *Pododdziay Antyterrorystyczne* (counterterrorist unit). Now the Cold War was well and truly over, his unit, the 22nd Special Air Service Regiment (SAS), was in demand as the governments of newly independent states attempted to stem the tide of international organised crime and terrorism. He closed his eyes; the last rays of the summer sun seemed reluctant to leave Poznan.

At twenty-four, Aidan Snow had been deployed to numerous hostile locations – some overt, such as Northern Ireland, and others strictly covert; some domestic, some international. His time with 'the regiment' had been eventful all right – not the life his parents would have wished for the son of a teacher and a diplomat.

He looked on as the rest of his team showed the Polish trainees the correct way to track and hit a moving target. A target had been attached to a pulley, which was strung between several trees. Some bright spark had pasted a photograph of Andreas Möller to it in a direct reference to the English soccer team's defeat at Euro '96. That summer, famously, Möller had scored the sixth-round penalty that had stopped England getting to the final. The trainees thought this was very funny. The SAS did not.

The team had made some real progress; for a police SWAT

unit they were good – ready, in fact, should a real incident arise. Training was still needed, however, to turn this SWAT unit into a truly elite CT team. Their next exercise, which Snow would lead, would utilise 'The Killing House' and hone Close Quarter Battle (CQB) techniques.

The regiment's killing house in the UK was a two-storey building. It was designed and furnished to look like an average two-up two-down, but had special rubber-coated walls to absorb bullets, extractor fans to clear out cordite, and video cameras in corners to record and play back the action in the rooms. Each room had at least one metal target and live rounds were used. The SAS team had built a less elaborate, mini version at the camp to train the Polish operatives in how to enter a room, assess the situation and neutralise any threats. Inspector Zatwarnitski, head of the Polish CT unit, had said a permanent killing house would be built to UK standards. It hadn't happened yet.

Snow sipped his tea. It wasn't a bad gig. The Poles were quick learners, as most of them, unlike their British Police counterparts, had already served time in the Polish army before joining up. This gave them an understanding, if somewhat rudimentary, of military procedure and firearms handling. Several of the men spoke passable English, which was good, as none of the SAS team spoke Polish! In cases of misunderstanding, Snow resorted to his Russian, which most of the Poles spoke as their first 'foreign' language.

'My men impress you, Snow?'

'They are very promising, Inspector.'

'Good.' Zatwarnitski sat. 'History is a funny thing. A few years ago, your being here would have been unthinkable; the West was the enemy. Our hope, our future, our security lay with our Soviet protectors. And then? Like dominos, it all fell. To be candid, we never really wanted to be on the Soviet side. That is why we need you here, Snow; we are tired of the old methods and, of course, want to learn from the best.'

Snow smiled politely. He had been present when Zatwarnitski made the same speech on his visit to Hereford, courtesy of HM Government. The Pole meant every word and fancied himself as a bit of a public speaker.

'Our biggest fear now is our old protector – Mother Russia. She is wounded and a wounded bear is the most dangerous kind. We really do appreciate your team, Snow.' The older man reached out to shake the SAS trooper by the hand.

'Thank you, Inspector, but we're just doing our jobs. It's your men that need to be thanked for working so hard.'

'Modesty is something I hope you also teach.' Zatwarnitski raised his mug in mock salute.

A shout came from the communications room; both men stood. Moments before, the radio had fallen from the operator's hand. The call was from central despatch. Armed men had entered SchreinerBank on Wroclawska Street. They were the nearest specialist unit, could they assist?

Zatwarnitski looked Snow in the eye. 'Are my men ready?'

'Yes.'

Minutes later, on Zatwarnitski's orders, the Poles and their SAS training team were in a convoy being led by a very nervous recruit. After eight weeks on the job, this recruit's first real 'action' was as the lead driver on what the SAS referred to as an 'immediate'. The young officer concentrated on threading his way through the traffic in his new police Omega. Never mind that his siren was blazing; the drivers of Poznan were none too happy to yield. In the passenger seat sat Zatwarnitski, with Snow, who trusted only his own driving, sitting behind.

Wroclawska Street, Poznan

Bull checked his watch. The local militia would be there in five more minutes. A dull thud came from the back room – his men

4

had blown open the safe. Another sound registered in the distance. *Sirens?* They were early! The men from the safe detail lumbered into view, weighted down, their Bergen packs now full. Giving the signal, he and his 2IC, Oleg, tossed smoke grenades into the centre of the room and out onto the street. It was now time to leave. He felt for the remote detonator, then the two men took up sentry positions on either side of the road to cover the bagmen as they sprinted across, partly concealed by the billowing white smoke. The heavily laden Bergen packs were hauled into the waiting cars.

The recruit slued around the tight bend and into Wroclawska Street, where he saw smoke pouring from the bank, and men… men in black with guns. Forgetting his training, the young Pole panicked and gunned the accelerator, sirens still blazing.

Bull looked up. '*Blat!*' This wasn't meant to happen; they weren't meant to be here so soon. He realised these weren't normal police vehicles. The lead car hadn't yet reached the van, but it would at any second. Dropping to one knee, he pressed the button on the remote detonator as his men opened fire.

The second car came into view. The explosion tore through the Opel van, hurling debris across both lanes of the road. The full force of the blast caught the second Omega, tossing it up and sideways like a child's plaything. It smashed into the façade of the post office. The lead car punched through the smoke, the recruit screaming as he lost control of his car. The force of the blast sent his charge headlong into the entrance of the bank. He and Zatwarnitski were killed instantly. At the end of the block the other van erupted, levelling a newspaper kiosk and gutting a bakery. The first BMW roared off and away.

As the remainder of his men delivered suppressing fire, Bull noticed movement in the first Omega. He moved to the devastated vehicle. The front of the car had been turned into a mass of twisted steel and broken glass but… a passenger in the back was alive!

The man was dressed in his own black coveralls. Bull looked down at the young, ashen face with dark-brown eyes. *Who are you?* he thought.

The mouth moved and, through the pain, a raspy voice whispered, 'Piss off!'

Had he spoken in English? Who were these police who had arrived so quickly? The man tried to move but was pinned to the seat; blood seeped from his mouth and ears. This hero would die soon regardless. Bull pulled up his balaclava and smiled, letting the boy look at the last face he would see on this earth. Shots zipped past his head. More black-clad figures were running through the smouldering debris, returning fire.

'*Blat!*' He cursed again and ran back to his car. Tyres screeching, they disappeared into the suburbs. Tauras 'Bull' Pashinski fell back against the leather seat and closed his eyes. He was now a rich man.

Chapter 1

July 2006. Pushkinskaya Street, Kyiv, Ukraine.

He was woken by the early morning sun warming his face and the excited barks of his neighbour's dog scampering around on the communal landing, waiting for his master to lock the door and join him. Outside, three floors below, the swish of the street sweepers tidying up the pavements with their birch-twig brooms echoed gently. Aidan Snow opened his eyes and tried to focus on the ceiling. Gradually the image sharpened as his eyes became accustomed to the bright sunlight. He rolled onto his side and his nose found the empty glass bottle of Desna Cognac nestling between his pillow and the arm of the bed settee. Snow was wide awake now and knew that, whatever he tried, he wouldn't be able to sleep. He was a morning person, which wasn't exactly a blessing after nights out. Swinging his legs out, he sat up. Never again, he told himself, and not for the first time. The parquet floor was sticky from spilt beer. Snow walked to the balcony doors and opened them, breathing in the fresh morning air. The street-cleaner van approached from the far end of Pushkinskaya Street with hoses spraying water over the dusty road and pavement. Kyiv glowed with pride in the morning sun, the workers

7

below intent on making her even prouder. A well-oiled Soviet machine that still worked fifteen years after the Union had ceased to.

Snow leaned against the balcony railings and gazed at the Ukrainian capital city he now called home; he had yet to tire of the view. To the left, his street, Pushkinskaya, crossed Prorizna Street and carried on downhill through a high, ornate, double arch into Independence Square. To the right it also sloped downhill, crossing both Bogdan Khmelnitsky Street and Boulevard Taras Shevchenko, before ending at Shevchenko Park and University. These were named after the great Ukrainian writer, their equivalent of Shakespeare, and not the Chelsea footballer, as his pal Michael had insisted. Carefree locals drinking beer and enjoying life were to be found at these meeting places at either end of Pushkinskaya, not to mention the bars that dotted its entire length. For the first time since Poland, Snow was at peace, or as near to it as possible. He took another deep breath – at peace, that was, except for the hangover he was battling.

It had been another night of cheap beer and ex-pat posturing at his favourite bar, Eric's Bierstube. There had been the usual faces: the TEFL teachers sitting in one corner, trying it on with their most promising or largest-breasted students, and the so-called 'serious businessmen' in the other, downing shots as toasts to clinch deals. The rest of the clientele had been made up of either 'new Ukrainians', trying to look casual in their Boss suits, or local university students sipping slowly.

Snow had sat in his usual corner, his back against the exposed brickwork, and looked on with Mitch Turney and Michael Jones, who played their game of 'guess the bra size'. As always, the Obolon beer had flowed freely. Michael had guessed at least one correct size before being called home by his wife, Ina. Mitch and Snow had then adjourned to the flat, where one last drink had taken three hours and resulted in five empty beer bottles and the end of the Desna. Mitch had fallen into a taxi and Snow had fallen on the floor.

He took one more deep breath and walked to the kitchen, collecting the empty bottles en route. His head swam. Never again. It was at times like this that being single was both a blessing and a curse. He had no one to tell him not to drink like a fool until all hours, but no one to come back to. So he drank and partied like, as Mitch put it, 'a college student on midterm break in Tijuana'.

Snow padded around his functional kitchen and removed a carton of yogurt from the fridge, which contained the bachelor's bare minimum: a block of cheese, milk, yogurt and a hunk of ham. The space usually taken up by beer had been liberated. He sipped the thick local strawberry yogurt straight from the milk-style carton and opened the kitchen window. July, and Kyiv showed no signs of cooling down.

He scratched the mosquito bite on his left buttock. The heat he liked, the heat he enjoyed, but the damn mozzies could be a pain in the arse! They seemed to hide during the day, only to break in and assault him at night if he forgot to plug in the repellent gizmo.

'You've grown soft,' he told himself. 'How did you ever pass selection; a man who complains about a few bites?' The former SAS soldier smiled to himself. 'Perhaps I have, but it bloody itches.' Snow pulled open a draw and took out a packet of pills. He popped two and chased them with yogurt. Never on an empty stomach, his mum said.

Saturday morning and in a couple of hours the streets of the capital would be teeming with people. The Kyivites shopping or promenading along the city's main boulevard – Khreshatik Street – and the visitors from other regions come to sightsee. Kyiv – he loved her. She was graceful, cultured and beautiful, yet overlooked by the West. He hadn't abandoned her for the holidays like his fellow teachers, but stayed to savour the hot Ukrainian summer.

This would be the start of his third year teaching at Podilsky School International and he felt at home. Kyiv had been the third-largest city of the mighty Soviet Union, but here in the centre, for all its grand buildings, it still retained a village-like atmosphere, with its inhabitants living just off the main shopping streets. Snow hated towns but Kyiv was different, with its vast number of trees – more than any other city in Europe (a local had told him) – several large parks and a river (again, according to the same source, the widest in Europe) running through the middle. It was both town and country in one. Snow was the only foreigner in his building and Kyiv wasn't yet spoilt by tourism. It was rare to hear a foreign voice on the street, and those he did hear he usually recognised, by sight at least, as belonging to ex-pats or diplomats.

Just over one more month and school would start again. These drinking binges would have to stop, or at least be confined to the weekends. But not yet. He finished his yogurt and dressed in his running gear. Saturday or not, he wouldn't allow himself to miss a run. It was a rule he had learnt in the SAS and one he wouldn't forsake now he was a civilian.

Snow took the steps down to the ground floor to warm up his leg muscles before starting his ritual of stretches in the street outside. It was just after 8 a.m. – later than he normally ran, but, as it was a Saturday, there were fewer people up. Running was something that had become second nature to him; it helped clear his mind. He ran most mornings, although this was tough in the Ukrainian winter, with an average temperature of -10°C. It wasn't the cold that made it difficult, but the ice. Walking up and down the city's hills was treacherous and running became suicidal. Thus far, Snow had found the solution by running around one of the city's central stadiums, either 'Dynamo', home to the famed football team, or 'Respublikanski', built and used for the 1980 Moscow Olympics. The fact that both of these were open to the general public was another Soviet legacy he embraced.

Satisfied he'd stretched enough, he moved off at a steady pace. He ran down Pushkinskaya until he hit Maidan. Dodging the stallholders setting up their kiosks, he pumped his legs up the steep Kostyolna Street. Cresting the hill he entered Volodymyrska Hirka Park. The morning air hadn't yet become dusty and a breeze blew in from the Dnipro River below. He was taking his weekend route, as he had nowhere to be in a hurry. Reaching the railings overlooking the river, he turned left, following the footpath. The park followed the river until it abruptly ended at the mammoth Ministry of Internal Affairs headquarters. As Snow ran past the building and towards the British Embassy in the adjoining street, he was once again taken by the sheer size of the place. Looking much like the Arc de Triomphe, but larger, he estimated, the Ukrainian government building wasn't on any international tourist 'must see' lists, but he made a point of staring none the less. It was one of the many things that made him want to stay in Kyiv.

Snow had grown up with a love for the unusual. His father had been cultural attaché for the British Embassy, Moscow, in the mid to late Eighties. As such, Snow had been at the embassy school there for much of his formative adolescent years. The upshot of this was that Snow's Moscow-accented Russian was all but flawless. Ignoring his parents' protestations that he go to university, he had joined the army immediately after his A-levels. Turning down a chance at officer training, he'd completed the minimum three-year service requirement before successfully passing 'Selection' for the SAS. He'd wanted to be a 'badged member' ever since seeing the very public 'Princes Gate' hostage rescue (Operation Nimrod) at the Iranian Embassy as a nine-year-old in 1980. His parents had laughed it off and bought him a black balaclava and toy gun, but, as the years passed, Snow's desire to join only increased. Then he was in. His boyhood dream fulfilled and, although begrudgingly, he knew his parents had been a bit proud. Then it all went wrong.

Snow slowed to a walk as he entered Andrivskyi Uzviz. The steep cobbled street, lined with souvenir stalls, art galleries and bars, was quite capable of inflicting a broken ankle on the unwary. He descended the hill. His right thigh had started to throb. The sensation always brought back memories of the accident in Poland, the unbearable pain he had felt, pinned to the backseat of the car, unable to move, unable to reach for a weapon to defend himself. The sound of flames and the vicious scent of petrol filling his lungs. Then that face, the serpentine eyes that had looked into his and pronounced sentence upon him.

Snow shivered in spite of the warm morning air. After the accident the doctors had said he would always walk with a limp; that the bone would be weakened and that the muscles might not knit back together. They advised that he be taken off active duty, given a desk or other duties. He ignored them and attempted to defy all medical opinion by pushing himself harder than he'd ever thought possible. He spent hours in rehabilitation, first with PT instructors and then, later, on his own. He was twenty-four years old and a member of the 22nd Special Air Service Regiment; no one was going to tell him what he could or couldn't do.

His effort paid off and the regiment doctor had signed him off as fit for active duty. No limp, just a scar. However, the one thing Snow hadn't admitted to anyone, least of all himself, was the toll taken by the mental scar. The nightmares, for want of a more macho term, that prevented him from sleeping and turned him from jovial troop member into withdrawn loner. Snow had sought professional help and then accepted the truth. He left the regiment within the year with an honourable discharge, his military career cut short.

He felt his leg ease as he reached the bottom of the hill and swore at himself for yet again allowing the past, something he couldn't change, to ruin a perfectly good day. The sun was now higher in the sky as he jogged through central Podil and headed towards Hydropark, the largest island and park in the Kyiv stretch of the Dnipro River. Perhaps he'd risk a swim?

Tiraspol, capital city of Transdniester, disputed autonomous region of Moldova

The two men embraced like the old comrades they indeed were. Bull regarded the face of his friend and former Spetsnaz brother Ivan Lesukov. 'You have grown fat, old man.'

'And you ugly.' Lesukov laughed heartily. 'I see that Sergeant Zukauskas has not changed – you still look like a pig!'

'That is why the Muslims hated me so much!' Oleg, the barrel-chested Lithuanian winked.

Lesukov raised his glass and the others followed. 'To fallen comrades.' The vodka was cold, having been stored in the fridge Lesukov kept in his office.

'You have an empire here, Ivan,' Bull said, congratulating his friend.

'I am the King of Chairs,' Lesukov replied, spreading his palms at the window, which looked out over the factory floor below. 'The main industries of our country are furniture and electronics, but we can't sell abroad because of those bastards in Chisinau.' He shrugged. 'Our products do not carry the Moldovan government stamp and, as our country of Transdniester is not recognised outside of its own borders, we cannot sell.' Lesukov refilled the glasses. 'But I don't care a shit about the electronics or even my chairs. What I have brought you here for today is to discuss how you can help an old comrade with his export business.' He raised his glass. 'To success.' Again, the glasses were drained.

Bull spoke first. 'I understand that, of late, you have been having some logistical problems?'

'Our "friends", the Russians, are understanding, if not supportive, of our "specific" situation. They let my goods pass freely through the security zone. In fact, some of my goods even originate from the weapons they are "peacekeeping over". He tapped his nose with the end of his index finger. 'So, with the Russians, here in Transdniester, I have no problem. They are good boys. It is the Moldavians to the west and the Ukrainians to the east that I am having problems with.' He balled his fist.

Tensions between Transdniester and her neighbours, Moldova and Ukraine, had been high since Transdniester separatists, with Russian support, broke away from Moldova in 1992, declaring independence. The short civil war that ensued had left more than 1,500 dead. An uneasy truce, brought about by Russian 'peacekeepers', had stabilised the region since then. In a strange turn of events, Europe's biggest Soviet Army weapons cache was now to be found not in 'Mother Russia', but near the Transdniestern town of Kolbasna, guarded by the two thousand Russian soldiers acting as 'peacekeepers'.

A 'confidential' 1998 agreement between Russia's then prime minister, Viktor Chernomyrdin, and Igor Smirnov, the self-appointed president of Transdniester, to share profits from the sale of 40,000 tons of 'unnecessary' arms and ammunition had made Lesukov and men like him very wealthy. However, once a copy of this agreement had come into the hands of the Associated Press, there had been protests in Washington and a scandal in the European media. Russia had denied the story as preposterous and Ukraine had condemned any potential arms dealing, stepping up the size of their border guards units.

Lesukov was beginning to feel the pinch as he found it harder and harder to get his goods out of the country.

Lesukov paused and refilled the glasses. 'How many of the Orly still serve with you?' It was a question to Bull. *Orly*, the Russian for 'eagles', wasn't a regimental title but a traditional name used to signify fearless fighting men.

'Of my Brigada, six; however, since becoming freelance we have many more good men.'

After leaving the Red Army Spetsnaz, Bull had recruited other former 'Special Forces' soldiers from numerous Soviet Republics. These were some of the most highly trained soldiers in the world, yet had been discarded when the Union crumbled. He had bought their loyalty for little more than a few hundred dollars each; as a hero of Afghanistan he already had their respect. For the past fifteen years he had built a reputation in several war zones as a ruthless leader, mercenary and surprisingly good business facilitator. He had brokered arms deals with the Mujahedeen, rebels in Georgia's breakaway Abkhazia region, and insurgents in Africa, to name but a few. Now it was only natural that one of the main suppliers of weapons should want his direct assistance.

'What had you in mind, my old friend?' Bull asked.

Lesukov smiled, raised his glass again. 'To women.' The other two followed. It wasn't that they especially wanted to honour women, just a Soviet tradition for every third toast. He placed his hands flat on the metal desk.

'The Ukrainians have their own group of Orly, called the "SOCOL". They are a highly effective anti-smuggling and anti-organised-crime unit. This I could normally admire; however, they have now turned their focus on my shipments. In the last two months alone they have intercepted three of them...' His voice trailed off as he totted up on his large fingers how much he had lost, then doubled it. 'They have cost me almost three million American dollars in profit!' His face had grown red and any hint of levity had passed.

He sighed and remembered the dusty mountains of Afghanistan some eighteen years before, and the young Spetsnaz captain who had fought next to him. 'You were the best in Kabul, saved us all. Now I ask you to save me again. I want you to stop this SOCOL team once and for all.'

Oleg, who had listened quietly, let his tongue run along the outside of his top lip. He loved action and had grown weary of 'business'. To take on a real target was what he lived for. He looked at his CO.

Bull folded his arms and nodded. 'It can be done, but of course there is a price.'

Lesukov's eyes glinted; he had anticipated this. 'I will give you ten per cent of each shipment that passes successfully into Ukraine.'

'Thank you. While that is a good offer, my friend, can I ask if you find it easy to export your "goods" from Ukraine?'

Lesukov paused and in that millisecond confirmed what Bull had expected. 'They are squeezing me from both ends. At one end I have the SOCOL and at the other border guards, customs officials who will not accept payments and...'

'Thirty per cent, Ivan.'

'What?'

'Thirty per cent and I take care of imports into Ukraine and exports out of the territory.' Bull folded his arms.

Lesukov scratched his nose. 'My margins are not that high, Tauras. I can give you twenty.'

'Twenty-five per cent and we can start today.' Bull held out his right hand. Lesukov momentarily paused then grasped it with his own.

'Deal. But you will not start today. Today we have a little fun, eh? I know an interesting club!' He refilled the glasses and then placed a call on his office phone.

This time Bull made the toast. 'To business.'

They drank. There was a knock at the door; Lesukov beckoned a young man into the room. 'Gentlemen, this is my nephew, Arkadi. He will take you to the hotel.'

'Zdravstvyite.' Arkadi Cheban greeted both men in Russian as he shook their hands. 'This way, please.'

Lesukov regarded his two comrades as they were led down

the steps and out of the factory. He had once been a Spetsnaz warrior himself, but now – he held his considerable gut – he was the director of a chair factory. Officially.

Regus Business Centre, London, UK

The City Chamber of Commerce and Industry pre-mission briefing for the forthcoming Trade Mission to Ukraine was held at a Regus business centre in Central London. The fourteen participating companies had, in the main, sent their representatives on this wet July day. Alistair Vickers was one of the first to arrive and had taken a seat, as befitted a man from the embassy and official guest speaker, at the head of the long oval table. To his right sat Nicola Coen, the mission leader who would be accompanying the group to Kyiv. On her right sat the official mission travel agent, Wendy Jenkins from Watergate Travel. Vickers had made a joke about the company name but, in Wendy's case, it had been heard by ears that hadn't understood. Nicola had smiled and looked down at her papers, not wanting to make fun of her 'travel management provider'.

The seat to Vickers's left was empty and reserved for the other guest speaker, Bhavesh Malik. Vickers had met him once before and on that occasion he had also been late. He picked up his copy of the handouts that accompanied the briefing and read the information about Bhavesh's father, Jasraj, which had been lifted from the company's own unapologetic website:

'*NewSound – a success story! At the age of fifteen, Jasraj moved to the UK – East Sussex, Portslade, in fact – to work for his uncle's hearing aid dispensing business. But by twenty-one, 'Jas', as he became known to all his friends and customers, was qualified as an audiologist and set to work designing his own aids. These were some of the first BTE (Behind the Ear) models to go on sale in the UK! Now, after forty-seven years of hard work, Jas's front-room workshop has turned into three manufacturing plants in the UK, Pakistan and Ukraine, producing high-quality hearing aids and covert listening devices.'*

Vickers skipped the more self-congratulatory bits and focused on the part the missioners had come to learn about:

'...Opened in 1999, the Odessa manufacturing site is based in what was formally a top-secret Soviet telecommunications plant. Initially aided by European Union money and taking advantage of Investment Zone status granted to the area by the Ukrainian government, it soon started mass production...'

Vickers replaced the handout on the table and picked up the mission brochure detailing the various British companies ever-hopeful of selling their particular brand of goods into Ukraine. These companies included, among others, a manufacturer of industrial chemical metering equipment, a management training consultancy, a nickel alloy welding supplier, a pharmaceutical manufacturer and distributor, a language school, a giftware company and, much to his amusement, a Savile Row tailor.

Looking around the room he saw that most of the missioners had now arrived and were just waiting for the final two to finish pouring their coffee and deciding which biscuits to put on their saucers. The tall double doors opened and in stepped Bhavesh Malik. He smiled at Nicola and Vickers and, after placing his umbrella in the stand and brushing the rain from his lapels, took his place.

Nicola started the briefing. 'Thank you all for coming today. I know that, for some of you, London isn't the easiest of places to get to. As you'll see, each of you has a briefing pack which includes our itinerary for today, the proofs of the mission brochure, and copies of the information Wendy and I will be giving you. But first I want to start by introducing our two guest speakers for today. Alistair Vickers is the commercial attaché at the British Embassy in Kyiv. He'll be giving a business overview of Kyiv and the rest of Ukraine.'

Vickers smiled and looked around the room, finding a sea of expectant faces.

'Bav Malik is managing director of NewSound UK and his company is somewhat of an export success story. He'll be letting you in on the secrets of how to make your business work in Ukraine. But first to practical matters, Wendy here, who I believe most of you will have spoken to on the telephone, has some good news. Wendy?'

Wendy unfolded her arms and opened an envelope; her accent, much to Vickers's chagrin, was estuary English. 'I'm happy to say that Air Ukraine International has now confirmed your seats and sent me the tickets. You'll be pleased to know that I've managed to get you all complimentary access to the business lounge at Gatwick and on your departure from Boryspil Airport.'

Vickers sipped his tea and listened as Wendy handed out tickets and, together with Nicola, went through the travel itinerary. These were the usual points that needed to be clarified, but Vickers didn't know why he had to sit through it. Nonetheless he pretended to look interested and not stare at the clock, its hands moving ever so slowly, at the opposite end of the room. The technicalities over with, the floor was his. Vickers delivered the prepared FCO (Foreign and Commonwealth Office) statement on Ukraine, told the story of the country since independence in 1991, and gave an overview of the investment climate, current government and, of course, the inherent risks of doing business in an emerging market. 'I am now happy to answer any questions you might have.'

'I saw a lot at the time about the Orange Revolution, in the press and on television.' It was the language-school rep – or Director of International Studies, to quote his mission entry. 'What do you think will be the long-term outcome of this and what will be the impact?'

Vickers nodded. He, of course, had two opinions on this: the official HM Government line and his own personal one. He decided to live dangerously. 'As I'm sure you must be aware, the former president had been in power for two terms so couldn't sit for a third. More reforms were needed and the new government promised to introduce these. The new president, Victor Yushenko, was a former prime minister and head of the National Bank of Ukraine. His party came to power representing reform and I believe that's what got the people's vote. The main rival candidate for his presidency, you'll remember, was the then prime minister, Victor Yanukovich. He was being backed by the then president.'

'Leonid Kuchma?'

'Yes, Kuchma. When Yushenko got elected, he wanted to form closer ties with the West; however, that was over a year ago. In the recent parliamentary elections, Yanukovich gained the most votes and now he's prime minister once again. He, it's fair to say, would rather strengthen ties with Moscow.'

The Director of International Studies raised his eyebrows. 'Do you think the parliamentary election was rigged like the first presidential election was?'

Vickers realised he was on thin ice. 'I can't comment on that. I think the electorate might have expected change to come too fast. Perhaps that's why we now have both Yushenko and Yanukovich, as it were, "in power". This, however, is only my opinion. The reforms are still going through and so far the business environment has seemed to improve. Yushenko, at least, is working hard to attract foreign trade and investment.'

The next question came from the pharmaceutical rep. 'In other markets I've visited there have been counterfeit versions of my company's products. Is this likely to be the case in Ukraine?'

'Ukraine is not yet a member of the World Trade Organisation but is hoping to join. It's quite common to see pirated DVDs, CDs and some fashion items in the open-air markets. There are imported medical products from the subcontinent which have been investigated. There are, however, many international brands trading in Ukraine and they've not reported any serious problems, either to myself or the Ukrainian Chamber of Commerce. But that's not to say some counterfeiting doesn't exist.'

The pharmaceutical rep made a note on his pad. The last question came from the gift company's export sales manager: 'Do you like living and working in Ukraine then?'

Vickers looked at the round-faced missioners and felt awkward. He really did like Ukraine but found it hard to put into words. 'I do. Kyiv's apparently got the highest number of chestnut trees of any European capital city, hence the city's leaf emblem. In May especially, when the trees bloom, the city is full of life. There are lots of parks and the old architecture makes it quite picturesque. I really feel it will be an important European city within the next ten to fifteen years. But no "Easy Jet" yet!' He was proud of this joke and it drew a couple of smiles.

It was then the turn of Bav Malik to talk about his company and how, as per the handout, it had taken advantage of a tax-free investment zone and set up a factory near Odessa. He spoke at length about what they had done and how they had done it. This elicited quite a few questions from the assembled party. Finally, the formal part was over and light refreshments and wine were brought into the room. Some of the missioners rushed back to their offices to complete their day's work while others lingered to chat, quiz Nicola and enjoy the complimentary Chardonnay.

Bav cornered Vickers with a glass. 'That went well. I see you didn't mention the cheap beer as the reason you like Ukraine then?' He sipped his free wine.

'I prefer the cheap vodka,' countered Vickers. 'I thought your father was going to be here?'

'He couldn't make it. He had some meetings in Odessa to attend so he deputised me.' It was Jas Malik, father to Bav, founder and chairman of NewSound, who was actually responsible for the success in Ukraine and many of their export markets. Bav, at thirty-seven, had followed his father and would eventually become 'chairman'; his cousin in Pakistan would then be the MD.

'Do you get over to Odessa much?' Vickers knew the answer but had to say something.

'I didn't used to but now they've scrapped the whole "visa" thing it's a lot easier. I can just hop on a plane.'

'That,' said Vickers, 'is the most positive thing the Ukrainians have ever done for tourism. It was originally for the Eurovision Song Contest. Did you see it?'

Bav smirked. 'Not quite my cup of tea.'

'Really?' It was Vickers's.

He let his mind wander back to May the previous year. There had been a real carnival feel to Kyiv, even more so than usual. Vickers had walked along Khreshatik with a broad smile on his face. Closed to traffic every weekend, the boulevard had become a huge pedestrian zone. This was one of the only edicts of the former President Kuchma that had been welcomed. Street entertainers juggled balls and bottles, comedians told anecdotes, tented bars had appeared like mushrooms overnight, and couples strolled from end to end. Many people still wore the orange of the revolution and the new president.

He, however, could not take full credit for the high spirits. That honour was shared with a raven-haired local singer called Ruslana, who, thanks to a very athletic dance routine, had won the 2004 Eurovision Song Contest for Ukraine, bringing the following year's contest to Kyiv. The United Kingdom was in the finals, as of course was host nation Ukraine, with the Orange Revolution's protest song *Razom nas bagato* – 'together we are many'. The song had been sung nightly in Independence Square by thousands in subzero temperatures the previous December to vent national outrage at the 'rigged' election results that had temporarily put Moscow-backed Victor Yanukovich into office.

By May 2005, with Victor Yushenko having been fairly elected, the Eurovision in town, and the world's media focused on them for positive reasons, the population felt huge pride in being Ukrainian. For several days the contestants had rehearsed by day and partied at night, giving impromptu concerts in local bars and clubs to the ever-grateful Kyivites. Vickers loved the Eurovision and had done so for as long as he could remember. His mum had been a fan of Cliff Richard but he preferred Bucks Fizz. This was a secret he didn't care to share.

Brought back to the present, he looked at his watch. 'I'd better thank Nicola.' Vickers held out his hand. 'It was nice to see you again, Bav.'

Bhavesh shook his hand. 'You too, Alistair.'

Vickers left the businessman and crossed the room to where the diminutive girl from Yorkshire was making small talk with several middle-aged men. 'Excuse me, gentlemen, but I must say goodbye to Nicola.'

Nicola looked up at the tall, thin figure and shook his hand with a surprisingly firm grip. 'Thank you ever so much.'

Vickers bowed slightly. 'Delighted. No trouble at all.' He left the business centre and took a cab to Vauxhall Cross. He had another, more important, meeting to attend, this one with HM Secret Intelligence Service.

Chapter 2

The two high-ranking officers from the GRU listened to the sound of boots approaching at a steady pace along the wooden-floored corridor. The colonel took the file the major had given him and looked once more at the release form. He shook his head in dismay. In Soviet times he could have refused point-blank to let such an outstanding young officer go, but this was the new Russia and times had changed. Now a skilled man such as this could earn hundreds of times his current salary in the business world. Russian Military Intelligence couldn't keep him if he didn't want to be kept, and that was the harsh reality of the 'new Russia'.

The doors to the cavernous room were opened by a low-ranking aide and the guest was let in. He drew nearer to the desk before coming to attention and saluting his two superiors.

The colonel returned his salute. 'At ease, Gorodetski. Please sit.'

'Yes, Comrade Colonel.' The young officer sat in the indicated chair.

There was a long pause while the colonel looked at the form

again, then at the man sitting in front of him. 'You are at the end of your second tour of duty, Captain. You have achieved much.'

'Thank you, Comrade Colonel.'

The older man furrowed his brow. 'You are still young; you have an extremely bright military career in front of you. One day you could be sitting here, and have these…' The colonel indicated his rank bars. 'So, that makes me ask why. Why do you not want to extend your duty?'

Sergey Gorodetski looked first at the colonel and then at his major, the man he had originally given his release form to. 'I am grateful for what the Russian Army has done for me but I now wish to pursue other interests. I have been offered an opportunity—'

The colonel snorted and cut him off. 'This is your opportunity, Captain.'

Gorodetski continued. 'With respect, Comrade Colonel, I have something I must do.'

The colonel was not moved. Before him sat a rare breed of soldier, the 'intelligentsia' of Spetsnaz. With his supreme language skills he could pass for a foreign national and was also deadly with a Dragunov sniper rifle. 'I knew your brother. You are better than he was.'

Gorodetski nodded. He didn't know how to take this comment. His brother, too, had been a Spetsnaz officer but he had been killed in Afghanistan. The colonel continued, 'You have made your family very proud and upheld your brother's name. But you can do so much more. Will you not reconsider your decision?' He didn't like to plead but damn it; this man was one of the best he'd ever seen.

Gorodetski shook his head slowly. 'I have made my decision, Comrade Colonel. I am sorry.'

'A Spetsnaz officer should never be sorry.' The colonel held out his hand and the major passed him a pen. He cast one more look at the young officer before signing the form and marking it with the official stamp. All three men stood. The colonel handed Gorodetski the papers. Gorodetski saluted and left the room.

'Fool,' muttered the major.

'Exactly the opposite,' replied the colonel.

Horley Community College, Horley, UK

'My dad says all the French are poofs,' Danny Butterworth stated to the class of fifteen-year-olds.

'Sam knows French, don't ya, Sam!' added his comedy partner, Dale Small.

Samantha was busy reapplying eyeliner and didn't look up from her mirror. '*Voulez-vous couchez avec moi?*'

'Everyone has, you slapper!' Dale shouted.

At the front of the class, Arnaud took a deep breath. 'That is enough!' He slammed the French textbook on the desk and glared at the offending class members. 'I have asked for silence and I will not ask again!' A hand went up at the back of the class. 'Yes, Danny?'

'Which page we on, mister?' Danny replied with a cherubic expression.

Arnaud paused and inwardly sighed before answering. 'Page sixty-nine. *Le Weekend.*'

There were sniggers around the room. 'That's when Sam does her French, sir – at the weekend,' shouted Danny across the classroom.

'Twat!' Sam put down her compact and raised her middle finger.

'Stand up.'

There was a pause and Sam, a heavily made up girl, her hair streaked bleach-blonde, stood up. Arnaud looked her in the eye she held his gaze. 'Wot?'

'What do you mean, "wot"?! I will not tolerate that kind of language in my French class!'

'But it is French, mister,' shouted Dale

'And she is a slapper, sir!' added Danny.

Sam threw her textbook at the two boys. 'Wankers!'

'Get out. Just get out.' Arnaud was turning red. Unbelievable, unbelievable.

Making as much noise as possible, Sam pushed her table away, scooped up her bag and left the room. Slamming the door, she added, 'I am twatting going!'

Danny and Dale looked at each other, Danny raising his right fist and Dale hitting it with his own. They were enjoying this, their weekly game of wind up the 'gay teacher', made all the better if they could also piss off Sam Reynolds. Danny leant back in his chair and put his feet up on the table and Dale opened a can of Coke. Arnaud, facing the whiteboard, was oblivious of this and continued to calm his breathing, writing the page number, date and title in his neatest handwriting. He would report this behaviour once the lesson was over; Sam was already on report and would be internally excluded for her outburst. Behind him the noise level in the class started to grow. He was about to turn around again and give them another telling off when suddenly it stopped.

'Put your feet on the floor, and you... put that can in the bin.' The man at the door looked at Arnaud, a stern expression on his face. 'Let me know the names of the ones who'll be picking up litter at lunchtime.'

Arnaud returned with an equally stern face of his own, 'Will do, Mr Middleton.'

Middleton nodded, glowered again at Danny and Dale, and shut the door. Outside he could be heard shouting. Arnaud let out a sigh, sat at his desk and opened his book.

'*Le weekend*. Can anyone tell me what that means in English?'

The remainder of the lesson was only slightly less chaotic. Sam

27

returned after having been spoken to by Middleton and sat solemnly at the front, refusing to work and doodling, while Danny and Dale were quiet because they were listening to their iPods. In fact, the only pupils working were the six on the front two rows. At ten-fifty the bell sounded and there was a sudden mass exodus. Chairs were left upturned and books lying on tables. Arnaud sighed heavily and made a note on Sam's report. She looked at it and then at him with a face full of hate, before she, too, left. This wasn't what teaching was meant to be like. He bent down to pick up a sweet wrapper and got a handful of sticky chocolate for his trouble. He wiped his hand on a piece of A4 paper and collected up the French textbooks.

Twenty minutes for break, then another two hours until lunch, and finally a free period for lesson five. Unless they gave him another cover! Two more Year Nine classes and then a bottom-set Year Ten. Now he knew why the government had paid him to train as a teacher! Still, he was nearly at the end of his NQT year and would be a fully qualified, respected teacher in September.

He shut the door and locked it behind him. Instantly, he was banged into as pupils pushed past in an attempt to get to the canteen and gorge on junk food as soon as was humanly possible.

He had grown immune to the knocks now. Arnaud had been at Horley Community College for almost two years, first as a student, when he was given easier classes, and then as an NQT – newly qualified teacher. The school had offered him a job and he, like a fool, had accepted it. 'Best to work in a difficult school – baptism of fire, as it were,' his mentor had told him. Yeah, right. At least it was a nice day outside, which was probably why the kids were so fidgety. He couldn't blame them. Who would want to be inside concentrating on French grammar or asking how much for a kilo of *pommes* when, just through the window, the summer had truly arrived?

One more week, he kept telling himself, and then the summer holidays and unemployment. Well, not quite. Having given a term's notice, his contract would finish at the end of August and the school had said there would be supply work for him if he still hadn't found anything. Supply work, in Horley? He laughed to himself as he entered the staffroom; Beirut sounded safer.

Arnaud sat wearily in the worn easy chair that occupied the corner of the room. Around him, teachers scurried to get as much coffee as their break would allow. He spotted the sexy blonde student teacher he'd seen on the train and wished her into the vacant seat next to him. It didn't happen. She sat between two fit-looking men in shorts. P.E. teachers! Puh! He sipped his hot coffee and burnt his tongue. Bugger.

'Heard any more about that job you applied for?' the Head of Foreign Languages, Richard Middleton, asked as he sat down heavily.

'Not yet.'

'Kyiv, wasn't it?'

'Yes.' He moved his tongue inside his mouth, feeling the burn.

'Ah, did you know that Kyiv is the birthplace of modern Russia?'

'No.' Arnaud turned in his seat.

'Kyiv-Rus was the original capital of Russia almost a thousand years ago, long, long before the Tsars, the Bolsheviks and the Communists popped up. Back then it was populated by nomadic tribes.'

Arnaud was impressed. 'Did you study Russian history at uni?'

Middleton smiled. 'No. I saw it on the Discovery Channel.'

Odessa Oblast, Ukraine, near the Transdniester border

Bull looked through the kite sight. Nothing yet. He and his Brigada were watching and waiting. If all went to plan, this would be the first step. He shivered in the cold of the pre-dawn. It brought back memories of a lifetime ago…

The chill of the Afghan night had all but disappeared, to be replaced by the weak warmth of dawn. In the half-light, the poppy field stretched ahead of them and west on the valley floor. A beautiful flower to some, but to others as deadly as any bomb. To the east, the unnamed village with its ramshackle huts. Bull lowered his binos and rubbed his eyes.

His Spetsnaz assault group had been given specific orders: attack the village, eliminate all Mujahedeen, burn the poppy crop. His men, the true elite of the Red Army, were ready. They lay prone on the ridge, waiting. To Bull's left and hidden in a dip, Captain Lesukov's fire-support team had their mortars ready; to his right were Lieutenant Gorodetski, Sergeant Zukauskas and the rest of the Brigada. The plan was simple, brutal and effective. Lesukov's men would commence shelling of the village, and then Bull's team would move from house to house, picking off anyone and everyone who survived. Intelligence supplied by a local informant had said the village was a sham, nothing more than a base for Mujahedeen fighters and Arab Islamic mercenaries to grow and distribute the death that came from the poppy in the field. The Red Army could not let this continue in a 'partner state'. Hence the unequivocal orders. Bull looked at Lesukov. 'Start firing your mortars in two minutes.'

Lesukov nodded. 'Good luck.'

Bull smiled. 'Ivan, we are Spetsnaz. We make our own luck.'

Bull's men moved silently over the ridge and into the valley. Thumph. Thumph. Mortar shells whistled through the sky. There was sudden movement from the village. A robed figure appeared and looked directly at the ridge. He yelled, raised his rifle and fired into the sky. As he did so, an explosion tore the very earth from under his feet. More shells landed, flattening the Afghan houses and destroying the beauty of the new day. Then, as abruptly as they had started, they stopped.

Bull's men now swept through the carnage before them. The dead and dying littered the village; many had been asleep, others in the process of grabbing weapons. Several had fled to the fields and were chased down by rounds not even the fastest could outrun. Bull reached the building he knew housed the village elder. The roof was intact even though part of one wall was now missing. The old man was sitting on a crimson rug in the corner, his henna-red beard specked with dust. His eyes angry, he showed no fear. He waited until Lieutenant Gorodetski had entered the room behind Bull before speaking words of venom.

'He says it is a trap; that we have all been tricked,' Gorodetski translated. The old man jabbed at them with a bony finger. Gorodetski continued. 'He says we are infidels, not men of our word, not men of honour.'

'Enough.' Bull stepped forward and crouched. 'We are men of honour. We did not break our agreement.' Drawing his revolver, Bull shot the elder in the face.

Shocked, Gorodetski looked down at his captain. 'Why?'

Pashinski stared at the young officer. 'He was Mujahedeen; that is all you need know.'

An explosion behind, then another. Bull turned as Gorodetski backed out of the house. On the ridge above, the fire-support team were under attack. Gathering up his Brigada, Bull charged back towards Lesukov's team. Reaching the ridge, wild rounds whistled past them. Lesukov's men had been taken by surprise; a group of fighters numbering more than twenty had flanked them from the west. Lesukov fired controlled bursts from his Kalashnikov at the Afghan hordes. Of the team of eight, only he and two others were left.

Zukauskas grabbed a mortar and turned it around to face the oncoming threat; one-handed, he dropped a mortar into the tube and fired. Unsighted, the bomb flew over the Mujahedeen and landed harmlessly, save for an explosion. Securing the tube on the ground, he sighted it while Gorodetski dropped in a new shell. This time the explosion landed just to the left of the advancing fighters. Some stopped, others carried on.

Bull joined Lesukov. There was a grin on Lesukov's face. 'We make our own luck!'

'No. We make it unlucky for them!'

A sound from below brought Bull very much back to the present. He raised the kite sight and saw three trucks moving slowly along the rural road. Shifting his weight slightly he looked to his left and could make out the hunched figures of the militia's SOCOL Eagle unit further down the incline in front of him. His lips formed a serpent-like smile as he depressed the switch on his covert transmitter twice. Seconds later, his ready signal was acknowledged by three bursts of static in his earpiece.

On the valley floor the lead truck slowed and stopped. The driver stepped out and made a show of kicking the tyre in disgust. The two remaining trucks concertinaed and also stopped. Soon all three drivers were inspecting the 'guilty tyre'. In the green haze of the night scope there was movement again as a larger but solitary truck appeared on the horizon, heading directly towards the convoy from the opposite direction. It joined them and the driver greeted his fellow truckers warmly and offered his help and advice.

As Bull had hoped, the stationary convoy made too good a target to pass up. The armed members of the SOCOL appeared on the road below and advanced towards the drivers, weapons up. The second SOCOL group on the hill now stood and started down the incline on a ninety-degree approach to the target. Bull pressed his switch again. SOCOL's 'plan' was going to plan. Here, twenty kilometres inside the Ukrainian border, they would intercept the latest arms shipment and punch a hole in this smuggling route. That was, until…

Bull's sign was met this time by two short, static bursts. From above and to the right, his men opened fire. A tracer flew towards the descending SOCOL 'cut off' group. Four fell without even knowing where their executioners were. The remaining two flung themselves down on the barren hillside and scrambled for the smallest piece of cover. On the road, the intercept team had just enough time to train their weapons. The lieutenant, whose reactions had been surprisingly rapid, managed to get off a single, low-velocity round from his pistol, which struck Driver Two square in his concealed Kevlar breastplate. Staggering back, he had fallen as Drivers One and Three let rip with armour-piercing rounds from short-barrelled AKs, all but cutting the officer in half. Further shots sought out the two attackers on the hill and the engagement was over within a minute. Like the Poznan anti-terrorist police a decade before, the Ukrainian SOCOL had met the Soviet Red Army Spetsnaz and lost. Bull stood, walked down the hill and joined his Brigada. The first part of his business deal had just gone through. He exchanged congratulatory glances with his men and retrieved a satellite phone from a padded pocket.

Tiraspol, Transdniester

Ivan Lesukov sat in the sauna and sweated. 'You have done well, my friend. And the other half of the bargain? You are a real man of your word, Bull.' He shut his flip phone and placed it on the wooden plank next to him.

'They have done it?' Arkadi Cheban was anxious to know.

Lesukov beamed. 'Yes, they have. The shipments will no longer be hampered by those Ukrainian "heroes".'

'That is great news, Uncle.' Cheban used the term as a sign of respect. Lesukov was actually the uncle of his wife. He had married into the business, leaving his days of being an interpreter behind.

Lesukov wiped his brow and looked at the younger man. He was ready. 'We are expanding on all fronts, Arkadi, and I have a job for you.' He noticed Arkadi's narrow chest swell with pride. 'I want you to organise our deliveries in London. Who knows, you may even be able to import chairs.' He tapped his nose.

Arkadi was ecstatic; he had been dreaming of permanently leaving this joke of a country for as long as he could remember. When he'd been ordered back from England by his uncle, he'd thought perhaps he'd done something wrong and even debated whether to return or not. He had, after all, only been there for three months. On the contrary, however, 'Uncle' had been impressed. 'Thank you, Uncle.'

'I know how much you will miss Yulia but trust me... she will be able to join you soon.'

In fact, during his time in London, Arkadi hadn't missed his wife at all. He was quite taken with the Polish girl who worked in the local coffee shop. 'I do hope so, Uncle; it is lonely without her.'

Lesukov liked this. Having no children of his own, his sister's daughter was very dear to him and he would have killed anyone who didn't treat her with respect.

Arkadi changed the subject. 'Why is Pashinski called "The Bull"?'

Lesukov held up his finger. 'When we were young conscripts together, about your age, we had a very stupid sergeant who asked Tauras his name. When he replied, the man asked him if he was a bull – like the star chart. I do not know why this offended him but Tauras hit him. You see, the sergeant did not like Lithuanians. Tauras was beaten and left outside in the snow, tied to a post, for three days. A month later the sergeant disappeared on a training exercise. For my part, I think he is more like a venomous snake.'

Chapter 3

Fontanka, Odessa Oblast, Ukraine

The best rooms were, of course, on the thirtieth floor. Here the penthouses had floor-to-ceiling glass walls that gave fantastic views of the landscaped gardens and private beach. The top five floors were VIP class with private clubrooms. Every room in the hotel had both a sea and inland view as the structure curved like a giant wave. The hotel was indeed fantastic, or would be, Varchenko reminded himself, once it was built. Yes. The architect had done a great job of transferring his vision from idea to plans to scale model. Now, it was the foreigners he needed to turn the model into reality, for his wealth alone could not bankroll this venture. A man of the world, he liked to think, since 1991 he had travelled to the best resort and gaming hotels in the world. This hotel would not be Nice's Hotel Negresco; it would not be Las Vegas's Caesar's Palace, New York's Four Seasons, the Sandy Lane of Barbados, London's Ritz or Dubai's Burgh Al Arab. This would be the Hotel Noblesse, and it would be his.

Meetings had been arranged with venture capitalists in London, New York, Zurich and Vienna. He had brought, at his own cost, potential partners to Ukraine. The diving would rival

Egypt (they would make a fake reef), the service would be seven-star. This would be the new principality of the twenty-first century and he would be the new prince!

Although he had a tear in his eye and the vodka bottle was empty, he was not a dreamer. Valeriy Varchenko stood, patted the roof of his hotel, and retired for the evening.

Odessa, Southern Ukraine

Sergey Gorodetski threw the grappling hook over the ledge of the warehouse, making sure it was fast before carefully hauling himself up the wall and onto the roof. He paused, counted to a hundred and, when he heard no sounds of alarm or noises from below, worked his way forward on the gravelled roof, all the while making sure to keep his body below the skyline. On reaching the edge of the roof, he leaned against the parapet and removed his rifle from its canvas carry case. He inspected it for dirt before looking down the sight to check for misalignment. Making the necessary adjustment, he carefully chambered the first round. It was two-forty-five and he had exactly five hours to wait for his prey, who was, by his very nature, a creature of habit.

Jas Malik pulled his trench coat around his body and stepped into the back of the Lexus. Ruslan had kept him waiting. Today's excuse: the local militia refused to let him turn right... or something. Jas didn't care why he was late, just that he was. Jas did not like this. His father had taught him the value of punctuality at an early age in Islamabad when he'd whipped him for having the audacity to be late for the family stall. Casting Ruslan a stern look, he urged him to 'bloody hurry up and get him to the factory'.

'Yes, sir,' replied the bemused Ukrainian.

'I have to open the factory at seven-forty-five, no later,' he ordered, shooting Ruslan a glare before transferring his attention to the heavy lifting cranes of the Odessa docks.

Ruslan slumped over the wheel and made faces in the mirror only he could see. A veteran of Afghanistan, he didn't suffer fools, such as Jas, gladly, but the fool paid his boss well. Besides, he got to drive this big Lexus and the women loved it.

Seven-twenty. Sergey took up his trigger position on the factory car park. He was invisible to those below unless they made the fatal mistake of staring directly up. Experience and training had taught him patience. What was that English saying his training instructor had told him? Ah, yes: 'Slowly, slowly, catchy monkey.' Never before had the saying made so much sense. His eyes started to water and blur his vision. He squeezed them shut and opened them again, blinking, fighting the urge to rub. He would not take his eyes off the trigger position, not now, not after what felt like years of waiting. He would do this now, and he would do it perfectly.

Jas liked the journey to the factory. Speeding past the mainly Soviet-era traffic, made up of Ladas, Volgas, Kamaz trucks and the odd Jigoli, he felt he had really arrived. He allowed himself to smile as he recalled the look he had seen on the faces of the so-called 'old men' of the business when he announced his successful bids for hitherto secretive state tenders in Ukraine, Belarus and Russia. Let the corporate Germans in Erlangen call him a tin-pot Paki now!

A car engine approached and Sergey made his final adjustments. The dark-blue Lexus rounded the corner of the warehouse and drew to a halt in front of the main entrance. Sweat formed on his brow despite the unseasonably chilly morning as he concentrated on the crosshairs of the Dragunov's sight. The door opened and the target started to rise. Let him get out, don't rush… apply second pressure to the trigger. The single shot flew along the barrel and covered the short distance to the target. There was a crack and suddenly a cloud of blood. The target was propelled backwards, striking the rear panel of the limousine before hitting the ground. The driver momentarily froze before throwing himself to the floor and scrabbling behind the car for cover.

British Embassy, Kyiv, Ukraine

Vickers frowned as Macintosh passed him the report, ashen-faced. 'It happened this morning Alistair. The driver was unharmed. Mr Malik died instantly. The militia think it was a professional hit.'

Scanning the two A4 sides of Cyrillic print, Vickers's brow furrowed even deeper than normal. 'Anyone would think this was sodding Moscow. I don't suppose the local militia have anything to go on?'

The ambassador shook his head. In his time at the British Embassy he had heard of two other assassinations; both had been foreign investors and both had been unsolved. 'The first Brit to open a manufacturing plant in Ukraine becomes the first Brit to be murdered in Ukraine. The EU isn't going to like it one little bit.' Vickers massaged his temples. 'I'll liaise with the SBU. We'll have to put out a press statement eventually. We don't want to undo what little commercial progress we've made thus far.'

'And his family?' the ambassador asked with a concerned voice.

Vickers, still scanning the report, looked up. 'Oh, yes, we should inform them.' He read on, suddenly arching his eyebrows. 'Surprisingly, the body will be on its way back to Kyiv tomorrow. Apparently the SBU don't trust the local coroner to carry out the postmortem. Once that's been completed I'll have consulate arrange passage to the UK.'

Macintosh nodded, looking decidedly pale. Vickers left the ambassador's office and asked his secretary to send him in a tea. Macintosh was a career diplomat and skilled at cocktail parties, but when the real world encroached on his delicate sensibilities, he really struggled. That's why I'm here, mused Vickers.

Nearing his own office, he remembered the email in his in tray from the CCCI mission manager in London. Bugger, that was his other hat calling. Alistair Vickers's official post was that of commercial attaché at the British Embassy, Kyiv. He wore another, albeit invisible hat, however – that of SIS man in Ukraine. Kyiv had been Vickers's second-choice posting after Moscow.

Sitting back at his own desk, he picked up a custard cream and crunched it between his teeth before sipping his now-cold tea, white Earl Grey with two sugars. A purist would never add milk but he liked it that way. He replaced the cup and saucer on his desk and leant back to concentrate on the report. He had, of course, met Jas on many occasions. The man wasn't afraid of self-advertising and had managed to get into most of the national newspapers as well as joining expatriate business groups such as the American Chamber of Commerce. In fact, he was probably one of the most well-known 'Brits' in Ukraine, which made his murder all the more curious.

Vickers liked to think he knew the feel of the place and he spoke regularly with his contacts in the SBU, the Ukrainian security service. He had been of the opinion that Jas had had a good 'Krisha', a 'roof' in other words; his local partner had protected him from any unsavoury interest from other businessmen, Mafia. Big business was, to some extent, still governed by the Mafia in Ukraine, and the more noise you made, the more likely it was you would encounter them. Jas's partner was ideally placed to protect him. The man was a former KGB general and Hero of the Soviet Union who had now amassed a fortune as a businessman. If anyone called the shots, it was this man, General Valeriy Varchenko. As close to an oligarch as you could get in Ukraine, Varchenko had his base in Odessa, Ukraine's pretty port city. Vickers crunched on another biscuit. Why would anyone pick a fight with Varchenko, for killing his business partner was surely an act of war?

Central Kyiv

'Da. I'm listening.'

Dudka cleared his throat. 'Please put me through to Valeriy Ivanovich.'

There was a slight pause. 'Who would you be?'

'Tell him it is Genna.' Dudka drummed his fingers on the plastic café table.

Another pause, noises in the background. 'OK.'

Dudka heard a rustling at the other end and then a muffled voice started to speak, 'Gennady Stepanovich, my dear friend, how are you?'

'Fine, my friend. Is this an inconvenient moment?'

'No, no,' Varchenko replied. 'I am in the middle of a rather good lobster. The next time you are in Odessa you really must try one.'

Dudka eyed his pathetic café sandwich. 'I have something I need to discuss with you.'

'Oh, and what might that be?' Varchenko's voice was now clear.

Dudka cast his eyes around the terrace; there seemed to be no one eavesdropping. 'Can we meet at the *dacha*?'

If any other man had received a call from a Deputy Head of the SBU, the Head of the Main Directorate for Combating Corruption and Organised Crime, they would have been justified in showing concern; however, with Valeriy Varchenko, retired KGB general, what registered sounded more like annoyance. 'It is not very convenient.'

'I insist, old friend.' Dudka held firm; after all, he was still the enlisted man, even though he turned a 'general' blind eye to the general in Odessa.

Varchenko sighed, more for effect than anything else. 'Very well. We'll meet tomorrow afternoon at three. I'll even have the chef here prepare you a lobster.'

'Agreed.' Dudka put the phone down. He knew where the chef could stick his precious lobster. He bit into his open sausage sandwich. The money and power had clearly gone to his old friend's head.

Chapter 4

Podilsky School International, Berezniki, Kyiv, Ukraine

Snow rubbed his right thigh, which was playing up again. Was he getting too old for this? He pondered a moment before dismissing the idea. 'You're thirty-four, not fifty.' He surveyed the class as they continued to jog around the small area of grass circling the playground. Some of these kids, especially Yusuf, the Turkish lad, could give him a run for his money. 'That's it, two more laps and you've finished.'

Would these same kids be so eager to join a running club if they were back home in a normal comprehensive? He thought not. International schools seemed to bring out the best in children. Most would be bilingual by the end of their parents' three-year stint. Snow blew his whistle and gestured that it was time to go in. Counting heads, he headed back to the school entrance along the small, paved path they shared with the residents of Kyiv's Berezniki suburb. Yusuf caught up with him and trotted alongside. 'Did you see how I run, Mr Snow?' he asked expectantly. 'I beat Ryoski and Grant.'

Snow nodded and smiled. Yusuf was twelve, quite tall for his age, and wiry. He had the perfect runner's physique and a real talent.

'Well done, Yusuf. I'm impressed.'

Yusuf smiled back, picked up his pace and jogged the remaining distance around the corner and into the main entrance. There was a banging; Snow raised his hand to screen the glare of the sun as Michael Jones opened the staffroom window.

'Hey, Aidan, have you seen this?' Michael's west Wales tones lilted to accentuate the question. 'Murder in Odessa. And to think I was there last weekend!'

Snow took the *Kyiv Post* and looked at the main page.

'*British investor slain in Odessa factory shooting.*' He scanned the story as Jones kept an eye on the rest of the runners ambling past.

'What d'ya think?' Jones's eyebrows arched in his usual show of curiosity.

Snow studied his friend's ruddy face. 'I'm glad I'm just a teacher and no one important.'

Fontanka, Odessa Oblast, Ukraine

The *dacha* was in the small coastal town of Fontanka, twenty kilometres from Odessa. During Soviet times it had belonged to 'the Party' and was for the use of high-ranking members of the YCCP. On Ukrainian independence, this and many other such properties had been sold off by 'the state' for hard currency to the highest bidder. The fact that many had been sold to the same person, who was acting as 'the seller' on behalf of 'the state', had been conveniently overlooked.

This particular *dacha* had been built in 1979 and used by some of the gold medallists from the 1980 Moscow Olympics. The new owner sought to commemorate this event and had the Olympic rings included in the design of his new nine-feet, wrought-iron security gates which guarded the entrance. The gates weren't the only part of the *dacha* to be modernised, '*remonted*'. The original three-storey building remained but an additional wing had been added at a right angle, forming an L shape. Italian marble adorned the surfaces of all the bathrooms, of which there were now six, and the indoor pool. The back of the house led on to a large terrace, with an ornate garden and views of the Black Sea.

Varchenko leant forward to smell a particularly nice rose. He was dressed in an expensive, dark-grey pair of slacks, a black polo shirt and a pair of Italian loafers. A matching dark-grey cashmere sweater was draped casually over his shoulders. He closed his eyes and inhaled deeply. Dudka exhaled and flicked his cigarette stub into the flowerbeds. Varchenko straightened up and frowned at his friend's disregard for nature's beauty.

'What do you know, Genna?'

Dudka met his gaze. 'I know your British business partner was assassinated in Odessa; I know it was a trained sniper; I know this is not good for general business; but I also know you now control the entire venture.'

'And you think I am so transparent?' Varchenko held his gaze.

'I have to look at all possibilities, Valeriy. You provided a *Krisha* for the Englishman, yet he is dead.'

'Yet he is dead…' Varchenko paused as Dudka fumbled in his jacket pocket for his handkerchief. 'Go on.'

Dudka blew his nose. 'Pollen.' How one could enjoy sniffing flowers, he did not know. He wiped his nose and returned the handkerchief to his crumpled suit pocket. 'That is all I can say on the matter. This partner of yours was a very high-profile businessman, liaised with his embassy, spoke at business lunches and drew much attention.'

Varchenko snorted. 'This is a difficult situation for me, Genna, old friend, as I am sure you are aware. I gave this man my word it would be safe to invest here, to work here, to live here. He had my word, you understand, my word on this. My best men guarded him; he was in no danger from normal "business threats". This murder places much stress on the status quo, on the relationship and understanding we share, Genna.' Varchenko looked him in the eye.

Dudka grunted, 'And you think I am not immune to this? Remember, I'm the one who has turned a "blind eye" to your business dealings here.'

'And for this you are handsomely rewarded.' Varchenko paused. 'Ah, my old colleague, so we are both in the same situation. What is bad for me is bad for you. But the agreement works. What crime we have here is now under control – ask any one of your SBU underlings to give you a report. I have worked hard to ensure this, but then, when I am on the verge of a successful endeavour, it is potentially snatched away. By whom? That is what I must know. Who is it who dares upset us?'

Dudka shrugged. 'You have no idea? I have seen some intelligence about the Turks and I have also read reports on the Moldavians.'

Varchenko closed his eyes to hide his rage. 'Turks! I am aware of the Turks and they would not dare attempt this! And the Moldavians could not spell the word assassinate! No, this must be someone new.'

So his old superior was worried. 'That, I am afraid, is all we have at the moment. We will, of course, be exploring all possibilities, Valeriy.'

Varchenko raised his finger. 'All possibilities? We are both decent men, Genna. We did not work all these years together to protect the people's interest to now be threatened in our golden years! We have kept it simple. Old-fashioned crime. None of the slavery, narcotica or weaponry…'

Varchenko's voice trailed off and Dudka nodded. It was true. Varchenko was a bandit, but an honest one. There was crime in Odessa but, because of him, it was petty; the large-scale arms smuggling, people and drug trafficking of the early Nineties had been severely restricted. Dudka felt his stomach rumble. 'Where is that lobster you promised me?'

Shoreham by Sea, United Kingdom

The morning sky was a brilliant blue, unusually so for this time of year, but Bav didn't notice as he headed towards Lancing. Under the supervision of his father he had been, on paper, managing director of UK operations while his cousin held the same title in Islamabad. Jas had held the position of chairman with overall responsibility for NewSound worldwide. Now, with his death, Bav, at the age of thirty-seven, had been left the lot. His own dispensing business would have to cease as he took the reins of the three plants. He had never wanted to go into the family business. His only concession, albeit a large one, was to train as an audiologist. He had then, of course, been 'persuaded' to recommend his family's products. And now he could hardly refuse his appointment as MD.

His old man was – *had been*, he corrected himself – a crafty one. All the while he had known deep down that Bav, and Bav alone, would replace him. That he, and not his cousin, Said Shabaz, would be the future head of NewSound.

He bit his bottom lip to stop the tears forming again. He could not stay at home and grieve; he had to carry on, open the factory – it was what his father would have wanted. Why did you have to die, Dad, why did you have to leave me? An old man who had only ever brought happiness had been snatched away by a bullet. It wasn't working. He'd have to stop. The factory would have to open later. He pulled onto the hard shoulder, stabbing the hazard-warning button with his left index finger as tears fell from his eyes.

Simon Macintosh extended his hand. 'Thank you for coming to see us, Director Dudka.'

Dudka took the proffered hand and shook it with a firm grip. 'It is least we can do, Mr Ambassador.'

Macintosh nodded and introduced the man standing at his side. 'This is Alistair Vickers. He will be liaising with London.'

Vickers and Dudka shook hands.

'And this is Vitaly Blazhevich. He is running investigation.'

Blazhevich shook hands with both British diplomats. The ambassador bade them sit.

'My English not as good as could be. I am sorry. I speak *Deutsch.*'

Dudka put his hand on Blazhevich's shoulder. 'But Vitaly is secret weapon.'

There was a knock at the door and Macintosh's secretary brought in a tray containing four cups of tea, a bowl of sugar, milk and custard cream biscuits. Dudka took a cup, nodded, blew on the surface of the tea, then took a sip. Momentarily his eyes flickered before he placed the cup on the table. '*Dobre Smak.*' It was a lie. The tea tasted peculiar.

'Earl Grey. Traditionally English.' Vickers poured milk into his own cup.

Blazhevich opened a file and placed it on the table. Dudka spoke in Ukrainian and Blazhevich translated into English. 'We are obviously very sorry for the loss of Mr Malik. We want to confirm that we will give our full support and resources to finding the person or persons responsible for this unlawful act.'

Blazhevich looked at Dudka. Dudka added two spoons of sugar to his tea and sipped. Vickers made notes on a PDA with a plastic pointer while Macintosh knotted his hands in his lap and nodded. The biscuits remained untouched. Dudka continued, with Blazhevich a phrase behind.

'Here are photographs taken at the scene. They are not appealing. The angle of the impacted bullet leads us to believe the shot came from above. Scuff marks on the roof of a neighbouring warehouse substantiate this.'

Macintosh, his face pale, passed the photographs to Vickers, who spoke next. 'What type of ammunition?' Vickers studied the image. '7.62?'

'*Tak.*' Dudka smiled and continued in English. 'Very common in former USSR.'

Vickers studied the image again. 'May we presume it was a trained sniper?'

'*Tak.* Our Red Army had many, many.'

Blazhevich added more information: 'As you have hinted, the profile of the suspect we have is a trained sniper. This further adds to our suspicion that the attack was professional and pre-planned.'

Macintosh placed his palms on the table. 'So we have a British citizen assassinated by a paid assassin, a sniper. Do you have any idea who the paymaster might have been?'

Vickers tried not to smile. For all Macintosh's professional abilities, investigating a murder was not one of them. He tried his best but sounded to Vickers like a le Carré novel.

'This is something we intend to investigate further,' Blazhevich translated. 'Can we ask you for any ideas you may have? For example, a list of Mr Malik's business and social contacts?'

'Alistair?' Macintosh looked at Vickers.

'We have searched all our files and of course asked the expatriate community; however, at this stage, we have nothing of any consequence.'

Vickers waited while his words were translated. 'We, of course, know that Mr Malik was in partnership with a Ukrainian joint stock company and believe they would be the only party to gain from this.'

Dudka's eyes narrowed for a moment before he spoke.

Blazhevich looked at Macintosh then Vickers in turn. 'We can assure you that we have started to interview all directors of Odessa-Invest in addition to a number of others. We will find those responsible.'

There was a pause as the four men pondered their positions. 'Well, gentlemen. I feel reassured that the SBU are actively working on this disturbing and unfortunate case, and that Director Dudka himself has taken a personal interest. I like Ukraine and like working here. Your country has made much progress towards becoming an investment and business power in the last few years, and the British Government will do all it can to assist in the continuation of this.' He stood and shook Dudka's hand again.

Vickers showed the two men from the SBU out into the hall. A minute later, after bidding them goodbye and thanking them again, he re-entered the room to find Macintosh with the plate of biscuits in his hand.

'Nice chaps; not like the old KGB. I feel they will do all they can.'

'I'm sure.' But Vickers was not.

Lingfield, Surrey, UK

A low burble crept into Arnaud's head. At first it mixed with the last-orders bell in the pub, until he realised it was a shrill electronic note and not the brass ding he'd expected. The busty barmaid who had been 'chatting him up' abruptly vanished.

'Oh, no!' Arnaud leapt from his bed and ran downstairs to the hall.

Now well into September; and still no permanent job. Arnaud had signed with a supply-teaching agency covering the Surrey and Sussex area. Sometimes he would get a call in the evening asking him if he wanted a day's work the next day, but mostly they would call in the morning, getting him out of bed and in general giving him a matter of minutes to get to the station and on his way. He had started a routine. Regardless of a call or not, each night he would iron a shirt, make a packed lunch and ready his 'schoolbag'. His mother was always offering to help, but since he had returned from university and was now living at home again, he felt somehow embarrassed he didn't contribute enough around the house. The fact that the agency would insist on calling the house phone downstairs rather than his mobile was also irksome. His father had complained on more than one occasion.

'Hello… hello… hello,' he said to himself as he reached for the phone in an attempt to get rid of his 'morning voice'.

'Hello?' There was a strange tone on the line. After a pause a voice finally answered.

'Hello. Is that Arnaud Hurst?'

'Yes, it is.'

'Hello, Arnaud. This is Joan Greenhill from Podilsky School. How are you?'

Arnaud tried to think who this woman calling him at ten past six in the morning might be; then he suddenly realised. Podilsky School, the international teaching job he had applied for. 'I'm fine, thanks,' he replied, slightly lost for words but no more awake.

'Good, good. Arnaud, I wanted to make sure I got you before you left for work… Oh, I'm terribly sorry, I've just remembered the time difference. We're two hours ahead of you. Oh, dear…'

Arnaud decided to be British and reduce her embarrassment. 'Not to worry. I usually get up at six-ish to go for a run so I was already awake.'

The voice on the phone replied, 'Oh, that's good.' It then took on a more professional tone. 'I'm sorry we didn't get back to you sooner. I expect you thought we'd forgotten about you?'

'Well, I did think the job must have gone to someone else.' It had been May when he'd originally seen the advert in the *TES* overseas appointments section, and June when he'd met with the American interviewer in London.

'Well, as a private school, we did have some staffing issues here, which meant we were unable to appoint over the summer, but I won't bother you with the details. Arnaud, the reason I'm calling is that I have some good news for you. Your application for the position of teacher of French and English has been successful.'

Arnaud smiled and sat on the radiator in the hall, ignoring the cold metal on his bare buttocks. 'That's great news. Thank you very much.'

'So you accept then?' Greenhill asked expectantly.

'Yes, I do.' Arnaud caught himself grinning in the hall mirror.

In Kyiv, Greenhill smiled and beckoned Snow into her office. 'I'm happy to hear that. Now, since you applied for the job, our teaching requirements have changed slightly.'

'Oh?' Arnaud held his breath. Was there a catch?

'Well, we originally wanted you for French and English as a Second Language, but now we would also need you to teach some P.E. Would that be a problem at all for you?'

'No, not at all, I'd be very happy to do that.' P.E.? Oh, well, at least it was better than maths.

Greenhill beamed at Snow and raised her thumb. 'Great. I didn't think it would be a problem for someone as fit as you must be, running every morning. I know it's quite short notice but can you start on Monday the 2nd of October, in two weeks' time?'

'Yes, I can; that's no problem at all. The sooner the better.'

'Wonderful. I'm going to put your offer letter in the diplomatic pouch leaving today, so, once it's posted in the UK, you should get it by Wednesday.'

'Thank you, Mrs Greenhill.' Arnaud could say goodbye to Supply once and for all.

'Call me Joan. Bye bye.' She put down the phone and looked

at Snow. 'There we are, someone to help you out with your running club.'

'Good.'

Greenhill continued, 'As long as you promise to collect him for me and look after him.'

Snow smiled. It would be nice to get another British teacher into the school; he and Joan were outnumbered three to one by the Canadians.

Chapter 5

Odessa, Kyiv Highway, Odessa Oblast, Ukraine

The silver 7 Series BMW pulled to an abrupt halt in front of the Maybach 57S, causing Varchenko to spill his cognac. 'What is this?' he shouted at his driver as his mobile phone rang.

'Don't be alarmed, Valeriy Ivanovich, I mean you no harm.'

'Who the hell is this!?' Varchenko threw the remainder of his cognac down his throat.

'I am in the car in front of you and would like to talk.'

Two men stepped out of the BMW and approached. They had their hands raised to show they held no weapons. In the Maybach's front seat, Varchenko's guard unholstered his Glock 9mm as the driver put the luxury saloon into reverse gear, ready to perform a J-turn.

A third man emerged from the BMW; this one had a phone to his right ear. 'I am getting out of the car and will now walk towards you. Your driver will open the door and let me in. He and your guard will then get out.'

'Like hell they will,' Varchenko roared into the Vertu handset.

'Come now, Valeriy Ivanovich; I am sure you would like to know who killed Mr Malik?'

Varchenko went cold. Were the killers of his business partner about to make contact or were they about to kill him? Impossible, his mind retorted. Did they not know who he was and what he stood for? Varchenko's curiosity got the better of him and he ordered the passenger door to be opened. By now his guard had called ahead and a backup car was on its way. While the two other occupants of the BMW looked on and exchanged professional glares with his own men, Varchenko was joined by his caller. The man pocketed his phone, calmly climbed into the car and shut the door.

Tauras 'The Bull' Pashinski extended his hand, but it was ignored. He shrugged and introduced himself. 'I am Olexandr Knysh, and I killed the British businessman.'

Varchenko shook in his seat with rage, his face turning crimson. 'You hold me up on the Odessa highway in the middle of the day and have the audacity to tell me this!'

'I am sorry. Should we have met in the restaurant you just left and caused a scene?'

'Who are you and what do you want?' Varchenko was still incredulous.

'I am just a businessman like you, Valeriy Ivanovich. A simple businessman and I am looking to invest in Odessa. I understand that you now seek a new partner and I am offering to be that very person.' Bull picked up a glass and poured himself a cognac.

'How dare you insult me in such a manner? Don't you know who the hell I am?' Varchenko grabbed the cognac bottle.

'Why, of course I do.' Bull drank the dark liquor. 'Very good. French? You are Valeriy Varchenko, former general of the KGB and Hero of the Soviet Union. You own several large companies, part-own a bank and four hotels in the Odessa Oblast, and you are also responsible for most of the organised crime.'

'You are well informed, if somewhat too concise.' His ego slightly massaged, he started to breathe more normally. 'What, however, gives you the slightest idea that you can strong-arm me?' The man had balls, he had to concede.

Bull placed the glass delicately back in the holder. 'It would be a pity if foreign investors were to avoid Odessa. Given the tax-zone incentive, they should be pouring money into the area and into your pockets.'

'So you are threatening me, Knysh?' Varchenko now knew how to play this.

'That is a very crude way to put my proposal, Valeriy Ivanovich. I believe that you have need of a partner who brings in not only capital but a wealth of experience in other business-related matters such as, for example, security and life insurance. Not to mention new export opportunities…'

Varchenko had now heard enough. He looked into the snake-like eyes of the man who called himself Knysh. 'I have no need for another partner, however experienced he may be. You have made a monumental error of judgement in approaching me. I do not want to see or hear from you again. Now leave my car before I personally strangle you!'

Bull held the old man's gaze impassively. 'My offer is still open. I will give you time to reconsider.' He exited the car.

The driver and guard got back in.

'Drive,' commanded Varchenko, 'but not fast.'

The Maybach manoeuvred past the BMW and moved up the road. Its 612bhp V12 Mercedes engine could propel it to 100kmph in five seconds, but he wasn't running away. This was his Oblast! Varchenko dialled a number and a phone rang in a fast-approaching Mercedes G Wagon. 'Ruslan, when you see them, run them off of the road. They must not get away. Do you understand?'

He leant back and poured a large cognac. This one he savoured. If you are a dog, do not attack the bear.

The arrivals doors at Kyiv's Boryspil Airport opened and, through eager crowds pushing to catch a glimpse of their loved ones, Snow spotted a tall, fair-haired figure. The man looked somewhat bewildered. He had a large case in each hand and a rucksack on his back.

'You must be Arnaud?' Snow called out above the heads of an elderly couple.

Arnaud looked up and smiled. 'Aidan?'

'Correct. Welcome to Kyiv.'

Arnaud pushed his way forward as best he could and Snow took one of the cases with one hand and shook Arnaud's with the other. 'Travelling light?'

'I didn't know what to bring, so I brought two of everything.'

'Well, as long as you've brought two pairs of socks you'll be fine. Follow me.'

Snow led them through the crowds of hopeful locals masquerading as taxi drivers and out to a waiting Lada. The driver, Victor, leant against the bonnet smoking. On seeing the pair he stubbed out the cigarette and opened the boot.

'Hello to Kyiv.'

'I think he means welcome.'

Arnaud held out his hand, 'Nice to meet you, old boy.'

Victor nodded and took the luggage. Once the boot was loaded, he gestured for them to be seated.

Arnaud sat in the back behind Snow. 'Is this a Lada?'

'Yep, the Subaru of the former Soviet Union. It's about forty minutes to the city centre and our place; sit back and enjoy the view.'

Arnaud nodded and looked out of the window at the passing forests bordering the Boryspil-Kyiv highway. Victor pressed a button on the radio and Queen's greatest hits filled the car. Arnaud let Freddie Mercury sing for a few bars then leant forward. 'How long have you been here then?'

Snow swivelled in his seat. 'This is the start of my third year at Podilsky.'

'Do you like it?'

'Yeah, I do. The staff are friendly and we tend to socialise outside of school too. Beats teaching in the UK.'

Arnaud clicked his teeth. 'I hope so.'

'That bad, eh?'

'I just finished my NQT year at Horley Comprehensive, or to give it the new "super" name, Horley Community College. Ever been to Horley?'

Snow shook his head. 'I've passed through.'

'Best thing to do. It's a toilet. The kids are half-crazed from breathing in the aviation fuel from Gatwick Airport. Where did you train then?'

'Leeds, and I did my NQT year in Barnsley.'

'Like it?'

'Probably better than Horley.'

Victor said something in Russian to Snow, who smiled and replied in the same language.

'What did he say?'

'He said it was his dream at school to visit London, so now, when he hears English, it makes him happy.'

'I'd better not speak French then; it may overexcite him.'

'That's right; you're bilingual. Dad or Mum?'

'Mum. And you speak Ukrainian?'

'I speak some Russian. I learnt it at school.'

'Private school?'

'I was an embassy brat. My dad was at the British Embassy in Moscow in the Eighties, then Poland, then East Germany.'

'Was he the ambassador?'

'Nothing so glamorous. He was the cultural attaché. He arranged exchanges with the Bolshoi Ballet, etc.'

'Oh. See many women in leotards?'

Snow laughed. 'Yeah, but I was too young to appreciate them!'

There was a pause as Arnaud stared at a Mercedes with blacked-out windows shooting past. Victor waved his fist and mumbled '*Jigeet!*'

Arnaud looked at Snow blankly. 'It means something like "road hog and menace" in Russian.'

'I thought they spoke Ukrainian here?'

'They speak a mixture. They were forced to learn Russian when it was still the Soviet Union. "Rusification", it was called. Since independence the official national language has been Ukrainian but everyone can speak and uses Russian. More so in Kyiv and in the east of the country. The further west you go, the more Ukrainian you hear spoken.'

'Sounds a bit like Wales.'

'Similar.'

Victor piped up again and Snow nodded. 'If you look to your right you'll see Misha the bear on the grass verge. Look there, see it?'

Arnaud looked and saw an eight-feet-high cartoon-style bear made of painted concrete. 'What is it?'

'He was the emblem for the 1980 Moscow Olympics.'

'Oh, I see. That was a bit before my time.'

'When were you born?'

'1981.'

'Jesus.' Snow frowned playfully. 'I've got shirts older than you!'

They passed a large sign welcoming them to Kyiv. The city was expanding fast as more and more high-rise tower blocks were built in the suburbs. The new builds looked like luxury hotels compared to the old Lego-box Soviet architecture. Arnaud stared at the roadside billboards and squinted until he realised he couldn't read the words because they were in Cyrillic and not because he needed glasses. They passed a two-storey shopping centre and then a McDonald's.

'That lot's only been here for the past five years,' commented Snow. 'They had to make do with proper food before that.'

'How do you say "Big Mac" in Russian?' Arnaud's mind drifted to his favourite film, *Pulp Fiction*.

'Big Mac,' replied Snow. 'They don't bother translating the words. I think Ronald McDonald is rather keen on brand awareness.'

Suddenly the tower blocks dropped away and they were at the river Dnipro. They crossed the bridge. The side they had just come from, the left bank, was littered with high-rise blocks; the right was covered with thick green trees. Several gold, onion-shaped domes poked out between them, reflecting the summer sun like mirrors. Arnaud recognised the Pechersk Lavra Monastery from his *Lonely Planet* guidebook and remembered it contained more mummies than all the pyramids and temples of Egypt. Next to the monastery was a tall metal statue of a woman. In one hand she held a dagger and in the other a shield. He couldn't remember what it was. Snow anticipated Arnaud's question. 'That's Brezhnev's mother.'

'What?'

'That's what they call it. Brezhnev ordered it built as a symbol of Mother Russia.'

'That's right.' He started to remember.

'You see the dagger? That was originally a sword but, after it was completed, the planners realised it was actually taller than the grand church tower at the Lavra Monastery. So it was made shorter. Brezhnev wasn't happy but in this case the Church beat the mighty Soviet State. It's still allegedly taller than the Statue of Liberty, but don't let the Yanks know! The statue is on top of the military museum. I'll take you there if you like; they've got loads of Soviet-era tanks, planes and helicopters.'

Arnaud stared. 'Cool. I'm into all that. You know, military stuff.'

Snow tried not to smile. 'Yeah?'

'Yeah. I was in the TA for a while at uni, even thought about becoming an officer.'

'What stopped you?'

'I'm not a fan of green. No; I met this girl, and anyway, I didn't in the end. I'm not a meathead. I'd rather not get shot by an Arab.'

'I used to be in the army.'

Arnaud blushed. Had he offended his fellow teacher? 'Oh?'

Snow paused to maximise Arnaud's potential embarrassment. 'The Salvation Army. I had to give it up, though; I got repetitive strain injury from banging my tambourine.' Snow held Arnaud's gaze for a second before both men started to laugh.

They reached the right bank of the river and took a road which suddenly became cobbled and wound its way between the trees and up towards the city centre. As they did, Snow pointed out the city barracks, 'Arsenalna', before they arrived at Khreshatik. Snow described it as a mixture of Bond and Oxford Streets, but four times as wide. Two minutes later, after fighting the traffic, the Lada mounted the pavement and parked in front of the arched gates of the apartment block. Victor opened the boot and handed Snow and Arnaud the bags. He then extended his hand and shook Arnaud's. 'Good day.'

'Good day,' replied Arnaud with a smile.

The Lada pulled back into the road and headed back down to Khreshatik. Arnaud looked around. Pushkinskaya ran parallel to Kyiv's main boulevard – Khreshatik. It was lined with six-storey apartment blocks at this end and a couple of government buildings at the other. On the ground floor of most of the blocks were restaurants, bars, a travel agent and a shoe shop. The road itself was just wide enough for two-way traffic. The pavement on both sides was almost as wide as the road.

'Not a bad street, eh? The architecture is a lot better here in the centre than on the outskirts.'

Arnaud agreed. From what he had seen so far, Kyiv's city centre reminded him of a much cleaner version of Paris, although his part-Gallic blood wouldn't allow him to vocalise this. 'So, where's the school?'

'Twenty minutes away by car on the other side of the river, I'm afraid, even though it's named after an area ten minutes' walk away. Come on, let's get inside. The quicker we dump your bags, the quicker I can show you the bars. Unless you're tired?'

'What, and miss out on a beer? Nah.' Arnaud looked at his watch. The flight had landed at ten-thirty, it had taken forty minutes to get his bags and clear customs, and about the same time to get here. It was almost midday. They walked through the door in the three-metre-high iron gates and round the back of the building. There was a small courtyard bordered by other apartment blocks from the neighbouring Prorizna Street. Snow led the way to a door and tapped in a code.

'The actual foyer and front door face the street but, for some bizarre reason, the other residents have decided to use the back door, and who am I to change this?' He shrugged. They walked through the door up three steps and into the dark foyer. The walls were painted a two-tone of cream and dark-green. Snow pushed '3' on the keypad and the small lift slowly descended.

'Here's something to remember. The floors are numbered in the American way. The flat is on the second floor but we need the third.'

'Right.' Arnaud frowned.

'This is not the ground floor but actually the first floor. Are you with me?'

He wasn't but didn't let on. On either side of the foyer sat rows of dark-green mailboxes, one for each flat.

'How many flats are there here?'

The lift arrived and they manoeuvred themselves and the bags in. 'Four per floor and six floors. But only one on the ground floor – the others are offices.'

The lift stopped abruptly and they stepped out. Snow walked

the five steps to the furthest corner and opened the padded metal door. Inside there was a second wooden door. Opening it, he beckoned Arnaud forward. 'Welcome to *Chez Nous*.'

'*Merci*.' Arnaud stepped over the threshold. 'Why two doors?'

Snow shrugged and followed. 'All the flats seem to have them. Security, I suppose.'

'They look like blast-proof doors. You know, like in the films.'

Snow laughed, 'Well, if you lose your key, please don't try to open them with a block of semtex.'

Laughing, they walked along the hall and Snow nodded at two doors. 'Your room is on the right.' Arnaud followed Snow into the room and they dropped the bags. 'Hope you don't mind sharing a flat too much?'

'Not at all, it reminds me of uni.'

'It was Joan's idea. She thought you could stay here until you found your feet. I had a spare room, so as far as I'm concerned it's yours. Stay as long as you need.'

'That's great, very kind. Thanks.'

'*Nichevo* – it's nothing, just happy to help. Grand tour?'

'OK.'

The flat had real wooden flooring throughout and light silver wallpaper. Snow led him in turn to the bathroom and kitchen before retracing his steps and heading into the lounge. Snow adopted an upper-class accent. 'If you will follow me, sir, you will find yourself entering the lounge with a south-facing balcony providing panoramic views of the city centre.' He dropped the act. 'My room is here, through the lounge.'

Snow opened the doors and they stepped on to the street-facing balcony. Arnaud looked up and down Pushkinskaya. To the left he could make out the top of a building with a large electronic clock. 'What's that?'

'That's the clock on Maidan, Independence Square. You can hear it chime each hour. It also has a thermometer. I have a picture of myself standing in front of it with a reading of minus twenty-five.'

'Cool.'

Southall Car Auction, London, UK

The hammer fell and the car was his. Arkadi Cheban was happy. The 2.5 V6 Vectra was a step up from his Escort and certainly a million times better than the beaten-up Lada he had left in Tiraspol. He had paid only £1,800 for the car, which was at least £1,400 less than the dealer price. He had waited outside the auction as the car was started, looking for any telltale blue smoke coming from the exhaust pipe and checking for oil leaks on the floor. Neither was present. The dark-green Vectra had a set of after-market 17' alloy wheels fitted and a transfer on the rear screen proclaiming it to be a Holden. Both of these he would remove. The car would perform better on a pair of its standard 16' rims, and it was a 'Vauxhall'.

Cheban knew about cars; he knew how to tune them and he knew how to drive them. These skills he had learnt in his native Transdniester, working on Soviet-made cars where only the ingenious managed to stay on the road. By the time he had finished working on his new car, it would be anonymous and fast, just what he needed to operate without being noticed. He had almost bid on the BMW he had seen but decided not to. A BMW was a bandit's car and, even though he was a bandit, he didn't want the world to know. He was happy to be back in London and decided it was now time to finally spend some of the money he'd earned from his 'uncle'. Shipments were coming in via Tilbury docks from the continent and he was always nearby observing, just in case anything went wrong.

On one occasion he'd believed the operation had been compromised when he saw a group of men watching from a van. He had kept his own watch on them and been very relieved to find they were from HM Immigration and were concentrating on a shipping company using illegal immigrants as labour. The fact that he himself was an illegal immigrant had not been lost on him. That had been close, as his shipment was due in the same day. But, unperturbed, he continued to lurk in the shadows with his pair of Leica, high-powered binoculars. He kept a 'birds of Britain' book in his glove compartment just in case anyone wanted to confront him. This, along with a false Ornithological Society of Latvia photo identification card and an RSPB sticker on the windscreen, would hopefully explain his strange behaviour to all but the very persistent. These he would need to add to his new vehicle.

He paid in cash for the car and drove it away. Sticking to the speed limit, he cruised out of South London and headed east for the Bluewater shopping centre in Kent. The traffic was mostly light at this time of day on a Wednesday, but built up as he approached the complex. He parked his new car by the House of Fraser entrance and entered the store. He was taken aback both by the range of goods and the prices. The shops on the streets of Tiraspol still displayed shoddy, Soviet-era clothes and cheap Chinese electrical goods. He still couldn't get used to the choices available to him here, especially now he was 'cash rich' – compared to many, that was.

He picked up a Ralph Lauren polo shirt and almost laughed out loud at the price: £55. Nevertheless, he chose four: two blues, a black and a dark-red. Next he picked up a couple of pairs of chinos and three pullovers before finally adding a jacket to the pile. The assistant had a happy look in his eyes as he rang up the total – in excess of £700. Arkadi smiled and paid in cash. The assistant was slightly perturbed by this but put the sale through anyway and, in his estuary accent, which seemed out of place in an upmarket shop, wished him a 'nice day'.

Cheban next picked up a mall map and studied the layout. He spotted the shop he wanted and entered. It was a small unit but full of authenticated celebrity items such as autographed pictures. He pointed to a photograph of David Beckham and said he wanted that one. The assistant informed him of the price; this time Cheban did laugh out loud but still laid down a pile of notes on the counter. Feeling happy with himself, he grabbed a large coffee before returning to his car and driving back to London. Later that day he would dress to impress and give the Polish waitress her present; he had overheard her say she liked the new 'England football captain'. First, however, he would work a bit on the car. He made a mental note to go to the nearest Vauxhall dealer and get a set of proper wheels. He was allowed to look flash but the car was not.

Odessa, Southern Ukraine

Varchenko put the large Crimean grape into his mouth and looked at Ruslan. He was a mess. Tubes were sticking out of his nose and greasy hair protruded from his bandaged scalp. He was now sitting upright and could finally speak.

'Tell me exactly what happened.' Varchenko held a cup to Ruslan's lips and he drank thankfully.

'We followed the BMW as you ordered, but, as soon as we got near enough to ram them, they opened fire.'

Varchenko had been given some information by the 'tame' local militia who had found the wreckage of the G Wagon and Ruslan, but he wanted to hear it firsthand.

'We had no chance; their weapons were automatic. I think I managed to return fire then my front tyres blew, and the next thing I can remember, the jeep is rolling off the road.'

'But it was armour-plated!' Varchenko gave him another mouthful of water.

'Then the bullets were armour-piercing. Valeriy Ivanovich, I did my best… What of the others?'

There had been three others in the Mercedes, each armed with Glock handguns. As employees of Varchenko's security firm, Getman Bespeka, he had personally met their families and dependants and provided financial recompense. 'They are all dead, Ruslan. You are the only survivor and that, I presume, is because they wanted you to live.'

Ruslan swallowed hard and closed his eyes. 'I will kill them!'

'No, Ruslan, you will not. They want me, not you.' Varchenko placed his hand on that of his injured employee. 'You will be well looked after here.'

Varchenko left the hospital and climbed into his waiting car. What he was dealing with here was more serious than he had imagined. He had to find out who these people really were, which meant losing face and calling his old subordinate, Genna.

Chapter 6

City Centre, Kyiv, Ukraine

Breathing deeply but steadily, Snow pumped his legs up the hill and past the Ukrainian parliament, the Verhovna Rada. It was 7.15 a.m. and he was halfway through his morning run. The guards outside were used to seeing joggers in the park opposite, but Snow was the only one to run on their side of the road and directly past them. It astonished him how close he could actually come to the entrance without being challenged. Cresting the hill he increased his pace and ran past the presidential administration building. His route, which he had now perfected, took him down Pushkinskaya, across Maidan and along Khreshatik, up the hill past the Hotel Dnipro to the Verhovna Rada, the presidential administration building and back down the hill, this time via the Ivana Franka Theatre, then through Passage before finally running uphill again and into Pushkinskaya.

On days that he felt he needed to push himself, he would stop halfway at the Dynamo Stadium and complete a few laps of the track before continuing on his way. Today, however, he felt hampered by a mild hangover. It was Monday morning and Arnaud's first day at Podilsky, yet they had both decided the night before to have 'a few pints' at Eric's. Snow was glad that Mitch was in Belarus on business and that Michael Jones hadn't made it; otherwise, it would have become a heavy session. Fifteen minutes later he was stretching outside the front of his building as the street sweepers made their way towards him.

'Fancy a coffee?' Arnaud was on the balcony above, cup in one hand, waving. Snow needed no second invite and within minutes was walking from the shower to kitchen. Arnaud had made toast and was busy buttering a thick slice as he read an old issue of the *Kyiv Post*.

'You should have told me you were going to jog. I'd have come too.'

Snow finished drying his hair and dropped the towel on the empty seat. 'After what you drank last night?'

'Hmm, maybe not.' Arnaud bit into his toast. As Snow poured himself a coffee, Arnaud noticed a faint, long scar on Snow's right leg, stretching from just below his boxer shorts to just above the knee. 'How did you do that?'

Snow sipped his coffee. 'I was in a bad car crash a few years back. Lucky to survive actually.'

'Sorry, I didn't know.'

'How would you?' It was too soon for Snow to share his past with his new friend. Snow surveyed the table. Arnaud had made a large pile of hand-cut toast and set out two plates. Snow sat and took a couple of slices. 'You'd make someone a good wife.'

Arnaud looked up, his lips caked in crumbs. 'I'm open to offers.'

For the previous day and a half, since Arnaud's arrival, he and Snow had mostly got drunk and ogled women. Snow found himself liking Arnaud and seeing in him himself ten years ago. They'd started with a tour of the city centre, beer bottles in hand, purchased from a street kiosk. Snow had led Arnaud up Prorizna Street and along Volodymyrska, pausing at the Golden Gate (the medieval entrance to Kyiv), the old KGB (now SBU) building and two cathedrals, which Arnaud had already forgotten the names of, before pointing out the British Embassy. 'If you ever get stopped by the police, just say "British Embassy",' Snow had advised. 'The local militia are a bit scared of stopping a foreigner and will think you're a diplomat.'

They then met Michael Jones and his wife in a small, open-air bar on Andrivskyi Uzviz, the steep, cobbled tourist area which led down to the oldest part of Kyiv, Podil. There Arnaud had been excited to see the vast range of ex-Soviet militaria on offer, in addition to paintings, amber jewellery and numerous *matrioshka* (Russian dolls) of all shapes and sizes. Snow managed to persuade him not to buy a fur hat; instead he bought two Vostok automatic KGB watches, a hipflask, and a set of *matrioshka* painted with the faces of Soviet leaders. The vendor said that if Arnaud supplied pictures of his family he could have a set of *matrioshka* hand-painted for him. Arnaud agreed and had already started mulling who should be the biggest and who the smallest. He finally decided on his dog, then his sister, but only just.

'How are you enjoying Kyiv, Arnaud?' Michael had asked, his wife, Ina, sitting at his side.

Arnaud looked down the street at a pair of local girls. 'The beer and the scenery are great.'

Michael, who had already finished three pints, or half-litres as they were served in Ukraine, let his face crease into a dirty-toothed smile. 'You'd have to be either bent or stupid to have an unemployed knob here!'

Michael sniggered while Ina nudged him in the side. 'What? It's true for sure.'

'So, which are you then?' Arnaud had looked at his flatmate.

Snow finished his mouthful of beer. 'The exception to the rule.'

Ina smiled and touched his hand and Arnaud felt slightly embarrassed. Was there something he didn't know about? 'How long have you been here?' he asked Michael.

'Me? Phew, too long!' He sniggered again. 'I came in 1996 for four months and stayed ten years. I could apply for a Ukrainian passport!'

'Has it changed a lot?'

'Some things. When I came here there were no supermarkets and people bought their meat on the street.'

'Michael, that's not true.' Ina felt the need to defend her country. 'We always could buy meat in the Gastronom or the market.'

'Which was on the street!' Michael quickly swigged more beer.

'Michael!' Ina was annoyed. When the men got together they became just as silly as the schoolboys they both taught. 'We have more shops now since independence and there are more places to go.'

'Expensive places,' Michael, who was known for his conservative spending on all things except beer and cigarettes, added.

'So, Arnodt, where are you from?' Ina ignored her drunken husband.

'Arnaud.'

'Sorry, what did I say? Arnod… Arnode. Your name is a bit difficult for me to say. I haven't heard it before.' She blushed.

'It's French. My mother is French, from Nice, and my dad is English, from Surrey – it's not "nice".'

'So you speak French and English fluently, Arnoode?' Ina was impressed.

'Yes, I've always been bilingual. For me, it's natural. What about you? Your English is good.'

Michael finished his fourth half-litre and, shouting at a passing waitress, ordered another round. 'Wasn't when we met. She couldn't say a word.'

'That's not quite true, Michael. I learnt English at school but never used it. In the Soviet Union we did not have the possibility to travel to England, so I never got to practise. Even my English teacher had never been to England, can you imagine that?'

'Wow. That's crazy. The basis of learning any foreign language is exposure to native speakers.'

'So…' Michael's eyes lit up. 'Ten years ago I exposed myself to her and she's never been the same!'

Michael roared with laughter and Snow almost gagged on his beer. There was a delayed reaction from Ina, who punched her husband in the ribs.

'Right,' Snow said, finishing his coffee and snapping back to the present. 'The school bus will be outside at eight. It'll just pull up on the pavement so we have to be ready for it. I'll finish getting dressed. Are you ready?'

Arnaud nodded. 'Yeah, just got to do my hair.'

Snow looked at his flatmate's blond mop. 'Sorry, mate, I thought you were wearing a woolly hat.'

SBU Headquarters, Volodymyrska Street, Kyiv

Dudka had received the call late on Sunday. His mobile was switched off; the call to his landline, a number only a very select few knew, had interrupted his meal. Sitting in his flat on Zankovetskaya Street, he had been looking forward to a little stroll with his dog before retiring for the evening. Now, however, his weekend had been shortened and he had to look at this. The deaths of Varchenko's employees had been kept very quiet indeed. A few thousand dollars here and there had reinforced Varchenko's position with the Odessa police and Dudka guessed that the relatives had also been paid off. Such was the way with bandits like Valeriy. He had sounded almost humble on the telephone, although not quite, when asking for Dudka's help. He had relayed the story of the meeting with Knysh that led to the shootings.

'Why did you not tell me this sooner?' demanded Dudka, now standing, arms folded, in the kitchen. 'This is a very serious matter. You have withheld information in a highly public SBU

71

investigation – in fact, possibly the most public investigation in SBU history!'

Varchenko, although humbled, was nevertheless angered by Genna's tone. 'This man threatened me and I took action. He is a danger to us both and needs to be stopped.'

Again, Dudka had to concede that Varchenko was correct. He had too much to lose himself. As he looked around his large, but still Soviet, flat, this, however, was not obvious. He had been very clever, investing his money in first his daughter's and now his granddaughter's education in Switzerland. It was they and his late wife who had benefited from his agreement with Valeriy Ivanovich, not Dudka himself.

'Very well, Valeriy. I will send you my best man and you will tell him all about this meeting in the car. You will give him a full description of this Knysh. He will carry a computer with photo-fit technology. He will be under my orders to speak to no one but you and me.'

Varchenko snorted at the other end of the phone but was nevertheless relieved. 'Genna, I hope for both our sakes that this is a man we can trust.'

Dudka rubbed his eyes. He hadn't slept well and morning had caught him unawares. His second cup of coffee finished, he called his secretary to bring another. She entered followed by Boris Budanov, who had been summoned by his boss. Dudka pointed to a seat and Budanov sat. Once the secretary had shut the door Dudka spoke.

'Boris Ruslanovich, I have a highly delicate and secretive task for you to perform. You will tell no one about this and speak to no one other than myself and the person you will be interviewing. Do I make myself understood?'

'Yes, Gennady Stepanovich.'

'Good.' He pushed an envelope across the desk. 'Inside you will find the name and address of the person you are to see and also $300. You are to use this money to purchase an airline ticket to Odessa and cover any other expenses. You will take a laptop computer with our photo-fit software installed and will compile an accurate image of our suspect. Any questions?'

Budanov swallowed hard. 'Does this relate to the Malik case, Gennady Stepanovich?'

'Yes. And before you ask, yes, that case is being handled by Blazhevich, but this is a new and confidential lead. Get to Odessa, get the photo-fit and bring it back to me as soon as possible. I cannot emphasise enough how critical this matter is.'

Podilsky School International, Berezniki, Kyiv, Ukraine

The journey to school had been interesting. Arnaud recognised a few of the places he had already been to but within five minutes was lost. The bus stopped in total four times to collect children. Unlike his secondary school teaching experience, at Podilsky Arnaud would be teaching Year Three primary right up to A-level, or Years Twelve and Thirteen, as they were now called. Smiley faces looked at Arnaud and asked who he was. Snow did the introductions. Forty minutes later they were at the school complex and the pupils were running to meet up with friends already in their classrooms or arriving by car. The teenagers were too cool to run and, wearing a mixture of predominantly black and purple baggy jeans and 'hoodies', ambled in at their own speed.

Arnaud took in the size of the building. 'Surely this isn't all the school, is it?'

'No. The building is a technical college and it rents out some of its rooms. We have the wing on the right. On the left is an auditorium we use for concerts, etc. There's also a small café and some other offices that are let to a couple of businesses.'

As Snow and Arnaud entered through the large aluminium doors, Arnaud's attention was taken by a figure approaching from the main road. He stood motionless for a second. 'Bugger me... look at that... she's bloody gorgeous...'

Snow turned and saw a woman approaching. 'Yep, that she is.'

Arnaud was still staring. 'Who is she? Please don't let her be one of the mums.'

'Close your mouth, you're dribbling.'

'What? Oh.' Arnaud raised his hand to his mouth but felt nothing.

The woman approached and removed her sunglasses. She looked directly at Snow, then Arnaud, who was blocking the entrance.

'*Dobroye utro.*' Snow bid her a good morning.

The woman nodded at him, gave Arnaud a weird glance, then made her way into the building and towards the left wing.

'You know her? Please tell me you know her?' Arnaud was almost begging.

'Her name is Larissa. She works for a Swiss watch importer and, yes, she is bloody gorgeous.' Snow put his hand on his friend's back. 'Come on, we better get inside.'

As they walked towards the sign saying 'Podilsky School International', Arnaud couldn't help but turn once more and stare. He was rewarded with a glance of Larissa's pert bottom as she disappeared through a door.

Chaika Sports Complex, Kyiv

The phone was handed to him by Oleg. Bull removed his ear protectors. '*Da?*' The voice at the other end told him there had been an interesting development. Bull raised his hand and the others stopped firing. The target range fell silent as he listened intently to his source. 'You know what must be done.' The voice replied that he had understood and could be relied upon. The call ended, Oleg gave his commanding officer a questioning look. Bull waved him away and readied his weapon. The range erupted once more as controlled fire ripped apart targets.

Podilsky School International

The classroom was full of teachers with cups of tea and coffee. Arnaud had already learnt that Ukrainians drank just as much, if not more, tea as the British. Arnaud sat at the back with Michael and Snow. Joan Greenhill was at the teacher's desk at the front of the room, reading notes. She looked up over her glasses and smiled. 'Are we all here?'

'Yes, Mrs Greenhill,' came the choral reply from well-practised members of staff mimicking children in assembly.

'Good, good. Now the first thing you have all probably noticed is this gentleman sitting at the back. Arnaud, wave!'

He did as requested. 'Hello.'

'Most of you will have met Arnaud already, but for those of you that haven't I'll just give a brief introduction. Arnaud has joined us from the UK and will be teaching French, ESL and some P.E.'

Arnaud was always a bit embarrassed meeting new people, especially women, and had turned a shade of pink. Greenhill then carried on with the rest of the agenda. Arnaud listened intently as he tried to soak up as much information about the school and its running as possible. Snow nudged him in the side. Arnaud looked past him and out of the window to see Larissa walking past. She was the most beautiful woman he had ever seen in real life and he couldn't take his eyes off her.

As the meeting finished, Michael tapped Arnaud on the shoulder. 'Drink?'

'You need to ask?'

'I know just the place.' It was Snow. 'We'll stop a car.'

The three teachers collected their bags and left the school. They walked to the main road where Snow held out his hand. A car stopped, this time a large Volga, and the driver wound down the window. Snow leaned forward, told the driver where they wanted to go and haggled over the price. He agreed and they got in, Snow in front with the others behind. Arnaud noticed the ubiquitous miniature icon on the dashboard of mother and baby. Even with all four windows open the car stank of smoke. The driver steered one-handed while his left hand moved from lips to window to flick ash. The car took them from the newer Soviet utilitarian left bank to the picturesque right and over the Paton Bridge before depositing them outside a street café.

Leaning back on his plastic, garden-type chair, Arnaud sipped what had now, after three days, become his usual: Obolon Temne – Obolon dark beer. 'That girl. Jesus, she is… oh, I can't describe…'

'Which one?' Snow knew exactly who but wanted Arnaud to squirm.

'Larissa, the one from the school.' Arnaud stared into the distance.

Michael smiled and spoke in Welsh-accented Russian '*Sto procent.*' He continued in English, 'One hundred per cent. Now if I had an unemployed knob…'

'How do you know her?' Arnaud turned to face Snow.

Snow sipped his Svetly – light beer. 'Just about everyone has tried it on with her and got nowhere. She doesn't even give me the time of day – as you saw.'

'Perhaps she likes the rugged, handsome type?' Arnaud adjusted the collar on his shirt.

'No, she turned me down,' Snow countered.

'That's because she's looking for a lover not a father.'

'Cheeky sod.'

'Could be a lesbo. If so, I'd like to watch…' Michael pulled on his cigarette.

'Well, she hasn't said no to me yet,' Arnaud retorted.

'Good luck.'

Arnaud took a large swig of beer. 'Who Dares Wins.'

'What?' Snow paused, mid-slurp.

'You know, the old SAS motto.'

'SAS.' Michael raised his eyebrows above the rims of his glasses and looked at Snow.

'Shoreham Angling Society,' Snow said, deadpan.

SBU Headquarters, Volodymyrska Street, Kyiv

Budanov arrived back at the SBU building on Volodymyrska just after eight in the evening. He had taken the first flight to Odessa, arriving at 11.40 a.m., where he had been driven to the address in Fontanka by a waiting car. He had been shocked by whom he was to meet and the implications this had for the investigation. Varchenko had been a legendary KGB officer long before Budanov was born, and to meet him was a privilege but chilling at the same time. Budanov had tried to control his nerves and acted as professionally as he could.

This special mission had placed far more pressure on him than anyone could imagine. During the return flight, which lasted one hour and ten minutes, he had sat alone, constantly checking and rechecking his notes and the computerised image. He didn't want to make any mistakes. He entered through the main doors and flashed his pass at the bored guard behind the protective glass who waved him past and continued to read the *Fakty* newspaper concealed beneath his desk. As he approached his chief's office he could see light seeping under the door. He knocked and was immediately told to enter. Dudka looked tired, the bags under his eyes even larger than usual, and for the first time Budanov could see a five o'clock shadow around his jowls. There was also a faint smell of pepper vodka in the air.

'You have the report?' Dudka glanced up from his papers.

'Yes, Gennady Stepanovich.' Budanov passed him the notes. Dudka looked at the handwritten sheets, which were surprisingly neat. 'I will have this typed up for you by nine tomorrow morning.'

'Very well.' He handed them back. 'Show me the photo-fit.'

Budanov opened his bag and powered up the laptop. 'Shall I print the image or would you like to look at it on the screen?'

'Show me on the screen. Later I'll connect it to my printer in this room.' He motioned to the large printer standing next to the filing cabinet.

The Fujitsu Siemens came to life and was placed in front of Dudka. The image appeared on the screen. The face was thin with round, dark-brown eyes and a wide mouth. There was a prominent chin. The hair was dark and swept back, the ears quite small.

'You are sure the man looked like this?' Dudka questioned.

'Yes, Gennady Stepanovich. General Varchenko was quite adamant.'

'He is no longer a general, Boris Ruslanovich.'

'He said that the eyes were most striking and the chin was prominent.'

'OK, Boris. You have done well. Was there any money left over from that which I gave you?'

'Yes, Gennady Stepanovich – $80.' Budanov pulled out his wallet and placed the notes and also his receipts on the table.

Dudka took the receipts and put them in his drawer. He then pushed the money towards Budanov. 'Thank you, Boris, you have done well. Blazhevich will now continue with the case. Take this and get that pretty wife of yours something nice.' He nodded at the SBU's rising star.

Budanov took the money and nodded in return. 'Thank you.'

'Goodnight, Boris Ruslanovich.'

Budanov rose and left the room. 'Goodnight, Gennady Stepanovich.'

Shutting the door behind him, Budanov pulled a handkerchief from his pocket and wiped his brow and hands; both were clammy.

Back in the office, Dudka continued to look at the image for a few minutes, consigning it to memory before shutting down the laptop and popping it into its bag. He opened his drawer and removed the half-bottle of vodka, poured two fingers, stood and walked over to the window. The street lights illuminated the cobbles. A faded, orange-and-yellow, electric trolley bus glided along towards the opera. He remembered, years before, going with his wife and half-smiled at the memory. Irina had loved the opera and loved him. They had made quite a pair, the then-dashing young KGB officer and the ballerina. Their careers had been good for each other. She had toured and he had sometimes accompanied her, gathering intelligence as he went.

The doors to the Opera House opened and patrons started to flood out, the street lights catching their brightly coloured evening gowns, further illuminating the night. He hadn't gone to the opera since her death; he couldn't bring himself to. Together they had been strong and in love, but cancer had killed her. It had torn him apart inside and he had never recovered – but this he had also never admitted to anyone. He watched for a few minutes more as humanity passed by. He downed the vodka, a silent toast to the past. It was a two-minute drive in his official car or a ten-minute walk, mostly downhill, to his empty flat, empty apart from his little dog. It looked nice out so he decided to walk. He picked up the laptop bag and locked his office.

Chapter 7

Podilsky School International

'I'm going to do it.' Arnaud drained his coffee and nodded.

'You're a braver man than I.' Snow finished his slice of pizza. 'Are you sure you want to shit on your own doorstep so soon?'

Snow and Arnaud were sitting in the small staffroom of Podilsky School. It was lunchtime and Arnaud hadn't been able to get Larissa out of his head. Michael bit into a cheese roll. 'Why not try? All that can happen is she slaps you.'

'Who's been slapping who?' It was Vanessa Taylor, a Canadian pre-school teacher, who had heard the end of the sentence as she opened the door.

'Just a silly-billy in my Year Three class. I made them sit in the corner,' replied Michael.

'Best thing for them. They should kiss and make up,' replied Vanessa as she grabbed a biscuit and left the room.

'There you are, just kiss her,' advised Michael.

Arnaud stood. 'I will.'

'Go on then,' Snow pushed.

'OK.' He wiped his lips, popped a mint into his mouth and left the room. He walked out through the reception, along the corridor and past the main entrance. The greasy smell of the Institute's café on his left, and their abominations, hit him as he passed. He turned the corner and saw three doors straight ahead and a staircase on his right. The writing on the doors was in Cyrillic but there was a small watch emblem on the first. He took a deep breath and knocked on the door. It didn't open. He knocked again and it was opened by a fat, peroxide-blonde woman. She said something in Russian which he didn't understand; he guessed she had asked him to sit, so he did. She shut the door and returned to the fax machine, which was disgorging a multi-page fax.

Arnaud looked on, wondering what the hell to do next. The blonde woman, who was clearly the receptionist, shouted into the back room and a man in a tie and shirt sleeves appeared and looked at the fax. He shouted at the woman and disappeared back into his office without even acknowledging Arnaud. The receptionist tried to fold the fax, which was still falling from the machine on a continuous roll of paper. Arnaud still had no idea what to do. He didn't speak the language, so couldn't ask for Larissa, and he didn't know what to say to the receptionist. He'd started to rise to leave when the outer door opened and in stepped Larissa. She was wearing a burgundy skirt which hugged her hips and a matching jacket that accentuated her bust. She glanced at Arnaud, puzzled, then the receptionist ran to her and pointed at the fax. Arnaud still didn't understand a word but knew he had obviously come at the wrong time. Larissa took the fax and scanned the pages. Her face looked serious. Arnaud stood to make his escape.

'Can I help you?' Larissa asked in accented English.

Arnaud stuttered, 'I... er... I... wondered if you...'

Larissa looked back at the fax then read the words aloud, quietly: '...*depuis de ton...*' Her brow wrinkled as she tried to make sense of the words.

Arnaud's ears pricked up; he had heard French. '*Vous parlez Français?*' he questioned.

Larissa raised her eyes for a moment, not comprehending, then spoke again in English. 'The fax is in French but we do not understand.'

A huge smile appeared on his face. 'Let me help you.' Arnaud took the fax and read it out loud. Both Larissa and the receptionist stood wide-eyed. The back room door opened again. The man looked at the stranger reading his fax. '*Bonjour.*' Arnaud smiled.

'*Bonjour,*' replied the man uncertainly. He turned to Larissa and spoke before retreating back into the room.

'Can you translate into English for me? It is very important, from our new supplier in Switzerland.' Larissa looked directly into his eyes.

Arnaud's heart started to pound in his chest. 'Yes, I can do that, but I do charge.'

'What is the cost?' Larissa asked.

'Go out with me in the evening?' His heart pounded faster.

'Go out?'

'Yes, meet me for a drink or a meal.'

Larissa closed her eyes momentarily and shook her head, a slight curl appearing on her lips. 'OK. I am free tonight.'

'Superb.' Arnaud's smile became so wide that his face hurt.

Kyiv Oblast, Ukraine

Heavy curtains hung at the doors to the club. The interior décor was dark and opulent. The several other clients who could be seen were partly hidden in their own secluded booths. Bull faced his guest. 'It would be an electronic transfer?'

The clerk nodded. 'The money would be sent from one account to another through the ether. It takes milliseconds.'

Bull refilled the clerk's glass. 'The client could then draw on it?'

'In theory, yes, but what usually happens is that the money is never seen at all, merely shifted from one account to the next. It is not like a personal or small business account; the client will not walk into the bank and demand cash.'

'But he could?' Bull enquired.

'Of course he could, but it would take several days for the bank to retrieve the funds.'

Bull was shocked. 'The bank has $100,000,000 in cash?'

'It would have to get it. If the bank has accepted the transfer then, through international agreement, the money would be allocated to the bank by the clearance houses. But can you imagine how heavy that amount of cash would be?' The clerk laughed and emptied his glass. He drank the expensive whiskey like a toast, quickly, too quickly to savour.

Bull smiled, refilled the tumbler and asked, 'How heavy?'

'I cannot estimate how heavy but it would fill ten vans at least, maybe more.' The clerk looked wistful. 'Imagine what you could do with that much money…'

Build a seven-star hotel in Odessa, mused Bull. 'So, tell me, how much could a client, in general, demand in cash?'

'It depends. At my bank, perhaps $80,000, perhaps $280,000; it all depends. Some clients deposit funds regularly. I know of one who deposits large cash amounts monthly.'

Bull's eyes flickered. 'How much?'

The clerk shifted in his seat and looked around before answering in a conspiratorial stage whisper. 'Between one and four million US dollars.'

'So that amount could then be withdrawn?'

'Yes, that is correct. It is a fallacy that banks hold millions. They have a reserve and whatever cash has been deposited before it is shipped off to be securely stored. Remember, Odessa Bank is quite small. Larger banks attract larger clients.'

Bull signalled for another bottle of whiskey 'So, to clarify… If one knew when a deposit was to be made, one could make a withdrawal of the same amount?'

The clerk smiled at the waitress, who was scantily clad and extremely beautiful, as she poured a large measure from the new bottle of Johnny Walker Blue Label into his glass.

'Exactly.' His gaze followed her and her long legs back to the bar.

'Perhaps I will need to make a large withdrawal in the future and would need your assistance.' Bull fixed the clerk square in the eyes and placed a thick brown envelope on the glass-topped table.

The clerk's left eyebrow twitched as he picked up the inch-thick package. 'I am happy to help.'

Bull nodded and abruptly stood. 'I am sorry but I have to leave you. Please stay and enjoy my hospitality.'

Bull took the clerk's hand in a firm grip. The clerk was unnerved by the piercing green eyes but more than happy with the deal. Bull left and was replaced by the waitress, who sat close to the clerk and placed her manicured hand high on his fat thigh.

Khreshatik Street, Kyiv

Arnaud waited impatiently outside the main entrance to Khreshatik metro station. He felt like a right plonker standing there. He checked his breath for the umpteenth time and then his watch. Unlike most young men, Arnaud was never late. He always liked to be the first anywhere so he could get the best seat at the best table for the best view. This, he knew, he got from his mother, who was forever hurrying his father up. Again he looked at the watch. Even though it was set five minutes fast – a fact he couldn't forget – she was now ten minutes late. He'd give her ten more and then leave to find Aidan and the others. Aha! There she was! Trying to suppress his excitement and the growing bulge in his jeans, Arnaud walked forward to meet Larissa.

'Hello there!'

'Hi,' Larissa replied, looking him up and down. What was he wearing?

'You're a bit late. Did you have to wait for a train or something?' he enquired, leaning forward in an attempt to kiss her lips. She turned her cheek.

'No. Where are we going?'

'Where are you going to take me?'

She looked him in the eyes. 'You are going to take me to Le Grande Café.'

'What's that?'

She looked shocked. 'You don't know what Le Grande Café is?'

'No,' he lied.

'It's the best French restaurant in Kyiv.' Surely he was playing?

'I thought we'd go somewhere Ukrainian?' he asked hopefully. Le Grande Café, he had heard from Michael, was as pricey as they came, and, according to Snow, survived primarily on the custom of new Ukrainians and corporate expense accounts.

'I hate Ukrainian food,' she replied and took his arm. They walked to the side of the road where she hailed a taxi.

Rock Café, Kyiv

Mitch Turney leant back in his chair and exhaled cigar smoke. 'I've forgotten. You ever been to California, bud?'

Snow lowered his glass. 'I've seen *Baywatch*.'

Turney nodded and took another drag on his Havana. 'Let me tell you, those women are pigs compared to here, baaaby.'

'Your ex-wife included?'

'My ex-wife especially.'

Mitch Turney, country manager for Perry & Roe, was a sleek, forty-two-year-old Californian who had been in Kyiv a year longer than Snow. Having just negotiated an eighteen-month extension to his contract he was in a celebratory mood. Having already consumed half a bottle of imported tequila before Snow arrived, and the rest after, he showed no signs of slowing down. The second bottle arrived. At over $60 a go, this made both waitress and bartender, who were anticipating a large tip, smile.

Turney continued, 'Don't misunderstand me, man. I mean, they take care of themselves there, but in the US you need a second mortgage to pay for all the damn cosmetics.' He stubbed out the cigar and cast Snow a look out of the corner of his eye. 'So, when are you going to hang up your chalk and get a proper job?'

'When are you going to stop selling sugar water?' Snow poured him a shot.

'Never.' He raised his glass. 'I'll make you a deal. You teach the kids how to drink my cola and I'll promise to become a feminist.'

'Deal,' replied Snow.

Mitch necked Mexico's finest. 'I've often thought of myself as a butch lesbian. Speaking of which, I got an email from Donna.'

Snow put his empty shot glass on the table. Donna was his ex-girlfriend. It hadn't ended well; she had dumped him. Snow folded his arms – a subconscious show of defence and insecurity, the old regiment shrink would have told him. 'What earth-shattering statement did she make this time?'

Mitch frowned and poured two more shots. 'She invited me to her wedding.'

Snow was stunned; it had been just a year since they'd split. 'Who's the unlucky guy?'

'Aidan, come on, man, don't be bitter. She wasn't for you. Call it fate, call it karma. Yeah, karma. Things happen. My ex-wife and I split – karma.'

'I thought that was Carnal?'

Mitch laughed. 'Yeah, that was carnal; I wanted to sleep with someone else. The point I'm making is you were too good for her.'

'Er, thanks, Mum.'

Mitch placed a hand on his buddy's shoulder. 'Aidan, man, you just gotta believe in karma. Until then, hey, join me in seeking out the carnal!'

Smile back in place, both men drank.

The 'date' had been a bit awkward and Arnaud was pissed off. They had arrived at the restaurant where he had been shocked by the prices and also by a couple of spelling mistakes on the menu. He had, however, managed to ignore this as he was with her and she looked even better than he remembered. They made conversation for a while, Larissa saying she lived on her own in Kyiv, her family being from a city Arnaud had never heard of. Arnaud spoke about his dad the banker in Surrey and his French mum. This she had found interesting, and at one point he felt he had made it when she asked if he would teach her to speak French. However, as he moved his hand to try and touch hers, he tipped her glass, spilling red wine all over her pale-green skirt. Arnaud shuddered. Things had gone downhill from there. Larissa had been highly annoyed and he had turned the same colour as the wine. She left in a taxi and he was left with the bill.

Still feeling a mixture of anger, exasperation and depression, Arnaud opened the door to Rock Café and made for the bar. He pointed at the tap. 'Beer. Big.'

The barman nodded and duly pulled him a half-litre of Obolon.

'Oi, Froggy!' a familiar voice called from the shadows.

Arnaud turned to see Snow at a corner table with another ex-pat. He collected his drink and ambled over.

'Nice night?' The ex-pat spoke first.

Arnaud sat. 'Ha!'

'This is Mitch. Mitch, this is Arnaud.'

'Nice to meet ya, buddy.' Turney extended his hand. 'Aidan here has been telling me all about you. So where'd she take you?'

Arnaud sat. 'Le Grande Sodding Café.'

Snow whistled and Turney took in a deep breath, 'No offence, but on what you guys earn?'

'I hope you made her pay, Arnaud?' Snow asked, grinning too much for Arnaud's liking.

'What! I even had to pay for the sodding taxi. I bet she thinks going Dutch is a sexual position, not that I'm ever going to find out!' He took a long gulp of beer.

'Ah, the price of love.' Snow squeezed his thigh.

'Get off!'

'You, my friend,' stated Turney as he lit another Havana, 'need a little trip to Mars.'

'Do what?'

Mars Strip Bar, Kyiv

Mitch pointed to an empty table to the left of the pole and handed the waiter a note. They were duly seated and the reserved sign was removed. By the time Arnaud had taken off his jacket, Mitch had a bottle of tequila and was filling the first of three glasses. 'Welcome to Mars.'

Arnaud looked around, his eyes now becoming more accustomed to the light. 'Looks more like the bar from *Star Wars*.'

'Strange taste in décor…' Mitch tapped the plastic rock-effect wall behind him. 'But the women are out of this world.'

From concealed speakers, an indiscernible Eighties' Madonna hit faded in, and through a red curtain stepped a peroxide blonde dressed in a lime-green bikini. She threw her arms above her head and started to lip sync and then bent over.

'Bottoms up!' Snow raised his glass.

'I'll drink to that!' Mitch beamed.

Arnaud pulled a face as the liquor hit his throat. 'Are Mexicans forced to drink this?'

Chapter 8

Petropavlivska Borschagivka, Kyiv Oblast

Bull refilled his young guest's glass. 'Your first time in Ukraine, Sergey?' Gorodetski nodded. 'You will find it an easier place to tolerate than Moscow. Your brother and I shared many a good time here. That is now sadly only a memory.' Bull raised his glass. 'Your brother!'

The two men touched glasses and downed the Nemirof, the ice-cold vodka not burning the throat but warming the stomach.

'You told me you had found him?' Gorodetski leaned forward eagerly.

Bull removed an envelope from his pocket. His eyes narrowed and his mouth twitched before he spoke. 'Here is the man who was responsible. It was his group of Islamic fighters who tortured and killed my friend, your brother.'

Gorodetski opened the envelope and removed the photograph. A balding, middle-aged Asian grinned and shook hands with a large man, chest heavy with medals. 'Who is he?'

'His name is Jasraj Malik. He is a British ethnic Pakistani.'

'Who's the other one?'

Bull snorted. 'That, my friend, is KGB General Valeriy Varchenko…'

Bull leant against the balcony railing, eyes transfixed, enjoying the sunrise. Oh, how simple it had been and how effective an instrument Sergey had proven to be. Now for the son, the one in England. This would prove more difficult. Not because of Sergey – he would accept if he was fed the right information – but because of the logistics of the operation. Favours had to be asked, and he would have to speak to Lesukov and have him arrange something with his men in London.

'Captain Pashinski?' Gorodetski was on the dot as requested. Oleg had let him in and led him upstairs. Bull turned and opened his eyes.

'Sergey!' He beckoned for the younger man to join him. Gorodetski surveyed the rooftops of the neighbouring houses and forest beyond, the first rays of warmth now glinting on the windows of the distant Kyiv apartment blocks in the early morning sun. 'I have some good news for you, Sergey.'

Gorodetski gripped the railing and turned to face his brother's friend.

'I have found another. This is the son who was present at the execution. It was he who carried out the father's order.'

'The man who murdered my brother.' It was more statement than question, his throat suddenly dry. Sergey shivered despite the unseasonable warmth of the autumn morning.

'Yes. He is in England and his name is Bhavesh Malik. It is he who has taken over from the father, and he who must in turn pay for what he did to your brother.'

Gorodetski's knuckles turned white as he gripped harder in an attempt to control the rage he felt inside. 'When can I go?'

'We will have to arrange for a suitable weapon. London is not Odessa, Sergey. Firearms are not commonplace there.'

'I want to do this at close range.' Gorodetski's jaw hardened as he imagined finally laying the ghost of his brother to rest. 'I want him to know who I am and why.'

Bull did not let his delight show. So the young soldier had real metal in his veins. He would use him again, perhaps if Varchenko stood in the way? 'Let me make a call and we shall have an answer.' Bull left his guest on the balcony, lost in his own thoughts.

Gorodetski wasn't your average assassin. Born in 1979, he'd grown up a child of Perestroika and Glasnost. His earliest memories were of his brother being fussed over by his mother on his first day in the Red Army. She was proud of him but didn't want to let him go. He also remembered when his brother, his senior by almost thirteen years, joined the Spetsnaz and how proud his father, an English-language teacher, had been of him. 'You will be the first of us to have a chance to speak to the Queen when we invade!' Father had joked.

Then things went wrong and he could remember his parents crying, inconsolable when his brother was sent to Afghanistan. Even among some Russians the war was not popular. Reports leaked out of Soviet soldiers captured and mutilated, yet all the while *Pravda* and the state-controlled media sang the Red Army's praises and said the Mujahedeen were tribesmen, 'savages with sticks'. One day there was the knock on the door. A month before the Red Army left Afghanistan for good. Sergey was off school with a bad cold and was there to see his mother fall to her knees at the front door and beg the soldier to check his facts, to insist he must have made some type of mistake. But he hadn't. Sergey was ten years old and the person he loved most in the world was never coming home.

The next two years passed with very little joviality. As the Soviet empire started to crumble, so did his parents. His mother threatened to leave his father and then she did. It was near his twelfth birthday. His father had taken him to Moscow's first

McDonald's and bought him a Big Mac. It was still a novelty and the Russian customers treated it like a proper restaurant, with everyone dressed as though they were at the opera. Pasha Gorodetski let his son eat the burger, then told him his mother was going away for a while; that she wasn't well. He had cried into his fries and Pasha had struggled to keep his own eyes dry. Mrs Gorodetski could not get over the death of her firstborn and was put into an institution; the calendar in her brain had stopped. For her, there had never been that knock on the door; her son was still coming home tomorrow.

However, things got better for father and son. Pasha Gorodetski got a job at the new American Moscow International School; this came with free schooling for Sergey. His already good grasp of English, taught to him by his father, was improved as he learnt from American teachers and sat next to the sons of diplomats and foreign industrialists. By the age of fourteen he was fluent. With his blond hair and square jaw he could pass for a Yank. He readily embraced all capitalism could bring; watching the Americans and Canadians arrive with their money, passing huge amounts of this on to the many new Russian business enterprises that had sprouted like mushrooms in the spring. But he never forgot his brother or the vow his ten-year-old self had made inside his head: that when he was a man he would hunt down those who had killed him.

When the time came for military service, he went gladly and was immediately transferred into the military academy. He was watched and his potential noted. After this, he took his brother's lead. He applied to join the Russian Spetsnaz, as it was now called. There had been no argument; his English was better than any other applicant that year and he was shown to be a keen shot. Soon his marksmanship was as good as his English. Two tours over and having achieved officer status, he was considering leaving the forces to pursue a business career when he got a knock on his door. Captain Pashinski, his brother's commanding officer, had found his brother's murderer. Now, at the relatively young age of twenty-seven, he had outlived his elder brother and would finally have his revenge.

'It is done.' Bull reappeared.

'When?' Gorodetski asked now with more determination.

'Be in London in four days.' He handed Gorodetski a Post-it note. 'Meet this man at this address.'

'*Spasiba*.'

'No. Thank you, Sergey.' Bull placed a hand on the younger man's shoulder. 'I know you are a man I can trust.'

Podilsky School International

Snow had been right to call it a night. They had returned to the flat at the right time. Unlike Mitch, they weren't the boss and couldn't turn up to the office when they pleased, which would have been useful after a midweek night on the tiles. Despite the curfew, Arnaud still had a sore head and had struggled through the first two lessons of the morning. Drinking when pissed off was never a good thing. Now, with his breaktime coffee, he was starting to come alive. How Snow had managed to get up and run was beyond him; but then he was a P.E. teacher.

Snow entered wearing a tracksuit. 'Feeling better?'

'Yeah.' Arnaud massaged his temples.

'Good, because you've got a visitor at reception.'

'What?'

'She said she's a private student of yours.'

'But I don't have any.' Confused, Arnaud stood and, together with the Mickey Mouse mug he was holding, made for reception. The sour-faced school receptionist was in conversation with a woman he recognised. The two women saw him approach and exchanged words.

'Hello, Arnaud.' Larissa smiled warmly.

'Larissa. Hi. I didn't expect to… How are you?' He placed his inherited mug on the counter.

'Can we go outside? Have you got time?' Her smile was even warmer.

Arnaud looked at the school clock above the reception desk. 'Sure, I've got about ten minutes.'

They walked out of the building and down the steps to the street. Larissa turned. 'Sorry. I wanted to say sorry for the restaurant, the way I left. It was an accident but I lost my temper. I have a bad temper, I know. People tell me. I have been thinking and I was very silly and rude.'

Arnaud looked down at her face and into her eyes. 'No, I'm sorry for staining your skirt. Please let me pay for it to be dry-cleaned…'

She put her index finger on his lips and shook her head. 'Now you are silly. It is only a skirt.'

They held each other's gaze for several seconds. Arnaud wanted to kiss her so badly but didn't want to mess this up. What if she was just being friendly? Then it happened. Larissa kissed him quickly on the lips.

'I am not busy tonight. Do you want to meet?'

His answer was a definite yes.

Inta Hotel, Vienna, Austria

Bernadette Nierman straightened her red waistcoat and pushed a stray strand of blonde hair behind her ear. She smiled at herself in the mirror. The uniform was tight in all the right places. It accentuated her full breasts and narrowed her waist. Turning side on she was pleased to see that, although longer than she liked, knee-length, the red skirt was tight across her bottom. Respectable, but only just.

She was excited. The email, addressed specifically to her, was from Mr Peters, Mr Mark Peters, the '*sexig*' American businessman who had stayed with them twice before. She had always served him and had noticed the way he looked down her top as she bent forward to draw directions on his map of Vienna. He wasn't much older than her, according to his passport, and did not wear a wedding ring. Now he would be staying again for one night, in three days' time. She had already arranged a shift change so that it would be she who checked him in, and she again who checked him out by noon the next day. She herself would be free in the evening after seven. She adjusted her black-framed glasses. Three days. She couldn't wait.

Chapter 9

Druzhby Narodiv Park, Kyiv

'Welcome to "the Hash", or to use the proper name, the Kyiv Hash House Harriers – the only drinking club with a running problem. For those of you new to the Hash, I am the Grand Hash Master. Thanks to Randy and Mr Clark from our beloved embassy for laying today's trail.'

It was just after twelve on Sunday when the group of ex-pats gathered in the wood. They were all members of the running club known as the Hash and met twice a month to run, drink beer and socialise. The Grand Hash Master, Mitch Turney, continued with his usual spiel and made the usual bad jokes, which were greeted with the usual mixture of groans from the usual Hash members.

Arnaud surveyed the assembled group. 'What are the rules again?'

Snow jutted his chin. 'Those two…'

'Randy and Mr Clark?'

'Yeah.' Snow chuckled. 'They have set a trail of arrows leading to a ribbon tied to a tree. This eventually leads to the Hare, who we have to find and catch. Whenever we find the trail we shout "On, on".'

'Right. Why?'

'It's an excuse to drink more beer and feel less guilty.' Snow patted his young friend on the back. 'Everyone ends up following each other around for an hour or so, then regroups again at the starting point for beer and "The Ceremony".'

'Ceremony?'

'You'll see later. Don't worry, it's not a religious cult.'

Across the circle Mitch blew the Hash Bugle and the race was on. The forty or so runners headed off into the forest. The more serious athletes were soon lost in the trees. Among these was Alistair Vickers. The stragglers, which this week made up two-thirds of the field, trotted or walked in pairs. For them the wearing of a tracksuit was exercise enough. Arnaud, dressed in his French rugby shirt, ran with Snow. Mitch fell into step next to them.

'Howdy, Snow-Queen.'

'Up yours, Grand Hash Master,' replied Snow.

'So, Arnaud, what Hash name are we gonna give you?'

'Hash name?'

'Snow-Queen didn't tell you?'

'Snow-Queen did not.' Arnaud smirked.

'The Hash Master here gets to give all new members a suitable name – unlike mine, I hasten to add.' Snow pretended to be none too happy with his.

Mitch continued between laboured breaths. 'We gotta think of a good one for you, you phallic symbol.'

'Gallic symbol?' Snow shot back.

'Hey, I resent that comment!'

At the front a shout of 'On, on' had the Hash trail all but double back on itself. Vickers slowed and was joined by Vitaly Blazhevich. 'The weather is terribly unpleasant today, old chap. I think it may rain.'

Vickers forced a smile. 'Is the SBU still teaching Noel Coward for Beginners, Vitaly?'

Officially, Blazhevich and Vickers didn't know each other. They had met to exchange information and ideas for just over a year and would often use the Hash as a meet. The route was always different, and new faces, although welcomed, were very obvious. It was also notoriously difficult to monitor a non-static outdoor conversation, especially among trees. Although no longer the enemy of the SIS, the SBU wasn't yet its drinking partner, unsurprising seeing as it was made up primarily of former KGB, who had simply donned new uniforms on Ukrainian independence. Vitaly Blazhevich wasn't one of those; he had still been at school in 1991 and was proud to enter the 'new SBU' to serve his 'new independent Ukraine'. Vickers begrudgingly respected him for that. It would be men like him who would lead the fledgling country after it sobered up from its 'Soviet hangover', a phrase he had used at many embassy receptions. When disgraced former prime minister Pavlo Lazarenko evaded the authorities and jumped on a plane bound for Washington, the CIA had known from their sources in advance, but the SIS had been caught napping. In light of this, Vickers and his predecessor had been keen to nurture their own assets.

'Anything to tell me about the Malik case?' Vickers asked between breaths.

Blazhevich shook his head. 'Nothing more. We are still interviewing those linked to the company.'

'That includes General Varchenko?'

'He has made a statement directly to Dudka. It is very annoying.'

Vickers slowed to navigate a fallen tree trunk. 'We need to get this one solved, Vitaly. The trade implications are serious.'

'Alistair, do not think that we do not understand this.' He wasn't going to be pushed around by the English intelligence officer.

'Anything else?' The Malik case wasn't the only worry he had.

'There is some activity at the moment concerning the Moldavians.'

'Aha.' Vickers had been monitoring the group from Tiraspol, Transdniester who had links with arms dealers. Ukraine was fast becoming the main supply route for east-west and west-east for weapons, narcotics and human traffic. Something the respective governments of both intelligence officers were eager to stop. 'And?'

'Our intelligence reports say they are arranging new shipments in Lymans'ke, near the Ukrainian border. A border guard team has been put on standby and will be there to intercept if this takes place.'

'Vitaly, our sources report more planned shipments within the next three months to a new buyer in Ukraine. We can't close the factories but we can cut off their distribution network. It is of the utmost importance that these Moldovan separatists cease trading.'

Blazhevich nodded. He and his colleagues within the department had stated the same. At least six factories were thought to be churning out grenades, rocket launchers, Makarov pistols, Kalashnikov assault rifles, mortar tubes and other relatively low-tech weapons under contract to the Russian military, and possibly skimming off surplus production to sell to arms dealers. The gangs were somehow evading capture and weapons were still working their way to, among other destinations, Afghanistan and Chechnya. If they could only make a dent in this trade everyone would be happy. The SOCOL team had been very effective until they had been ambushed. This had been played down by the Ukrainian government, for various reasons about which Blazhevich could only speculate. If this had been happening in Latin America, the 'North Americans', thought Blazhevich, would have had Delta force teams and laser-guided bombs taking out the plants. So much for the real war on terror.

'On, on.' This time it was Arnaud who had spotted the arrow and sprinted like a maniac into the undergrowth, leaving Snow in his wake, with Mitch and his hangover trailing.

Twenty minutes later and it was all over. Mitch had his ridiculous foam jester's hat on and the Hashers were once again in a circle.

'Assembled Hashers, we have just two virgins to indoctrinate today. Step forward, virgins!'

Snow pushed Arnaud. '*Bon chance.*'

'Who gives up these virgins to the Hash?' Mitch's voice resounded in the forest clearing like an evangelical preacher. Snow stepped forward, as did Peter Poland. Peter, who, as his Hash name suggested, was from Poland, went first. He stood next to his virgin, Svetlana, and introduced her. Snow then made his introductions. Arnaud and Svetlana were placed back to back in the centre of the ring and each was given a large soup bowl of beer. Mitch started the song.

'*Swing low, sweet chariot,*
Coming forth...'

The rest of the Hashers joined in, '*CUMMING!*'

'*...to carry us home. Swing low, sweet chariot,*
Coming forth to carry us home...
Why was he born so beautiful, why was he born at all?
He's no bloody use to anyone; he's no bloody use at all...'

Mitch nodded to the virgins, who raised their bowls.

'*Drink it down, dowwwn, down, dowwwn, ON YER HEAD!*'

Arnaud caught on quicker than his fellow virgin. As the chant finished he triumphantly tipped his all-but-empty bowl over his head, while the unfortunate Svetlana, who'd only sipped hers, received an unexpected shower. Mitch and Randy exchanged a knowing smile. Another local girl who wanted to impress the ex-pats.

'Sveta...' Mitch held up his arms in an exaggerated manner. 'Peter Poland has told me all about you. For ever more you will be known as "Hot Legs". Arnaud, you are half French so you will be known as "Frogs' Legs".'

A groan resounded around the party. Arnaud, meanwhile, grinned and cracked open the can Mitch had tossed him.

'Snow-Queen… music, if you please!'

Snow pressed play on the CD multi-changer in Mitch's SUV and the woods filled with the sound of Bryan Adams. Arnaud crossed to Mitch. 'Your music?'

'Sure is, Frogs. You like it?'

'My dad used to listen to him.'

'Your dad! Jeez, Frogs, don't go and make me feel old. I've got women to impress.'

With the social part in full swing, Blazhevich slipped away to his own car and returned home while Vickers was cornered by an American wanting to know the best place to stay in London.

Inta Hotel, Vienna, Austria

The taxi passed St Stephen's Cathedral and turned down a side street, depositing the passenger and his luggage outside the Inta Hotel, Vienna. He paid the driver in US dollars and apologised for not having any local currency. The driver, used to such things, especially from Americans, courteously accepted the green notes without pointing out that the visitor had in fact paid double. Holding a cabin-luggage-sized Samsonite case in his left hand, the American walked through the double doors and entered the hotel. He breathed in the scent of several voluminous vases of fresh flowers, which almost covered the smell of fresh paint and barely trod carpet. The bellboy hurried over from the bar area and apologised profusely for not having seen him arrive, saying how nice it was to see Mr Peters again in Vienna. At the desk he rang a bell and, while they waited for the receptionist to appear, asked if the flight from Bern had been a good one. The guest was about to speak when a tall, blushing blonde appeared from the back room. She touched her lips with a serviette to remove a crumb.

'Welcome back, Mr Peters. It is very nice to see you again.' She smiled.

'It's great to be back, and to see you too,' replied Sergey Gorodetski.

Bernadette touched her glasses self-consciously. 'Your room is ready for you, Mr Peters. Just sign here.'

The express registration process completed, Sergey was led into the lift and up to the fourth floor. Bernadette looked on from her post. Yes, he was definitely handsome, but Americans certainly were funny. Why was he wearing that silly beanie hat? Making idle chat, the bellboy showed Sergey into his corner room. Don't worry, he explained – as a regular guest he had been given a complimentary upgrade. Sergey thanked the boy, who was in fact a year older than him, and gave him a ten-dollar bill.

Shutting the door, Sergey took off his coat and threw it onto the king-size bed. He walked to the very corner of the room and noted that, if he opened the window and stood on tiptoe, he could just catch a glimpse of the grand cathedral around the corner. He shut the window and, kicking off his shoes, padded over to the bathroom – a long, white affair with a huge mirror opposite the bath. He stared at himself. Mark Peters stared back, only Mark Peters was not yet Mark Peters. Sergey removed his black-framed glasses and then his hat. His blond locks tumbled out; he'd need to dye those before he set foot outside the room. He yawned, wanting to sleep but knowing it would be bad trade-craft to risk it now before he was ready. He left the bathroom, opened his case and removed his toiletries bag. He put the Do Not Disturb sign on the outside of his door, then retrieved a 'wash in wash out' sachet of hair colour. Mark Peters had natural ginger hair.

The drive from the Hash had been just over half an hour. Arnaud sat wide-eyed like a child at Christmas as Mitch navigated his company Porsche Cayenne along the new streets of Petropavlivska Borschagivka. Five years before, the place had been just a small village on the outskirts of Kyiv, three kilometres from the nearest metro station. The houses were ramshackle and belonged to farmers and locals who bussed into the city to work. Horse-drawn carts were a common sight jostling for space with ancient Ladas. Now, however, these houses fought for space among the new mega *dachas* of the rich and famous. The price of land had rocketed from $5,000 for a house-sized plot up to well over $100,000. Myriad styles and colours met the eyes. In the UK, houses of this size would have been at the end of secluded drives surrounded by hedges, but here the area looked like a giant-size Barratt development.

As they turned into Mitch's street they passed a four-storey pink castle sitting next to a dilapidated bungalow. Arnaud had to admit that someday he'd love a castle of his own, although perhaps not pink. They sped along the narrow road; Mitch was showing off for his young friend. Snow's knuckles were white on the dashboard and his face was emotionless. Mitch broke the silence. 'See that one on the right?'

'Yeah.' Arnaud looked at the six-storey building.

'The locals call it "Titanic". You can't see from this angle but the back is shaped a bit like a boat. They have a swimming pool on the second floor!'

'Jesus. How much would that cost?'

'There's the funny part. It's been empty for two years. It was up for sale for $80,000 but no one wanted it and now it's on the market again for $250,000.'

Arnaud frowned. 'But if it didn't sell, why put the price up?'

'Ukrainian economics, my friend. The owner didn't want people to think he owned a cheap house.' Mitch slammed on the brakes as they arrived at his house. They went through the electronic gates which duly shut behind them. Mitch looked at Snow, who gave him an unimpressed stare.

'Next time I drive.' He exited the car.

'Bloody hell, this is larger than my parents' place!' Arnaud took in the three-storey house in front of him.

'Impressive, eh?' Mitch beckoned them to follow him inside.

'Nah, you've seen one, you've seen 'em all.' Snow winked, regaining his composure.

Mitch handed Arnaud and Snow a bottle of beer. 'Actually, that's true. This one and the two behind are exactly the same, designed and built by the same people.'

'So, how many bedrooms have you got, Mitch?' Arnaud looked at the large chandelier hanging in the open-plan lounge-dining area.

Mitch ticked them off on his fingers. 'Seven. One for each day of the week. In fact, when I first moved in, I slept each night in a different bed to see which I preferred.'

'And which one was that?'

Mitch pointed. 'The couch. I fell asleep watching the baseball. I'll give you a tour later if you're interested.'

'So, how come you've got such a large place then?' Arnaud couldn't stop gawking.

Mitch sat at the breakfast bar and bade the other two do the same. 'My life story so far.'

Snow placed his bottle on the table, yawned and headed for the toilet. 'Call me when he's finished.'

Unperturbed, Turney continued. 'I've been with the company since I graduated UCLA. Before I came here I'd only worked in the States, but all over, y'know, where I was needed. Anyhow, just before I was offered this gig, the wife and I decided to go our separate ways.'

'She didn't understand him,' Snow shouted through the open toilet door.

'She understood me OK; it was the Puerto Rican maid I was screwing she couldn't understand.' He took a swig of beer. 'I know it shouldn't have happened but I'm a bastard and it did. So hey. I looked at my options. The company wanted to expand here, so I asked for the job, and hey presto. Anyway, I took over from the last guy they sent here; he had three kids, so I inherited this palace. That's little me rattling around this place like Macaulay Culkin but with only a cleaner for company.' Another swig of beer and a grin spread across his face. 'Best of all, I arranged to have my salary part-paid into a Swiss account. She can't touch it, the ex-wife.'

'You're a hard man, Mr Turney.' Snow rejoined them.

'So, seeing as we're swapping stories, are you going to tell him yours?' Mitch looked at Snow pointedly.

Arnaud noticed Snow's eyes flicker angrily at Mitch before he batted away the suggestion with his hand. 'Nah, I don't want to give the poor kid nightmares.'

There was a pause and Arnaud sensed he was either witness to a private joke or something they weren't going to share. He broke the silence. 'What are the neighbours like? I saw there were several Mercedes parked next door.'

'Mafia. The lot of them.'

'Really?' He leant nearer.

'Who else could afford these places? Actually, that's not quite true. Come, I'll show you.' Mitch walked through the French windows and into the garden. 'Right; you see that one, three houses along – the light-pink one?' Arnaud nodded. 'It belongs to a famous Russian singer. Apparently she's sold more records than Tina Turner.'

Arnaud was impressed. 'Any good?'

'Dunno. I've never bought her CD but sometimes I can hear her singing in the garden. I think it's her, or it could be next door's cat.'

'And the other houses?'

'OK, next door there's a Dutch guy. I think he works for Unilever – he just moved in so I haven't had chance to say hello. On the left there's an old guy. I haven't got a clue what he does but I know he's got a pair of gorgeous daughters.'

'You hope they're his daughters,' noted Snow.

'Now the two houses at the back, the ones the same as this… one's empty and the other is owned by a businessman. I think he bought it about six months back. I've seen him around the centre when I've been entertaining clients; you know, Le Grande Café and places like that.'

'Yup.' Arnaud did know.

'Funny thing, though… there's always at least one light on, people coming and going and always several cars. My bet is he actually is Mafia.'

'Don't tell me you fancy his wife?' Snow asked with mock concern.

'I don't think he has one.'

'That's good. Otherwise he might make you an offer you can't remember.'

'What are you on about?' Arnaud was staring at the barred windows.

'*The Godfather.*'

'What?' He turned, puzzled.

'Jesus, Arnaud, how old are you again? Quick, Mitch, take his beer before we're arrested for corrupting a minor.'

Chapter 10

Horley, United Kingdom

The mass of uniformed schoolchildren pushed past him like a tidal wave. Dressed in baggy black blazers they reminded him of Emperor penguins, their head feathers replaced by unkempt hair. They were desperate to get home. Boarding the train, Sergey forced his way up the carriage until he found one spare seat among a group of teenage boys. He looked at the seat next to the window and the boy whose feet were resting on it, his dirty white tennis shoes poking out from beneath a pair of regulation black trousers.

'Can I sit down, please?' Sergey asked politely. There was no reply as the youths exchanged amused glances. 'Your feet are on the seat,' Sergey now stated curtly.

The youth and his mates looked up. 'Yeah,' came the reply, another statement of fact. 'And?'

The boy looked at the American but his face changed from amusement to uncertainty when he met his gaze. There was something about this geezer that was weird. The American stared back, his eyes not blinking, and stepped forward. 'Move them, move them now.'

The teenager started to say something but thought better of it. 'I'm out of here,' he stated with a grunt, barging his way out of the carriage. Sergey sat in the vacant space, placing his rucksack on his lap. He smiled and called a loud 'thank you' after the departing youth.

'Danny,' another youth shouted, 'hold on.' The five remaining group members left, muttering obscenities and making hand gestures.

Sergey looked around. Diagonally across from him, next to the opposite door, a middle-aged man peered over a copy of the *Daily Mirror* and nodded. 'Buggers, the lot of 'em.'

Sergey smiled although inside he was feeling far from jovial. Mark Peters had left Vienna early that morning, taking Austrian Airlines Flight 451 to London Heathrow. Mark would stay for one night and fly back to Vienna on Saturday afternoon, his business meetings in London completed. Back in Vienna, Mark Peters would again disappear and Sergey would board the Ukrainian International Airlines flight to Kyiv, a tourist who had spent a few days with friends in Austria.

As an American businessman, Mark's passport had been given a cursory examination and duly stamped. He had taken countermeasures by riding the tube to Blackfriars, changing twice to check for a tail before backtracking to Victoria. There, he again made certain he wasn't being followed before checking his overnight case into left luggage and boarding the train to London's other international airport – Gatwick. He wouldn't be returning for the case, which contained a change of new and unworn clothes purchased with cash in Vienna.

The 'pickup' had been simple. On arriving at Gatwick he had taken another train to Horley. There, sitting in an uninspiring car in an uninspiring car park, he had met a man with an Eastern European accent who had given him the Uzi and kit. The delivery boy, who called himself 'Igor', was paid in cash and asked no questions. Sergey had spoken in his American English and could have been George Bush himself as far as 'Igor' was concerned. He again took countermeasures, catching a train to East Croydon before doubling back to Gatwick Airport to take the Littlehampton service.

So here he sat, on the Littlehampton-bound train, with a highly illegal machine pistol inside his rucksack and hordes of escaping school kids. Sergey closed his eyes in an attempt to focus his mind. He was very near now, so very near to avenging his brother that he could almost smell the cordite from the spent shells. The train stopped; he opened his eyes and read the sign that said 'Haywards Heath'. Most of the school kids disappeared. There was a banging on the outside of the window as the expelled youth found a new confidence and shouted 'Knob off, tosspot' at him. Sergey smiled and ran his index finger along his neck to signify a throat being cut. The youth's expression changed to one of confusion as the train pulled out of the station.

Sergey closed his eyes and ran through the plan in his head. By the time he arrived in Lancing it would be dusk. He would make his way down to the beach via the target. As he passed the target he would be partly hidden by the failing light and workers returning home, so would perform a quick close target recce, choosing a place to lie up later. On the beach he would wait for darkness and hope no one had a mind to use the beach on a dark October night. At 2 a.m. he would put on the oilskins and move from the beach to his chosen lying-up position and await the target.

At the next stop a young mother and daughter sat opposite him. The mother busied herself with reading a magazine while the little girl stared directly at him with a serious face.

'*Da*. For sure.' Arkadi Cheban negotiated the roundabout with one hand. 'I make drop-off in thirty minutes.'

Business had been good for Cheban; including the meet with the American the day before, he had made two drops this month. He exited the roundabout and immediately had to swerve to avoid a learner driver who had taken the corner too wide and half-mounted the opposite curb. He swore in his native Moldovan. The instructor held her hand up and smiled cheerily while the spotty teenager wrestled with the gear stick. Cheban gave the instructor a one-fingered salute in return and accelerated hard up the road.

'Here comes another punter.' PC Wilks aimed the speed gun. 'Forty-eight point seven, Geoff. Stop him?'

PC Thorpe nodded; it had been a slow morning. 'Go on then, Rodge.'

Wilks climbed back into the patrol car and Thorpe entered the flow of traffic, on the tail of the speeding Vectra.

Cheban saw blue flashing lights in his mirror and his heart almost stopped. He immediately dropped the phone, leaving his contact talking to himself. He couldn't be stopped, not now, with his consignment hidden in the boot. He assessed the road ahead. The traffic lights had turned red. He indicated left and pulled over. The police Astra came to a halt behind him, the passenger door opened, and a police constable stepped out and walked towards his driver's side window. Back in the patrol car, Thorpe, as per usual, accessed the DVLA database to check if the vehicle had been reported stolen. Reaching the Vectra, Wilks peered through the open window.

'Good afternoon, sir.' He adopted his best 'you've been naughty' face.

Cheban nodded.

'Can you turn the engine off, please? Is this your vehicle, sir?' He removed his notepad and pen.

'Yes.'

'I'd like to speak to you about a safety issue. Are you aware you were travelling at forty-nine miles per hour in a thirty zone?'

Cheban's hands started to sweat. 'Yes, officer, I am sorry. I have to meet a friend and I am late.'

Wilks nodded and listened to the accent, not knowing quite where it was from. 'Well, that's all well and good but forty-nine is a lot faster than thirty, sir. There are several schools in this area, which is why we must enforce this limit.'

Cheban kept quiet and nodded, a bead of sweat forming on his temple.

'I'm going to have to issue you with a fixed-penalty ticket for driving in excess of the speed limit. Now, if I may take your name, Mr —?'

'Trillevich, Igor Trillevich.'

Wilks made a note. 'How is that spelt? T – r – i – l...'

'T – r – i – l – l – e – v – i – c – h.' Cheban tried to stay calm.

'Do you have your licence with you, Mr Trillevich?'

Cheban swallowed. 'I keep it at home. Is safer than to keep in car. What if the car gets stolen?'

Wilks smiled. 'You never know who's about, do you? OK, just one moment while I speak to my colleague.' Wilks returned to the Astra.

Cheban lifted the phone and spoke rapidly in Russian before ending the call. In his mirror he could see the two police officers conferring.

'It all checks out, not reported stolen. Registered to a Richard Lewis of Horsham.' Thorpe tapped the screen.

'He said his name was Trillevich.'

'Oh. In that case it doesn't.' Thorpe squinted at the display.

Cheban wiped his forehead on the sleeve of his T-shirt and his hands on his jeans. It was now or never. He started the engine, put the car into gear and floored the accelerator. The Vectra shot forward, tyres squealing. Reaching the junction in seconds, he swung left through the lights, which were again red, and entered Newton Road on the Manor Royal trading estate.

'Cheeky bugger!' Thorpe floored his own accelerator and, sirens flashing, followed. A double-decker Crawley bus slammed on its brakes and narrowly missed the patrol car.

Cheban sweated profusely as he worked the Vectra up through the gears. Into third and hitting sixty, past the Gatso camera, which flashed obligingly, and the BMW dealership, through a pedestrian crossing and on towards the roundabout. Wilks called for backup and Thorpe fought to keep up with the more powerful car.

'That's right, right, right at the roundabout.' Thorpe gave a running commentary for his colleagues in order to help locate the chase. The Vectra had increased the gap and was now at the next roundabout, joining Crawley Avenue, the M23 slip road. Cheban's drop-off was in Croydon but he didn't want to lead them there so he powered around the roundabout and hit the M23 south. 'What now? What now?' he shouted at himself in Moldovan, mind fully in 'panic mode'. Head south and take a turn-off, lose yourself in any number of country roads and villages, get to the coast and a boat?

Two miles to the north, at Gatwick's South Terminal, a high-powered police Subaru Impretza joined the chase. The advanced police driver eased the cruiser on to the motorway. He was in no doubt that his 155 mph 'Scuby' would soon catch the Vectra, especially with the tailback caused by roadworks at Handcross Hill.

The Astra maxed out at 102 mph, and while Thorpe cursed his luck at being given a shopping cart to drive, Wilks talked the Impretza into the chase.

In the fast lane, lights flashing other road users aside, Cheban hit 110 mph. His vision became limited to the road ahead as he concentrated on getting as far away as possible. Traffic in his peripheral vision became just a blur as he flew south.

Wilks and Thorpe slowed to 90 mph as the Impretza catapulted past them. The lunchtime traffic pulled to one side and more than one envious sales rep re-evaluated their chosen profession.

Cheban saw the distant blue lights in his mirror and realised they were getting nearer. He pushed the Vectra's V6 engine further with the needle dancing now.

The Impretza tore on like a bullet, the advanced police driver, although outwardly concerned for the general motoring public, secretly hoping he could enjoy this speed for a while longer.

Signs cautioned the end of the motorway; further signs signalled the road narrowing to two lanes. Cheban's lane abruptly disappeared and he swung left in front of a BMW Z4, which had been happily cruising at eighty-five. Down Handcross Hill now, and he had to use his brakes. Ninety – he dared go no faster. Down the dip and up the next crest, right bend and – *suka*! Cheban saw the queue of traffic stretching ahead and his mind went into overdrive. He slammed on the brakes harder than ever and tried to swing left into a fast-approaching 'B-road'. The front wheels fought to bite the asphalt, the combination of torque steer and ABS making the Vectra understeer. Touching the grass verge it lurched sideways, the rear of the car suddenly swung out as two tyres found traction in the mud. Unable to steer, Cheban froze in terror as the vehicle rolled into a ditch. Momentarily he saw earth and sky swap places before the airbags inflated at the moment of impact and his world went black.

Seconds later the Impretza came to a halt in the slow lane, the passenger getting out and placing a warning triangle on the road. The Astra arrived a minute later, Wilks and Thorpe both keen to see what had happened. The Vectra had come to rest on its driver's side in the ditch. Wilks could see the driver lolling inside the crumpled wreck against the imploded side window. He was motionless. As the driver of the Impretza called for an ambulance, the passenger was in the ditch trying to get to Cheban. Thorpe inspected the rear of the vehicle, which seemed to have taken the brunt of the impact. The boot had been ripped open and he could see the contents.

'Bloody hell!' Stunned, he raised his radio to his mouth. 'This is Thorpe. Alert the anti-terrorist squad!'

Chapter 11

NewSound UK's office was situated in Dolphin Close, a crescent-shaped cul-de-sac in Lancing Business Park. A large timber warehouse was placed haphazardly in the next road. The roof of this would have afforded Sergey a grandstand view of the target had it not been too far away for his Uzi. This time he was using a CQB weapon designed to inflict the maximum amount of trauma at short range, not the precision sniper's rifle he had used on the father.

The driving rain cut down visibility, which was good for him. Sergey lay on the damp concrete under the builder's truck, his left side leaning against the cold steel of the skip. His dark-blue waterproofs kept most of the rain out except for the continuous trickle which worked its way down his cuff, where it mixed with the sweat on his damp skin. Wearing jeans and a heavy pullover under the oilskins, he would change his appearance after the attack and head back to Gatwick Airport. Mark Peters would then return to Vienna and the warm arms of his new girlfriend.

Lights started to come on in the timber warehouse as the first

115

workers began to arrive. The business park, however, remained silent. As 7 a.m. arrived, the sky lightened but the rain did not, continuing to pound on the steel of the skip and the bonnet of the builders' truck parked next to it. Sergey's view was limited to what he could see directly ahead between the truck and skip, and to his right, under the vehicle. If anyone approached on foot he wouldn't see them until they were directly on top of him. This included the owner of the truck, who may or may not return. It wasn't an ideal OP but Sergey was now committed. He put all thoughts of comfort to one side and continued to await his prey.

Dave Ossowski felt none too good. Like most nineteen-year-olds he had been out drinking the night before. Unlike most nineteen-year-olds, however, he had had to be up the next day for work. It wasn't that he minded giving up the occasional Saturday morning, more that Saturday morning came right after Friday night! This Saturday morning, especially, was a bugger. His mum was doing a double shift at the hospital so had wanted the car. Hopefully Bav would give him a lift home; he was usually good like that. Dave pulled the hood of his parka up over his head as he stepped off the bus and leant forward into the rain.

Bav entered the Shoreham tunnel and lost the radio reception and the rain. His wipers scraped against dry glass briefly before the automatic sensors turned them off. Bav sniffed; he was coming down with a cold. He seemed to have a permanent cold recently. The stress of running the company was affecting his immune system – or so his wife, the resident doctor, had told him. He should take echinacea, vitamin C and zinc. He'd agreed, as usual, but continued to sip his brandy when she'd gone to bed.

Since Jas's death he'd spent more and more of his time at the office taking charge of everything, from updating data sheets to testing returned aids. Today was the turn of the website, specifically the NewSound news section. He had written a fitting tribute to his dad and now wanted this to be added properly, with new photos. Exiting the tunnel, the rain beat on the screen until the wipers decided to work once more. In the distance Bav noted that the sea didn't look too dark, with distant patches of blue sky. Perhaps today wouldn't be so bad after all?

Sergey felt rather than saw the first timber shipment arrive. The trucks could appear any time after the transporters had cleared customs at Newhaven and been offloaded. For this reason the warehouse was always staffed. It was now almost eight. Sergey stretched in an attempt to relieve his cramped muscles. In an ideal situation he would have had something to lie on, but then, in an ideal situation, it would also be dry and there would be no risk of witnesses.

His mind started to repeat over and over the words Bull had said to him. How it had been Bav who had carried out Jas's orders; how the son had complied with the father's death sentence only after Sergey's brother had been burnt, torn and tortured. Inside his overalls Sergey Gorodetski started to sweat more heavily as a white rage shook his body. They would pay for his brother's murder, all of them; the father, the son, and the cousin in Pakistan.

Dave heard the car horn over the rain and turned. Bav flashed his lights and drew alongside. 'Get in and try not to drip too much on the leather.'

'Cheers, Bav.' Dave shut the door.

The headlights of a car cut briefly across the close and brought Sergey back to the present. His mouth dry, his body suddenly stopped screaming at him for warmth and comfort. He readied the Uzi.

Bav handed Dave the factory keys. 'No sense in us both getting wet. You open the door and I'll follow you in.'

Dave rolled his eyes and pulled the hood back up over his head. 'Thanks, boss.'

Splashing from the reserved parking bay through the puddles, Dave arrived at the entrance porch and reached for the lock. He thrust the key in and turned. He stepped inside and started to punch the code into the alarm keypad.

Flashes of light erupted and an explosion of sound hit him from behind. Dave jumped and fell forward against the wall in shock. He crouched there for a second, trying to understand what he had heard. He stood and gingerly took a step back out to the porch. What he saw, his brain momentarily could not comprehend. Bav lay sprawled against the bonnet of his Mercedes, his arms out at either side. His white shirt, plastered to his skin by the rain, was turning a bright crimson as streams of blood poured out of his chest and stomach. He tried to sit up, only his head rising clear of the car. Three feet in front of him stood a figure in blue oilskins with a machine gun in its hands. Bav seemed to sense Dave's presence; his mouth moved as he attempted to voice a warning. But his words had no time to escape. The assassin raised the weapon, shouted something at Bav, then pulled the trigger. Bav's body convulsed as the red-hot metal ripped through his flesh and into the car below him. Dave turned on his heels and half fell through the front door. Hands shaking, he managed to lock it behind him before crawling behind the receptionist's counter where he threw up uncontrollably.

Sergey repeated his proclamation, but this time to a lifeless corpse. 'This is for my big brother...'

He heard a noise from behind. Had there been a passenger in the car? Shit. He had let his passion rule his head and acted as an amateur. He moved towards the entrance and slammed another magazine into the Uzi. He pushed the heavy industrial door. Locked. Should he look through the small window? No. He jogged back across the waterlogged car park to his hiding place, collected his small backpack and placed the weapon inside. This done, he ran as fast as he could out of the industrial estate.

Cheban sat in the interview room chain-smoking. He felt like, in his own words, 'shit'. His left arm was in a sling, his shoulder heavily taped, and he wore a surgical collar. He had been very lucky according to the doctor who had examined him. No sign of brain damage or internal injuries, just a broken collarbone, three cracked ribs, a heavily sprained left ankle and severe whiplash. Cheban had disagreed, saying he was very 'unlucky'. The doctor had reluctantly given medical consent for the patient to be released from medical care and interviewed.

'I am a dead man. You understand me? A dead man. If I go to jail, I die; if you let me go, I die.' In Cheban's own mind his future was very bleak.

Furr frowned and looked at the Moldovan. 'Who wants to kill you?'

Cheban held up his right hand, the only one he could, and waved his cigarette. 'No. No. You make deal with me, I tell you everything.'

'Arkadi. You're in no position to make a deal. You're facing a very long sentence for possession and supply of firearms. This is before we even look at possible terrorist charges and traffic offences.'

Cheban stubbed out the cigarette. 'No. You listen to me, Mr DCI Furr. If you sentence me, I die and you will learn nothing. They recruit another and, bingo, you have more AK on streets.'

Furr cast a glance in the direction of the two-way mirror where he knew the guvnor was watching. 'What type of deal had you in mind?'

Cheban lit another cigarette. 'You give me protection – new identity – and I tell all. I tell who I get work from, where I get shipments, where I drop off, the works. Who pay me and when. This is very big operation, like Mafia.'

There was a knock at the door and a uniformed officer entered and gave Furr a note. Furr read it and stopped the digital tape recorder after saying, 'Interview suspended at 10.28 a.m.; DCI Furr leaving the room.' He spoke to Cheban. 'I'll be back.'

'OK, Arnie. I no go anywhere.' Cheban looked at the empty cigarette packet. 'You bring me another packet?' Coughing, he winced in pain.

Lancing, West Sussex, UK

The adrenaline of the kill had passed and he felt nauseous. Exfiltration, however, was not to be rushed. He sat staring out of the window of the bus, just another passenger on this wet and miserable Saturday morning. Gorodetski had run to the beach, where he placed the Uzi in his day sack, weighted it down with pebbles, and then waded out into the sea. Removing the oilskins and waders, which he placed in his second bag, he then walked the mile and a half to the Worthing bus depot, where he caught the coastline bus from Portsmouth to Brighton. The driver, underpaid and not happy at doing the early shift, paid no attention to the American accent and gave him a ticket for Brighton. The bus retraced Gorodetski's steps back towards Lancing. By the time Brooklands Pleasure Park was in view, the driver had become even less happy. Flashing police lights had caused rubbernecking and both access roads to the industrial estate were blocked. On the other side of the coast road an ambulance approached, sirens blaring, pushing its way past the morning traffic of early shoppers. The lights changed and Gorodetski's bus moved off. Unable to resist, he shot a glance at the mayhem he had caused. His head spun and he tasted bile in his mouth. Was this what revenge, justice, felt like? Finally the men who had murdered his brother were dead. Tears formed in his eyes and he wiped them on the sleeve of his woollen sweater. The bus made slow progress along the coast road, passing through

Shoreham, Southwick, Portslade, Hove and finally Brighton. He alighted from the bus near the Palace Pier and turned left into town, where he got into the lead taxi in the rank.

The driver folded his paper and asked, 'Where to?'

'Gatwick Airport.'

The cabbie was surprised. 'You'd be better off getting a train, mate. There's a direct one from Brighton station. I can take you there if you like?'

Gorodetski hadn't expected the cabbie to be so helpful. 'No, I'm in a bit of a hurry. I'm meeting my girlfriend and I'm late.'

'Ah. Gotcha. OK. It'll cost about forty quid?'

'Worth it if it keeps her happy.' He didn't understand the word 'quid'.

The car pulled into the traffic. 'Women, eh?' commented the driver. 'Can't live with 'em, can't shoot 'em.' Unseen by the driver his passenger squirmed. The driver shook his head and tutted. 'So, where you from in the States then?'

Gorodetski didn't want to enter into conversation but thought the driver would be more likely to remember a rude American then a polite one. 'Boston.'

'Oh, yeah? I like their Red Sox. You a fan?' He made eye contact via the rear-view mirror.

'When I can catch a game.'

'Yeah, know what you mean. Can't get it much on our crap telly.' Gorodetski nodded and the driver continued. 'If you don't mind me asking, what you doing here then? On holiday?'

'Kinda. Meeting friends, travelling some.'

'You have a nice one. England isn't just London, you know. You should get around a bit.'

'I plan to.'

The driver went silent as he negotiated the mini roundabouts by Preston Park then asked, 'Mind if I put the radio on, mate?'

'Not at all.' He was glad of the diversion and leaned back in his seat, closing his eyes. The tension and fatigue had finally caught up with him and he began to drift off, his head lolling and tapping the door. Waking with a start he heard the radio news. '…A shooting on an industrial estate on the outskirts of Worthing. At least one man is reported to be dead. The police are believed to be…'

The driver switched stations. 'Don't like the news. Never nuffin good.'

Gorodetski nodded, now wide awake and very alert.

Worthing Hospital, Worthing, West Sussex

The doctor said he was suffering from shock and might develop post-traumatic stress, have a panic attack or a 'flashback'. It was true; Dave couldn't stop shaking and was sick again. However, in an attempt to be macho, he put this down to his hangover. 'I was sick over the receptionist's chair,' Dave murmured as he sipped his hot, sweet tea.

'Dave, I wouldn't be questioning you now unless it was absolutely necessary.' DCI Reed was fifty-five, had a soft, round face, and tended to put those he questioned at ease. These were unusual traits for someone from the anti-terrorist squad.

'I know. I'm OK, just got a hangover. I was hammered last night.' The sugar had perked him up. Reed looked at his brief notes. 'Ossowski, that's an unusual name.'

'It's Polish. My grandma and granddad were from Gdansk.'

Reed remembered the TV news from the Eighties. 'Ah. Solidarity, shipyards and Lech Walesa.'

Dave nodded but was too young to understand.

'Do you speak Polish, Dave?'

'Nah. My grandparents used to speak it to me but that was years ago.'

Reed leaned forward and smiled. 'Dave. Tell me what happened?'

Dave sipped his tea. 'Bav asked me if I wanted to work some overtime – I'm in charge of the website – so I said yes and had just got off the bus. Then Bav saw me and gave me a lift the rest of the way onto the estate.'

Reed nodded and held his hand up. 'OK, Dave, that's good.' The shock was making the boy speak too fast and Reed had to slow him down in case he forgot any details. 'So you were in the car together?'

'Yeah. I got out of the car to open the door.'

'What time was this?'

'About half eight? No, eight-fifty. Yeah, I saw the clock in reception.'

Another nod. 'Where was Bav?'

'He was still in the car...'

Reed knew it was difficult but had to press. 'Dave, what happened?'

'I opened the door and heard the gun...'

'OK, Dave, you're doing very well. Tell me exactly what you saw and what you heard.'

'I turned and Bav... Bav was lying on the bonnet of his Merc and... and... a man with a machine gun... was shooting him.'

Reed's voice remained calm. 'What was he wearing?'

'Dark overalls, like a mechanic. No, they were waterproof.'

'Oilskins?'

'Yeah, like a fisherman but not yellow.'

'Did you see his face?' The most important bit now.

'No. But he said something.'

Reed edged further forward on his plastic chair. 'Can you remember what he said?'

'It wasn't English. I think it was Polish. Yeah, it sounded Polish.'

Polish? Reed showed no outward surprise. 'OK, Dave, exactly what did he say?'

'Sounded like, *Za mayevo Brata.*'

'Are you sure?' Reed wanted to be certain.

'Yes. That's what he said before he...' Dave put his hand over his mouth and abruptly stood. Reed watched as he raced once more to the bathroom. The police officer shook his head. Something like this could really mess up a young kid. He'd make a note to reassure him, tell him it wasn't his fault, that there was nothing he could have done. He opened his phone and called 'the office'.

Paddington Green Secure Police Station, London

'Interview with Arkadi Cheban resumed at 10.40 a.m. Officers present: DCI Furr and PC Reynolds.'

'You bring me cigarettes?' Cheban held out his good hand.

'Here.' Furr handed him a fresh packet.

'Lights? You think that I am concerned for my health from cigarettes?' He lit one.

'Maybe not, but I am,' replied Furr.

'So why you keep me waiting? I am a busy guy.'

Furr dove straight in. 'Have you sold a semi or fully automatic weapon in the past two months?'

Cheban exhaled, smoke pouring out of a mouth whose edges had curled into a grin. 'You give me deal, I tell you.'

Furr pursed his lips. 'Look, I promise I'll get you a deal – but I need something from you, a token of good faith.'

Cheban shrugged. 'For sure. I supply an American yesterday with an Uzi 9mm – like Terminator.'

Furr blinked. 'American?'

'This one I give for free – nice faith? Yes. Bring picture and I pick. I have very good memory for faces.'

Furr almost knocked over PC Reynolds, who was guarding the door, as he left the room.

At Gatwick Airport, an Orange pay-as-you-go mobile phone had the battery and SIM card removed. Each of the components were then dropped into separate rubbish bins. In Kyiv, another untraceable phone, a UMC pay-as-you-go 'Sim Sim' Motorola, bleeped to alert the owner to a text message. Bull read the message and punched Oleg's heavy shoulder. 'He has done it.' He then tossed the phone out of the speeding BMW and into the river. The driver, Dmitro, looked back in the mirror but made no comment. He knew better than to ask his new commander what had made him smile. A former Ukrainian Special Forces member, Dmitro was an asset and knew the roads of Ukraine like no other. Bull and Oleg had recruited others too, loyal and proud to once again be among the 'Spetsnaz'.

Paddington Green Secure Police Station, London

Wheels moved fast. Within four hours HM Immigration had compiled a list of all American and Polish citizens who had entered the UK over the past two weeks and were working back a further month. Reed's information had been crosschecked with Furr's. The cases had without doubt been linked. An automatic weapon of any type was unusual in the UK. Cheban's description had been circulated and a short list of twenty-five red-haired men drawn up. Cheban was presented with the CCTV images taken at all London airports in addition to the Channel Tunnel and major seaports. This time Furr had an offer for Cheban which was quickly accepted. Cheban looked through the various images, dismissing five Americans for being too fat and four Poles for being too thin. Of the remaining sixteen he picked one face. 'This man.'

Furr looked at the name. 'Mark Peters.'

Chapter 12

The Forbidden City Restaurant, Odessa, Southern Ukraine

'General Varchenko. Perhaps you will shake my hand this time?' The restaurant was gourmet, Chinese, trendy and owned by Varchenko. Bull applauded his taste.

Varchenko looked up. 'You!'

Bull sat and took a prawn cracker. 'May I?' Varchenko tried to reply but couldn't finish chewing in time. 'I have some news for you, straight from London. Malik's son is now dead.'

'What?' Pieces of bean sprout shot from his mouth.

'He was assassinated this morning.' The green eyes bored into the general. Varchenko was speechless. Pashinski continued. 'This is purely a business situation but you made it personal by sending your men to kill me. You can understand why the second Malik had to die. Now we are even again.'

Varchenko stood, tipping the table, his rage rising like never before. 'You are a madman!'

'No, General. A madman kills for no reason.'

Varchenko's eyes darted around the restaurant. He couldn't see his men on the door and, in fact, even the waiter had vanished.

'Now, about my offer…' Bull stated in an even tone.

'Your offer!' Varchenko made for the door but stopped dead. Two huge men stepped over the threshold. How could this be? He was General Varchenko of the KGB; he had held the power of life and death in his hands. He took a deep breath and turned to face his tormentor. 'What is your proposal?'

Bull righted the table and sat. Varchenko warily joined him. Oleg and Dmitro led Varchenko's smaller bodyguards into the restaurant. Bull's men had 9mm handguns in their hands; Varchenko's men's hands were on their heads. The party sat in the far corner, Oleg and Dmitro keeping a safe distance. Bull nodded. 'I admire you, General. You have been a model for me; you have made the transition from Party man to bandit and now capitalist with ease. You have a company which exports to Pakistan and Europe, several restaurants, part ownership of a bank and now plans for a major hotel development. Bravo.' He clapped his hands.

Varchenko's face showed no outward sign of emotion as his grey eyes gazed at the younger man. 'I am glad you approve.'

Bull clasped his hands together then formed a steeple with his fingers. 'What I propose, General, is that you assist me to do the same. First, I have certain goods that could be readily exported with the use of your existing distribution network, and second, I would like to invest my profits from this "venture". As one patriot to another, I feel that your hotel project would be perfect. This would bring investment to Ukraine.' The green eyes widened slightly and Bull smiled.

Varchenko noticed the stoppered bottle of Chinese wine on the floor. 'May I?' Without waiting for a reply he reached down and retrieved the Huadong Chardonnay Shangdong. He poured himself a glass without offering his guest one, and drank. 'You have a direct way of doing business, Mr Knysh. You kill my partner – creating a vacuum – this I understand; but you then want this to be put aside? A mere business strategy? Now you come here… What is this in business terms, a "hostile take-over"?'

Bull was enjoying this. He really did admire the general for his past achievements, which were legendary, and respected his metamorphosis. 'Not hostile, just an earnest interest. I have buyers who want their goods and, better still, money which they want to give to me. However, such sums may cause suspicion if they were to be, how shall we say, deposited directly into a standard bank account. But if these funds were to be invested, they could be increased tenfold.'

Varchenko snorted. 'I am not a laundry service and my company is not a freight forwarder.'

'But if you were to be, we would all benefit.' Bull hadn't thought this would be easy; but the old man was in business and surely wouldn't ignore such an opportunity. 'For every successful shipment you would of course receive a handling fee.'

Varchenko emptied his glass. 'I do not make deals with criminals.' The photo-fit image he had given the SBU was a very good likeness. This man would soon be in custody.

Bull let another smile crease his chiselled face. The man couldn't be trusted unless the deal was too good to refuse. 'You are throwing away immediately one million American dollars. I have a shipment ready to leave which would earn you at least that if we were to agree upon a partnership.'

Varchenko's nose twitched at the sum. It wasn't large for a man of his resources but was more than Malik had delivered in his first two years. 'This is a sum which you can guarantee me, Knysh?'

Bull spread his hands. 'As soon as the shipment has left Ukrainian territory, the money is yours.'

'Half now or no deal.' It wouldn't hurt him to accept; he could always inform customs on the goods' arrival.

'That is acceptable.' Bull raised his right hand and one of his men on the door handed him a leather case. 'As agreed.'

Varchenko gawked at the case then cautiously opened it. Inside sat neat wads of hundred-dollar bills. He could have asked for more. 'Hmm. I will have this tested and counted.'

'Still no trust?' Bull nodded. 'It is understandable. I will send you details of the first shipment. I hope that this can be the start of a very profitable business for us both.'

Varchenko closed the case and stood, as did his new business partner. Bull extended his hand and this time it was accepted. The handshake was held for longer than necessary as the two studied each other. Bull nodded and left the room. Varchenko scowled at his men, who returned to their guard positions. He then counted his money.

British Embassy, Kyiv

His inbox was brimming with new messages and automated circulars, sent over the weekend or from different time zones that were already well into Monday. He checked his email religiously at the office; but, of course, he didn't have a home connection. Broadband hadn't yet been introduced in Ukraine so, as Vickers saw it, there was no point. If anyone really wanted to get in touch he had his Nokia. Scrolling through the electronic messages he saw one from Patchem. It had been sent on Sunday night and asked him to call on the secure line once he was in the office. Vickers looked at his watch. It was 8.30 a.m. in Ukraine, which meant it was 6.30 a.m. in the UK. Patchem lived for the SIS but Vickers doubted he would be in yet. Instead Vickers clicked reply and asked his boss to let him know when to call. It was to be a busy day. The arrival of the trade mission the day before meant he had an embassy briefing to deliver at 10 a.m. This also necessitated a reception at the embassy in the evening, at which invited guests were to meet hopeful British companies. He had also been asked to a meeting with the Kyiv city council, who wanted to discuss investment and a partnership of some sort. In addition to his emails and any other business which might pop up, he couldn't see himself sneaking out for a bite at lunchtime. His secure desk phone rang, he picked it up, and there was a second's pause as the scramblers at each end electronically shook hands.

'Alistair.' It was his boss, SIS field controller, Jack Patchem.

'Jack, good morning.' He was in early.

'I doubt you missed this over the weekend but there's been a shooting in Worthing.' Patchem came straight to the point.

'Yes, I saw it reported on BBC World. They were a bit light on details, as one would expect.' Vickers was curious.

'We have it confirmed that the dead man is Bav Malik, the son of Jas Malik.'

Vickers was stunned. 'The son dead too?'

'I'm afraid so, Alistair. Did you know him?'

'We met on a couple of occasions.' Vickers thought back to the mission briefing.

'I'm sorry.' Patchem coughed. 'Whatever we have on our hands here isn't limited to Ukraine. I'll send the details over to you. The method is different – point-blank range, automatic weapon. Up close and personal, one could say. "Five" already has someone in custody who may have supplied the gun. Be prepared to speak to them if they contact you and also our friends at Interpol. I don't think there's much more you can do there, other than put pressure on the SBU.'

'Of course.' Vickers's mind was racing as it tried to think of anything that might help. 'What have Five got at the moment?' Like Patchem, he used the nickname for HM Secret Service.

'Hmm.' Patchem showed he wasn't happy. 'Nothing concrete, meaning nothing they're prepared to pass over yet.' There was no official turf war but, on occasion, the Security Service and the Secret Intelligence Service didn't cooperate to the best of their abilities. Vickers shook his head. Was this a vendetta against the

Maliks that just happened to have spilled into Ukraine? Was Malik Senior's business in Ukraine a factor? Vickers had an answer to neither of these questions and that bothered him. He hated not knowing what was happening. 'Alistair?' Patchem interrupted his train of thought.

'Yes, Jack?'

'Enjoy the rest of your day.' The phone went dead. Patchem, as always, did not waste words.

Vickers leant back in his chair and looked at the ceiling. Two hats; always two hats and just one head. It was nine. He had just an hour before he was to brief the missioners.

British Consulate, Kyiv

Classical music played softly in the background and waiting staff offered canapés to the assembled guests. For a modern building, this room had 'come up' better than expected, although Vickers much preferred the smaller but more interesting rooms in the embassy to these large and characterless ones at the new consulate building. The fourteen members of the trade mission mingled with their invited guests. Some mission members, such as the Director of International Studies from the language school, had more guests arriving than others. In fact, the Savile Row tailor seemed lonely. He looked longingly at the four attractive women buzzing around the school rep. Vickers scanned the faces; some names on the list he had known, but most he did not. These were small businessmen – and women, he corrected himself – who had come on the trade mission. Multinational companies seemed to jump in with both feet then complain to him they were out of their depth. He heard giggles from another invitee when the giftware export sales manager gave her an 'orgasm keyring' to try. She pressed the button and it made groaning sounds. Vickers shook his head. What were these people trying to sell? And furthermore, why would Ukrainians want to buy?

'Tom Watkins, Thomas Watkins Associates.' The businessman held out his hand.

'Alistair Vickers, Commercial Attaché.'

'Yes, I saw you at the briefing this morning – sorry I couldn't stay afterwards and say hello; I've had so many meetings.'

Vickers took the business card. It was in English on one side and Ukrainian on the other. 'You've done your homework.' He had lost count of the number of foreign businessmen who had come to Ukraine with only English-language versions of their corporate brochure and product literature.

'I pride myself on that, knowing the market.' He looked around the room. 'The last two of these things I've been on were to Saudi.'

Vickers made an appropriate face. 'Really?'

'Yep. Two receptions, two years running, and both times the same ex-pats turned up to drink "legally" at the embassy.' He held his neck and pretended to choke. 'I couldn't live there.'

'Well, you won't run dry here, I can assure you of that. Jesus may have walked on water but Ukrainians run on vodka.'

Watkins did a double-take. 'That's good. I'll have to remember that one.' He closed his eyes for a second to file the quip.

'Have your invitees turned up?'

'No. I only invited one person – I already had meetings arranged with other potential clients.'

Vickers ran through the invitees in his head. He had a near-photographic memory – a prerequisite for an intelligence officer – but couldn't recall any who had been invited by Thomas Watkins Associates. The businessman continued, 'Oh, I didn't fill out any of those cards – I didn't think I needed to.'

Vickers concealed his annoyance. 'Hmm, the thing is, we can't just let anyone into the consulate – security reasons, etc.'

'Oh.' Watkins took a red caviar sandwich from a passing waiter. 'Sorry.'

Bondarenko, one of the local embassy employees, appeared at the door and beckoned Vickers over. 'Well, no harm done. If you'll excuse me, I believe I'm wanted.'

'Of course.'

Vickers crossed the room. 'Yes?'

'We have an invitee at the door that is not on the list.'

'I see.' Vickers looked back at Watkins, who was busily helping himself to a second glass of wine. 'Have they been invited by Thomas Watkins Associates, by any chance?'

'Yes. Here is the name of the person.' He handed Vickers a card.

Vickers looked at the card. It read, *Valeriy Ivanovich Varchenko, General Director Odessa-Invest*. Vickers swallowed. General Varchenko had been invited by Watkins? Vickers didn't let his surprise show for long and acted matter-of-factly.

'That's fine, show him up.' Vickers straightened his tie and waited for the former KGB general. Watkins was still busy, now choosing another nibble, so didn't notice when Vickers greeted the latest arrival. Varchenko entered the room, head held high like an old-school actor appearing onstage, and surveyed the other guests. He was used to attention and had been treated with an almost celebrity-like reverence in the old days, when he had been awarded the Hero of the Soviet Union medal.

Vickers approached. 'General Varchenko, how very good to see you here on British soil.' The consulate and its grounds legally constituted British territory.

Varchenko smiled and replied in English. 'It is not the first time that I have invaded, Mr...?'

'Alistair Vickers, Commercial Attaché.'

'Pleased to meet you, Alistair.' Varchenko liked to use first names when speaking to foreigners; he felt it made him more cosmopolitan. 'I have been invited by a Thomas Watkins. Is he here?'

Vickers pointed. 'There he is, General.'

'Thank you. If you will excuse me, Alistair.' Varchenko nodded regally and crossed the room. Watkins was drinking wine, oblivious of the fact that he had several crumbs on his tie. Inwardly, Varchenko sighed. Why were British businessmen so scruffy? Why couldn't they wear $4,000 suits like he did? The reason, of course, was that he was a man of means.

'Tom, how nice to see you again!' Varchenko had his game face on once more.

Vickers looked on. This was a very peculiar incident. A second British citizen with a link to this guest had just been butchered, yet here he was, bold as brass, in the consulate, on British soil. An audacious idea made him smile. He could arrest the general; Ukraine did not have jurisdiction inside the building. A team from London could then question him. It would cause an international incident if word got out but it could be done. Why the father and son? What had they done and to whom? His mind wouldn't be able to rest until he knew why. He was an intelligence officer, yet here he had no intelligence at all. Vickers loved puzzles but hated those he couldn't solve, like the ten-thousand-piece jigsaw with the missing bit. He felt a tap on the arm. It was the tailor.

'That man looks remarkably well dressed.'

Vickers's train of thought was broken. 'He's a multi-millionaire, so he can afford to be.'

The tailor gulped. 'Who is he? I wonder if you could… if I could…?'

'He's a former KGB general turned businessman. I suggest you give him your card.'

The tailor nodded enthusiastically, flattened his laps and trotted towards his prey. Vickers continued with his thought process. Varchenko had to know something, may even have authorised the killings. They would not have been his first. Had he just come to the reception to better his cover story? Vickers had to call London; this was too big for him to handle. He couldn't hold a foreign national, let alone a Ukrainian oligarch, without a direct order. Vickers left the room and made for the nearest secure telephone.

Chapter 13

Mars Strip Bar, Kyiv

The waitress removed the reserved sign and they sat. Without a word, a tequila bottle and four glasses were placed on the table. Mitch was mother and poured Snow, Arnaud, Michael and himself a shot in turn.

'Whoa! This stuff doesn't get any better,' complained Arnaud.

'I personally prefer a good malt,' commented Michael.

'I'm happy to drink anything if Mitch's paying,' stated Snow.

Mitch held up his middle finger. 'Sod the lot of you then, tossers! Is that better, Arnaud?'

'Yep, we'll make you a Brit yet.' Arnaud had been trying to teach his new friend real 'English' English.

The lights dimmed and Snow's favourite, the blonde in the green bikini, entered through velvet curtains. She danced to the techno beat and gradually removed, first, her long, white gloves and then her top. 'And the British judge gives her a nine point eight for artistic interpretation.'

'I'd give her one.' Michael made his usual joke.

'I have,' said Mitch between puffs on his Havana. 'She told me I had the body of a god.'

'Yeah… Buddha,' retorted Snow.

The stripper came nearer and rubbed against Snow's crotch before turning and whispering in his ear. Snow put a twenty-hryvnia note into her bikini bottoms and was rewarded with a close-up of her pert, round buttocks before she moved on to the next table. The song over, she disappeared through the curtains, holding her costume, and a second dancer appeared.

'She's new.' Mitch knew all the girls by name and a couple better than that. The new stripper cavorted on the small stage then moved from table to table before landing next to Mitch. 'I'm Peaches,' she whispered.

Mitch was in his element. 'Hi, Peaches. Have you seen Cream recently?'

The stripper paused, mentally translated the comment, and started to giggle. She retreated as the music ended.

'Was it something I said?' Mitch adopted a pained expression.

'Right, I'm off for a leak.' Snow stood and moved towards the toilets.

Background music started again but this time the lights didn't dim as a gypsy violinist accompanied by a belly dancer started their routine.

'Do you think she likes to fiddle?'

'Michael, they're getting worse,' groaned Mitch.

'What, you can't stomach them?'

The waitress passed in front of their table, followed by a group of men in suits. She removed another reserved sign from the table next to the stage and they sat.

'Hello, there's my neighbour.'

'Russian Tina Turner?' Arnaud stared at the stage expectantly.

'No, the Mafia guy.'

Arnaud turned. 'Where?'

'Over there by the stage, Mr Subtle.' Mitch motioned with a nod.

'Looks mean,' Michael commented, 'but probably just buys and sells on eBay.'

'Yeah, auctions off the odd AK-47 when he needs a bit of cash.' Mitch raised his hand in acknowledgement as the neighbour looked over. The man smiled and did the same. The entertainment continued with the belly dancer wobbling, almost knocking Mitch's neighbour over as he made for the toilets.

Snow could hear the belly dancer's music, albeit muffled, through the toilet door. He splashed cold water on his face as another customer entered the room. The man walked to the basin and washed his hands. Without looking directly at Snow, he acknowledged him in Russian. '*Zdravstvyite.*'

Snow replied with the same in his Moscow Russian. The man continued to scrub his hands, drying them before he adjusted his dark tie, making sure it sat well on his colour-coordinated shirt. Snow dried his face and looked up. Less than a metre away, he looked into a pair of green, snake-like eyes. After ten years the eyes and face had hardly aged. A chill ran through him and he felt his body quiver. Snow tensed; his fight or flight instinct had suddenly been switched on. He wiped his face again and kept his hands raised to protect and obscure his face. The man continued to adjust his tie and then pushed an errant hair back from his forehead. Snow stepped away from the sink and towards the door. The man didn't seem interested. Passing through the toilet doors, Snow immediately turned left and exited the club. He quickly, but not hurriedly, walked up Karl Marx Street, putting himself further away from the club, Khreshatik, Pushkinskaya and his flat. At the corner of Karl Marx and the Ivana Franka Theatre square he sprinted up the hill towards the presidential administration building and the safety of its armed guards. Reaching the top he leant against the railing, looking back the way he had come. The two guards across the road eyed him with suspicion but lost interest when he started to use his phone and they heard him speaking English. Arnaud's phone rang in his pocket. Unheard over the music, it went to voicemail, which never let him leave a message, before going dead. Snow swore, waved at the guards, and then tried Mitch.

The stripper spoke into Mitch's ear. 'You are vibrating.'

For a moment Mitch thought it was a compliment, then realised that his phone in his pants pocket was ringing. He pushed his hand past the stripper's naked buttock. 'Turney.'

The background noise almost drowned out the voice but Mitch could hear it was Snow. 'Where are ya, buddy?'

'I'm outside. Listen, you have to leave.'

'What? I can't hear ya. You outside?'

It was hopeless. A booze-and-lust-upped Mitch was like a dog with a bone. 'You have to leave. *Now*.'

'What? Leave... what...?'

The phone went dead as Bull shook the hand of his American neighbour. He liked mixing with the foreign business people; it gave him an air of respectability. Returning to his own table he had a bottle of Mitch's favourite sent over to the American. He was in a celebratory mood.

'Where's Aidan?' Arnaud had taken his eyes off the girls long enough to see that Snow still wasn't back.

'I think his homing beacon went off. He gets like that sometimes when he drinks; he goes home,' Michael explained. Arnaud accepted this, too drunk to find it unusual, and downed his shot.

British Embassy, Kyiv

Vickers leaned back in his chair and munched on a custard cream. He'd received two breathless messages on his mobile from Aidan Snow demanding a meet. The call had been made at 11.35 p.m., and at 8.30 a.m. the next morning Vickers found Snow sitting opposite him in his office.

'Shouldn't you be at school?' Vickers quipped with a smirk.

Snow, dressed in his usual mock-tweed fleece and black jeans, ignored the comment. 'Alistair, I told you... I wanted to speak to the embassy's Six man.'

'The Six man?' Vickers copied Snow by using the nickname for the Secret Intelligence Service. 'Aidan, with respect, you surely can't expect me to allow any Tom, Dick or Aidan who barges into the embassy to be allowed to meet a representative from HM Intelligence. What makes you think we even have one stationed here?'

'Don't mess about. I've got some urgent information I need passing on.' Snow had expected this.

Vickers sighed, even though, inside, he was intrigued to hear what his acquaintance, the ex-pat teacher, had to say. 'You can talk to me. If it's important I can arrange for the "right people" to hear it.'

'Alistair, this is no time to play games.' Snow started to feel angry but reined himself in. Getting annoyed at Vickers wouldn't be helpful. 'I take it you've signed the Official Secrets Act?'

'Of course, as a serving civil servant.' Vickers's interest grew.

Snow rolled his eyes in resignation. 'Fine. What I'm now going to tell you puts me in breach of the Official Secrets Act.' Vickers's eyes widened slightly but he made no comment. Snow continued, 'In 1996 I was a serving member of the British Army. I was involved in a training operation in Poznan, Poland. My team was training a Polish paramilitary police unit in CT techniques...'

'Counterterrorist techniques?' Vickers interrupted. 'This would have been a training team from Hereford?' Vickers fished for confirmation of his sudden suspicion.

Nodding, Snow went on. 'It was a three-month assignment to help bring their boys up to standard.' Snow continued with the explanation, giving only as much information as was absolutely necessary. He told Vickers how his SAS instructor group and their trainees had been the nearest police unit to the 'robbery in progress' call on SchreinerBank, the subsequent firefight and the losses sustained. 'The two transits were rigged to explode. We lost eight team members in the first blast. That included the driver of the car I was in, the Polish inspector in the front seat and two lads from the regiment sitting in the second car.' His mouth suddenly dry, Snow took a sip of his embassy Nescafe. Pulling his mind back from the events of that day, he continued. 'They escaped with approximately four million Deutsche Marks. Where they went after that we never knew. The cars were found abandoned outside Poznan; locals reported seeing a military helicopter.'

Vickers no longer showed any sign of humour. 'Go on.'

Snow inhaled deeply. 'Last night in Mars I saw their leader. The same man who pushed a gun in my face in 1996. He's here, Alistair, in Kyiv.'

Offices of Perry & Roe, Horizon Tower, Kyiv

Within ten minutes of leaving the embassy, Snow arrived at Horizon Tower. He nodded at the security guard. 'I have a meeting with the director of Perry & Roe.'

Hearing English, the guard immediately straightened and called upstairs. On getting the OK from Mitch's receptionist, Snow was ushered into the lift. Getting out on the twelfth floor, he was met by Mitch's gushing secretary, Vera, who led him to Mitch's large corner office.

'Come.' Mitch attempted to sound professional. Snow entered, shut the door, and sat.

'Morning.'

Mitch looked at his watch; it was 10 a.m. 'Middle of the night, man!' Mitch was wearing, as per usual, a crumpled blue Oxford shirt and stripy tie.

'Don't you own an iron?' It was a running joke.

'It's a non-iron shirt.'

'It is now.'

Mitch poured them both a ridiculously strong coffee from his private pot. 'You've decided to come and work for me? Well done. Have a cigar.'

'No.'

'OK, shoot. Why are you messing up my office?'

'Last night I saw someone from my time in the regiment.'

Mitch's smile vanished, his face becoming serious. 'Like who?'

'Someone who tried to kill me.'

Mitch whistled. 'Ya sure?' There was a silence as both men drank the American coffee.

'He was in the toilet in Mars.'

'Ya shitting me, bud?' Mitch winced.

Snow ignored the pun. 'Dark suit and tie, athletic, mid-forties, shoulder-length hair gelled back like a footballer, green eyes.'

Mitch almost dropped his coffee. 'I'm scared, man. You just described my neighbour. He came in when you were in the can.'

Snow frowned. 'The Mafia guy?'

Mitch gulped. 'Uh-huh.'

Snow stretched and ran his hands through his thick, dark hair. 'He didn't see us together, but, just in case, you need to leave town.'

Mitch held up his hand, as in his business meetings. 'Hey, hold on. Ya told the police?'

'I've told the British Secret Service; they'll tell the right people.'

Mitch stood and walked to the window. The view over central Kyiv was one of the best in town. 'What are you gonna do?'

'The guy, if it is him, is dangerous.'

'So why would he be after you?' Mitch leant against the window, staring at the traffic.

'I saw his face. I'm the only one who can ID him for the Poznan job. He'll come for me.'

'Are you sure it's him?'

'It's him, Mitch, believe me.' Snow had told his friend he'd been in the regiment and even about Poznan; but not about the nightmares he'd suffered after. In these, the face with the green eyes stared at him.

Mitch turned and folded his arms. 'Right, so we've gotta get to him before he gets to you. Let's get us a plan.'

Snow welcomed Mitch's spirited response but brushed it away with upturned hands. 'Mitch, it's too dangerous. Look, if you want to help, get out of here, today. Go to your office in Belarus and see that Natasha, or go to your Warsaw plant.'

'What about Froggy and the Welshman?' Mitch thought about the other members of their 'drinking party'.

'Michael lives hidden out in left bank like a native, even looks like one. It's Arnaud I'm worried about. I'll speak to them both. If this is your neighbour, I want to be certain. Can you give me a key? I want to check him out.'

'Sure, you know where the porn is stashed.' Mitch opened his desk and threw a key at Snow. Snow gave him a questioning look. 'You never know, I may lose my keys, may get locked out, or I may have given this key to a certain former female employee.'

Nothing about Mitch shocked Snow any more. He had hand-picked his new hires and had his own vetting system. 'Thanks.'

Mitch looked at his buddy and drinking partner, honest concern on his face. 'Seriously, man, I wanna help.'

Snow held up the key. 'You just have; now ask your secretary to book you a flight.'

Mitch sighed and nodded. 'OK, but I hate to run. A marine never leaves his men.'

Snow shook his head. 'Mitch, you were never in the Marines.'

'True, but I got a copy of *Platoon*.' Both men regained their smiles.

As he passed the principal's office, Arnaud saw Snow sitting with Joan. Puzzled, he continued on to the staffroom and poured a coffee. Snow had left a note in the kitchen telling him to take the bus to school without him. Arnaud had a free lesson, so sat and looked at his French textbook.

'Morning.' It was Snow.

'Hey, what happened to you last night? Homing beacon go off?'

Snow sat, his own mug in hand. 'Something like that.'

'And late this morning?'

'Hey, sorry, Mum.' He held his hands up. 'I had to go to the embassy and see Alistair. There's a problem with my work permit or something.'

'Oh.' Arnaud had no reason not to believe his flatmate. 'Throwing you out for being an undesirable?'

Snow sipped his coffee and ignored the jibe. 'Are you still going to Lviv for the weekend?' Snow hoped his young colleague would be leaving Kyiv as he'd mentioned earlier in the week. His relationship with Larissa had got 'serious'. Putting a twelve-hour train ride between him and potential danger wasn't a bad thing.

'Yep. Larissa's got us booked on that posh private train at eight this evening. You ever been?'

'Yeah, like you, when I first got here. Don't worry, it wasn't with Larissa.'

'In your dreams.' He smirked. 'What's it like?' Arnaud was keen to explore.

'The dream with Larissa?' Arnaud frowned. Snow smiled. 'Lviv's an old place, lots of cheap bars, Opera House, used to belong to Poland. They speak Ukrainian there.'

'Hmm. And the train?'

'Not bad, from what I can remember. Private cabin, two single beds, en-suite washbasin, and they have waiter service. I got a bottle of cognac to amuse myself last time.'

Arnaud winked. 'Oh, we can think of ways to amuse ourselves.'

'I'm sure you can. So it's a dirty weekend in Lviv?'

'Hardly. We're staying with her grandparents. That's why I need to know if the train's any good.'

Snow laughed. 'Arnaud Hurst. You are a naughty boy.'

SIS Headquarters, Vauxhall Cross, London, UK

The phone range in his Vauxhall Cross office. 'Patchem.'

The caller apologised for circumventing protocol and again calling the SIS field controller, but he had just received some information which perhaps couldn't wait for his weekly report.

'Perhaps?' questioned Patchem. 'Alistair, I'd like to see what you classify as urgent.'

Vickers related the meeting with Aidan Snow, a former member of the SAS, and reported on his fears. Patchem, cradling the receiver between neck and shoulder, made notes on a pad. 'OK. Tell this Snow character not to go anywhere – we may need to call him in.'

'Have you got any more information about the second Malik murder?' Vickers wasn't quite sure what to call Bav's death.

'Interpol are trying to trace a suspect who arrived in Vienna the same day from Gatwick. They believe him to be either American or Polish. Quite confusing. They have someone in custody who says the shooter was a young American and another witness who says he heard the man speak Polish.'

Vickers thought. 'Could it be that he's Polish but speaks American English?'

'That would be my guess,' Patchem acknowledged. 'But we can't rule out the possibility that he's Ukrainian or Russian-speaking.'

'Or American.'

Patchem shuddered. 'That would be problematic. Do you still believe Varchenko may be implicated?' Patchem had been as surprised as Vickers when the general had attended the mission reception at the consulate. Vickers's fleeting idea of holding the former soldier in British custody had been dismissed. Both men had agreed it was too sensitive and not justified by anything more than circumstantial evidence. Besides, they weren't police officers.

'I think there's some link, somewhere; they were his business partners. But I have no more clues.'

Patchem looked at the notes he had made. 'I'll have someone here check up on what you've told me about Snow. I think that's all for now.'

Patchem replaced the receiver and sucked on the end of his pen thoughtfully. Never one to delegate, a trait some said had stalled his career, Jack Patchem closed his eyes. 1996, Poland? Did he remember? Hmm. He tapped a couple of keys and called up the relevant computer file. He traced the number on the screen with one hand and dialled with the other. At the other end of the line, in Hereford, a clipped voiced answered.

Chapter 14

Le Hotel Imperial, Vienna, Austria

Varchenko had chosen the venue for maximum effect. Built in 1863 for an Austrian prince, the palace had been converted to a hotel ten years later and immediately become one of the most prestigious in Vienna. The grand 1863 façade and two-storey, wood-panelled lobby, made complete by a green-and-cream marble balcony and giant chandelier, immediately impressed on guests that they were in a former palace and that he was holding court. Other important men, like him, preferred to appoint people to do the talking for them; but not Valeriy Varchenko. For him it was all part of the fun. To pitch an idea, however big or small, and get a result was a thrill, and he was good at it. He looked at the important men in suits.

'Gentlemen, recent trends in Ukraine's hospitality industry suggest that, although the shortage of quality hotels remains an issue, the industry has been exhibiting strong signs of growth. Several international operators successfully entered the market last year, *but* small, privately owned hotels have also been proliferating, in western Ukraine.' He paused for effect and met the gazes of his potential investors. 'In excess of $400 million was invested in improving Ukraine's network of hotels in 2005, a forty per cent increase from the year before. And who invested this?' Again, a dramatic pause. 'Foreign investors, like you. Radisson SAS, $57.3 million, the Turkish hotel operator Rixos, a similar amount. Are these companies misguided?' He raised his eyebrows theatrically. 'No. Will these be the last foreign investors? No. Hilton International have announced that they will open their first hotel in Ukraine. This will be a $70-million, five-star luxury hotel in Kyiv, completed in mid-2009. Gentlemen, this niche of the hotel market will only continue to expand in the near future!'

In the small audience of twenty-five, Tom Watkins of Thomas Watkins Associates nodded vigorously and, watching from the corner of his eye, made a mental note of who else was too.

Varchenko sipped from a glass of Perrier before continuing. 'The Schengen visa zone is right on Ukraine's border, EU and many foreign nationals no longer need visas to visit Ukraine, and the number of visitors from neighbouring countries is growing.' He clicked the projector remote control and a table of figures appeared on the screen behind him showing new hotels, the number of rooms each had, their occupancy rates and locations. 'We now have new luxury hotels appearing in western Ukraine, in Lviv and Truskavets, and in Kyiv. This is in addition to the existing Oreanda Hotel in Yalta and the Londonskaya in Odessa. But these are not exclusive hotels. They are fine for the casual Western tourist or visiting businessman, but not for cultured people like you and I.' He paused and smiled at the audience, wanting to fluff their egos. 'The Hotel Noblesse will be.'

He pressed another button on the controller and a DVD of the completed hotel and its surroundings played. For this he had employed a very expensive British production company who supplied the same mixture of live footage and CGI techniques to Hollywood movie studios. He surveyed the audience; they were transfixed. Thomas Watkins caught his eye and nodded ever so slightly. Varchenko was very proud. He could feel his body tingling with anticipation. In this room sat the real decision makers, some of the biggest venture capitalists in the industry, and they were buying it. 'Gentlemen. The time to invest is now and the Hotel Noblesse is the place.'

Café Einstein, Vienna, Austria

Half a kilometre away, a smaller party of two had gathered. '*Guten Tag, Herr Peters.*' The waiter remembered the young, bespectacled American from his previous visits. He was with the tall blonde again, lucky fellow. She probably swooned over his exotic accent! Once again they ordered the Einstein steak and a stein of local beer. Very simple tastes, Americans, mused the waiter.

Gorodetski looked the girl in the eyes. What had, in his mind at least, started as a bit of fun now felt like something more. She touched a napkin to her lips as she replaced her beer glass.

'Perhaps you should drink something else?' he asked.

Bernadette shook her head. 'Don't you like women who drink beer?'

Gorodetski laughed. 'I love girls who drink beer. It's girls who don't I can't stand.' He raised his own beer and tapped hers cheerfully.

'I never used to like beer, never, never. Then once, it was summer and very hot, I was with my friends from college at the lake. We'd forgotten to take any water with us so one of the boys gave me a beer. It was cold and it was then that I realised I liked beer.'

'And the boy? Did you like the boy?'

Bernadette blushed. 'No. He tried to kiss me, we were young.'

Gorodetski smiled. 'We're young. Can I kiss you?'

She frowned for a moment, not quite understanding, but then she moved forward. Gorodetski kissed her on her full lips. He closed his eyes as he felt tears form. His brother's death, the faces of the two men he had killed, flashed before him, but he felt a huge sense of relief. He realised they had been kissing for longer than was decent but he didn't pull away and neither did she. There was a cough. The spell broken, he opened his eyes. The waiter stood over them with their orders.

'*Danke*,' Gorodetski said with an American accent.

'Would that be all, sir?'

Gorodetski smiled and winked at Bernadette. 'I hope not.'

The waiter nodded curtly and left.

Chaika Sports Complex, Kyiv Oblast, Ukraine

Bull replaced the magazine in his AK100. The smell of cordite from spent shells hung in the still morning air. Something was troubling him but he didn't know what it was. He fired off another burst at the Huns Head target at the far end of the range… His memory was trying to tell him something… That was it: the man at the club. He looked at his own black fatigues. He'd seen the face before, but where? The noise of his men firing rounds at their own targets triggered a memory, a door had been opened…

BLAT! Bull switched his AK to fully automatic; his anger ran white-hot through him. The magazine emptied in seconds. The hero from the Poznan operation… the young English face… the only person who could link his past with his present. He moved away from his position, his rifle hanging on its sling, his fists now balled. He looked skywards. All he had worked for, all he had done to distance himself and his Brigada from the past… faked his death, created his new identity. This man could take it away.

'And there we have it.' Patchem paused and sent Vickers an electronic copy of the dossier, his face surprisingly clear via the secure video link. 'Their leader was believed to have been a former Spetsnaz officer by the name of Tauras Pashinski. Known by the nickname 'The Bull'. A veteran of the occupation of Afghanistan, he left the service in the early Nineties around the time of the first budget cuts. His name was then linked to a series of "incidents", for want of a better word, across Eastern Europe and the former USSR. This includes the robbery in Poznan. The last of these was over six years ago. Interpol tried to track him, as, apparently, did his own FSS and GRU. Eventually he was cornered in Vilnius where he was killed in a high-speed pursuit. That was December 1999.'

There was a slight pause caused by the encrypted line. Vickers looked at the file. It contained the Polish police report into the Poznan raid. These included eyewitness accounts, blurred enlargements taken from CCTV footage, and badly photocopied excerpts from Soviet service records. He studied the only clear photograph, that of a serious-faced sixteen-year-old with piercing eyes. Patchem had anticipated his question and continued from his office in London, 'Yes, that's the only photograph we have. Understandably, the Russian intelligence services are somewhat guarded about providing us with any more.'

'So we're certain he's dead?' Vickers wanted to hear his controller confirm this.

'The folder, Alistair, is quite convincing.'

Vickers clicked to the relevant pages and saw that the Vilnius automobile accident was indeed well documented, including witness statements, a coroner's certificate, and the obligatory horror shots showing a corpse embedded in the steering wheel. 'I agree. How do you want me to play this, Jack?' Vickers spoke at the screen displaying his boss's face.

'Alistair, I don't need to tell you how to run your shop. Dig around a bit if you like, but in my opinion what we have is an ex-soldier chasing ghosts. Look at Snow's psych record. Pashinski is the reason he left the regiment, the reason for both his injuries and the flashbacks.'

Vickers nodded. 'Again, I agree.'

Patchem continued, 'Remind Aidan Snow he's still bound by the Official Secrets Act. If he does "see" this man again, he should tell you. Otherwise, he needs to keep quiet and just get on with the rest of his life.'

Chapter 15

The old man poured the liquid into the shot glasses and handed one to Arnaud with a grin. Arnaud returned the smile and, together, he and the two other men downed their shots. The rest of the family looked on with expectant faces. Arnaud suddenly gasped.

'*Samogon*,' said the old man.

'Moonshine,' translated Larissa. 'Homemade vodka.'

'How strong is it?' His throat was burning.

'Maybe sixty per cent.' She shrugged with pretend indifference as the rest of the family laughed.

The old man, Larissa's grandfather, shook his head and said in heavily accented English, 'Ninety degrees.' Although he spoke no English he remembered some phrases from his time as an engineer in the Soviet Army. Larissa's grandmother passed Arnaud a bowl of red soup.

'*Borsch*?' he asked.

The old lady nodded and spoke in Ukrainian, Larissa once again translating. 'My grandmother said that she made it herself. Just for you.'

Larissa ladled *Smetana* (soured cream) into the bowl and Arnaud tried it. '*Doozja Smatchno*,' he said, using his two words of Ukrainian. 'Very tasty.' Again, smiles all round. Their foreign guest had now tasted both grandparents' cherished recipes.

Arnaud and Larissa had been welcomed at Lviv railway station by Larissa's grandparents and driven to the flat they owned on the outskirts of the city. Unlike many other apartment blocks, this one wasn't Soviet but newly built. It had been designed by the Germans, managed by Poles, and built by Ukrainians. Larissa had bought the flat with money she had made in Kyiv. Arnaud was impressed. Larissa's mother and father sat opposite him, her aunt next to her on one side and Arnaud on the other. The table was piled with homemade food. Many things he didn't recognise, including a type of fish pâté and several layered salads. A three-litre glass jug of homemade vodka sat dead centre. Arnaud's glass was refilled and Ivan, Larissa's father, raised his glass to make a toast. Arnaud held his glass and sat mute. Larissa whispered a translation into his ear.

'He says that he is glad to see us both in Lviv, that he hopes you like our city, and that he wishes you health and love.' She blushed and under the table placed her hand on his crotch.

The glasses were emptied and Arnaud's eyes again watered, much to the amusement of the others. 'Thank you.'

They ate the *Borsch* and soon the family started to chat. Arnaud heard his name mentioned occasionally but couldn't understand a word. The quickfire Ukrainian was even less intelligible than the quickfire Russian of Kyiv. The second course arrived and this time it was his turn to make a toast. Lost slightly for words, he thanked the family for their hospitality, said he was happy to meet them, and wished them health. Prompted by Larissa he repeated the toast in French. Larissa's mother cooed at the French and her father raised his glass proudly. This time the *Samogon* seemed almost palatable.

Alone in his flat, Snow woke with a start. He was wet from sweat and shivering. He checked his watch; it was just past three in the morning. The nightmares had returned; the face with the evil eyes stared at him as he lay unable to move. Now the dream seemed more real than ever, the detail of the face and the gun aimed at him. Even the shot that never came was all too real. It was as though the last ten years had never happened.

In his hospital bed Snow had looked at the images the Polish police had shown him. None of the faces had been the one: the man with the green, snake-like eyes and chiselled face. He had worked with a police artist who had produced a sketch. He had also helped to provide a photo-fit. Meanwhile, the police forensics department had found traces of the plastic explosive used in the vans. The chemical footprint was familiar to the expert, who had formerly been enlisted in the Polish army. The origin of the explosive was Russian military. In the hope of finding their man, the Polish authorities sent images of the suspect to both the Russian FSB, post-breakup successor to the KGB, and their military intelligence counterparts, the GRU. In the spirit of *Glasnost*, the GRU cooperated and found the man to match the face. A heavily censored copy of his military record was handed over to the Polish police. The man was identified as a former Spetsnaz captain, Tauras Pashinski, also known as 'The Bull'. The GRU did not add, however, that Pashinski was wanted for questioning in Russia.

The Polish investigation continued but without result. Eventually, after a year, the case was shelved, the only lead gone. Snow had returned to Hereford and physically recuperated; however, unable to rid his mind of the nightmares, he had left the regiment in mid-1997. He felt a failure but had tried to put his military past behind him, becoming a mature student.

In late December 1999, during the build-up to the millennium festivities, the FSB informed the Poles they had found Pashinski. He had reappeared with a group of former Red Army veterans in Kaliningrad, the small Russian enclave sandwiched between Poland and his native Lithuania. Here he had been observed meeting with known criminal groups and had only been recognised by chance when a Russian who was under surveillance was introduced to him. The FSB Special Operations Centre ordered Pashinski to be followed and launched a snatch operation with their counterterrorism commando unit, Alpha. Their extreme force was met with his, and Pashinski managed to break out and through the Lithuanian border. His luck ran out as he entered the outskirts of Vilnius where, on an ice-laden road, his BMW spun, colliding with a large Kamaz truck. As a civilian, Snow hadn't been informed by HM Government of his tormentor's documented demise. For him, the green-eyed nemesis was still alive.

Snow sat up and wrapped the duvet around his naked body. Every noise had him tensing; with each movement of the lift, he imagined a black-clad Spetsnaz team getting nearer. He stood in the darkness and again checked both the inner and outer doors to the flat. Both were secure, both were locked. Arnaud had been right; it would take semtex to open them.

He smiled despite himself. Arnaud, the lucky bastard, wasn't only giving Larissa one but getting in with the family. Snow suddenly craved the normality he had always run from. Why had he spited his parents by joining the armed forces? Why had he not gone to university at eighteen like his peers and then done something with his language skills? He could have been an international banker or even in the Foreign Office like his father. He shook his head and saw Alistair Vickers's face. No. He had made the right decision by joining up, and yes, he had eventually got his degree, albeit as a mentally scarred mature student, and now he was doing something rewarding with his skills. But was it all for nothing? His past had reappeared and was trying to reclaim him, to take him back to the world of death and nightmares. He shuffled into the kitchen and took a cognac bottle from the cupboard. Tomorrow at the Hash he would speak to Vickers, see whether he had discovered anything. If not, he would have no choice but to try himself; but now he had to sleep, if not sober then so be it. Snow opened the bottle and took a large slug.

Pechersk Lavra Park Gardens, Kyiv

Randy wore the Grand Hash Master's hat. He explained that Mitch was away on business. The Hashers had met outside the Hotel Salute near the Pechersk Lavra Monastery. The route had taken them through the parks and ended up at a monument overlooking the river. This time there were no Hash virgins so they went straight to beer. A tired and hungover Snow leant against the railing and watched a barge pass by as he sipped his 'hair of the dog'.

'Alone today?' It was Vickers.

He continued to watch the river. 'Yep. Frogs is in Lviv. He's being presented to his girlfriend's parents. They live there.'

'Very historic.'

'The first time always is,' Snow replied, deadpan.

'I meant Lviv.'

'Good friend of yours?' Snow gestured towards Blazhevich, who was speaking to a pair of Canadians.

'Just a hasher like you, works in the EBRD, I think.' Vickers had made contact with Blazhevich during the run; the European Bank of Reconstruction and Development was a cover the SBU officer used on such occasions.

'Important banker then?' Snow continued to sip. 'How long you worked for Six?'

Vickers was taken aback at the mention of his real employer.

'I can't talk about that, Aidan.'

'I know. Neither could my dad. Funny, eh?'

'You went to school in Moscow if I remember?' Vickers changed the subject.

'Yep. According to my file, which I presume you have a copy of? Together with my psych report etc.?' Vickers sipped his beer as a 'no comment'. Snow continued, 'So. Any news?'

Vickers finished his mouthful. 'It's Sunday, Aidan; things are shut for the weekend.'

Snow felt his own anger rise but outwardly stayed calm. 'I'm sorry, but this is more important than a lost airline ticket or passport, don't you think?'

Vickers looked around to make sure no one could overhear them before nodding, 'I've spoken to London and you are who you say you are. They've sent me some information and as far, as we can make out, this man of yours is dead. He died in 1999.' Vickers paused to gauge Snow's reaction.

Snow hadn't expected this. He looked back at the river for several seconds, trying to organise his thoughts before replying. 'How did he die?'

'Car crash. Vilnius. It's all documented; they even have his dental records.'

Snow continued to stare, not sure what to feel. 'Alistair, I saw him. I swear I saw him.'

'You think you saw him. They say we all have a double, a doppelganger. I personally am waiting to meet Cindy Crawford's.' He chanced a half-smile.

Snow conceded and faced Vickers. 'Perhaps you're right, but I was so sure.'

'Look, Aidan, if you do see, or think you see, this person again, I'll dig around a bit for you. Deal?'

Snow felt as though he was being patronised but appreciated Vickers's offer nevertheless. 'Thanks, Alistair.' He crunched his empty beer can in his hand and went to get another, starting to feel a sense of relief.

Chapter 16

Arnaud and Snow counted the heads as they re-entered the school. All the members of the running club were accounted for. Arnaud looked up the corridor wistfully.

'Stop pining; you'll see her in a couple of hours.'

'Yeah, I know.' Arnaud had a faraway look in his eyes.

'I'm surprised you can walk with all the "exercise" you've been getting!'

Arnaud laughed. 'Those bunks on the train are for midgets; still, better than Lviv – her parents made us sleep in separate rooms!'

'How was it? Meeting her parents, I mean.'

'Cool. I got very pissed. They gave me this homemade vodka. It's evil.' Arnaud had a bottle in his bag for Snow and would give it to him later. He had come to school straight from Larissa's flat, where he had tried to make up for the loss of intimacy.

'Did you go to the opera?' The Lviv Opera House was allegedly the fifth best in the world.

'We got a box. Shared it with some bloke but we had to leave early to get the train back.'

'What a pity.'

Arnaud smiled 'Yeah, real shame. Now I'll never know if the rich Count got to deflower the peasant girl or not. Suppose you got shit-faced as usual?'

The receptionist looked up, nonplussed. Both teachers smiled; she glared back and answered the phone, clearly not liking their language.

'Sorry!' He rolled his eyes at Snow. 'Does she ever smile?'

'Only when she farts,' whispered Snow.

They reached the staffroom. At mid-morning break it was popular.

'Good morning, Mikhail Romanovich.'

Mikhail Klimov took his bag off the spare seat. 'Hi.'

Arnaud sat and frowned. 'So, what's all this *Ovich, Evich* business then?'

'It means "son of". Like the Scandinavian,' explained Snow.

'Magnus Magnusson?'

'Yeah, and Eriksson.'

'But not Sony Eriksson,' added Mikhail Klimov

Arnaud groaned. 'So I would be Arnaud Paulovich?'

'That's right, and I'm Aidan Phillipovich. Mikhail's son is Olexandr Mikhailovich.'

'Hang on, why Olexandr? Does the first name change too?' Arnaud leaned forward across the table and frowned even more.

'Mikhail, you explain,' Snow delegated.

'We are in Ukraine. Olexandr is the Ukrainian version of Alexander. If you want to sound Ukrainian, even if you are speaking Russian, you can use the Ukrainian version of the word. Galina…' He raised his mug to the Russian language teacher at the photocopier. '…Could be called Halina.'

'So what's the Ukrainian version of Arnaud?'

'There isn't one, it is not a Slavic name,' replied Klimov.

'Well explained, Misha.' Snow poured Klimov some coffee from the pot.

'Misha?'

'That,' added Snow, 'is the shortened version of Mikhail.'

There was a pause while they all sipped their coffee. Klimov winked.

Galina finished her photocopying. 'I was once translator for American businessman. He had same name as his father, but he was George Layton the Second. When I introduce him he sounds like he is a king! He was not.'

British Embassy, Kyiv

Vickers scanned the file again and looked at the face. His desk phone rang. He answered, telling Bondarenko, on reception, to let the visitor in. He rose from the desk and walked along the corridor. Blazhevich was standing staring at a watercolour of a cricket match. Vickers spoke in Russian, '*Dobre Den Vitaly Romanovich.*'

'Good afternoon, Alistair Vickers,' Blazhevich replied in English.

'The County Ground, Sussex County Cricket Club. My grandfather used to take me as a boy.'

'I never could understand cricket.'

'Neither can most of the spectators, Vitaly.'

'I do like your rugby.'

'Yes. Our last ambassador was very keen on that. I believe he even coached your national team.'

'One day, perhaps, we could be welcoming the Lions to Kyiv?'

'Perhaps. If you'll follow me I have something to show you.' Vickers led the way. A pot of tea and a plate of custard creams greeted them. Once seated Vickers handed his SBU contact the photograph.

'Who's this?' Blazhevich studied the image.

'In 1996 there was a rather messy bank robbery in Poznan.

Several members of the Polish and British armed forces were killed. This man was responsible.'

'I am sorry but I was sixteen, why show me this?'

'A reliable source says he saw this man in Kyiv five days ago.' Vickers exaggerated Snow's credibility.

Blazhevich raised his eyebrows. 'Is this not a job for the Militia and Interpol?'

Vickers shook his head. 'No, because this man died six years ago.'

Back at his own desk, Blazhevich checked his files. He had come to a dead end with the Malik investigation and his other minor cases were under control. He pulled out the Polish file Vickers had given him. It contained details of the Poznan robbery, the testimony of an unidentified eyewitness (for security reasons all mention of Snow by name had been deleted) and the heavily edited military record. These records he would attempt to get in full; later he would also check the state security files, including the old Soviet ones.

'How goes the Malik case?' Budanov leant against the door-frame.

'It doesn't,' replied Blazhevich as he fished in his desk drawer for a paperclip.

Budanov's hand shook and tea spilt from his mug onto his light suit trousers. A sudden tightness gripped his chest. It couldn't be. He steadied his hand and drank a mouthful of tea, his throat dry. 'Who's that?'

Blazhevich clipped a handwritten note to the bottom of the photograph. 'Someone who should be dead.'

Pushkinskaya Street, Kyiv

Snow stood on the balcony of his flat. Arnaud handed him another beer. 'Thanks.'

The two teachers stood and drank in silence as they gazed at the city streets in front of them. Getting back home at four each day had its advantages. They beat the rush-hour traffic when the roads became gridlocked and the commuters packed the underground like 'herring', as the Russian idiom went. But if anyone were to say to Arnaud that teaching was a soft option, not a full-time job, they would get a slap. He was shattered, having today decided to start on his health kick, running with Snow before work, then again with the lunchtime running club. He looked at his flatmate, who was ten years his senior yet seemed twice as fit.

'I don't know how you do it, Aidan.'

'Do what?' Snow was lost in thought.

'Get up each morning and run, then run again at school. I'm so knackered I can barely hold my beer!' Arnaud's health kick involved drinking less, when he remembered.

'I'm used to it. Been doing it a long time, I suppose, and now it feels weird if I don't run or train.' Snow liked to get in at least three sessions a week at the little local gym he had found. He had booked Arnaud in there with him tomorrow.

'You need discipline, I suppose. Like being in the army.' Arnaud took a swig.

Snow turned and looked at his young friend. There was something he had been wanting to tell him, something that, in light of recent events, he couldn't keep a secret any longer. Now they had known each other for a while, Snow had decided to trust him. 'Exactly like being in the army. When I joined up I soon learnt discipline.'

Arnaud gave Snow a strange look; he hadn't thought to ask what Snow had done before he became a mature student. 'What do you mean?'

'I used to be in the British Army. I left eight or so years ago.'

'Really? Why?' Arnaud was impressed; he'd never taken Snow for a 'squaddie', especially as he had a retired diplomat for a father.

'Why did I join or why did I leave?'

'Err, both?'

'I joined to spite my parents who were trying to make me into them; my dad especially wanted me to get a good degree and enter the Foreign Office. He said it would be a disgrace if I wasted my language skills.' Snow drank some more beer.

Arnaud nodded. His father had seen him as an international investment banker. 'Why did you leave?'

Snow patted his leg. 'Remember that car crash I told you about?' Arnaud nodded. 'I was actually on a training mission in Poland when it happened. A bomb detonated as we passed and I got trapped in the wreckage. I was pretty busted up physically.'

'A bomb?' Arnaud was shocked but suddenly very interested. 'Terrorists? Was it the Baader Meinhof?'

'Cheeky sod, that was the Seventies. I'm not that old! It was a bank robbery, pure and simple. A group of Russian ex-Spetsnaz had decided to do a little freelance financial work. I was trying to stop them making a withdrawal. They planted a couple of car bombs outside the bank and boom!' Snow leant against the railings. In his mind he was starting to relive the attack again.

'Jesus.' Arnaud was very impressed and didn't know what to say. He then frowned. 'Why was the British Army trying to stop a bank robbery? Why not the police?'

'We were training their SWAT team; I was in charge of weapons.'

'You sound like James Bond!' Arnaud smiled broadly.

'Nothing so glamorous. I was in the SAS.'

Arnaud's jaw dropped. He now felt slightly embarrassed, especially as he had read the entire works of Chris Ryan and Andy McNab and would on occasion quote from them.

Snow continued, 'I'm sorry if I've been acting a bit strange but last week I thought I saw the gang leader from the robbery in Mars – Mitch's neighbour. Remember?'

Arnaud vaguely remembered a man in a suit; his eyes had been on the strippers. 'Right.'

He finished his beer. 'But I now know I was wrong.'

Petropavlivska Borschagivka, Kyiv Oblast, Ukraine

The security gates opened and the Volkswagen Passat pulled into the drive. Oleg showed Budanov into the house. Bull sat on a cream leather settee in the cavernous lounge. CNN was on the huge plasma television screen. It amused him how the Americans believed the entire world was interested in what they had to say. 'Sit down.'

Budanov sat in an armchair; despite the cool air conditioning his shirt was already clammy.

'What is it that is so important it cannot wait?' Bull looked wholly unimpressed by his presence and Budanov noticed that, for the first time, he wasn't in a suit, rather a black T-shirt and matching tactical trousers.

'This photograph of you was on the desk of my colleague.'

Bull snatched the proffered 10x8 print. It was an image he hadn't seen for almost thirty years; of himself in full parade dress. There was a long silence before Bull stood quickly and walked around the back of the settee, his face turning a dark red. Budanov had never seen the impeccably composed businessman like this. Bull grabbed the nearest object, a bottle, and threw it against the wall. Budanov flinched.

'Explain how this came to be on the desk of an SBU officer?' Bull leant now on the back of the settee, his face close to his informer's. A vein in his forehead twitched.

'It was given to him by a contact. He says a reliable source has seen this man – you – in Kyiv.' Budanov's voice was shaky.

'Who is the contact and who is the source?' demanded Bull.

'I do not know. Blazhevich has his own people.'

'Guess.'

Budanov struggled for an answer. 'He is close to the British.'

Bull kicked the settee and shouted for Oleg. The massive sergeant appeared at the door. Bull shouted at him in their native Lithuanian. 'He knows who I am.' He returned his attention to the man from the SBU and used Russian. 'Who else has seen this image?' Bull had another bottle in his hand but this time was pouring a shot.

'Perhaps just Blazhevich, but he will show it to Dudka.'

'And what will Dudka do?' Bull knew the names of the high-ranking officials.

'I don't know. I do not think that Blazhevich has linked this to Varchenko or Malik.'

Bull emptied his glass. 'That is not good enough.'

'For a positive ID they need the source, an eyewitness.'

'Then we eliminate the source.' It was Oleg.

'Whom he does not know.' Bull spoke again in Lithuanian.

Oleg replied in the same tongue. 'The Englishman?'

'Who else can it be?' Bull sat and pointed at Budanov, speaking in Russian. 'Go back to your office. You are no good here. Get a list of all British citizens, with pictures, currently in Ukraine. Then come back here. Understand?'

Budanov nodded, rose and tried to leave, but Oleg blocked his path. 'Remember, Budanov, that I know where your wife and child are. If you cross us they will die.'

Budanov tried not to shake. 'Please. I… I… won't say anything. Y… you can trust me.'

'Get out,' Bull gestured, and Oleg stepped aside.

Once Budanov was out of the door Oleg spoke. 'We have to kill him.'

'Not yet. The fat man has his uses. Once we get the address of the Englishman and have silenced him, then you can kill him, Oleg.'

The former Spetsnaz sergeant smiled. 'I will do it slowly.'

Chapter 17

Central Kyiv

He could hear Michael, still haggling with the taxi driver, as he reached the opposite side of Khreshatik. Kyiv's main drag was empty with the exception of the ever-hopeful cabbies waiting at the bottom of Passage. Michael spluttered past in an ancient Volga and yelled out of the window. Snow smiled and waved goodnight with his middle finger. The two ex-pats had been among the last to leave the Cowboy Bar, a regular occurrence. The bar generally lived up to its own advertising and stayed open 'until the last customer leaves'.

He looked at his watch. Christ, 3.40 a.m.! Hadn't he told Michael 'Just one more' at around half two? He chuckled to himself. Who cared? It was Saturday night – or Sunday morning, rather, Snow corrected himself. He started the short climb up Prorizna to the corner of Pushkinskaya and the safety of his empty but inviting bed. Michael had gone home to wake up his long-suffering wife, Mitch, still abroad, was probably working on his latest conquest, and Arnaud was busy 'stress testing' Larissa's bed.

It had been a year since his last relationship had ended but it still hurt. Donna had been American, part of Mitch's company, and gorgeous. Snow had seriously thought she might be the one, but then she left. No goodbye, no excuse. Just returned to California to continue her life without him. If he hadn't liked her so much he wouldn't have cared. He had opened up to her, told her more than anyone else about his history with the regiment, the accident, the nightmares. For him it was something serious, yet for Donna, as he eventually found out via text message, it had been a 'vacation fling' while she had been working away from home. What was wrong with him? Here he was in a country full of beautiful women, mourning the loss of someone who didn't deserve him. Snow realised he was getting maudlin. Sod it. He'd have a dram or three and watch the four o'clock news on BBC World before passing out alone.

The black-clad figure, lying prone on the first-floor balcony of a rented apartment, depressed his pressel switch twice, giving the alert that the target had been sighted. The Englishman was getting nearer and would pass within ten feet of his head. A whisper via the earpiece asked, 'Is he alone?' One squeeze on the pressel as an affirmative. Oleg imagined he could see the others getting ready in the van, two of them pulling down their masks and readying weapons, while the third sat at the wheel. The target got nearer. Oleg held his breath. The target took the short cut through the square and onto Pushkinskaya. He spoke into his throat mic. 'Target has crossed road. I no longer have visual.'

'I have,' came the reply from the van. 'Pull back to secondary position.'

'Have that.' Oleg waited until Snow had disappeared around the back of the apartment block before standing and wiping the icy sweat from his brow. He dropped his rope over the edge and swiftly, hand over hand, made for the street. Landing with a practised delicacy, he moved silently for the cover of the Gastronom's porch entrance and continued his watch in silence. With the exception of the two Berkut guards, clock watching in their command box outside the Uzbek Embassy, Pushkinskaya was asleep.

Snow pushed open the back door to the flats, called the lift and rode up to the 'Ukrainian' third floor. He swayed at the threshold and opened the door on his second attempt. He pulled shut the outer door and secured the inner one with three turns of the lock. He pushed the connecting double door to the hall shut with his foot and, without kicking off his shoes or removing his fleece jacket, dropped on to the Polish sofabed. He flicked on BBC World. An advert for a new brand of Indian car filled the gap before the news headlines. Staring past the TV, through the open double-dividing doors, he could see Arnaud's clothes and books strewn across both bed and floor. Messy bugger. He hauled himself up and leant against the doorframe, and as he did an explosion ripped through the front door.

The circular charge blew both locks inwards, immediately followed by a second deafening noise, a burst of light, and the first of two men in black military assault coveralls. The assaulters ran into the flat, CQB weapons covering large arcs, looking for movement and targets. Ears ringing and sitting dazed on the floor between the lounge and bedroom, Snow recognised the noise as 'flash-bangs' – stun grenades. He saw shadows through the remaining frosted glass in the hall. His training, dormant for the last seven years, took over, and in seconds he had covered the distance from the bedroom to the balcony. Crouching, he opened the balcony door and moved towards the edge. Another crash and the doors to the hall had been demolished by heavy boots.

Time seemed to stop. Rounds ripped past Snow's head and he clambered over the railings. Sparks flew as hot lead impacted inches from his hands. He lowered himself as best he could until he was hanging by his arms, then let go. Dropping one floor, he landed in the wire mesh designed to catch stray icicles in winter. Snow was no icicle and the mesh broke loose a second later. This was all that was needed to save his life as he fell the remaining ten feet to the pavement. Landing heavily on both feet, bending his knees and rolling on to his side, he hid under the footprint of the balcony as more bullets rained down over the railings, peppering the pavement ahead. Two figures ran towards the building. They were too near to see him in the shadows.

Gasping for air and holding his side, Snow pushed himself up and away from the building. He felt no pain from his legs, just a sudden wave of cold which raced through his body. He collided with the first figure, who fell to the pavement with a shrill shout. Grabbing the attacker's gun he shot a burst at the other just as he was raising his own firearm. Only metres away, the second figure crumpled to the ground without opening his mouth. Reaching the corner of Pushkinskaya, Snow detected movement to his left and swung the weapon. A line of bullets raced towards a figure that dived back into the shadows. The magazine empty, Snow discarded the gun. Throwing one leg after another and praying they would hold his weight, Snow hurtled down the undulating pavement of Pushkinskaya towards Maidan Nezalejsnosti and the river.

Picking himself up off the floor, Oleg drew his weapon but knew it was too late. The target was out of sight. He cursed, using all the American expletives he could remember and a few he'd made up. Lights had started to flick on in apartments all around him. Pushkinskaya was no longer asleep.

Hydropark, Kyiv

Snow walked quickly across the footbridge. He had to disappear now. Shards of moonlight illuminated the gloomy blackness of the Dnipro River beneath him as he made for the opposite shore and the relative safety of Hydropark. Had anyone seen him head this way? He would soon know. His escape and evasion instincts had kicked in; he was once again the SAS trooper. The distant trees rose like a giant wave as he crested the centre of the bridge. No sound except for the heavy metallic echo of his feet on the footbridge. Breaking his stride, he stumbled down the three or so broken steps as he left the bridge and aimed for the gloom of the tree cover. He rushed into the trees and steadied his breathing. No stir from the trees or the bridge. Twenty seconds' wait. Still no stir. He rose slowly, circled, listened again, then joined the path leading further into the woods. Four o'clock on a November morning would hardly be rush hour but Snow still had to take care. He'd use the path but stick to the relative gloom of the edge, ready to burst into the undergrowth at the slightest hint of pursuit. As he walked on he studied each new trunk that emerged from the shadows, while forever turning to watch his rear.

Petropavlivska Borschagivka, Kyiv Oblast, Ukraine

Bull, fully clothed, slept on top of the bed. It was a habit he had developed while enlisted and one, when alone, he found hard to break. His boots stood at his bedside, a 9mm Glock nestling in the one on the left. The phone on the bedside table warbled. In an instant Bull was sitting up, his eyes open. '*Da?*'

It wasn't good news. Holding the handset, he swung his legs on to the floor and stood. 'Come here now.'

Hydropark, Kyiv

After a quarter of an hour, Snow reached the far side of the island – away from the main tourist area with its kiosks and stray dogs. Crouching just in the tree line, he slowly counted two minutes as his ears adjusted to the sound of waves gently lapping against the shore. He looked at his watch dial, trying to make out the two hands: 4.48. His eyelids were becoming increasingly heavy. The adrenaline of the chase was now wearing off and he could feel the after-effect churning his stomach and pounding at his temples. He was going to feel like crap in the morning but at least he'd have a morning. He started to shiver and turned the collar up on his jacket. He was dressed for a night out and not a night out 'on belt-kit' as they had called sleeping rough in the regiment. He'd spent endless hours trying to perfect the art of ignoring the cold and wet, only to realise it was impossible. He had jarred his good knee in the fall from the balcony in addition to hurting his side. All pain, however, had been put aside as he'd run for his life. Now, sitting ten feet back from the tree line with his back against a tree trunk, the pain started to really register. He drew his legs up to his chest, winced, and tried to stop the shivers. With a thin covering of soil over sand, here the grass was less damp, but he could still feel it seeping into his jeans. His heart was still beating raggedly as he suddenly remembered Arnaud. Would he go back to the flat after all? Would they try to snatch him too? Was Larissa's place being watched? Snow tried to rationalise the situation in his mind but to no avail. He unzipped his fleece and pulled out the Nokia. He punched in Arnaud's number and pressed his ear tightly against the speaker. It seemed to ring for an eternity before being picked up.

A groggy female voice answered. '*Allo?*'

He spoke in Russian; if he was to be overheard by anyone, it would be better to be taken for a local and not an ex-trooper from Worthing.

'Larissa, it's Aidan. Is Arnaud with you?'

'Aidan, what you want!? We sleeping!'

'Give the phone to Arnaud. It's import—' He frantically pressed redial. Engaged. Shit. Why was she so bloody awkward! He tried again but this time the call went straight to voicemail. Arnaud's message sounded deafening in the still night air. 'This is Arnaud. Leave a message only if you are sexy or owe me money…'

Snow spoke clearly and with purpose. 'Arnaud, it's me, Aidan. This is very important. Do not go back to the flat. OK? Do not go back. I can't explain why now. Call Alistair Vickers in the morning. You have to trust me. I'll call you when I can.'

Arnaud's voicemail was as temperamental as Larissa. Despondently, Snow ended the call realising he'd sounded like a bad 'B movie'. He checked the phone's illuminated display – two battery bars left; if he was going to use it he would have to conserve power. He tapped in a text message to Arnaud and repeated the warning then switched off the handset. Again, his mind raced.

Whoever had attacked him wasn't playing or trying to scare him; they knew exactly what they were doing: plastic charge on the door and flash-bangs. But why not snatch him on the street? Why make it so overt, unless that was the point? Was there some kind of message? Snow creased his eyes shut and pressed his fingers to his temples, forcing his beer-addled brain to think. It had to be the work of Pashinski. Who else would try this? He had to assume the man was not dead, that he had been recognised by him, and that this had been some kind of snatch squad. Snow opened his eyes. Things suddenly became clearer. The only member of the SAS training team able to positively ID Pashinski and link him to the Polish raid; the only person who could say Pashinski was alive. Snow felt nauseous. Pashinski was coming for him.

On the other side of the city, Arnaud rolled over in Larissa's bed. He was in no mood to text anyone now. It was probably another of the lads in London forgetting, yet again, that he was two hours ahead. 'Tossers,' he mumbled to himself and drifted back to sleep.

'You were a team of four against an unarmed man!' raged Bull. He threw the coffee cup across the room at Oleg, hitting him square in the chest before it fell to the ground and shattered at his feet.

Oleg took a deep breath. 'We followed him as planned but he did not surrender, did not give himself up, he just jumped.'

Bull massaged his temples with both hands. 'Were you aiming high as requested? Did you hit him? Was he injured when he "jumped"?'

'We did not shoot at him, but to him,' Oleg paused for a moment, trying to tell if he was making sense. 'A man does not run away from two Berkut if he is injured.'

Bull wanted the Englishman alive; he wanted to be the one to pull the trigger himself and finish what he had started in Poznan. 'You left the rifle?'

'*Da*, of course.'

Bull nodded; the backup plan at least was in effect. The SBU would no doubt be alerted by the noise of the attack, investigate the flat and find the Dragunov sniper rifle. And if the SBU found him then Bull could get hold of him. Bull took a new cup and poured himself coffee from the steaming pot.

Outside the terrace window the sky was still pitch-black. He checked the living-room clock. 'It's almost five. First light will be in an hour. He won't run yet. He'll go to ground and then try to get lost in the crowds. The question is where?' Bull sipped the coffee, impervious to the heat, then started to think aloud. 'He'll contact MI6 at the embassy. Will they get him out, a man wanted by the SBU? Watch the embassy and the airport.' Bull positioned himself in Oleg's face. Oleg's bloodshot eyes betrayed no emotion. 'You find this teacher for me or I find you a plot in the cemetery.'

Oleg nodded; he had only seen his commander this angry

once before, and on that occasion eight Afghans had been executed.

Hydropark, Kyiv

The sound of splashing woke Snow with a jolt. Instinctively tensing for a moment before remembering where he was, Snow relaxed his arms, silently cursing himself for having fallen asleep. Sitting motionless against the tree he concentrated hard to locate the source of the commotion. A bark from behind. He took a deep breath and prepared for the worst. First one, then another mongrel slipped through the trees and trotted in the direction of the beach. They were dirty, emaciated strays, not the pursuit dogs he had feared. He gingerly pulled himself to his feet. Wincing in anticipation of the headache, which he knew would soon follow, he took a step. Sure enough it arrived with a vengeance. Feeling shaky and damp to the bone, he negotiated the tree roots. His left knee was especially bad and his thighs felt as if he had run a marathon wearing clogs. The sun was beginning to alter the colour of the sky above, replacing the dark ink-blue of night with the pink of early morning. Alerted to his presence, the dogs drinking at the water's edge trotted away.

Only now did he look at his watch. 6.10. He'd been asleep for just over an hour. Taking a deep breath, he filled his lungs with the biting morning air in an attempt to shake off his tiredness. The oxygen rushing to his brain relieved his headache temporarily. No one around; the first metro would be running in twenty minutes, bringing with it the hardcore fishermen who would race around the island claiming their prized spots. With Chernobyl only thirty-five miles upstream, Snow had never fancied the indigenous fish. At the water's edge he washed his muddied hands and splashed his face with the icy river water. He wetted his hair just enough to push it back and flatten it. Another deep breath;

this time he took the path towards the metro station and main road. With any luck no one would give him a second glance boarding the train; if they did they would wonder who the hell was leaving Hydropark at 6.20 a.m. on a Sunday. Still, he had no choice, was in no mood for walking, and attempting to flag down a car would cause further suspicion.

Volodymyrska Street, Kyiv

Alistair Vickers sipped his first tea of the day. How he missed the fresh morning paper. The Saturday edition would have to do until Sunday's, flown over from London by BA, was delivered after lunch. He hated being out of touch, out of 'sync' with the world. The local press was a joke; in fact, the only thing that kept him sane was BBC World.

He pulled on his New Balance running shoes. Today would be a nice day, he persuaded himself; first he'd go for his run, finish his admin work, then head over to O'Brian's for a spot of lunch and a pint. It was the only place in Kyiv that offered anything remotely resembling a Sunday roast. He checked his appearance in the mirror and then the phone rang.

Hydropark, Kyiv

Two dogs slept by the hot air duct at the entrance to the metro, and broken glass glistened in the morning sun. Snow pushed open the large steel and glass door and entered the station. Just past the counter a pair of stout, middle-aged women stood, arms folded, deep in conversation. One wore the equally stout blue cotton overalls and orange jerkin of the metro maintenance team, the other a fluffy purple cardigan, skirt, woollen stockings and large slippers. On noticing him they paused momentarily before

176

continuing their philosophical debate. Snow waited politely for several seconds for 'Slippers' to serve him. With a thud she sat down on the stool behind the glass. Reaching into his pocket he found a one-hryvnia note, cursing that he didn't have a metro token. Without a word his note was converted into two *jetons*, two blue bits of plastic.

The tick of the clock, informing travellers of both the time and how long since the last train had left, echoed across the empty platform. He could see the deserted kiosks on one side of the line and the cafés and bars on the other. In the distance, Snow could just make out the entrance to the outdoor gym. The gym, which had been the brainchild of a frustrated local fitness fanatic, had become an institution for the residents of Kyiv. Consisting of bits of heavy old machinery, Soviet tanks and planes, it was all but indestructible. Bugger a London loft conversion. If he ever became famous and fat and had to make a fitness video, he'd do it here. A low rumbling sound broke his train of thought. Gliding to a halt, the metro doors opened and Snow stepped inside.

Volodymyrska Street, Kyiv

'*What* happened?' Vickers was incredulous.

Vitaly Blazhevich repeated the events again in clear and precise English that even Vickers could understand.

'Bollocks.' His hand was over the handset but he didn't really care if his contemporary at the SBU heard him or not. 'Where is he now?'

'We do not know, Alistair Phillipovich. All we do know, all we suspect, is that Aidan Snow, a British citizen, survived an attempt on his life and is now in hiding after shooting a member of the Berkut Diplomatic Protection Squad.'

Vickers fell into the armchair. Snow would surely try to contact him. 6.35 a.m. If he hurried he could still get to the stadium for his daily run. He'd take the car and save the twenty minutes it took to jog.

'Is there anything we should know about this Snow?' questioned Blazhevich. 'Something perhaps you have not told us?'

Vickers answered too quickly for Blazhevich's liking. 'Nothing I can think of. What of his flatmate, Mr Hurst? Have you spoken to him yet?'

'No, we are expecting him to return home sometime this morning. However, if you do have his mobile telephone, perhaps, this would be very useful?' Blazhevich replied.

I bet it would be, thought Vickers. 'Sorry, can't help you on that. All I know is that they live somewhere on Pushkinskaya. If they contact me, I'll let you know.'

'Good, Alistair Phillipovich. Enjoy your run.'

Vickers collected his car keys and mobile, and left the flat. He'd inform the ambassador as soon as he himself knew more. Snow and Vickers had often seen each other on their morning constitutionals, so if Snow wanted to make contact, this would be an opportunity.

Hydropark, Kyiv

The train pulled off and, within minutes, had slowed to enter Dnipro station, where the metro line plunged into the darkness, tunnelling down deep under the Pecherska Lavra Monastery. Snow looked at the floor and thought long and hard about the incidents of the night before. The door had been blown minutes after he had entered the flat. Why had they waited? Why not grab him before he got inside or as he opened the door? It didn't add up, drawing attention to the snatch attempt. Nor did launching yourself off a balcony, running like a madman and sleeping rough; not the easiest thing to do at the best of times and making no sense at all when half-pissed!

'Jeez.' Snow ran his hands through his damp hair; he had been lucky. His thoughts turned to survival. Pashinski, the face from the past, had to be behind this. He had to get somewhere safe and soon. Shit! Nine years since he'd left the regiment and now here he was, grabbed firmly by the scrotum and hurled back into the fire. He closed his eyes and opened them just as the train pulled into his station.

Snow let the barrier bang against his right leg as he exited through the glass doors at Arsenalna and into the daylight once again. He was taking a huge risk surfacing so close to the city centre but he had to catch Vickers during his morning constitutional. If Pashinski's men were professionals they would have eyes on every major tube station, Voksalna – the central railway station – and both airports. Perhaps he was being paranoid, he thought briefly, as his feet negotiated a broken paving slab; but you make mistakes, you die. No one, however brazen, would risk snatching him here next to the city barracks.

Minutes later, concealed behind the rows of plastic chairs, Snow sat on the cold concrete ledge in the stadium and shivered. From his perch up high he saw Vickers arrive, park his battered, dark-blue Land Rover Defender, and jog into the stadium complex. Jogging around the empty stadium in his yellow and sky-blue 'British Embassy Cave Inn' rugby shirt, Vickers was nothing if not conspicuous, nodding at the occasional pensioner in their monotone tracksuits as he bounded by.

Although he had run far less than usual today, Vickers found the going harder. His mind wasn't clear and he wasn't concentrating on his breathing. He scanned the rows of empty seats for any hint of a watcher or surveillance team. He hoped that Snow was somewhere out there and could explain what the hell was going on.

Snow waited until Vickers had finished his requisite eight laps, watching him slow to a fast walk. Hands on his hips, he started his ascent out of Dynamo Stadium, through the park exit, leaving his Land Rover Defender in the car park.

Snow eased himself up. He'd catch Vickers before he crossed the road by the Cabinet of Ministers building. Taking a path parallel to Vickers, he retrieved his Nokia and put it to his ear, pretending to make a call. Alistair appeared, walking slightly faster now. Snow crossed in front of him and turned to face him.

'Alistair! What a surprise – just go along with it – how are you?'

'Aidan, what the hell?'

'I need answers. I need answers now.' Snow extended his hand, they shook. 'Who, why, and what are you going to do about it?'

Vickers's face showed no surprise; in fact, he struck Snow as looking relatively calm. He tried to withdraw his hand but Snow held it tighter.

'You tell me, Aidan?'

'I was jumped as I got home. They blew open the door, shot at me, tried to kill me. I grabbed a weapon. I think I got one of them and ran.'

'Are you crazy?'

Snow let go, puzzled. 'What?' Indicating for him to walk, they continued along the path.

'You shot a Berkut officer. A Berkut officer guarding a bloody embassy! For Christ's sake!'

'Shit.' The face of the guard outside the Uzbek Embassy flashed back into his mind. What had he done? Snow felt his empty stomach churn.

Vickers faced him and nodded. 'He's not dead but the SBU are looking for you.'

'I don't care what you have to do, just get me out of here.'

'There's nothing I can do. I can try to stall them but I can't do anything. I wish I could. You're not in the regiment anymore; you're not an SIS operative. You are a civilian British citizen working in Ukraine. You are the main suspect in the shooting of a member of the diplomatic protection force. For all I know you could have made this Pashinski business up as a cover. But, for what it's worth, I believe you and I believe an attempt was made on your life. I should hand you straight over to the SBU but I won't. Aidan, one friend to another, get the hell out of Ukraine.'

Snow clenched his teeth; he was incensed. Things had just got worse.

Chapter 18

'Gennady Stepanovich.' Vitaly Blazhevich extended his hand and shook that of his boss. 'What brings you here on a Sunday morning?'

'Vitaly Romanovich. If that is your idea of a joke you should not give up your day job. Now tell me; what do we have here?'

His boss was not in a good mood, it seemed. *Did I drag you back from the* dacha, he wondered? Blazhevich took a biro from his pocket. 'We have a large hole where the lock would have been.' He poked at the hole with his pen for dramatic effect.

'Circular charge. Quite neat.' The old man circled his hand.

'Premade plastic charge, Gennady Stepanovich. It took the lock clean out. A very professional job.' He led Dudka through the hallway and into the lounge.

'Who would have access to that, Vitaly?'

'Army, SOCOL snatch squad, Mafia…'

'And your guess is?'

He shrugged his shoulders. 'Discount the army; we are not at war. There were no SOCOL operations last night. My guess is a criminal gang of some sort. We're dusting for fingerprints

182

now but my bet is that we don't find any. We've got blood, though.'

Gennady Dudka rubbed his chin. 'Go on.'

Blazhevich pointed. 'Two types, here and here.'

'Neighbours?'

'Heard the gunfire, felt the explosion, saw… nothing.'

'Gunfire? Then you must have shells, Vitaly?' Dudka asked rhetorically.

'Of course.' Blazhevich bent down to retrieve an evidence bag from the coffee table and placed it in Dudka's outstretched hand. 'Standard 7.62. AK, Uzi, Heckler & Koch. Take your pick.'

'No witnesses at all?' The boss furrowed his brow.

'Two.' Blazhevich walked on to the balcony and pointed to the pavement below. 'The Berkut guards from the Uzbek Embassy next door. One of them was shot. He is in a critical condition. He's not talking but the other is. He's nursing a broken collarbone. He says, if you believe this, that they heard an explosion and shots, and had got to about there, just below the balcony, when this figure came flying out of the shadows, grabbed his gun, shot his colleague and ran off!'

Dudka leant against the railing and lit a cigarette. 'You mean to tell me he jumped out of the window, disabled two armed members of the Diplomatic Protection Squad… and just ran away?'

Blazhevich nodded and winced involuntarily. He knew it sounded too preposterous to be credible but it was all they had thus far. Dudka raised his eyebrows and flicked his ash on to the street two floors below. 'What do we know about our "flying" man?'

'The resident of this apartment is—' Blazhevich held up Snow's passport '—British, thirty-four…'

'Foreign national? *Blin!* That's all I need.' There would be repercussions.

'A teacher.'

Dudka almost choked on his Mayfair. 'What did he teach, for Christ's sake? Advanced terrorism?'

'No. Physical Education.' Blazhevich reddened as Dudka cast him a withering look.

Arnaud had a spring in his step despite his lack of sleep. Larissa had been insatiable and he had been the lucky man on the receiving end. Oh, why hadn't he come to Ukraine sooner? He took a sip from his can of Coke and almost walked into the militia officer on the corner of Pushkinskaya. Giving him a wide grin, he said good morning in Russian with his best English accent.

'*Dobroe Utro!*'

The police officer mumbled, frowned and let him pass. The street was unusually busy. Two more officers were standing on the street opposite at the café entrance, smoking and generally looking grumpy. A TV film crew were interviewing the owner of the café, and a small crowd had gathered while more militia officers kept an eye on them. Arnaud finished his Coke, crushed the can and put it in the bin. TV crews weren't an uncommon sight in the capital city now, more so with the new government's promise of more press freedom. Arnaud ignored them. He would get back to the flat, have a shower and go to bed. No doubt he, along with Snow and the others, would be on the sauce again by lunchtime. And then once he'd got his strength back…

He walked into the lobby, called the lift and rode to the third floor. What was this? The door to the flat was open and there were uniformed men inside. Arnaud took two steps forward and was met with a firm grip on both biceps. 'What the flying f—?'

'Bring him in,' Dudka ordered.

Arnaud, still bemused, felt himself being dragged into the flat. The front door had a large hole in it and was hanging off its hinges and there were what seemed to him to be about six militia men rooting through his stuff. The oldest, dressed in civvies, gave a quick command in Ukrainian.

'What the hell are you doing in my flat?' he blurted out before he realised what he'd said.

'Hell? You Englishman too?' No reply. Dudka nodded to the two restraining the new arrival. Their grip tightened. 'Who are you?'

Arnaud pulled his arms but it was no use; they weren't letting go. 'British Embassy.'

'You diplomat?' Dudka raised his eyebrow. That would make it tricky.

'British Embassy.'

'Passport, please.' Just his luck.

'Hands off, please!' Arnaud snapped back; they were beginning to annoy him. Again the man barked in Ukrainian and a third officer, also without a uniform, gingerly searched through his pockets. Retrieving the passport, Blazhevich gave it to Dudka and placed the rest of the contents of Arnaud's pockets on the coffee table. Dudka looked on. A comb, mini-toothbrush, an empty three-pack of condoms and some chewing gum. He read the passport.

'Arrnoode Hurrrssstt.' Was that really a British name? 'Where were you last night?'

No reply. He repeated the question as Blazhevich now scrutinised the passport of the man he had seen at the Hash.

The militiamen tightened their grip; unintentionally, Arnaud swore out loud in protest. 'Fucking…'

'I can well believe that, Mr Hurst.' Blazhevich impressed his boss again with his near-perfect English.

'What?' The man looked familiar. 'I… my girlfriend, she… I was with her in Obolon.'

There was a sudden call from the second room and another militia officer entered. He held a long rifle in his two outstretched gloved hands.

'You come with us now, Hurrrssstt,' Dudka barked.

Arnaud's nose twitched; the room was dirty and musty. He didn't know whether it was an interview room or an interrogation cell; after all, this had been the Ukrainian headquarters of the dreaded KGB. But what he *was* certain of was that it smelt like a toilet. If he hadn't been so scared, he'd have been quite excited. He sat at the table, his arms folded. Two militia officers in their blue-grey uniforms sat opposite him.

'*Imia.*'

'What? *Ya ne pon-iy-my-oo. Ya Englayski,*' Arnaud answered in his fledgling Russian. 'I don't understand. I'm English.'

The officer shook his head. '*Ya ne pon-iy-my-oo Englayski. Imia.*'

'*Imia*... Name. What your name?' the second added, helpfully.

'You know my name. You've got my passport.' Although worried, he was starting to get annoyed.

'You are British?' the officer said, looking at the travel document.

'Yes.' *Morons*, he almost said out loud.

The first officer read the charge sheet, pointed to it with his index finger, and spoke quickly in Ukrainian to the second.

'Ruslan, he no speak English, he want to know why then you have French passport in suitcase?'

'I have dual nationality.'

'This is not possible under Ukrainian law. Are you Englishman or are you Frenchman?'

'My mother is French and my father is English. I have dual nationality. Two nationalities. Two passports.'

'You entered Ukraine on British passport?'

'Yes. But I have dual nationality.'

'So, here you are Englishman.'

Arnaud put his head in his hands and breathed in deeply. Why was he sitting here with these two clowns? What about the English-speaking officer who'd been at his flat?

A figure paused momentarily and peered through the window in the door before continuing along the dimly lit corridor. Boris Budanov was annoyed; he had not been informed of any new arrests. 'Vitaly Romanovich,' he called out to Blazhevich, who was heading towards him. 'Who's the American?'

'Englishman, Boris Alexandrovich. He lives in the *Kvartira* where that trouble was last night.' As if it was any of his business.

'What trouble would that be then?'

Was he being serious, Vitaly wondered. The explosion and firefight were the talk of the entire bureau. 'Door blown off with a plastic charge, gunfight involving foreign nationals, officer down.'

'What?' This was outrageous. Inside, Budanov silently seethed.

'*Tak*. Regular Saturday night in the Wild East.'

'Shit. I was out of town,' exhaled Budanov. Why hadn't he known about this? They hadn't told him the attack on Snow would be so soon and so overt. He had missed the chance to run this part of the investigation. The ambitious officer cursed again.

'A couple of my best boys are working on him now. Playing the "I know nothing routine",' Blazhevich stated, matter-of-fact. The SBU used members of the militia on occasion for low-level interviews when they themselves wanted some distance. It was a ploy that worked well, an extension of the good cop, bad cop cliché that Blazhevich used to cringe at in American movies.

'Well? Was he involved? Does he know anything?' He had to get onboard this case before he lost his chance.

'Not easy to tell. He wants to speak to the embassy.' *Always questions, Boris Alexandrovich*, thought Blazhevich. *You writing a book or something?*

'And you've phoned them?' Budanov started to try to exert his authority, to take over from his slightly more junior colleague. He, after all, did have more experience.

'I spoke to their duty officer, told them it wasn't important. Let him sweat for a bit. Besides, he has a lot of explaining to do.'

A good move, thought Budanov; he would have done the same. 'That's against protocol but could be useful. Why?'

Blazhevich waited, gauging his colleague's interest. He was enjoying this. Anything to 'outdo' Budanov, the SBU's rising star, who always seemed to be in the right place at the right time. Not on this occasion, though. 'We found a rifle in his room. We think it's linked to the hit on that British investor in Odessa. That potentially leads us to the UK assassination also.'

Blazhevich noticed Budanov visibly change colour and his mouth twitch. 'You are a lucky man Vitaly. If you need me to assist your case I will offer my full support.'

'That's very kind of you, Boris, but Gennady Stepanovich wants me to handle this personally.' He let himself smile in what he pretended was a reassuring manner, but one both men knew was triumphant. Dudka had asked him, not Budanov, to investigate.

'The offer is there if you need it.' Budanov had been beaten and knew it. He patted Blazhevich on the back. As Blazhevich made for the interrogation room, Budanov hurried up the corridor, past the main desk and out into the courtyard at the back of the SBU building. He had to find out what was happening. Pulling out his keys he quickly unlocked his Passat and got inside. He looked around to make sure no one could overhear him, turned on the radio, then dialled a number on his mobile phone. At the other end a tall, thickset man in an Italian suit opened his tiny, shiny mobile telephone. '*Da?*'

'It's me. Listen. We have a problem. The Englishman is here. No, the other one. Yes, there are two. He is being questioned by Blazhevich's team as I speak. Why wasn't I informed that it was going ahead? This could have seriously jeopardised my position!'

Oleg ran his tongue along the outside of his top lip. As expected, their informer, the fat man, was fretting. They had been right not to tell him when the snatch was going ahead. A second Englishman? That was unexpected, but this could be very useful indeed; in fact, it could well be the key to getting hold of Snow. He listened as Budanov carried on complaining.

'I am no good to you if they find out!'

'They will not find out, Officer Budanov, unless you tell them, and if you do, you know what will happen.' Oleg would enjoy putting an end to this annoying one.

Budanov swallowed hard and wiped his forehead on the back of his hand. He could feel the car shrinking around him and the SBU building rising over him. He continued to listen to his new employer's instructions as the feeling of dread increased.

'I can't do that! It's impossible!' he blurted into the handset, but before he could protest any more the call ended. Budanov sat frozen for several seconds before shaking his head in an attempt to control his fear. He turned up the radio; some American rapper was proclaiming the enormity of his dick. *Shit, shit, shit*! Budanov pulled out of the car park, just missing a trolley bus. He couldn't do this anymore, could he?

'I am sorry I kept you waiting, Mr Hurst. I hope my two officers were polite?' The two militia men rose and left the room, closing the door behind them.

Arnaud looked at the plain-clothes officer and felt a wave of relief. He recognised him from the Hash. Blazhevich saw the recognition in his eyes; his cover, at least with the ex-pats, would now be no more. 'Hello, Arnaud. My name is Blazhevich, Vitaly Romanovich, and I work for the Ukrainian Intelligence Service, the SBU.'

'I've seen you at the Hash. Were you spying on me?' Arnaud became paranoid.

Blazhevich smirked. 'Should I have been?'

'No.'

Blazhevich walked towards the table and handed Arnaud an A4 manila envelope. Sitting, he indicated that Arnaud should remove the contents. 'Holiday "snaps" taken in Odessa. Not mine you understand.'

Arnaud took out the photographs and gasped. The body of a male lay on a tarmac road. The body, immaculately dressed in a dark-green suit, had no face. 'Why are you showing me these?'

Blazhevich held up his right index finger like a teacher correcting a slow pupil. 'We already know "the how" – the rifle in your apartment. We would like you to tell us "the why".'

Arnaud's head had begun to spin and his cheeks burn. He put the photograph face down on the table. 'You think I had something to do with this? You think I shot a man dead?'

Blazhevich held Arnaud's gaze for several seconds before shrugging his shoulders. 'Tell me about yourself. You have a French mother and an English father?'

'Yes.'

'What does your father do for a living?' Blazhevich removed his glasses, which were a prop, and took his time cleaning the lenses.

'He's a banker.'

'And your mother?' He folded the lens cloth.

'She arranges flowers.'

'Ah, how very interesting.' Blazhevich replaced his spectacles, then suddenly slammed his fist on the table. 'Tell me why their son became an assassin.'

Arnaud flinched. 'I'm not. I don't know what you're talking about. This happened a week after I came to Kyiv.'

'A train to Odessa takes twelve hours and a coach eight.' He looked him in the eye. Was he telling the truth?

There was a silence. Arnaud looked down. He could feel his heart pounding in his chest and his throat getting very dry. 'What happened to my flat?'

'You don't know? Very well, I shall tell you.' Blazhevich picked up the incident report. 'At approximately 4 a.m. there were several explosions and reports of gunfire emanating from Pushkinskaya 2/4–7, your flat. Two guards from the neighbouring Embassy of Uzbekistan, who came to investigate, were attacked. One had his collarbone broken and the other was shot. A man was seen running away from the scene carrying a weapon of some sort. Was it you?'

Arnaud tried to speak but only managed a raspy, 'What?'

Blazhevich smiled in what he hoped was a reassuring manner. 'Calm down, Mr Hurst… Arnaud. I do not think you were at home at the time, so if you give me the address of your lady friend we will ask her to confirm this. What does concern me, however, is the sniper's rifle found in your bedroom.' He retrieved the image. Blazhevich held up his hands. 'We will test for your fingerprints and then the ballistics will be checked against those we have for Mr Malik's murder. We will know the truth soon enough.'

The truth? What truth? Arnaud couldn't believe this was happening. His voice cracked as he tried to speak. 'It's not mine, I've never seen it before.' He started to shake. 'I'm… I'm… not the only person who lives there.' What had he done? He had given up Snow without even thinking.

The reassuring smile again. 'I know. Can you tell me more about your flatmate, Aidan Snow?' Inwardly Blazhevich became excited; his technique had been successful.

'He's also a teacher.' The words tumbled out of the Englishman's mouth.

'I see, and what else can you tell me about him?' He leaned forward and clasped his hands. He could see Arnaud fighting the temptation to speak. 'Arnaud, I am trying to help you. I know you didn't shoot anyone, but not everyone here shares my belief. If you can tell me as much as you know, I can help you and your friend.' There was something the English teacher knew; he could sense it.

Arnaud closed his eyes, as if to avoid seeing the moment he would betray his friend. 'He used to be in the army.'

'Army? British Army?' At last, a real suspect. Blazhevich's eyes widened behind his glasses.

Arnaud looked up. He'd gone this far, so he couldn't stop; they wouldn't let him. 'He used to be in the SAS.'

'The SAS?' Blazhevich's heart almost stopped; he wanted to be sure he understood.

'Special Forces, 22nd Special Air Service Regiment.'

'The British Spetsnaz?' It was now the interviewer's turn to feel the blood pumping to his cheeks. This was their man, had to be their man! He was trained in assassination techniques. 'I see.'

Arnaud crossed his arms. 'I want to talk to somebody from the British Embassy. I'm not going to answer any more questions until I speak to someone from the British Embassy.' Arnaud felt sick. Blazhevich would now grant the young teacher access to the embassy. In fact, he wanted to speak to them himself.

Petropavlivska Borschagivka, Kyiv Oblast

On the top floor, Snow lay on the mattress under the window. He was unarmed except for the Russian Army commando dagger he had liberated from Mitch's collection. The telescope Mitch used to 'perv' on his neighbours' women was fixed on a tripod just in front of his eye. All around, the house was still. He had come there straight after leaving Vickers at the stadium and laid up. Having returned from Belarus, Mitch was now back in the States for a week, seeing his kids, and the 'maid' wouldn't come to clean for another three days, so until then he would be undisturbed.

It was early afternoon and the sun cast sharp shadows across the garden and into the room. Snow had kept an eyeball on the house for the past five hours, fighting the cramp in his legs and having to piss into an empty Pepsi bottle; Mitch would have approved. He didn't have a plan as such and hoped that any information he was able to glean might suggest something.

There were two sentries on duty; neither had weapons on display but, judging by the bulges in their leather jackets, were clearly carrying. He could only see the back of the house and part of the left side, but decided the guards weren't overly concerned as they would routinely disappear for minutes at a time and cigarette trails could be seen wafting in the air. The house was an exact copy of Mitch's and Snow had sketched a plan, which was on the mattress next to him. Unless Pashinski had changed the internal layout, Snow had a good idea of who was where.

The veranda doors opened and two figures stepped out on to the terrace. The terrace had security railings running from floor to ceiling to deter any opportunist from attempting to break in; this, however, did nothing to prevent a sniper's bullet. Snow focused on the men. He didn't recognise either of them. One was tall, at least the same height as Snow, but barrel-chested, like a wrestler. His head displayed a thick grey mane. His maroon shirt was tight around the chest but loose at the waist where it met his trousers, a sign to Snow that he was in good physical shape. The second man was overweight, suited and much smaller. He was nervous-looking and used his arms for expression. The bear-like man pushed him in the chest to emphasise a point. The smaller man stumbled but nevertheless nodded. They both retreated inside. Moments later Snow observed a silver Volkswagen Passat on the road, moving away from the house.

Chapter 19

Arnaud opened his eyes and realised he was shivering. He had had the worst night's sleep of his life. No matter what he did with the blanket they had given him, he hadn't been able to get warm. He'd dozed, even falling into a shallow sleep at times, only to be woken by footsteps outside, the slamming of steel doors or shouts from other prisoners. He'd lost track of time but from the amount of traffic noise now outside he estimated it was rush hour. He stood and stamped his feet. Holding the blanket over his shoulders, he moved to the door and shouted:

'Hello! Helloo! Will someone let me out of here?' His night in the cell had empowered him somehow, not breaking his spirit but making his resolve stronger. He would be buggered if he was going to feel scared again. He felt a sense of shame for telling the SBU officer about Snow, but then he was sure his friend, flatmate and fellow teacher was innocent. He could hear a muffled conversation and feet approaching along the corridor. The observation slit opened and a pair of bloodshot eyes peered at him and bade him sit on the bed. Arnaud sat and the door opened. The militia officer stepped to one side to let a plain-clothes officer pass.

Budanov looked Arnaud up and down. 'Mr Hurst, you can go home now.' He paused to gauge the reaction on his prisoner's face. 'My colleagues and I believe what you say is true, that you are no killer.' He smiled at his use of words; he had been practising.

Arnaud shivered. 'About bloody time too.'

'I'm sorry?' Budanov did not speak English as well as his rival. 'Thank you.'

A second militia man entered the cell with a plastic tray, which he placed on the bed. Arnaud took the bootlaces and rethreaded them into his Gortex boots. The jailer handed him his jacket and took the blanket.

'We will keep your passports for the moment. We may want speak to you again.'

Arnaud looked up darkly as he struggled into his coat; he was way past the point of argument.

Arnaud stepped out of the SBU headquarters on Volodymyrska Street and turned right. He needed a drink, regardless of what time it was, and would take the next turning, cutting through the side streets to O'Brian's, and sit in the ex-pat joint. They did a proper breakfast. On impulse – he couldn't wait, he was starving – he stopped at the Mister Snak sandwich bar. Unseen from across the street, Oleg cursed and made his way through the traffic, leaving the others in the car. By the time he entered the bar, Arnaud had a toasted sandwich and a large plastic glass of Slavutech. Oleg sat in the corner and kept his eyes on Arnaud's back. Ten minutes later he was following him on the street doing the same.

Arnaud turned off Volodymyrska. He was sated but still livid; he had only just noticed they'd kept his mobile. Why? All his numbers were on there. Now he'd have to buy a phone card and chance his arm at a payphone. Bloody militia would probably sell it and split the cash.

There was a sudden jolt of pain as firm hands gripped his

right arm and shoulder. At the same moment a silver saloon swept around the corner in front of him, its back door opening. Before he could register what was happening he was pushed roughly into the car. The door slammed shut behind him and a cold piece of metal was pushed against his right temple. Arnaud almost lost his beer as his stomach heaved. He was hauled upright into a sitting position. In the driver's seat, Budanov pulled away nervously, looking in his mirrors, collar up, his face partly obscured by a baseball cap. He cursed Pashinski for making him do this so close to his own office. His hands were damp on the wheel and, beneath his jacket, his Egyptian cotton shirt was already wet on his back.

They headed for the river, running parallel before taking the bridge and the route towards Boryspil. No one spoke. Arnaud craned his neck as much as he dared to look at the gorillas sitting on either side of him. His anger of earlier had turned to dread on realising that these were not the same state-employed thugs who had already questioned him. His heart pounded and his temples throbbed. Every muscle in his body was tense for fear of moving and giving his abductors an excuse to use their guns, the nearest of which was now pressed firmly into his gut.

Boryspil-Kyiv Highway, Kyiv

Bull stood in the corner of the room, his arms crossed. The restaurant had been empty ever since the last owner had stopped paying his monthly 'insurance premiums'. To the outside world, however, the only change was a sign proclaiming a grand reopening in one month; until then, the deep-red velour curtains remained drawn. The restaurant occupied part of the ground floor of a four-storey building bordering the forests on the outskirts of Boryspil village. The rest of the building was empty with the exception of an office-supply company next door. Traffic

196

passed here but seldom stopped as it sped on across the round-about to the airport. Bull wondered how the place had actually made any 'real money'. He looked down at Larissa, who sat bound and gagged at the table in front of him. At the far end of the room the door opened. Bull remained where he was. Arnaud was first in, followed by Oleg.

'Larissa!' He tried to reach her but was pushed to the floor. He skidded on the thick plastic sheeting covering the new carpet.

Bull spoke slowly in accented English. 'This was a nice place before. Good food, heavy food.'

Arnaud rose to his knees. 'If you've done anything to her I'll kill you!'

Bull tutted and dismissed the threat with a wave of his hand.

'Who are you? What do you want?'

'The SAS man, Aidan Snow.'

Arnaud got to his feet. 'Why?'

'We are old friends. I want to say hello to him. You tell me where he is now?' He smiled and barked an order to Oleg in a language Arnaud didn't recognise. Oleg pushed Arnaud down again and walked towards Larissa. As Arnaud watched, he undid the top three buttons of her blouse and put his hand inside. Larissa's and Arnaud's eyes met, her eyes widened. Arnaud jumped to his feet, his anger uncontrollable.

'Stop that!' He ran at Oleg, who swiftly stopped him with a punch to the stomach. Arnaud dropped to the floor in pain and vomited over Oleg's shoes.

'You shit!' Oleg kicked him in the face. Arnaud felt his nose crack before everything went black.

'Enough!' Bull pulled Oleg away. 'If he cannot talk he cannot tell us where the English soldier is. Now clean him up.'

Oleg's eyes showed contempt for his victim but he followed Bull's orders and lifted Arnaud to his feet. Arnaud's arms fell limply at his side and his head lolled to the left. Panicking, Oleg quickly placed him on his side on the nearest clean bit of carpet, opened his mouth and pulled the tongue forward. He then arranged him in the recovery position. 'He is unconscious.'

'You are a fool.' Bull pushed him away. 'Water. Bring him some water.'

Oleg turned and headed for the kitchen. Bull returned to Larissa and noted the tears in her eyes. He buttoned up her blouse and delicately wiped the tears on the back of his finger.

'Sshh, my little rabbit. We will soon have both of you away from here. I am a soldier, not a killer, and you are a civilian.' He looked into her eyes and noticed through the redness and the tears a strength which he had rarely seen. Such a pity he had not met her somewhere else. There was a sudden electronic 'beep beep'. Budanov, who had been standing just outside the room watching the road, now entered.

'Here.' Budanov, hand shaking, held out the phone. 'I took it from evidence.'

Bull sat on the nearest chair. Sure enough, a message had arrived. He read it: *Snogging a fat bird*, and the sender it was assigned to, *Steve B*. He closed it and went on to the next. He smiled and banged his fist on the table. 'Here it is.' *Very Important. Arn do not go to flat. Dangerous. Will explain later. Contact Vickers@embassy. Trust me.* Sender: *Aidan S mob*. There was a time, date, and yes, the sender's number.

Zankovetskaya Street, Central Kyiv

'We have a suspect.' They sat at the kitchen table. Dudka blew his nose.

'Someone who works for Knysh?' Varchenko did not conceal his glee.

'That I do not know, Valeriy. The man is English, ex-Spetsnaz.'

'Hmm. This Knysh has a long reach but we have bigger hands.' He raised his glass and drank. Dudka did the same.

'A Dragunov sniper's rifle was found in his *Kvartira*. The ballistics are a match. The weapon fired the shot that killed your British partner.' Dudka handed Varchenko a copy of Snow's work-visa application form, the passport-sized photo enlarged. Varchenko held it at arm's length to focus, while he searched his pockets for reading glasses.

'Aidan Snow… teacher of Physical Education and English… Podilsky School International… And you really think that he is responsible?'

Dudka shrugged. 'Looks highly likely. Trained sniper, in Ukraine, may even have known Malik, teacher – perfect cover?'

Varchenko nodded and filled both shot glasses. 'Has he confessed? What has he said?'

'*Nichevo.*'

'Nothing?'

'We do not have him. He has disappeared.'

Varchenko narrowed his eyes in disappointment. 'Then he must be the man.'

'Something is not right, Valeriy. There was an attack on his *Kvartira*.'

Varchenko studied his friend. 'I am confused. Who attacked his apartment?'

'How do I know?' Dudka sipped. 'The door was "opened" with plastic explosive; we picked up the other resident – another British teacher – and found the rifle.'

Varchenko thought for a moment. 'Set-up or tidy up? Was he a loose end?'

Dudka lowered his glass. 'I am under immense pressure from those above and the British Embassy. The evidence might seem circumstantial but what could be better for us than to prove it was one of their own? Our reputation is restored and it is apologies all around. And of course the SBU looks effective. The new president will like that.'

'I am not concerned with catching the killer but stopping the paymaster, Knysh.' The man was a thorn in his side.

'He is elusive. The photo-fit you provided has provided no leads.'

'Do you have a copy of it here? Perhaps I can add more detail?'

'As you wish.' Dudka stood and shuffled out of the kitchen and into his study. He returned with his briefcase. Sitting, he sifted through the contents and removed a buff-coloured folder. 'Here. The report from Budanov.'

'Very bright boy.' Both men emptied their glasses again and Dudka duly raised the bottle to refill them. Varchenko focused. 'This is not Knysh.'

'What?' Dudka's hand shuddered and he poured onto the table.

'This is not the man who calls himself "Knysh". This is not the face I described to your Budanov.'

'*Blin.*' Dudka swore, sank the vodka and quickly poured himself another. 'But that is the image Budanov gave me.'

'Then he is either a fool or a felon. The eyes are the right shape but should be green, the face is too narrow – too weak, and the chin is bulbous and not square. I admit that there is a passing resemblance but this is not the image we created on his computer.'

Dudka starred forlornly at his ex-boss. 'He is my best man.' He paused, something falling into place. 'Which is why he was chosen by Knysh?' Varchenko nodded. Dudka suddenly remembered another image he had hurriedly popped in his case. 'Valeriy, I have another photograph.' He removed the file that Blazhevich had been eager to give him.

Varchenko snatched the image. 'This is him. This is Knysh.'

Snow was sore and extremely stiff. He had intended to stay awake, prone on the mattress all night, but fatigue had beaten him and he had ended up sleeping fitfully, waking with a start every few minutes. Cursing himself and slapping his face, he had eventually taken to pacing around the dark bedroom and doing press-ups to ward off sleep and muscle stiffness. It was awful operating procedure but this was his second night without sleep; his body was fighting his training and, for the first time, winning. All night, at least two lights had been on in the house opposite and there were constant shadows in both garden and interior.

Snow had left his OP briefly to grab a free tray of Perry & Roe's finest 'Energy Blast Cola' from Mitch's large stash and to piss. This time not into a bottle. Sitting upright against the back of an armchair, he'd manoeuvred to the head of the mattress, Snow was awake but jumpy, the taurine- and caffeine-filled cola had seen to that. His head still throbbed but now the hangover from the day before had been replaced by natural exhaustion. It was almost 8 a.m., night had long since vanished, and brilliant sunlight filled the room; he would have to keep still again now.

The Nokia suddenly vibrated on the wooden floor next to his hip. Snow carefully felt for it without taking an eye off the target house. He held it up to his face then almost dropped it in surprise. The display showed the stupid drunken snapshot of Arnaud and said he was calling. Snow held it to his ear. 'Arn? Are you OK?'

Snow could hear laboured breathing on the other end before finally a foreign voice spoke. 'Aidan Snow. We have your friend and his *deavooshka*. If you want them to live you must come to see us.'

Snow held the phone harder to his ear, as if not believing what he had heard. 'Who is this?' he asked, his head suddenly pounding.

Again a pause. 'An old friend. We met in Poland.' Snow felt

a chill run through his body and his stomach heave. The caller continued. 'You come alone. Tell no one or they die.'

The phone went dead. Snow took it away from his ear and stared at it as if it would provide him with more information. He fell back against the chair as the sudden enormity of the situation hit him. But he had no proof, no proof they had Arnaud or even that he was alive. Could it even be someone who had found his phone? Seconds later, as he was still running through options in his mind, a multimedia message arrived. It was from 'Arnaud'. It showed a picture of Arnaud and Larissa – both bound and gagged – and gave a time and an address. His stomach heaved.

He had a decision to make. Either way, someone would certainly die. The question was: would it be him or Arnaud? A voice inside, that of a coward, said *run, leave him, he's not family, save yourself, call their bluff*. He sat forward, put his head in his hands and rocked. Why was this happening? Why were they doing it to him!? Snow took a deep breath, a decision made. He stood quickly; he didn't have much time.

British Embassy, Kyiv

The phone barely had time to ring before Vickers answered it. 'Vickers.'

'It's Snow. Listen. They've kidnapped Arnaud.'

'What?' Vickers was stunned but stretched for his pen. 'Who has kidnapped Hurst?'

'Whoever attacked me – it has to be Pashinski. They also have his girlfriend.'

'Where are you now?' He needed an address.

'I'm on my way to the trade. It's me they want, not him.'

Vickers felt his pulse quicken. 'Don't be a fool, Aidan. They'll kill you. Give me the address – I'll tell the SBU.'

'No. That way everyone dies. I have to go alone but I'll need your help afterwards.'

'Aidan, listen to me. Give me the address... Aidan? Aidan!' Snow had ended the call. Vickers stood, kicking his chair in anger, then made a decision. He tapped in the memorised number on his desk phone. 'Vitaly. It's Vickers. Hurst has been kidnapped. They want to exchange him for Snow.'

Blazhevich stepped outside the Gastronom and on to the pavement. He had his usual morning cup of café coffee in one hand and his phone in the other. 'Hurst has been released?' The surprise was evident in his voice.

'You didn't know?' Vickers's mind whirred.

'No.' Blazhevich leant against the railings. 'OK, do you have the address?'

'No. Snow is on his way to the trade.'

'Snow contacted you?' Blazhevich was trying to understand what had happened.

'Yes.'

Both men were thinking as fast as they could. 'How long ago?'

'Two minutes.' Vickers hadn't wasted any time.

Blazhevich had had suspicions and now was the time to confirm them. He would confront the man he believed was responsible for Hurst's release.

Boryspil-Kyiv Highway, Kyiv

Budanov answered the call via his Bluetooth headset. '*Da.*'

'It's Vitaly. You released Hurst. Why?'

Budanov swerved slightly in his lane. He had known the call would come; but not so fast. 'We had no evidence; he is just a kid.'

'It is my case!' For the first time he shouted at the older officer.

Budanov tried to placate him, 'He told us all he knew, Vitaly.

We can always question him again if you wish.' Budanov slowed and pulled the Passat to a halt. He had begun to sweat again.

'He has been kidnapped. I have information that he has been taken by the same people who attacked Snow.' Blazhevich was angry but now managed to keep his voice controlled. Emotion wouldn't help the young Briton. 'Where are you? Gennady Stepanovich wants to see you.' He had taken a chance and relayed his suspicions to Dudka, who, he was surprised to find, accepted them without question.

There was a pause as Budanov stepped out of the car. He was suddenly queasy. 'I'm near Boryspil. I'm on my way.' Budanov leant against the car and was sick in the gutter. He wiped his mouth with the back of his hand and straightened up. He looked along the Boryspil highway. One way led back to the restaurant and on to the airport. The other led into the city. One way leading to Knysh and damnation by the SBU, the other possible death for him and his family if Knysh was not stopped. Budanov opened his wallet and looked at the picture of his wife and son, now a toddler who had just learnt to say *tatus* – 'daddy'. All he'd ever wanted was the best for both of them: the clothes, foreign bank account, holidays in Dubai, Egypt, and the house in Cyprus. The man he used to call 'Knysh' had paid for this and more, in exchange for an insider in the SBU. Now, caught between two worlds, he knew who Knysh was and what he had to do. The traitor Budanov got back into the car and accelerated towards Kyiv.

Chapter 20

Kyiv-Boryspil Highway, Kyiv

Bull looked at his watch. 9.40 a.m. The SAS man would be here in twenty minutes. Inside, a voice said he already was. Why? Because Bull knew he would do the same himself. During his full service career in the Soviet Union's Red Army Spetsnaz he had never directly faced them, the British Spetsnaz, the 22nd Regiment Special Air Service. There had been rumours of them training the Afghans with weapons donated by America's CIA and carrying out covert operations in and around Kabul, but he had never seen them. For this he was deeply disappointed. It would have been a fine thing, he mused, to have the world's two best Special Forces units collide in real combat. The Americans were too soft, too sensitive; even their Delta and SEAL commandos relied heavily on electronics and equipment. No. In his mind the British were the best and, much like the Soviet Spetsnaz, relied upon training, human intelligence and physical strength. They were not that different, he told himself, he and Aidan Snow. But unlike Snow, who seemed happy to forget his skills and squander his training, Pashinski had utilised them for maximum profit. He hadn't just bitten the hand that fed him but eaten the master too. Now he was to take over the running of his house. He allowed himself a smile. Business. The boardroom wasn't all that different from the battlefield.

Opening his eyes, Arnaud could see Larissa's face. For a glorious moment he thought it had all been a nightmare and that he was still in bed, safe with her in Obolon; but then he realised they were on a concrete floor and that Larissa had tape across her mouth. Her eyes widened as she met his gaze. They were both gagged and unable to speak but she nodded in reply to his unspoken question: *Yes, I am OK.*

Arnaud tried to move and found he was 'hobbled' at the ankles with his hands fastened behind his back. A table leg was passed through the gap at both hands and feet. He pulled and the table moved ever so slightly. They were in a storeroom packed with unused restaurant furniture. Larissa seemed to be tethered to the same chair as before, like a 1930s damsel in distress. It would have been comical if he wasn't so scared. Arnaud looked up. The table was piled with wooden restaurant chairs haphazardly stacked one on top of another. It wouldn't be that heavy to move but would cause one hell of a noise if the chairs came toppling down on to him and the concrete floor. He tried to pull his hands and feet apart but the rough rope dug into his skin. Next he tried his tongue, pushing it through his lips at the tape. Whoever had gagged him had been concerned he might not be able to breathe through his broken nose, so had cut a small airhole in the middle. The tape cut his tongue but he didn't give up and pushed harder. There was pain, as he tasted his own blood for the second time that day, but the hole increased. He then tried to open and close his mouth and eventually the tape gave way.

'Are you hurt? Did they do anything?'

Larissa shook her head as tears started to swell in her eyes. He ignored the pain which seemed to come from all over his body, but especially his face and ribs. 'Aidan will come to get us. He must know we're here.'

Bending his hands, he grasped at the table leg with his fingers.

He tried to push it up and away. He felt the leg rise ever so slightly but the pressure on his wrists was too much and it slipped away, jarring his arms. 'Shit. I can't get enough of a lever.'

Pushing against the floor with all her might, Larissa rocked her chair. It tottered on its legs but did not fall. She tried again, this time leaning forward as much as she could, then pushing her spine against the backrest. The chair tottered some more. She then pushed and rocked again and again as hard as she could. They was a cracking sound as a leg started to give way, then a sudden crash as she fell backwards to the floor. The rear leg had splintered along the join with the seat base. Larissa let out a muffled whimper, the gag stopping her cry of pain. Her left forearm had taken the brunt of the impact, her arms tied as they were around the seat and back of the chair.

Both lay still, waiting for their abductor to open the door and investigate. A minute passed but nothing happened. Arnaud beckoned her and she shuffled towards him on her side before pushing herself up against the table until, using her back, she pushed, as did Arnaud. Between them they managed to raise the table legs by two inches. Arnaud tugged, wriggled, and was free. He tried to sit upright. A stabbing pain hit him in his chest. He winced and tried again. 'Turn around and I'll untie your hands.'

Larissa shuffled around until her back was against his. Arnaud felt for the rope and tugged at the knot with his fingers. Patience had never been one of his virtues and he swore under his breath, ever mindful of the fact that their cell door could be flung open at any moment. Larissa kept her eyes glued to the door, still mute. 'Try now, pull your hands apart.'

With a grunt her hands became free. She tensed her lips and ripped at the tape on her mouth. Gasping as it came off, she looked at the man she now realised she loved. She reached forward and carefully peeled the tape from his mouth. His nose was misshapen and covered in blood, his eyes were bloodshot, but he still had his silly French smile. She kissed him gently.

The Volga pulled up a hundred yards short of the address. Snow thanked the driver and gave him a twenty-hryvnia note. The driver shut the door and, with a happy wave, headed towards the roundabout. Snow crossed the road and took advantage of what little cover there was. He wanted to get a visual of the address before entering. He stopped almost opposite and stood just behind the bus shelter as if casually awaiting a bus. The building was four storeys high. The ground floor looked to be some sort of restaurant, probably Georgian. The far end of the building faced the large roundabout and the main highway towards Boryspil. The woods started within feet of the roundabout and continued at the back of the building. It was this exposed corner facing the roundabout that the restaurant occupied.

Snow squinted to read the number on the building. The restaurant was indeed the target address. There was a main double-door entrance, the heavy looking red doors in a slight shadow cast by a porch. The windows either side were shuttered. Snow waited for several minutes to determine any sign of movement, or anything at all that could help him in his rescue attempt. He couldn't see any other visible entrance or exit to the restaurant but had to figure there would be at least one at the back as a fire escape. He needed to do a complete close-target recce but was thwarted both by lack of cover – he couldn't move forward without being seen – and lack of time.

Snow was just about to retrace his steps and cross the road in the dead-ground further back down the street when his eyes caught movement. A shape momentarily rose above the parapet. Back across the road now, Snow made his way to the other end of the building. This end was occupied by an office-supplies showroom. Snow slowly rounded the back of the block. The fire exit was just around the corner. He flattened himself against the wall by the side of it. At the far corner there was a second exit with steps and railings leading down. He counted at least four ground-floor windows. There was no visible hostile presence. He had to think fast. His options were limited. He was unarmed, with the exception of Mitch's commando knife, and without backup, facing an opponent of unknown size, commitment and alertness. He could enter the forest and covertly work his way along the perimeter so that he faced the back of the building; but how to gain entry? No. He would follow the line of the wall and keep flat against it, making it impossible for anyone on the roof to see him, and then try the door. He checked his watch. Shit. He had ten minutes. Get to the RV by 10 o'clock or both Arnaud and Larissa would die. Of that he had no doubt. He moved as fast as he could without making a noise, along the wall. Through the open windows of the supply company he could hear the radio and the catty chat of at least three women.

Arnaud and Larissa heard footsteps approaching and quickly moved back into their original positions as best they could. Larissa sat on another chair and Arnaud leant against the table legs.

Oleg opened the door. 'Your friend is coming for you now.' He leered at Larissa and then grunted at Arnaud on the floor. 'Maybe you see him before he die, maybe I let you say goodbye.' A wide smile creased his piggy face as he shut the door. Oleg walked towards the back of the building and nodded at the man on sentry duty – one of the better men they had recruited. 'See anything, Dmitro?'

'No, he can't get past me.'

Oleg nodded and slapped him on the back. 'I'm happy to see standards in the Ukrainian Army have not dropped.'

Oleg walked past him and turned the corner to start his check of the perimeter. The sentry's smile beneath his baseball cap froze as his head snapped to react to a movement in his peripheral vision.

'You're expecting me.' Snow's arms were quickly around the sentry's neck, applying pressure into the nerve inviting unconsciousness. Dmitro's hands flailed and a suppressed semi-automatic burst of 7.62mm lead impacted the trees. Snow sprang forward,

209

throwing himself and the guard through the doorway and into the wall. The Kalashnikov dropped. Snow increased the pressure on the guard's neck before his body became limp. Snow let go and the Ukrainian fell to the floor, banging his head. Snow grabbed the suppressed short stock of the Kalashnikov and pointed it first down the corridor, then back through the door. Nothing, no shouts or footsteps. Moving slowly but tactically forward, Snow edged further into the building. There were two doors on the left, one with a window, one without. Snow peered through it. A small toilet, empty. He got to the next door and noted the heavy padlock on the outside. That was where they would be holding them, he reasoned. There was a faint noise, from where he couldn't tell, but there were shadows ahead. Without thinking, Snow moved towards them.

Outside, Oleg noted that Dmitro had gone. The giant Lithuanian advanced inside and saw the guard's unconscious form on the ground. He bent down to search him for weapons. None. A huge smile on his face, Oleg moved forward, his sidearm drawn.

A heavy curtain let only a chink of light spill through. Snow cautiously placed his eye to the gap. The dining hall was directly in front of him and so, too, was a figure he recognised.

A scrape from behind. Snow span round to be met by a fist. His head snapped back and before he had time to react a second blow hit him in the stomach. Snow doubled up, winded, his head suddenly dizzy. The AK fell away. He had a split second to act while his attacker thought they had the initiative. The Lithuanian's left hand extended to balance him as the right moved to perform an uppercut. Too slow, thought Snow. He twisted and grabbed the right fist with his left, making Oleg pivot, and then pushed him against the wall and through the curtain. Oleg held on and threw Snow to the floor. They skidded on the plastic sheeting. Oleg scrabbled up to his knees and pushed his pistol hard into the Englishman's neck, breaking the skin. 'Stop. Up now. Get up.'

Snow released his grip and held his arms up. Oleg, now regaining his composure, stood and swung his boot into Snow's groin. Stars erupted in Snow's head and he desperately tried not to pass out.

'You are lucky that I do not shoot you now, but that honour belongs to another.' Oleg pushed him further into the room.

Snow stayed stooped in an attempt to soak up the pain.

'Hello, Snow.' It was Pashinski. 'Please take a seat.'

Still winded, Snow fought for breath, and was manhandled into the opposite chair. 'Where are my friends?' he demanded. Pashinski spoke in Lithuanian, and Oleg left the room. Snow locked eyes with his would-be murderer. 'I'm here, so now what?'

'Now we can talk.' Pashinski smiled. 'I have never met an SAS man, not at a time when I could have a conversation with him.'

Snow continued to stare at the eyes, the same eyes that had haunted him in his sleep, the eyes he could never forget. He noticed the powerful but wiry physique under the suit jacket and the pancake holster holding a Glock 9mm. He was determined not to let his fear of this man show.

'You look well for a dead man, Pashinski.'

'Pashinski died in Vilnius. My name is Knysh.'

'Your name is Tauras "The Bull" Pashinski. Former captain in the Red Army Spetsnaz.'

'And you are Aidan Snow, former SAS trooper.' The mouth smiled but the eyes remained cold. 'Are we now formally introduced or should I show you a picture of my mother?'

'What are you doing in Ukraine? Planning to rob banks?'

'You joke? Knysh is establishing himself as a valuable business leader. As I am sure you are aware, there is much opportunity for men such as us.'

'Such as us?' Snow felt like spitting. 'I'm not the same as you. I'm no murderer.'

'You have killed for your Queen and I for the Politburo. We are not that different.'

'Killing Jas Malik, who was that for?'

'I did not pull the trigger but I have killed for business purposes. I accept that. It has not been personal. As for Malik, I had nothing against the man but it is better for business that he is dead.'

Snow felt a chill run through him. He had never been in the presence of one so ruthless, a man so soulless that murder was just a business strategy. 'So, you are in business – and then what?'

'Politics. Our governments do not care for men like you and me. They discard us when we become too expensive, too old, or know too much. We are left to work in degrading positions for a salary that would not feed a wife and child. We are heroes, we are men who have given everything for our motherland, but we are not respected. For men of honour that is an insult worse than death. I see the value in our kind, and what we can do. I have a vision to unite these men of honour. The Orange Revolution is over, dead. Who will lead the next? It is time for Ukraine to have a new Hetman.'

Snow looked at his tormentor; the eyes remained cold even when he spoke with passion about his megalomaniacal vision. 'That's not going to happen.'

Bull looked intrigued. 'Why? Because a former British soldier thinks that I am someone he has met before?'

'There are others who know who you are.'

'True, the mighty KGB – sorry, SBU – have a picture, my picture; but they need you to identify me. Now I have you. You are a hard man to catch, Snow.' His insincere smile widened. 'Like your name, you melt away in the hand.' Bull paused. 'So now we talk. We talk about the Spetsnaz, yours and mine, yes?' The mouth smiled but the eyes did not.

'You are one sad Russian.' Snow spat the words at Bull.

Bull stood and slammed both fists on the table.

'I am Lithuanian!' His eyes flickered momentarily before he regained his composure. 'I hate Russians. For three generations my countrymen, like those of Ukraine, were subjugated by Mother Russia. We were worked the hardest in the fields, were assigned the most dangerous tasks, and used as human shields on the battlefield. We did what it was beneath a Russian to do. My own family starved because Russians took their harvest.' His eyes had now grown wide with an uncontrollable anger and a vein on his temple throbbed. 'Never call me Russian.'

There were steps from behind; Arnaud was pushed into the room. Snow looked at Arnaud and saw the belief in his face, the belief that he would save him. Bull removed his Glock from his shoulder holster and waved it in Arnaud's direction. 'Now I have no use for him.'

'Wait! Let them go.' The words came out of Snow's mouth but they were meaningless, he realised.

'*Niet.*' The arm straightened and he took aim.

'No!' Snow tried to move; unseen, the butt of a Kalashnikov impacted with his neck. A shooting pain raced down his spine.

'Not yet.' The arm relaxed. 'You can say goodbye first.'

Oleg's radio cracked and he raised his left hand. 'You are certain? OK, ready positions.' He looked at Bull. 'ALPHA units have arrived.'

Bull aimed the gun at Snow. 'You told them you were coming here. That was very foolish, SAS man.'

'I told no one.' How had they found them? Snow's heart raced in his chest.

There was a burst of gunfire from outside as two men on the roof laid down suppressing rounds at the arriving Ministry of Internal Affairs anti-terrorist troops. One of Bull's Brigada ran across the room to the window, positioning his rifle just below the shutter as he readied to repel the assault. Dmitro, now conscious, joined him at the second window. They both fired. Arnaud saw his chance; this was it. As fast as he could he sprang at Oleg, his loosened ropes dropping. Oleg batted him away with his Makarov pistol but Arnaud held on to the arm. A shot rang out and the bullet zipped across the room. Bull ducked and Snow threw himself sideways, using the table for cover. Bull fired and the chair back shattered. Snow reached up into the small of his back for Mitch's Soviet commando knife, swung his right arm wildly, and plunged the blade into Pashinski's thigh. Pashinski staggered and moved away, the knife grating against bone. He shot again, this time hitting the table. There were shouts at the windows and an explosion outside.

'Exfiltrate,' Bull shouted above the gunfire. He staggered towards the corridor and the fire exit, sending another round towards Snow. Dmitro left his position and grabbed his commander under the arms, hustling him away. Smoke grenades flew in through the shattered windows, the last soldier manning them cut down by an ALPHA bullet.

Snow turned and moved towards Arnaud. He was hanging onto the huge soldier's arm and kicking him with his right foot, Oleg's left hand pounding against Arnaud's face. The gun went off and Arnaud dropped. Snow's fist hit Oleg in the throat and he fell, the gun spilling from his hand. Snow grabbed the Makarov and fired, Oleg squirmed, and the round entered his stomach. Automatic gunfire ripped into the carpet around him and Snow rolled into cover behind another table. Oleg scuttled away, helped by two pairs of hands. The firing ceased. Snow grabbed at Arnaud. His chest was covered in blood, his eyes suddenly wide. 'I knew you'd come Aid… knew…'

No time for sentiment, no time to grieve; Snow could see his friend was dying. 'Where is Larissa? Where is she?'

'Storeroom… down the corrid…' Arnaud tried to sit up as blood seeped from his mouth. 'Sorry… I fucked it all…'

'No, mate, it was me. You were superb.'

The eyes had glazed over. There was an explosion at the door. Move it. Snow dropped the teacher and ran for the back door. He frantically tried the storeroom door; Larissa cowered in the corner. 'We've got to go!' He grabbed her hand and dragged her towards the back door.

'No,' she yelled above the gunshots as the ALPHA troops entered the restaurant from the main street. 'Where is Arnaud? Where is Arnaud?'

'Outside. He's outside.' No time to waste; have to get out.

There were shots ahead now but the exit was clear. No time to wait. '*Davai Davai* – go, go, quick, this way.'

Holding Larissa's hand, Snow ran down the steps. In his peripheral vision he saw assault troops exchanging fire with Pashinski's men. Rogue rounds zipped over his head and now from behind. They crashed into the tree line, breaking branches and ripping their skin. Larissa screamed as a limb sprang against her forearm but did not slow. The ground dropped away below them and they hurtled down a slope; losing their footing, they started to tumble and slip through the undergrowth. They landed at the bottom in a heap, bruised, battered, but alive.

The acrid smell of smoke and cordite from spent shells hung in the air as Blazhevich stepped into the restaurant. Around him the ALPHA troops had secured the building and were now trying to ID the dead kidnappers. In the dining hall he met the gaze of the assault leader, who was crouching over a body; he shook his head. *Blat!* They were too late. Blazhevich moved nearer and nodded. He recognised the body of his fellow hasher, the young British teacher who had run and drunk with him on several Sundays. 'We are too late.'

SBU Headquarters, Volodymyrska Street, Kyiv

Budanov looked up as Dudka entered the cell. 'You are now responsible for the death of a young British citizen. I hope you can forgive yourself, because I, for one, cannot.'

Budanov suddenly felt dizzy. 'W… what? But… but I gave you the address.'

'We were too late. He was shot.' Dudka looked down at the pathetic man who sat on the metal cot bed. The man who had betrayed both him personally, and the SBU.

'We have Pashinski?' Budanov was anxious.

Dudka sat heavily at the opposite end of the bed. 'We? For you, Budanov, there is no "we".' His nostrils flared as he tried to regain his composure. 'No, "we" do not have him. They were well prepared. They opened fire on the ALPHA team and many escaped – including Pashinski.'

Budanov felt himself suddenly age at the realisation of what he had done and what would now happen to him and his family. Tears began to roll down his face and in shame he hung his head.

Dudka looked on, nonplussed. 'Where are your wife and child?'

'Cyprus.'

'How convenient.' Dudka grunted.

Budanov desperately raised his head, tears falling from his face. 'You must send someone to protect them, Gennady Stepanovich.'

'And why is that?' Dudka could guess.

'Pashinski said that he would kill them if I told you anything.'

'Pray.' Dudka rose and banged on the door. It was opened, and then shut behind him. As he walked away he heard a mixture of sobbing and desperate screams from his former protégé. The fact that Dudka had already sent word to the consulate in Cyprus was something Budanov need not know about. Not yet.

Boryspil Village, Kyiv Oblast

The gunfire was loud behind them as they picked themselves up from the muddy ground.

'Where is he? Where is Arnaud?' Larissa had become frantic

and suddenly realised she couldn't see her boyfriend. Snow held her arms firmly and looked her in the eye. This would be the worst moment of her life so far.

'He's dead. I'm sorry. I was too late.'

Her mouth started quiver. 'No… he can't be…' Her face froze as the words registered in her brain. She let out a moan and started to thrash her arms in an attempt to break free from her rescuer.

'We have to move.' Snow pulled her forward but she dug her heels into the ground. This was not the place to grieve; that would get them both killed.

'No. I want to see him.' Her words were almost unintelligible through the anguish.

'We have no time.' Snow tugged harder and she toppled over. In among the trees they moved forward. Tears fell from Larissa's eyes. There was shouting behind them, rounds zipped past. Larissa screamed and Snow threw her to the ground at the foot of a tree. He landed on top of her and pushed her into cover. Snow hurriedly removed the Lithuanian's Makarov from his jacket pocket and took aim. On the crest above, figures followed their path into the woods. They were Bull's men attempting a retreat, firing controlled bursts back towards the street. The ALPHA assault group, however, hadn't given up and a lot of fire was rained down on them. Rounds flew into the woods, pinging from branches and falling wildly.

Below him Larissa was shaking. Snow held the pistol steadily; if they got too close he would have to use it. A black-clad figure ran towards him holding a short AK74. More rounds flew past and one hit the figure. He fell forward no more than six feet from Snow's face. His eyes crazed with pain, he saw Snow and scrambled to bring the automatic weapon to bear. Kill or be killed. Snow fired a double tap into his face. The bullets flew into his brain with deadly speed. Snow stayed still and again felt the pressure on his pistol grip. Above, the movement had stopped, but the gunfight had not. Snow rolled and dragged Larissa to her feet. This time she made no attempt to resist and they ran forward. The trees gave way to grassy fields peppered with newly built *dachas*. The first of these was at least four hundred yards away, on the edge of a village.

'We have to get to that house.' Snow's voice was raspy as he fought for air. Larissa did not reply but quickened her pace in line with his. There was no cover and he felt extremely exposed as they took the only escape route possible and dashed towards the end of the field.

Oleg scuffled into the back of the Volga. Dmitro had the wheel and a second man was returning fire at the ALPHA in an attempt to keep their heads down.

'GO! GO!' Oleg screamed at the wheel man.

Door still open, they pulled into the street as bullets impacted the bodywork of the Soviet car. Oleg held his stomach and lay down. Blood seeped from beneath his right hand; his left hung on to the back of the front seat as the Volga bucked over potholes. Oleg heard sirens but could do nothing about them. The inside of the car went dark around him as he lost consciousness.

The first *dacha* was unfinished. Snow pushed past this building and made for a tumbledown house that made up part of the village. He gingerly opened the gate and was greeted by a squawking goose. Concealing his pistol he knocked on the green wooden front door. There was no reply; he knocked again, this time with more force. Larissa pushed back her hair and wiped her makeup from under her eyes. A curtain twitched and an elderly face looked at them. Snow smiled. The face disappeared and there was the sound of a bolt being removed from the door. A two-inch gap appeared. Snow spoke in his Moscow Russian. 'Can you help us, please? We need to use your telephone.'

The old lady looked at the face of the smiling young man and the very pretty girl by his side. She opened the door further and put her hand by her ear. Snow repeated his request and they were beckoned inside. The house was dark and smelt of stale cabbage. Larissa had stopped crying and gone into shock.

'We had an accident on the highway.' Snow pointed in the direction of the road and smiled. 'Our car was hit by one of those *Jigeets.*'

The old lady looked concerned and beckoned them along the hallway. She took Larissa's hand. 'Are you all right, my dear?'

Larissa nodded and wiped her eyes. Snow replied on her behalf. 'It was her first car. She's a bit shaken.'

'I'll make some tea. The telephone is just there.' She disappeared into the kitchen, leaving Snow and Larissa by the hall phone.

'Can you call your cousin to pick us up? We have to get away from here.'

Larissa nodded and dialled the number. She started to talk in grief-stricken Ukrainian; Snow could only make out one word in ten. The tears fell again as she described where they were. The kettle started to boil on the gas ring and the old lady bade them sit at the kitchen table.

'Her cousin will be here in about forty minutes. Is it OK for us to wait?'

The old lady smiled. She had bright eyes and an oval face; even now, Snow could see that she had once been beautiful. 'Of course you can.'

Larissa had started to shake and tears once again welled in her eyes. The old lady took her hand and clasped it between both of hers. 'Have you lost someone, dear?'

Larissa looked up with reddened eyes and nodded. The old lady held her hand tighter. 'It will heal, it always does.'

Chapter 21

Petropavlivska Borschagivka, Kyiv Oblast

He had taken a taxi to the city centre where he had got on the metro, twice changing direction before being satisfied he wasn't being followed, then caught a passing car to Petropavlivska Borschagivka and walked the final half-kilometre to Pashinski's house via the woods. The gates were not opened immediately and the voice on the intercom sounded drowsy. Gorodetski noticed that the door was ajar. He paused, sensing things were not right, before cautiously entering the house. Then he saw the blood-soaked towel lying on the table.

'Over here, boy…' It was Oleg, lolling on the expensive cream leather settee.

Gorodetski drew nearer and could now see the skin was pale and the eyes bloodshot. An empty vodka bottle stood on the table in front of him. 'Get me another,' the former Spetsnaz sergeant ordered the Spetsnaz sniper.

'Where is Captain Pashinski?' Gorodetski was confused.

'Vodka… vodka now…' Oleg coughed and blood sprayed from his mouth.

Gorodetski took a bottle from the cabinet, opened it, and

handed it to him. Gorodetski noticed the large dark wet stain on the sergeant's shirt. Oleg took a swig and poured a third on to his stomach. He screwed his face up in pain.

'What happened?'

'Shot in the belly. The bullet is still in…' Oleg winced and pushed his hand over the wound. 'Should be removed…'

'I'll get a doctor.'

'*No*…! No use. Too late…' Oleg coughed again and drank more vodka. 'We have to celebrate… you killed the Paki. Bull very happy.'

Gorodetski sat in the armchair and surveyed the dying soldier. 'There's nothing to celebrate. I did it for my brother. Now he can rest in peace.'

Oleg started to laugh but it turned into a bloody coughing fit. 'He can rest in pieces.'

Gorodetski didn't understand what he had heard. 'What?'

'Your brother can rest in pieces!' He spat between coughs.

Gorodetski flashed with rage. '*What!?*'

Oleg's eyes started to roll but then he regained his composure. 'After we kill him we cut him up.'

Blood rushed in his ears. '*What* did you say?'

The eyes rolled again and then the gaze held firm. Even on the brink of death the soldier's eyes were piercing. 'You are a fool, boy… Your brother… Lieutenant Gorodetski was a traitor…'

Gorodetski lunged at the older man, grabbing his neck. 'WHAT?'

Oleg's lips curled in a swine-like smile and he made no attempt to break free. 'Do it… *Do it*…' Gorodetski released his grip and sat, ignoring the warm blood that had sprayed over his face. 'We were doing business… the Afghans have the poppy… but need the gun… we have gun… we have the gun…' The coughing returned.

'*And?*' His whole body was tense.

'And… we have brave men who need the poppy… your brother asked us to stop.'

Gorodetski's head started to spin and his vision narrowed. The rushing sound in his ears increased.

'…It was just business… but Lieutenant Gorodetski, he said it was immoral… against our honour code… he betrayed us…'

'*Who killed my brother?*' It was a demand, not a question.

'Bull shoots him… he falls, gets up… will not die… Bull stabs him… still he will not die… we both stab him… then we get Afghan sword…' Oleg raised the bottle to his lips. 'For fallen comrades.'

Suddenly everything went white and his ears rushed like never before. Gorodetski sprang forward and shot his right palm up into the bottom of the bottle. It shattered into Oleg's palate. The arms flailed as the Afghanistan veteran fought back but all strength was gone. Gorodetski delivered a punch to the wounded stomach. Oleg doubled up, blood pumping from face and abdomen. Immobile. Moving to the kitchen, the young veteran of Chechnya picked up a meat cleaver. Returning, he pulled Oleg up by the hair into a sitting position.

The eyes focused on him one last time. 'Traitor. Tra—'

Gorodetski swung the heavy blade through flesh, artery and vocal cords. The body jerked slightly then became limp. He let go and the lifeless corpse slumped on the settee. One of his brother's killers was now dead. In a trance he walked to the bathroom. He didn't recognise the image in the mirror; veins throbbed at the temple and blood striped the face. His eyes stung as it dripped into them. He ran the tap, filling the basin with icy cold water before submerging his head. Removing it, he again recognised his face and the resolve it now displayed. He dried his hair. He knew what he had to do. Captain Pashinski must die.

The Dnipro Hotel bar had recently been refurbished in the hope it would become the next trendy ex-pat hangout. This hadn't yet happened, so it remained the reserve of new Ukrainians and visiting foreign businessmen too lazy to venture further afield. Larissa walked to the ground floor bar and ordered a Desna, not her usual Rémy Martin; a shot of the strong local stuff was what she needed. She downed it in one, involuntarily shuddered, and ordered another. The barman raised his eyebrow but passed no comment as he completed her order. Holding on to the bar for support she caught a glimpse of her image in the mirror and reminded herself that she did indeed look better than she felt.

Yulia, Larissa's cousin, had collected her and Snow from the village and taken them back to her flat in the left bank region of Troieschyna. They were lucky their route missed the police cordon around the restaurant. The car journey had been silent but on arrival at the small flat there had been much sobbing and screaming. Larissa had at first been angry, then numb, and finally had physically attacked Snow, blaming him for Arnaud's death. Snow hadn't defended himself, absorbing the blows she landed on him. Larissa was right and he knew it. If it weren't for him and who he was, their friend would still be alive. Arnaud had been the bait and was expendable. Eventually, on seeing her draw blood, Yulia pulled her cousin off, holding her while both women cried.

At that moment Snow experienced self-loathing as never before, a hatred of himself for who and what he was. He sat on the dining-room chair and held his head in his hands. He couldn't let it finish like this; he couldn't let Arnaud's death be meaningless. He raised his head. The longer he stayed in Kyiv, the slimmer his chances of escaping from the SBU. If caught, he would lose any hope of finding the killer. Shutting his own emotion out, Snow decided on a course of action, a plan. He took a deep breath and, through the tears and accusations, persuaded both women to go along with it. Larissa had eventually agreed, as had Yulia, who awaited them in the flat.

Snow kept his eyes on the foyer and flexed his hands on the steering wheel of Yulia's Polo. His neck and back hurt like hell, as did his side and left leg. He popped two more painkillers. He'd parked thirty feet behind the taxi rank facing the main entrance to the Dnipro. From here he could see both up and down the main road and across to the spur that led around the park. Two taxi drivers leant against the lead taxi, putting the world to rights. A third sat in the last car, attempting to read his paper in the fading afternoon sun. Snow would wait twenty minutes, as planned, before entering the hotel and sitting in the foyer. He would keep an eye on Larissa and direct her to the most likely looking candidate. The eventual decision, however, would be hers, as she would be in a much better position to see any possible likeness. At this time of day, just after twelve, it was far too early for the 'hotel whores' to be on duty and for the hotel security to be alert.

Dietrich Schaeffer sat at the far end of the bar and leant against the wall finishing his club sandwich. Ah, how he loved Eastern Europe and, though he'd been forced to learn it at school, the Russian language. To him, Russian, not French, was the language of love. No, definitely not French. He'd take the sound of dogs barking any day over that of doves cooing. Who wanted to fuck a dove? He ate another fry. He'd been very excited when his company had finally given in to his request to visit Ukraine. They had market share in Poland, so, with a potential fifty-two million end users, Ukraine, he had argued, was a 'logical progression'. It was to be his first evening in Kyiv and he expected great things. His colleague, Henrik, returned from the toilet, his eyes gleaming.

'For sure, Henni, we find what we are looking for here.' Dietrich smiled and jabbed at his colleague's ring finger with a spiral fry. 'You hide that. If they don't want money, they want to marry.'

Henrik smirked and pulled off his wedding ring. 'It has been getting a bit tight,' he replied as his eyes fixed hungrily on Larissa's rear end nestling against the bar.

Dietrich followed his gaze and nodded approvingly. 'You know that girl I had in Warsaw?' Dietrich continued, looking wistfully at Larissa. 'Well, now I do private business with her, *ya*? I phone her last week and say come to hotel now. I meet her in foyer and we get a room on the fourteenth floor.' He took a slurp of his Kilkenny as he savoured the memory. 'She stands on the balcony and I do it from behind. It was super kinky, *ya*, with panorama of the city!'

Henrik snorted into his beer, staining his tie. 'Hey, I am meant to be the Viking, but you, Dietrich, are the biggest one!'

Larissa became aware of eyes looking intently at her. She glanced again into the bar mirror and saw two men in their late thirties at the far end. One had square, thick-rimmed, black glasses, dark hair and a goatee beard. He wore a leather waistcoat over the top of a white work shirt and black jeans. The other, dark blond, fatter, but more formally dressed in a grey business suit and blue shirt, sat at his side. As she continued to stare, the taller one finished his beer and ambled over. Propping himself up directly next to her he ordered two more beers. Larissa fought the urge to flinch, relaxed her shoulders, turned slightly, and took a sip from her glass. Six months ago she might have courted the attention, but then she had met Arnaud. He wasn't the businessman she had angled for; he wore jeans and blue and green Gortex boots. But she had felt something for him and now... he was gone. She could feel the tears starting to form but quickly dabbed at her eyes with her index finger. She was doing this for Arnaud, she reminded herself; Aidan had to escape if he were to have any chance of catching his killer. She swallowed hard and faced the man. He was looking directly at her, his eyes flicking from her eyes to her lips, then her breasts. Smiling, he offered her a cigarette. As she leant forward to accept her phone vibrated in her bag. She smiled apologetically and answered it, taking a step away and holding it to her left ear, the side of her head farthest from Dietrich.

'The one next to you,' Snow's voice boomed in her ear. 'Take him if you can.'

'OK, Oxsana, I'll meet you at one-thirty,' she replied nervously and ended the call. 'My name is Olga,' she said in accented English, taking the extended cigarette and letting Dietrich light it for her.

Snow, now in the hotel lobby, observed. An opened copy of the *Ukrainsky Visnick* newspaper lay spread out on the table in front of him. It was risky as hell sitting in the foyer like this but he had no choice. The man with Larissa was a similar height to himself but heavier and older. He felt his own face; at a push his four days' growth could pass for a neatly trimmed goatee and, besides, the specs would help alter his face. Larissa was his main concern. Would she be recognised again by any of those present? Probably not. She had the 'Khreshatik look' about her: shoulder-length, low-lighted, chestnut-brown hair, prominent cheekbones and long, slender legs. A photo-fit would resemble any number of local girls, especially at the more opulent bars and restaurants. She'd be OK; just colour her hair a different shade and lay low for a couple of weeks. Snow looked to his right. Across the hallway the receptionist busily checked in an elderly Canadian couple. Snow noted the CCTV camera above the desk and the other just past his table. He hoped his calculations were correct and that his face wouldn't be picked up.

Larissa and the man joined his friend at the end of the bar and introductions were made. A seat was pulled up for her and she sat between the two. 'Come on, come on,' Snow mumbled to himself. The faster they did this the better. They needed to get the passport and get out as quickly as possible. The taller of the two men, Snow named him Lucky, stood up and took Larissa's hand. He walked the pair of them out of the bar area and towards the lifts. Snow remained still and observed the second man order another beer and share a joke with the bartender. The receptionist eyed them suspiciously as they entered the lift but said nothing. Snow slowly counted to thirty, flexed the muscles in his legs, and headed for the stairwell. He kept his eyes fixed on the entrance to the lifts, lest Larissa and Lucky should reappear. The light illuminated the eighth floor and Snow started to climb the stairs. As he reached the fourth flight he speed-dialled Larissa's mobile. It rang five times before being picked up.

'Room number?' Snow could hear the sound of the shower running.

Larissa walked towards the door, stepping over Dietrich's boots. Dietrich was having possibly the fastest shower in his life in expectation of what he was to get. Checking the bathroom again over her shoulder, she spoke quietly. 'Eight-one-four.' Her voice cracked. 'Be quick, please.'

Snow clicked 'end', pulled on a pair of surgical gloves Yulia used when highlighting her hair, and hastened his pace up the stairs. The lift might have been quicker but he didn't want to risk having to share it with anyone. Sixth floor, seventh. 'Come on, move it.' Catching his breath he leant against the wall momentarily to put on the stocking mask before pushing open the door to the eighth floor. The hall was empty apart from an unattended maid's trolley at one end. He started to control his breathing and counted the numbers down to the one he wanted. Eight-one-four was in the middle of the hallway, an equal distance from the fire escape and lifts. Snow stood, his back pressed against the wall next to the door – if he were caught now he would need a bloody good excuse – counted silently to twenty, and then knocked. A German voice from within shouted at him with what he guessed to be an approximation of 'piss off', but Snow persisted and knocked again.

The door opened inwards and Snow threw himself into the room. Larissa was knocked to the ground, landing awkwardly and loudly on an open Samsonite case. She let out a cry and pulled her arms around her chest. Snow continued forward, lowered his head, and shoulder-barged the naked German on to the bed. Lucky's arms flew out sideways with his right slamming into the top of the bedside cabinet. Snow pushed himself up by forcing his left hand on the German's throat. Shock showed in the man's eyes. His feet twitched yet his arms remained as though glued to the bed. Snow swung his right fist into his face with as much force as he could muster.

'Don't move!' Snow's Russian was slurred. 'You, *Blat*, shut the door before I kill you too!'

Larissa shakily pushed the door shut from her place on the floor. Fear had now also gripped her and she sat in the corner, unaware of the blood trickling down her forearm. Snow gradually moved his knees so that all his weight was concentrated on Lucky's legs, just above the knees. He looked into the face of the German who had started to look more angry than afraid. Snow pulled the pistol out of his waistband and forced it into the cheek of his victim.

'I'm going to get up and you are not going to move. Understand?'

The German nodded. Slowly, Snow moved his left leg until his foot hit the carpeted floor, which transferred his weight off of the bed. 'I am going to do the talking. When I ask you a question you will nod or shake your head. Understand?'

Again, the German nodded. Blood had started to run into his mouth from his nose. He held eye contact with Snow. Snow noted the look in his eye; one of outrage, not a trace of fear. In that instant both men realised the other was no stranger to violence.

'Is your passport in your coat?' Lucky nodded. 'And your money?' He nodded again. Snow stood and walked to the desk just past the bed, all the time keeping the barrel of the Makarov pistol pointed at his victim's head. He picked up the jacket and threw it to Larissa. 'Take it all out.' Standing, Larissa retrieved the items. 'Where is he from?'

'Cologne,' replied Larissa shakily.

'And his name?'

'Dietrich Schaeffer.'

Dietrich's nostrils flared. This wasn't how he had hoped to be spending his Monday afternoon. The Russian knew what he was doing, of this he was in no doubt... But the girl, was she working with him? He looked at Larissa, who he could see visibly shaking. No, the girl was petrified. Surely she wouldn't be this scared if they were a team? Nervous, perhaps, but not like this. He'd tell him to take the lot, money and laptop. Three thousand euros wasn't that much and, besides, it wasn't his money to worry about.

'Lie facedown and put your hands behind your back,' he commanded. Dietrich cautiously did as requested, wincing in pain as he moved his right wrist. Snow picked up the German's trousers and removed the belt. He thrust it towards Larissa. 'Tie his hands tight. Remember, both of you – I have the gun.'

As she did this Snow darted into the bathroom and took the towelling belt from the bathrobe. This he quickly bound around the man's ankles. Schaeffer began to squirm but all notions of escape were quickly dismissed by a cuff to the back of the neck. Schaeffer slumped into unconsciousness. Finishing, Larissa cupped her hand over her mouth and ran into the bathroom. Snow knew he didn't have much time left so moved quickly. Opening the pilot case on the table, he left the computer but removed the trade literature on water filters. Crossing to the upturned Samsonite he pulled out a pair of slacks and a shirt. They were two sizes too big but the length looked about right. These he put into the case along with Dietrich's grooming kit from the bathroom and the chocolate and water from the mini bar. He put a couple of miniatures in his coat pocket for good measure before finally stuffing the recumbent German's leather waistcoat on top and forcing the bag to close. He cautiously leaned over Dietrich and checked his breathing, propping him up as best he could on his side. He didn't want to suffocate the bastard. In all his naked splendour Dietrich resembled a giant baby. Snow noted the tattoo of a cherub on his stomach and, looking at Larissa, stifled a nervous laugh.

'Now, remember to act normal. You go down first. As you leave, wave at his friend in the bar; smile – you've just earned $200. Then walk down the street. I'll follow in the car and pick you up.'

Larissa nodded, started to say something, then thought better of it. She opened the door and shakily left the room. Snow shut the door and breathed a huge sigh of relief. He looked around before grabbing the pilot case, Schaeffer's long leather overcoat, and glasses.

Larissa sat in silence holding a handkerchief to her forearm. She hadn't said a word since getting back into the car with Snow. It had been a long and terrifying day for them both. Arnaud's body would now have been taken to the morgue and the embassy informed. The real owner of the restaurant would be questioned and it wouldn't be long before Larissa joined Snow on the wanted list. Wanted for questioning, at least. He had to move fast and distance himself from the events of the last two days until he could regroup.

'How's the arm?'

'So, what do we do now?' she replied, unable to meet his gaze.

'Now,' answered Snow, 'we go to the central ticket office and you book Dietrich Schaeffer on the Grand Tour to Lviv. Book both bunks, I don't want any company.' Snow held up the *Reisenpass* and studied the picture as he drove. It was a few years old, which was good for him as it was nearer his own age. The beard was still there, as were the glasses, but the hair had less grey. This might just work.

Vickers stared. The body was pale from blood loss, almost marble in colour. The mortuary assistant pulled up the sheet. Vickers closed his eyes and remained still for a minute before he left the room and rejoined Blazhevich in the corridor. Neither man spoke as they exited the dimly lit government building.

Troieschyna, Kyiv

The water was wonderfully warm and Snow's mind started to drift as it massaged his scalp. As his mind relaxed, the events of the past few days flashed before his eyes. The explosion on Pushkinskaya, Bull… but most of all the image of Arnaud as the life bled out of him. Pashinski was going to pay.

Entering without knocking, Larissa looked him up and down, taking in his tightly muscled physique and the scars on his left leg. Snow met her gaze. She handed him a towel. 'He was fatter and… not as you are.'

Snow wrapped the towel around his waist. 'I'm sorry for what I made you do at the hotel.'

Tears again welled in her eyes. 'It was horrible.'

'I'm sorry. If there had been another way to get a passport, I…'

'I know.'

Snow nodded. 'We have to hurry.'

The grime washed away, he stepped out of the shower, patted his face dry, and looked in the mirror. 'Time to become German.'

He picked up the pink canister of lady shave gel and applied it to his face. Taking his time, he carefully cut away the five-day growth with the disposable razor. Larissa looked on with a critical eye and made sure the beard was even.

In the bedroom he put on Schaeffer's clothes. Larissa passed him the shoes.

'Jeez, he had small feet. You know what they say about small feet?' Snow didn't continue. Unable to squeeze into the shoes, he slipped his own boots back on.

'I need to make your hair white.' She leant forward with a talcum powder-coated hand.

'You mean grey?'

'*Da*. Grey. Sit still. Your hair is still wet a little so this should stick. We used to do this in school for school plays.' She applied the powder to Snow's temples. 'Good, let me brush. Finished. You look like Daniel Craig.'

'James Bond?'

'*Da*, but older,' she replied and kissed him on the cheek.

He looked into her eyes. Tears started to fall. He reached forward and held her. Larissa collapsed into his arms and sobbed like a child.

Petropavlivska Borschagivka, Kyiv Oblast

Bull scanned with the night-vision binoculars. The two militia Ladas and the ambulance were still outside his house. An American-style body bag was now being carried out by figures dressed in white. An old man stood in the courtyard and lit a cigarette as a younger man read from a notebook with a penlight. Every light in the house seemed to be switched on and there was movement in all windows. Bull seethed as he imagined SBU agents swarming like ants through his belongings. It was only his strict adherence to the Spetsnaz SOP that had saved his life. A perimeter of lookouts had been placed two hundred metres away from the restaurant, alerting all inside to the arrival of the ALPHA unit. Expecting to negotiate with hostage takers, the ALPHA had been taken by surprise by his attack. Yes, he had sustained casualties, but he had escaped along with seventy per cent of his men, an acceptable ratio on the Soviet battlefield. What, however, he had not accounted for was the betrayal by Budanov, the fat SBU toad. That betrayal would cost him and his family their lives. Sergey would silence them, Bull told himself, once he had briefed his pet assassin. That would be his last job; Oleg could then kill him as promised.

Lying facedown in the forest, Bull was finding it hard to control his rage. He pushed his hand against the stab wound in his leg inflicted by Snow and found some comfort and focus in the pain. He had lost everything; the house, the cars, and, most of all, his identity. It seemed the SBU now knew that Knysh was Pashinski. What to do? Leave the country, see a surgeon, and have the face altered like so many others? From somewhere deep inside, for the first time in his life, a voice was counselling a complete withdrawal. *You have the money in the Swiss account; take it, admit defeat, and disappear.*

He looked around at his men lying with him. Not many of the originals left, but a loyal unit still. These were the real heroes of Mother Russia, men who had fought in Afghanistan and Chechnya to be rewarded with a pittance. The state had turned its back on them but he could not. They would retreat, but after a victory, a rewarding victory. They had a cache of weapons and equipment stored at the Chaika Sports Complex, one kilometre away. With any luck the authorities wouldn't think to watch the small airfield with its light private pleasure planes.

Dmitro appeared at his shoulder with another Ukrainian, Taras. They had dropped Oleg off at the house then set out to find their medic, only to return to find they had been beaten by the SBU.

'They have the roads in and out manned and are circulating your photograph.'

Bull let his head drop so his forehead rested on the moist forest floor. 'What about Chaika?'

'If we head across the fields we can bypass them.' Taras knew this part of the city especially well.

'*Dobre.*' Bull unintentionally used Ukrainian. 'Tell the rest of the men that we are on the move.'

'Where are we going?' Dmitro was a Kyivite and did not want to live in exile.

Bull raised himself to his haunches and regarded the former Red Army soldier. 'We are going to make sure our shipment arrives on time.'

Kyiv Central Railway Station, Kyiv

Walking with a stoop and carrying two large, heavy-looking, cheap plastic holdalls, Snow approached the central railway station. They had parked around the back of an apartment building while Larissa quickly shopped for some throwaway clothes for him at the market. Now, wearing a leather cap and cheap padded suede coat over a fake Adidas tracksuit, Snow looked like any other down-at-heel Ukrainian traveller. His bags were the same as those used by the majority of the street sellers who journeyed into the capital in the hope of selling their goods before returning home in the evening to outlying small towns and villages. Snow made a conscious effort not to make eye contact with anyone. It was a safe bet that Pashinski, the SBU, or both were watching the station. It was just after seven-thirty and crowds of people still gathered on the street outside. Some waiting for loved ones, others waiting for connecting minibuses to their villages not served by the rail network. Snow spotted more than a dozen 'possibles' who could either be Pashinski's men or SBU. The problem was that the 'rent-a-muscle look' was popular, so large men with very short haircuts and leather jackets were everywhere. Below his baggy tracksuit Snow wore the oversized trousers of the German; the rest of the outfit was in the bag he held in his left hand. Nearing the entrance now he noted two men talking to a group of five or so militia officers, SBU agents. He continued past, keeping them in his peripheral vision, something he had learnt on surveillance in the regiment.

Four more militia officers were on the central concourse and he had no doubt there would be more posted on the platforms. It had been several hours since he'd taken the German's passport and time was running out before he was discovered. Snow had left the 'do not disturb' sign on his hotel room door but his colleague would soon start to wonder where he was. There was even a chance the militia were waiting to pick Snow up as he boarded the train. He had no other choice; he would have to 'brave it out' and control the situation.

Snow took a left inside the newly refurbished station building and entered the toilets. He moved past a man shaving in the mirror and entered the end cubicle. He placed the lighter of his two bags on the floor – this one was empty except for some flattened old boxes he had picked up. He now carefully took off his new market clothes and placed them in the bag. Opening the second, he retrieved the leather pilot case and dressed in his 'German' outfit. Now he steadied himself, took a deep breath, and opened the door. The shaving man was splashing his face with water and paid him no attention. Out on the concourse once more, Snow walked towards two militia men standing by the stairs leading down to the platform.

'Do you speak German?' he asked in German-accented Russian.

The two militia men looked at each other before the shorter spoke. 'Very small English?'

Snow shook his head and carried on in German-accented pigeon Russian. 'Can you help? I am lost. I need to find train "Grand Tour". Can you show me? I not want miss.'

'Take the steps down, then you have to go up and over the

platform until you see the sign saying "Grand Tour", the taller replied in Russian.

'I, err, no understand. Can you show, please?'

'Just take the steps…'

The second officer stopped his colleague. 'Follow me.'

Snow smiled and nodded. 'Thank you, thank you.'

He followed the officer while the other remained at his post. Snow kept searching for anyone who might have recognised him from the corners of his eyes, all the while his left hand holding the Makarov pistol concealed in his pocket. They reached the start of the platform. The militia officer stopped and pointed.

'There, Grand Tour.'

'I want say thank you for help.'

Snow placed his case on the floor then put his right hand into his pocket and removed a ten-dollar bill. The officer looked first left, then right, before taking the note, nodding, and walking away. It was no secret that the salaries of the militia were usually paid late, not to mention being woefully behind inflation. Internally Snow relaxed slightly. The militia were not yet looking for either Dietrich Schaeffer or someone attempting to travel on his stolen passport. Snow walked along the platform, found his carriage, and boarded the train.

At the central ticket office, Centralnaya Kassa, Larissa had helped the 'German' buy two SV tickets on the Grand Tour train to Lviv. The SV was the Soviet equivalent of first class and, on the pretence of being proletariat, had two beds. Those wanting to travel alone bought both. Once in Lviv, Snow would make his way into the mountains and attempt to exfiltrate over the border into Poland. He looked at the ticket number and found his compartment. He pulled back the sliding door and put the pilot case on the right-hand bunk. He shut the door and fell on to the bed. The train moved off. A wave of tiredness washed over him as the adrenaline left his body. It was twelve hours to Lviv and he planned to lie low. A lone German businessman might cause some interest on any normal train, but the Grand Tour, owned by the Lviv hotel of the same name, was frequented by foreign business people and tourists alike.

Without realising it, Snow had fallen asleep. Shit! He woke with a jolt, hand finding the concealed Makarov. There was a knocking at the door and the waiter, dressed in a red, velvet waistcoat, white shirt and black trousers, cautiously opened it. He asked him first in Ukrainian, then English, if he wanted anything from the trolley. Snow spoke in German-accented English and ordered a bottle of Desna, two packets of peanuts, and several chocolate bars. The transaction over, he shut the door, took off his belt, and threaded it through the handles. There had been cases of guards on normal trains opening the doors for a cut of whatever the thief could steal. This had not, to his knowledge, happened on the Grand Tour but Snow was in no mood for any unexpected guests. There was still a chance the SBU or Pashinski had men on the train.

Alone in his carriage, his thoughts returned to Arnaud. He had been an innocent, a kid like any other, who just wanted to have a laugh and shag for England. Snow found it hard to get close to people but Arnaud had been different. They had bonded almost immediately; his brash but kind nature and his outbursts had reminded Snow of himself ten years ago. He would miss him bitterly, all the more so because Arnaud wasn't meant to die, not like a soldier for Queen and country. It would somehow have been different if he had been killed on operations; they had all dealt with that back at Sterling Lines by sinking pints and telling tall stories about the antics of their mate who had failed to 'beat the clock'. He had mourned mates from the regiment but Arnaud had never agreed to take the Queen's shilling, never agreed to give his life. At the end, Arnaud had been brave, if foolish, to tackle the monstrous soldier. This one act had set Snow free but signalled his own death. If only Snow had been faster, just a second quicker to snatch the gun and take the head shot, the bullet wouldn't have struck his young friend's heart. But he had been too slow. For the first time in twenty years, Snow started to cry. The ex-SAS man had messed up.

Snow splashed his face with water from the basin. He stood and raised the bottle. 'To you, my friend, wherever you are…' He let his words trail off then swigged a third of the contents in one gulp. Within minutes the bottle was empty and Snow had fallen into a deep sleep as the train sped westward through the Ukrainian night.

Chapter 22

Varchenko sat in the penthouse of the Premier Palace Hotel. He still had his flat in central Kyiv but much preferred to be pampered and away from his wife. He also liked mixing with the international business elite in the overpriced bar. Today, however, he wasn't here for pleasure. Two members of the ALPHA stood outside the room in addition to his own personal security guards. Dudka bit into a peach and added another stain to his tie.

'Former Spetsnaz captain now with his own private army. What did you do to anger this man, Valeriy?' The question was rhetorical.

Varchenko opened his bloodshot eyes and reached for the very expensive Scottish single malt whiskey. 'Business is a dangerous game, Genna. The trick is to know when you have lost.'

'And have you?'

Varchenko slurped. 'Look at me, Genna, look at me. I have businesses all over the Odessa Oblast, more money than I can ever spend, a beautiful daughter, a wonderful granddaughter, and a wife I hardly ever see. I should be happy. I should be respected, but no. *No*. People try to threaten me, to kill me. I

239

am worried, Genna. I think that it is time to stop playing the game, old friend.'

Dudka dropped his peach stone in the wastepaper basket. 'It is not a game when people are killed, Valeriy. The son in England assassinated two days ago. Now, today, an English teacher. Who will be next?'

'Me, of course. If we don't stop Knysh, Pashinski – whatever name he uses – I will be next. Why? Pride. His pride will not let him lose. I know him, Genna. We are the same.'

'So you want to hide? You want to run?' Dudka had never heard 'General' Varchenko talk like this.

Varchenko shook his head. 'I have never run in my life and you, most of all, should know that, Genna. I am tired of playing. It now stops. Tomorrow I will go back to Odessa and wait for him. We have a business meeting after all, a shipment to safely transport.'

'You still think that he will come?' Dudka was puzzled.

Varchenko had not told his old friend of his handling fee. The fact was that Pashinski's money would have been very useful now Varchenko was almost legitimate. He would have let several shipments go and then turned the younger man in when he wasn't expecting it. 'A man like Pashinski does not simply walk away, Genna. I believe that he cannot afford to let this shipment slip.'

'A shipment of weapons to be sold to the crazies.' Dudka was angry he hadn't been able to stop this particular trader before, but now he knew the full picture he would.

'What I cannot understand, Genna, is why a patriotic Ukrainian would want to supply weapons to our mutual enemies?'

'He is not Ukrainian, Valeriy; he is not even Russian. He is Lithuanian.' Dudka left this piece of information hanging in the air.

'A-ha.' Varchenko nodded, sipped the Scotch, then filled in the gaps. 'So he wants to hurt Russia for…' He let his voice trail off. There was hatred of Russia in many quarters for what she had done under the banner of the Soviet Union, especially so among the Baltic States, who had been the last to join and the first to leave the Union. 'Then I was correct. He is crazy.'

'Tell me more about the shipment.' Dudka eyed up another piece of fruit.

'He called me. It will arrive in two days.'

'From where?' Dudka reached forward, grabbed a banana.

'He did not say but I can tell you that he wants it on my cargo plane to Pakistan.'

'You need to give me details of this plane, Genna.'

'Of course. The flight plan is the same each week.'

'And you are expecting him when?'

'We have an agreement. He is to oversee the loading of the first shipment on Wednesday. We are to meet at the *dacha* then drive to the airport.'

Dudka shook his head. 'You must realise that he knows you have given us a description of him? He will want to silence you. This game, as you put it, is very dangerous, old friend. The man has no fear, but we will stop him, Valeriy.'

Varchenko leaned forward. 'What I want from you is an ALPHA team to strengthen my own men. I agree that we will stop him, Genna, and then I will retire from the game.'

Zankovelskaya Street, Central Kyiv

It was 10 p.m. and he had called Blazhevich away from home. Both men had already been working late due to the day's developments. The dead man at the house in the exclusive area of Petropavlivska Borschagivka had been identified as Oleg Zukauskas, a former Spetsnaz soldier who had served with Pashinski. A search of the house had been ordered but, while it had been confirmed that 'Knysh' had lived there, they still didn't have any physical evidence that Knysh was Pashinski. They had, however, found an airline booking confirmation for a return ticket from Dubai to Islamabad in the name of Mark Peters. This was with an envelope containing $8,000. Blazhevich had sent a telex to Interpol regarding this mysterious passenger. It had not yet been answered. Blazhevich was still hopeful that, as the search continued, something else might turn up. Dudka opened the front door of his flat.

'Come in, Vitaly Romanovich. This way.'

They walked along the hall past closed doors to the kitchen. Blazhevich was impressed by the size of the flat and the height of the ceilings, at least five metres. The dark wood panelling added to the stately demeanour, a world away from his flat in the Obolon district, with its thin walls and noisy neighbours.

'Sit, Vitaly.' Dudka gestured towards the kitchen table. 'I have called you here on serious business. I have something to tell you.' Dudka briefed him on his conversation with Varchenko and developments regarding Pashinski. He explained how Pashinski had sought to use Varchenko's network to transport illegal arms to the East and heroin to the West (he wasn't sure about the narcotics but took an educated guess) and that the first shipment was due in two days. Dudka confirmed Blazhevich's theory that Pashinski had been responsible for the murder of both Maliks and surmised that this was a show of force meant to impress General Varchenko and warn him what would happen if he did not cooperate.

Blazhevich took in the information but there was still something that troubled him. 'What about Aidan Snow?'

'What do you think?' Dudka replied with a benevolent curl of his lips.

'I do not think that he is the assassin.' Blazhevich had felt this for a while but not expressed it due to lack of evidence.

'He was the perfect suspect, especially as the rifle was found in his room, but I agree with you, Vitaly Romanovich. Why would Pashinski hire an outsider when he has his own Spetsnaz Brigada? Why also seek to eliminate this man in such a way?'

'I do not know, Gennady Stepanovich. Perhaps to confuse, to throw a false trail? There must be some connection that we do not know about.'

Dudka nodded. 'Perhaps. I am sure that if we ask the traitor Budanov nicely he will gladly tell us.' He clasped his hands together before relaxing. 'Pressing matters. We have three objectives in our operation, which you will coordinate, Vitaly Romanovich.' Blazhevich sat up straighter. Dudka continued, 'One: prevent the shipment from leaving the airport; two: protect General Varchenko; three: apprehend Pashinski.' He paused for effect as his subordinate retrieved a pen and notepad from his coat pocket. 'Put down your pen, I do not want this recorded.'

Blazhevich raised his eyebrows. 'Sir?'

'Listen, Vitaly. This will be a "grey" operation. You have my full authority but we will not be informing the border guards or the local militia. They simply cannot be trusted.'

Blazhevich was shocked but sat a little straighter.

'You will be taking an ALPHA team to Odessa to observe and, if need be, secure both the airport and the general's *dacha*. You will speak to the commander today.' Dudka folded his arms. 'The troops go tomorrow.'

Blazhevich was surprised by the timeframe but nevertheless excited. 'Yes, Gennady Stepanovich. Are we sure that Pashinski will take the bait? Will he show?'

'In this life we can be sure of nothing; but let me ask you, Vitaly, could you write off several million dollars? In my opinion neither can Pashinski, and we must catch him.' Dudka uncrossed his arms. 'You will meet Varchenko and his head of security at the Premier Palace Hotel tonight. We have no way of knowing when Pashinski will show, but the transport plane leaves Odessa Airport on Wednesday evening. Vitaly, you will plan whatever you see fit. Remember, Varchenko was a general once, but now you are in charge.'

'Thank you, Gennady Stepanovich.' Blazhevich felt honoured as well as apprehensive to have this much responsibility thrust on him.

'That's it, you can go.' Dudka stood and removed a paper package from the fridge. He noticed that Blazhevich hadn't moved. 'You want to watch me eat?'

Blazhevich tried not to blush. 'No, sir.' He rose and left the flat. Dudka watched him leave. A good boy, but too polite, too sensitive.

Blazhevich shut the car door and placed his phone in the holder. He'd switched it on again after his meeting with the boss. As he made his way towards the ALPHA barracks he noticed three missed calls, all from the same person. He called the number; it rang once.

'Vickers.'

'Alistair Phillipovich, good evening.'

'Vitaly. Have you got an update?'

They hadn't spoken since Blazhevich had had the unenviable task of informing Vickers earlier in the day of the death of Arnaud Hurst and accompanying him to the mortuary. This had saddened and shocked both intelligence officers, especially Vickers, who had been on speaking terms with the young Brit. Vickers had just finished informing the next of kin. Blazhevich mulled over how much to tell his British contact and then made a decision. 'Snow is no longer a suspect in the Malik murder.'

Vickers, who had his own phone jammed to his ear, nearly fell off his chair. 'Repeat that, Vitaly.'

'I said Snow is no longer a suspect. We have reason to believe that it was a business rival. Pashinski.'

'Pashinski?'

Blazhevich negotiated a junction. 'Yes.'

'He is alive?' Vickers was incredulous.

'We believe so. I can now confirm that he is the main suspect in the Hurst murder.' He could have told Vickers this earlier but had chosen not to as he didn't have the whole picture. Both men paused; the death was still too real.

'Any news on the woman or Snow?' Vickers asked with urgency.

'None since we spoke last. Remember, he is still wanted for shooting the diplomatic protection member on Pushkinskaya.'

'What's the victim's status?' Vickers had momentarily forgotten about that shooting.

'He'll live. I have to end now. We have a major manhunt on our hands, Alistair, but I'll keep you informed.'

'Many thanks, Vitaly.' Vickers stood and paced his office. Snow had saved one life but not the other. Had it been Snow's fault or his own for not believing him? You have to make a decision on the evidence you have, on what you can see and not on what you cannot, not on speculation. Regardless of the blame, Snow and the girl had to be found. Vickers left his office and walked towards the kitchen. At this hour he shared the embassy with only the security guards and they wouldn't make him any tea!

Where would Snow go? He tried to think as he walked. Snow would now be into escape and evasion mode and attempting to put as much distance between himself and Kyiv as possible. He didn't have his passport; Blazhevich had this and, besides, the airports had been watched. What did that leave? A car; he didn't own one but could easily pay a cab, or a bus. Snow could pass for a local so could hide among the crowds, but both of these solutions seemed too precarious somehow. Ukrainian roads weren't made for high-speed travel and, besides, he might get stopped. Then it hit him. Where was the girl from? He poured the water into his cup. Hadn't Snow once said? Vickers closed his eyes and asked his usually photographic memory for help. At the Hash. He had said he was alone because Hurst was in Lviv with his girlfriend. That was it, it made sense. Her parents were from Lviv. Snow and perhaps the girl would be heading for Lviv and then would try to leave the country.

Vickers left his half-made cup of Earl Grey and ran back to his office. He tapped a few keys on his computer and was on the official Ukrainian railways website, www.uz.gov.ua. He searched the timetables and found several slow trains to Lviv before he saw what he wanted: the Grand Tour. Snow must have taken the Grand Tour. He checked the times; the train left at 8 p.m. and took approximately twelve hours. Snow would be arriving at 8 a.m. Vickers switched to www.Ukrainefare.com and checked flights to Lviv. The next would leave in the morning. Shit, he couldn't get there in time on a commercial plane. Options? Ask the SBU to stop Snow at the station? No, he could be armed and so could they. Contact the Warsaw embassy and ask his counterpart, Horner, to get to Lviv? Again, he wouldn't be able to get there in time. The SIS officer paused, then picked up the secure desk phone and called Blazhevich to ask him a large favour. Before Blazhevich had a chance to ask why he was calling, Vickers said, 'I need a plane.'

Chapter 23

Lviv Central Railway Station, Western Ukraine

Vickers looked down the platform at the arriving train. It had been a guess and he would soon either be very relieved or very embarrassed. Blazhevich had insisted on coming with him; after all, Snow was still wanted, although not, to their mutual relief, for murder. Vickers knew Blazhevich had somewhere to be, not from what he said but by the phone calls he kept making. Vickers also knew that his SBU contact had stuck his neck out by arranging the plane and letting Vickers run the show. The local militia hadn't been informed, and neither had the SBU, apart from the two rookie agents Blazhevich had brought along to watch his back. If all went well, Blazhevich would tell his boss where he was and what he had achieved; if not, then there would be a great deal of explaining to do. Vickers had informed Patchem, who was fully behind him if the proverbial were to hit the fan.

'Your men will stay outside as you asked?' Vickers just wanted to be sure.

'Yes, as arranged, Alistair. I'll remain here and keep you in sight.' He drummed his fingers on the office windowsill.

'Right.' Vickers left the office and took the steps down to

the arrivals level. Lviv's station was grand, art nouveau, a relic of the days when the city was the capital of Habsburg Galicia. Vickers made a quick mental note to return when all this was over and take a longer look. The guard stood on the platform and raised a flag. Doors opened and passengers streamed out, most pulling wheeled cases. Vickers stood partly concealed next to the newspaper kiosk and studied the faces. Passengers moved past him, some returning home, others just arriving. A couple of Western-looking businessmen were taking their time as they stopped to observe and pass comments on the workings of the station.

Vickers disregarded them, then focused on a group of three. Two of them were elderly women; one was a man who was carrying their bags. He was smiling and chatting as they walked. Vickers continued to watch. The trio moved closer and Vickers could see the trousers that seemed slightly too large, the unkempt hair brushed back, and finally the brown leather Gortex boots. He felt his phone vibrate, the signal that Blazhevich had spotted him too. They reached the end of the platform and then Vickers stepped out into the open. He kept his eyes on the face of the man until the suspect turned his head. Their eyes locked. Without losing eye contact Vickers heard the man, in Moscow-accented Russian, tell the old women he had been happy to help.

'Welcome to Lviv.' Vickers spoke first.

'Alistair, you needn't have come all this way to welcome me personally.' Snow was still but his eyes now darted around.

'Where's the girl?' Vickers meant Larissa.

'She didn't come with me.' So they didn't have her yet, Snow realised; that was a good sign.

'The SBU know you didn't shoot Malik. You're no longer a murder suspect.'

Snow's eyes returned to Vickers again. 'How?'

'They have testimony from an insider. Pashinski ordered it.'

'Pashinski and his men also killed Arnaud,' Snow stated, trying to control his anger. 'Where is Pashinski?'

'Sorry, don't know.' Vickers shrugged, then took an involuntary step back, believing Snow was about to explode.

Snow inhaled deeply and in almost a whisper said, 'I'm going to kill him.'

Vickers believed him. 'Look, we have a plane waiting to take you back to Kyiv. The SBU want to talk to you.'

'And accuse me of attempted murder?' Snow was none too happy with the offer.

'That can't be avoided.' Surely Snow wasn't going to do a runner now?

'Perhaps it can, Alistair.' Blazhevich appeared from behind Snow. 'I think that it is in our best interest to put this aside until Pashinski is caught.'

'Aidan, I've told Agent Blazhevich you can ID him.'

Snow took a side step so both men were facing him. He studied the two.

Blazhevich spoke. 'We will drive to the plane then fly back to Kyiv Zhulyany Airport. I have some questions to ask you on the way.'

Snow sighed and replied in Russian, '*Pyedem.*' Let's go.

Kyiv Zhulyany Airport

They were on the final approach to land when Vickers felt his phone vibrate. 'Vickers.'

'Alistair, it's Jack. I've just come into some information by way of Five.'

Vickers looked around the small plane. Snow sat opposite him with Blazhevich further ahead, talking to the pilot. The two agents were looking out of the window.

'Go ahead.'

'Bav Malik's assassin was supplied with a weapon by a Moldovan, name of Arkadi Cheban. He says he works for his uncle, Ivan Lesukov.'

Vickers listened. Lesukov had been discussed and he had been accused of being behind the recent increase of illegal arms sales. Patchem continued, 'Lesukov is a former member of the Red Army Spetsnaz and served with Pashinski in Afghanistan. According to Cheban, Pashinski has been contracted to "facilitate the transportation" of Lesukov's arms shipments through Ukraine.'

'That explains a lot.' For Vickers, the pieces of the puzzle were fitting together nicely.

'It was Cheban who said the shooter was American, but then one of Malik's employees, a David Ossowski, said he thought he heard the shooter use Polish.'

Vickers was silent for a moment. 'Did the Viennese authorities get anywhere?'

'No, the suspect, a Mark Peters, disappeared. Both hotel staff and a waiter in a local restaurant were questioned but don't know where he went. All were adamant he was American.'

'What do the Americans think?' Vickers would have liked to have seen the look on the London CIA station chief's face when Patchem spoke to him.

'They are helping us with our enquiries.' Patchem scrolled through the digitised dossier. 'I'm sending this to you now. You should pass it on to the SBU. It could be that we've stumbled on something quite important.'

'Will do, Jack. How fresh is the intel?'

Patchem sighed. 'The police had this the day of the shooting and Five have been holding on to it since then.' Vickers shook his head. The inter-service rivalry between MI5 and MI6 was again getting in the way. 'Speak more later.' Patchem ended the call.

Snow looked up. 'Care to tell me what's happening?' He had heard Vickers's side of the conversation.

Dudka folded his arms as Blazhevich entered the room. 'Vitaly Romanovich. Please explain again why you are in Kyiv not Odessa?'

Blazhevich cleared his throat. He had tried to explain on the plane but obviously not well enough for his boss. 'Gennady Stepanovich. I have gained vital intelligence from the British Secret Service.'

Dudka remained silent for a second. Vickers entered the office. Dudka stood, walked towards him, and shook his hand. He spoke in English. 'It is good to see you, Mr Vickers.'

Vickers replied in Russian, 'I am pleased to see you, Gennady Stepanovich, and thank you for letting me call this meeting.'

Dudka raised his eyebrows at hearing the embassy man speak Russian. His English, too, was better than he let on. He decided to continue the meeting in Russian and let the Englishman show off. 'Please take a seat, Mr Vickers.' Vickers sat. 'Vitaly. Can you confirm that the ALPHA team are in Odessa?'

'Yes, Gennady Stepanovich. They arrived two hours ago. Major Bodarctski has given them orders.'

Dudka was now slightly less concerned. 'So what have we that is so urgent?'

'Mr Vickers has passed on to me information from British Intelligence that points to Pashinski's direct involvement in cross-border arms smuggling and the assassination of two British citizens, Mr Malik in Odessa and his son in the UK.'

'This is corroborated?' Dudka asked Vickers.

'Yes. We have a Moldovan in custody who is the nephew of Ivan Lesukov.' Vickers repeated what he'd been told by Patchem and handed Dudka a hard copy of the file, which he had printed at the embassy. It was in English but he doubted that would cause any problems.

It was Blazhevich's turn to speak; he didn't want Vickers to take all the credit. 'Gennady Stepanovich, if you remember, we found an airline booking confirmation at Knysh's house in the name of Mark Peters.' Dudka's brow was furrowed as he attempted to scan the file but he nevertheless nodded.

'That is the same name the British have for the person suspected of shooting Bav Malik in England.'

'Good.' Dudka looked up. 'So we have an actual link between Pashinski and the murders as well as the arms shipments?'

'Not quite. We have a link with Knysh, but not Pashinski.'

Dudka frowned. 'But Knysh is Pashinski.'

'We do not have that proof yet.' Blazhevich looked at Vickers.

'That is where I can help. I have a British citizen who can physically identify Pashinski.'

'Where is this person now?' Dudka liked this Englishman already.

Blazhevich wanted to impress. 'He is in our holding cell, Gennady Stepanovich. The witness is Aidan Snow.'

'Then bring him up, Vitaly Romanovich.'

Blazhevich left the room; Dudka smiled at Vickers but said nothing. The sound of traffic from the street below was all that broke the silence. A minute later the two men entered. Dudka spoke first.

'You are Aidan Snow?' It was a rhetorical question.

'Yes.' Snow sat with his back straight.

Dudka wanted to cut to the chase. He handed Snow the old photo from the Polish file. 'Can you identify this man?'

Snow looked at the photograph and answered in Russian. 'He was older when I met him, but yes, I can identify this man. He is the man who tried to kill me ten years ago. Tauras Pashinski.'

Dudka nodded, concealing his surprise at Snow's Russian, and passed him a second image, this one a photo-fit from the informer Cheban in the UK. 'And this man?'

'It is the same man.' The image was a good, if not perfect, likeness.

'You are certain?' Dudka wanted to be sure.

'Yes. If I were to point a gun in your face I think you would remember mine.'

Snow didn't want to waste time persuading yet another official.

Dudka ignored the Englishman's sarcasm. 'When was the last time you saw this man?'

'Yesterday, here in Kyiv.'

'You are positive?' Again, he wanted to be certain.

Snow could no longer hold himself in check. Inside he raged. If he had been believed at the time, Arnaud wouldn't be dead. He looked at Vickers, who sat away from Dudka's desk at an angle. Vickers was looking at his notes, not wanting to make eye contact. 'Yes, one hundred per cent.'

Dudka looked at the three other men in the room. 'If you were to see him again, you could positively identify the man?'

Snow knew it was important so made a supreme effort. 'Yes, Director Dudka, I could.'

'Good.' He paused. 'When we have him in custody I will ask you to identify him.'

Snow rose from his seat. 'Just a minute, what do you mean?'

Dudka remained seated although Blazhevich stood. Dudka spoke. 'When we have arrested him, you will be a valuable witness for the prosecution.'

'You listen to me.' Snow spoke for the first time to the SBU with force. 'I want to identify this man as you capture him, not after. I want to be on the ground.' Snow steadied his breathing.

'Not possible, Mr Snow. You are a foreign civilian and we cannot have you put any further in harm's way.' Dudka used his fatherly tone.

253

'I'm sorry, Aidan. This way is the safest.' Vickers broke his silence.

Snow slammed his fist on the desk. 'This man has tried to kill me; he was responsible for the deaths of my friend and of two members of my regiment. I cannot stand by and have others...' Snow ran out of words as the images of the last few days replayed in his mind.

Dudka, although slightly surprised by the outburst, wasn't angry. 'I think you underestimate us, Mr Snow.' He opened a folder and handed Snow a picture that Vickers hadn't seen. 'This is, I believe, one of Pashinski's men?'

Snow studied the bloodied corpse with the head all but severed. 'This is the man who shot Arnaud Hurst.' Glances were exchanged around the room. Vickers looked up, his jaw slack. Snow continued, 'I didn't kill him but I am responsible for the gunshot wound he has in the stomach. Who finished him?' Snow felt some satisfaction that Arnaud's murderer was now dead.

Dudka shrugged. An anonymous caller had told the SBU to check the address. 'Thought you could tell us? OK, so now no one knows. We must speculate.'

Blazhevich addressed Snow directly. 'Aidan, you must let us take this from here. We have information that Pashinski will surface in Odessa and we will be ready for him.'

'Really?' It was sarcasm that only Vickers picked up on.

'Yes, really, Aidan. We have two ALPHA teams in place.'

'Vitaly.' It was Dudka. 'Explain to Mr Snow about the digital devices.'

'Very well, Gennady Stepanovich. We have high-definition digital monitoring equipment that will stream the images in real time. You can watch the operation from the control room and will be able then to identify Pashinski.'

Snow was unconvinced. Such equipment had been used primarily by America's Navy SEALs and Delta Force in the war against terror with varied results. In his opinion, 'space age' had yet to work in the 'real' world.

'I want to be on the ground.'

'No. This is final. You are responsible for shooting a member of the Berkut assigned to the Diplomatic Protection Squad. Mr Snow, I think that, in these circumstances, I am being more than accommodating.' Dudka looked him in the eyes. 'Please do not hinder us any further.'

Snow had lost and knew it. Dudka stood and gestured towards the door. 'Let us waste no more time.'

The meeting was over. Vickers shook the hands of both SBU men and followed Snow and Blazhevich out of the office and down the steps to the investigation rooms. Snow was to give a full statement to the SBU of everything that had happened since he had escaped from his flat. This included shooting the diplomatic protection member, injuring Oleg Zukauskas, and rescuing Larissa. Snow knew he was in the shit but didn't care. They could throw the book at him, they could pelt him with an entire library – he was beyond caring about himself. His sole purpose now was to get his hands on the face that haunted him: Pashinski. Blazhevich passed Snow over to another agent who led him into a room. The door was shut behind them.

Back at reception, Blazhevich held out his hand. 'Thank you.'

'What for?' Vickers was surprised.

'For bringing in Snow, for sharing your intel with us.'

'Vitaly, I told you I wanted to forge closer bonds with the SBU – take this as proof.' They shook hands. 'So, now you have a plane to catch?' Vickers was fishing.

'That's correct. I am to fly to Odessa to join Major Bodaretski and the assault team. They will be protecting General Varchenko and awaiting Pashinski and his shipment.' Blazhevich had nothing to hide.

Vickers was happier; things really were starting to move. 'Let's hope this can put a serious dent in their trade.' The respective governments of both officers would also be happy. Both men left the building. Vickers walked the five minutes to the British Embassy and Blazhevich raced, sirens flashing, back to the government jet at Zhulyany Airport.

Chapter 24

Varchenko stood on the terrace overlooking the sea. He felt invaded with the ALPHA men swarming over the house but this could not be helped. At least they were not in uniform; each had a Kevlar chest plate and thin black balaclava they would put on when the action started. Balaclava, Varchenko grunted to himself: an invention of the British when they fought his countrymen in the Crimea, that they had outrageously named after the town. What else was his nation famous for? Chicken Kiev – invented by an American restaurateur who wanted a cheap dish to entice the Russian immigrant; Chernobyl – the world's worst nuclear accident; the Antonov 255 – the world's biggest plane that now no longer flew? Still, things were improving; last year they'd won the Eurovision Song Contest and now Andrei Shevchenko was one of the world's best footballers.

He bent forward and tore a dead head off a rosebush. Ukraine deserved more; it was, after all, a noble country that had been battered by eighty years of communist nonsense. He imagined the views from his hotel again and the influx of elite tourists demanding to stay there. Out in the bay motor launches and yachts would vie for space. He felt noticeably more relaxed. A cold breeze blew in from the sea and he buttoned up his cashmere coat. The English tailor was a true craftsman. Once this business was all over with he would devote himself to the hotel and put something real back into society. He had another meeting arranged with his country's president and would again stress the urgent need for more investment in tourism. Tourism, after all, was the new heavy industry of the twenty-first century.

'General Varchenko.' Blazhevich approached the legendary figure.

The old man turned and regarded the newcomer. 'You are Director Dudka's new best man?' He didn't mean to be sarcastic but it was his nature.

'Yes, General.' Blazhevich had no time for false flattery. 'We have three different possible target vehicles approaching, each on different routes.' The two-hundred-and-fifty-mile Ukrainian border with Transdniester was mostly made up of unguarded fields broken by stretches of fir trees and riddled with twisting dirt tracks along which a small vehicle could pass if it had to, and when it came to smugglers, frequently did. 'Each is heading in the general direction of the airport.'

'*Dobre.*' Varchenko waited for more information.

'Is your cargo plane ready?'

'It sits on the tarmac awaiting its cargo as it does every Wednesday.' He had already told the SBU this.

'I'm sorry.' Blazhevich held up his left hand and retrieved his mobile from his trouser pocket with the other. He listened for a few seconds before smiling. 'And you are certain of this?' He listened to the reply. 'OK. We will get into position.' Blazhevich closed his phone. Varchenko raised his eyebrows expectantly. 'One of the vehicles is being accompanied by two cars. One of the cars has changed course and is heading for this location. I think that we should now get ready, General.'

Varchenko straightened and seemed to grow taller. 'Get the men into their positions. We cannot afford any errors.'

Blazhevich remembered Dudka's words but could see from the steely gaze of the former KGB general which of the two of them was now in charge. 'Very well, Comrade General.' He managed to resist the urge to salute.

Half a kilometre away from the house, ALPHA men dressed in DPM – disruptive pattern material – took positions in among the hedges and ditches that lined either side of the approach road. It was their job to monitor the road, confirm that the target vehicle had indeed passed, and prevent any unexpected surprises. The team leader radioed ahead as an ancient boxy Lada saloon bounced up the road. At the house the remainder of the men had taken up defensive positions covering the gates and driveway. Three snipers lay on the roof covering all angles. Two of Blazhevich's men had replaced Varchenko's own on the gate – they had their breastplates concealed under oversized jackets. From the road all looked normal; the extra men could not be seen. Varchenko stood in a first-floor window behind bulletproof glass, Blazhevich at his side; both men had their eyes fixed on the road.

The blue Lada came round the bend in the road and approached the house. It had Moldovan licence plates and two men sat in the front. Varchenko sneered and Blazhevich scratched his head. It arrived at the gate and the security men let it into to the compound. Once in the compound the occupants were in the crosshairs of numerous weapons. The driver got out. He was wearing a leather cap and matching jacket with fur collar, his trousers were baggy and looked as though they'd once belonged to a suit. He looked up at the house with wide eyes. The second man tried to exit the vehicle but was 'asked' to remain seated by one of the guards – the other had started to frisk the driver. He had no weapon. The guard radioed up to Major Bodaretski, 'He is clean.' Bodaretski, who was also on the first floor, but monitoring the digital surveillance equipment, told them to keep searching the car.

Varchenko and Blazhevich were down the steps and approaching the visitors within seconds. The general ignored all security precautions and addressed the driver. 'Who are *you*?'

The driver took his hat off to reveal greasy thinning hair and bowed slightly to the taller, imposing figure. 'I am Konstantin Doga. I am the driver for Knysh Export.' He inclined his head. 'It is my son in the car.'

'Doga?' Varchenko was angered and perplexed.

'It is a Moldovan name, sir. I have a message that I must give to Valeriy Ivanovich.'

'I am he.' Varchenko glared at the man. 'Well, what is it?'

Doga reached into his jacket. One guard raised his weapon, the other pulled Doga's hand back out. It held a piece of paper. Varchenko sighed and extended his palm. Doga gave him the note and the two guards took a step back. Varchenko unfolded the piece of paper. It was on letterhead from Knysh Export. He read aloud so Blazhevich and the monitoring equipment could hear.

'*Dear Valeriy Ivanovich, let me thank you for accepting my business. We are a small export company and have found it hard to enter new markets; however, with your support I am sure we will succeed. I must apologise that I cannot be with you in person but other business matters preclude this. Kindest regards, Knysh Olexandr, General Director Knysh Export.*'

Varchenko handed the note to Blazhevich. 'Where is he?'

Doga shrugged. 'He is a busy man, Valeriy Ivanovich.'

Varchenko had turned red. 'Your director was meant to meet me here.' Doga was speechless. Varchenko held up his hand and several ALPHA men wearing balaclavas appeared and cuffed the two men. They made no attempt to struggle and seemed more shocked than scared as they were led away towards the garages.

Major Bodaretski spoke to Blazhevich on the radio. 'The target vehicle has reached the airport.'

'Let's watch.'

Varchenko agreed with Blazhevich. 'Inside.'

The two men took seats around the makeshift command centre. Three large, flatscreen monitors showed clear images of the airport and the truck as it passed through the gates. A cursory inspection of the driver's documents was made by the guard before he was waved on. The truck stopped in the designated area. Here it would await a customs inspection. On the military side of the facility the observation team had a high-powered camera set up. They were hidden inside a Ukrainian air-force building and had two minibuses parked out of sight.

'Where is he?' It was Varchenko again. He was frustrated that Pashinski hadn't showed.

'The second car?' Blazhevich thought of many explanations, including one that had Pashinski dead due to injuries sustained, but put this aside. Most probably Pashinski had decided enough was enough and had vanished again. If this was the case then all this was in vain. The landline for the house rang. Varchenko's bodyguard-cum-servant answered it; he had been instructed to carry on as normal. He entered the room and handed the wireless handset to his employer. Varchenko snorted. Now was not the time for calls.

'Yes?'

'General Varchenko, I do hope that I find you well?'

Varchenko almost choked on his tongue. It was Pashinski. He pressed the speakerphone button. 'I am as well as can be expected. Where are you?'

Blazhevich looked on. This was totally unexpected. Could the technical people get a trace?

'I have been delayed due to unforeseen circumstances, General. I am genuinely sorry that I cannot be with you. I take it that my shipment has arrived at the airport?'

'How would I know?'

Bull paused. 'Of course. Forgive me, you are at your *dacha*. General, I am trusting you with the safe passage of my goods. It would be embarrassing if they were to be stopped by customs for any reason.'

'They will not be.' Varchenko was taken by the audacity of the man, even now making veiled threats.

'I am glad. So, General, I will see you soon to celebrate our business, but for the moment I must say goodbye.'

The line went dead. The assembled men exchanged looks. What had the conversation meant?

'Vitaly Romanovich, you'd better look at this.' Major Bodaretski pointed at the screen, which showed the stationary truck at the airport, rear doors facing the camera. A large Mercedes saloon had parked next to it. As they watched, three men in suits stepped out. Blazhevich couldn't quite make out their faces. The customs officers tried to get the car to move but seemed to be placated by a document one of the passengers handed to them.

In Kyiv, Snow sat motionless and watched the live feed. Next to him sat Vickers and several agents who were in contact with Bodaretski. Unseen by all, Dudka had entered at the back of the tense room and taken a seat.

Vickers spoke. 'Is that him?'

'The height looks to be about the same but I can't make out the face.' Snow peered closer, willing the camera for more definition.

In Fontanka, the same thoughts were running through the minds of Blazhevich and Varchenko. 'All the action is there and I am here.' Varchenko wasn't happy to be dealing with this at arm's length. 'We must go to the airport.'

'*No.*' Blazhevich was being firm. That was a crazy suggestion.

'You dare to order me around?' Varchenko's voice echoed in the high-ceilinged room.

'We stay here at the command post. Those are my orders.' He didn't have time for this.

Varchenko stood; Blazhevich and Bodaretski kept their gaze on the screens. Suddenly realising he was being blanked, Varchenko sat again and folded his arms. From his seat he could see the battered blue Lada. 'Get that thing out of my sight,' he bellowed over his shoulder. He wasn't used to being ignored and didn't quite know what to do.

On the screen, the loading doors of the truck were opened by the driver, the ramp lowered, and the two customs inspectors climbed aboard. Bodaretski spoke directly to the team leader at the airport.

'Any suspicious movement?'

'Nothing.'

'OK. Get the men in their ready positions. Once the inspection is over move in.'

'Understood.'

There was complete silence in both the control room in Fontanka and the monitoring room in Kyiv. Time slowed as many pairs of eyes scrutinised the feed. At the airport the assaulters retightened Kevlar vests and pulled down balaclavas, webbing was checked, and weapons were readied. The three cameras at the airport panned, zoomed in and out in an attempt to spot anything. The only movement apart from traffic at the gate came from customs officials popping in and out of the truck. Finally, after forty long and tense minutes, the two officials left the truck and handed the paperwork back to the driver.

'Stand by.' Bodaretski gave the ready signal; he checked in with the team leader then gave the order. 'Go. Go. Go.'

All the action happened at once. Two mini buses raced across the tarmac from the military side of the airport; the first stopped, disgorging armed men who fanned out around the customs inspection area. The second bus continued on towards the main gate where, as it was about to block the entrance, a car entered. The airport security on the gate drew their weapons but lowered them as the van flashed its sirens. Two assaulters jumped out and asked the guards about the car. The ALPHA driver now blocked the entrance. More ALPHA men tactically moved to the customs area from the adjacent hanger, weapons up. Three suited figures emerged from the customs office. They saw the armed assaulters and froze. Two raised their arms, the third kept his by his side.

Ivan Lesukov acted outraged. 'What in God's name is the meaning of this?'

His driver and the other passenger were pushed to the floor and plasticuffed, but he refused to move. The team leader, Ruslan Budt, arrived just in time to see Lesukov pushed face first into the floor. Suddenly a light went on. Budt turned to see a TV camera being pointed at the men, a woman holding a microphone one step behind. 'Turn that off!'

Two team members pushed the news crew back and hustled them into the customs building. Each of the three men on the ground was turned face up and Budt held his own camera close to their faces. Lesukov wasn't going to accept this without a fight.

'Who the hell are you? I'll have you arrested! I am a Moldovan businessman! Let me up!'

Snow spoke. 'He's not there. Pashinski isn't there.'

There was silence in both rooms once more. Dudka eventually spoke, causing heads to turn. 'Let us look at the shipment.'

The order was relayed to Budt, who had the 'prisoners' moved into the customs building and guarded. Budt entered the truck and, with a crowbar, opened the first case. It splintered open and so did its contents. Without showing any care for these, he dug around until he was sure that all the case did indeed contain was a pair of ornate wooden chairs.

Unknown location, Ukraine

Bull looked at the assembled men. There were only six of them: two of the Orly – the originals – and four others. They were his best men; he had ordered the others to leave. 'Any questions?' There were none. Bull continued. 'This will be our last operation in Ukraine. I know that for some of you this is your home. The risks are great but so is the reward. I will be leaving after this; if you choose to come with me you must understand that life may be very short and very dangerous.' The Orly would come, that went without saying; they had been with Captain Pashinski since Afghanistan. The remainder, who had worked for Knysh for the past few years, would, he believed, choose to stay. Bull nodded. 'We will attack tomorrow at midday.'

SBU Headquarters, Volodymyrska Street, Kyiv

'A shipment of wooden chairs!' Dudka had never been so angry. He stomped around his office and waved his arms.

At the other end of the telephone Blazhevich wasn't happy either. 'A consignment of chairs. The paperwork is one hundred per cent legal and stamped by the Moldovan customs authorities in Chisinau. Knysh Export is a fully legal Moldovan registered company.'

Dudka fell into his seat and placed the phone on his desk, pressing the speaker button. 'Exporting wooden chairs!' They had been hoodwinked. 'And what of Lesukov?'

'We have had to release him. We have no firm evidence on the man. He is the supplier of chairs to Knysh Export.'

'What!' Blazhevich repeated the information as Dudka poured himself two fingers of the pepper vodka he kept in his desk for special occasions. 'Sometimes, Vitaly, I feel as though the universe is against us.'

Blazhevich didn't know what to say so changed the subject. 'We still do not know where Pashinski is. We were unable to trace his call. I believe that General Varchenko may still be in danger.'

'I agree. Leave some bodyguards with him and bring the rest back to Kyiv.' He put the phone down and threw the vodka down his throat. The SBU had messed up again and this time very publicly. Questions would be asked in the Verhovna Rada. The prime minister's party would attack, demand resignations. The bandits from Donetsk would try to take over but his president would defend. What a farce. He poured the remainder of the bottle into his glass and drank again. Perhaps things had been easier under communism, when he could have shot a scapegoat or at the very least sent him to Siberia.

Chapter 25

Volodymyrska Street, Kyiv

Snow had been released and sat in Vickers's apartment in central Kyiv. Having given a full statement the SBU were content he didn't work for Pashinski and that he hadn't intentionally tried to kill the Berkut guard. The guard, who had now regained consciousness and was healing in a military hospital, had been approached by Dudka and agreed the case should go no further. Vickers was in the kitchen making them something to eat. Snow was absolutely shattered. The mental and physical toll on his body had been immense. He chased a couple of strong painkillers with the contents of his bottle of Obolon and watched the Ukrainian TV news. He couldn't believe what he was seeing, so turned the sound up. 'Alistair, you'll never believe this!'

Vickers appeared from around the corner. 'What?' He noticed the screen. 'What!'

Ivan Lesukov's indignant fat face filled half of the screen and the rest was taken up by the airport behind him.

'I want to press charges against these thugs who have attacked my employees and me!'

The reporter went on to ask him more questions as footage

played of the ALPHA team throwing him to the floor then attempting to snatch the camera. Lesukov's face was grave as he continued, 'I am a manufacturer of chairs. I have wanted to export for a long time and now have finally found a partner who can help me with this. Your prime minister and mine met to ensure that such exporting would be painless. I have followed all the rules and am here to say that it is not! Moldova continues to be oppressed by Ukraine!'

The interview continued for another minute with Lesukov hamming it up.

Snow started to laugh hysterically before choking on his beer. Vickers gave him a strange look. 'What's so funny?'

He knew it was the adrenaline release but couldn't help himself. 'It would be hard to arm the Taliban with Moldovan chair legs.'

Vickers looked on. He was not amused. The SBU had moved partly on his say-so, on intel he had got from Lesukov's own nephew. 'They'll try again. When things are quieter they will try again.'

Snow recovered. 'I know.' He became deadly serious. 'Pashinski is still out there somewhere.'

Vickers fetched the food; he enjoyed cooking. Penne pasta with feta cheese and rocket, the dish should have been, if he had managed to find a single place in Kyiv that sold rocket. They ate. Snow stuck with his beer while Vickers chanced white wine.

'Is this the end?' Snow asked the intelligence officer. Had Pashinski left?

Vickers held up his fork and furrowed his brow. 'Assessment. We now know that he is alive; we also know that Knysh was a "legend" he used to start a life here in Ukraine.' Vickers used the intelligence-officer term for a false identity. 'He has lost that life and any assets that may have gone with it. His house, his cars. So what does he do, we need to think; what does he need?' Vickers took a mouthful of pasta.

Snow swigged his beer. 'Money?' He drank some more. 'If he

was hired by Lesukov it must have been a big fee, large enough to make him take the risk. But now he won't get that.' Vickers concurred; Snow's reasoning was straightforward but logical. 'He's lost face too. He's ex-Special Forces like me, hates to lose.'

Vickers cut in. 'So maybe he won't let himself? Maybe he still thinks he can win.'

Snow wanted to follow. 'Explain?'

'Who's the person who made him lose face, the person he threatened?' Vickers's eyes were bright; he had something.

'Me?' Snow was still worried.

'You knew who he was – that was why you were dangerous – but now his cover is all but blown.'

Snow sipped more beer. 'OK, I get it. So now I'm no longer important to him he'll try to get…' Snow thought for a moment, his mind dulled by fatigue and alcohol. 'General Varchenko?'

Vickers gripped his fork like a lance. 'Correct. He tried to force Varchenko to export his weapons so he could get paid. He shot Varchenko's business partner to show he wasn't afraid of anyone. What did Varchenko do? He went to the SBU and they would have stopped the shipment.'

'If it had been weapons.'

'True,' Vickers conceded.

'So Varchenko owes him on both counts. Loss of face and loss of money?'

'Exactly.' Vickers was pleased. 'So he will not disappear, he will collect his debt.'

Both men ate the pasta in silence as they tried, through tired brains, to think of something.

'Have you got a file on Varchenko?' Snow had finished his plate.

'Yes, but I don't have it here. Why?'

'What does he have? What assets has he got that Pashinski can go after?'

Vickers closed his eyes in order to visualise the page from the dossier. 'Several small Soviet-style hotels, a couple of restaurants and part-ownership of Odessa Bank.'

'That's it!' Snow stood, unable to control his actions.

Vickers was taken aback. 'The bank?'

'What was Pashinski's MO?' He paced around the lounge; Vickers signalled that he should continue. 'He targets banks. Poznan, remember? He robbed the bank, so that's what he'll do now. He wants the money back that he's lost, and then some.'

Vickers was now on his feet and reaching for a pile of magazines. He retrieved the pocket-sized Kyiv business directory and found the banks section. He read the entry. 'Odessa Bank. Head office in Odessa, ten branches throughout Ukraine. Three in Kyiv.'

Fontanka, Odessa Oblast, Southern Ukraine

'We believe that Pashinski may attempt to rob your bank.' Blazhevich addressed the general in his study.

Varchenko's eyebrows arched. 'Then stop him.'

'If you help me I am sure we can.' Blazhevich had grown tired of the old man's superior manner. 'The bank has ten branches. Which would be the best target?'

Varchenko leant back in his study chair. 'The main bank is in Odessa, as you know. That is where the bigger safety deposit boxes are stored. But security is very tight and the bank is on the main street. The three in Kyiv deal with more money than the regional towns.'

'So you would suggest that he attacks one of the Kyiv branches?'

The man could be a fool, Varchenko thought. 'Yes, he will attack the branches in the capital.'

Blazhevich nodded; he had thought as much. 'Any idea which one?'

'They are equally large.'

Blazhevich turned to leave the room. Varchenko raised his voice. 'You are not taking back your men, I hope? He may still attack me here.'

Blazhevich leant on the doorframe. 'Some of "my men" will stay.'

'Perhaps I should employ this Snow?' Dudka mused. 'After all, Vitaly, he has provided us with this new lead.'

Blazhevich noted the dour tone in his boss's voice, even through his earpiece. 'We must move fast, Gennady Stepanovich; I believe the attack will be imminent.'

'Vitaly Romanovich, I have already ordered non-uniformed men to go to each branch and stay hidden. Others will pose as customers.' Kyiv had been the obvious choice but all three branches had to be covered. 'Come back to Kyiv.'

'Very well, Gennady Stepanovich, I am on my way.'

Chapter 26

Volodymyrska Street, Kyiv

Snow had slept fitfully. Images of Arnaud and Pashinski battled for space in his head. While his body had tried to shut down, he felt as though his brain had not. The theory was that dreams, and nightmares, were an attempt by the brain to figure out problems or file them away. Opening his eyes in the gloom of the near dawn, Snow felt nothing had been solved and that if his brain had been a room, the filing would be scattered across the floor. He was covered in sweat and shaking. He slowly untangled himself from the damp sheets and stood. His eyes adjusted to the inky blue light streaming through the window. It was just after 5 a.m. He walked to the bathroom, being careful not to bang against anything in the alien environment of Vickers's flat. Quickly and quietly he showered and dressed.

All had agreed he had better not return to his own flat. Bondarenko had been shopping and got him several fresh sets of clothes. The jeans were slightly baggy but his belt soon corrected this. Slipping on his own boots and fleece jacket, Snow left the flat and walked down the stairs. The early morning air was crisp and frost clung to the pavement. No traffic yet on the roads and only the occasional window light. Vickers would have tried to stop him from going but Snow would have gone anyway.

From his pocket Snow removed the page torn from the Kyiv business directory and looked again at the addresses he had already memorised. The first branch of Odessa Bank wasn't far from Vickers's flat. It was on Ivana Franka Street, a small avenue opposite the university botanical gardens that ran at a ninety-degree angle to Boulevard Taras Shevchenko at one end and Bogdan Khmelnitsky Street at the other. The bank nestled in between the Siemens Ukraine office and an upmarket restaurant.

Snow quickened his pace up the street. He had no idea what he expected to find but felt compelled to CTR each bank. After five minutes he arrived at the first address. He stayed across the street and leant against a building. As expected, nothing seemed out of the ordinary. A couple of parked cars sat on the pavement with the blue Siemens logo emblazoned on the side. The bank was silent. Its orange neon sign glowed eerily in the morning light. Snow crossed the road and walked past the building, glancing casually at the bank as he headed towards the junction with Khmelnitsky and the city centre. It was almost 6 a.m. as he passed the Opera House and headed for Khreshatik; the city had woken up. He saw one team of street cleaners with their water van, filling it at the side of the road, and several old women with traditional broomsticks sweeping the leaves and dust from the pavements. Soon the winter snows would come and then the equipment would be changed.

Snow liked this time of day; it was his time, when he could clear his mind and concentrate on pushing his body harder as he ran through the near-empty city streets. Only today his mind wasn't blank. He had a very serious objective; he had to find Pashinski. He passed Teatralna metro station and the early commuters who now hurried along the streets, getting the first metro or trolley bus of the day. Hitting Khreshatik he turned left past Tzum, the giant Soviet-era department store, and towards

Maidan; he didn't risk taking Pushkinskaya, which ran parallel.

The second branch was ahead. This was larger and on the far corner of the square. It, too, was empty and, with the exception of two uniformed men in their little guardbox outside, looked asleep. He stood on the other side of the road and took in the location. Roads passed the bank on either side at the corner, a hill, the music academy, and a cinema overlooked it from above, and the Hotel Khreshatik was opposite. Snow stood on the Maidan Square in front of the glass-fronted Globus shopping centre. The bank was very exposed. It seemed a likely target except for the fact that here, in the very heart of Kyiv, there would be thousands of people milling around who would either get in the way or report what they saw.

Then he saw it. A silver VW Passat arrived at the bank and three men stepped out. Two of them moved with confidence while the third, who was smaller, retrieved a bunch of keys from his pocket. Snow froze, his eyes locked on the bank as the heavy front door opened and the night security guard warmly shook hands. As the three men entered, Snow saw the other two being introduced to the watchman. As if to confirm his suspicion, Snow noted the government-issue number plate of the Passat as it pulled out into traffic and drove off uphill. He cursed. SBU undercover agents. If he'd seen them, he was sure Bull had too. He continued to observe for a few more minutes before crossing the road and walking past the bank and making for the third branch, which was in Podil.

Vickers felt a throbbing at his temples as soon as he sat up. He had never been a big drinker and now, after hitting forty, could handle the effects even less. Perhaps he should eat more and run less? He suddenly remembered why his head hurt and stood. He pulled on a T-shirt and pair of tracksuit bottoms, and left his bedroom. He knocked on the door of the spare room: it moved, unlocked. He looked in – the bed was empty. He rushed to the bathroom, then the kitchen. Snow had gone. He admonished himself and picked up his mobile. At the other end the phone rang but wasn't answered. What the hell was Snow thinking? He had spoken to the SBU and warned them of their fears. The SBU would take care of it, not him – and not Aidan Snow.

Podil, Kyiv

Snow looked at the display. *Alistair Vickers*. He ignored the call; he'd call later, once he had looked at each branch. He was now walking through central Podil, the oldest part of central Kyiv, just passing a café. The branch here looked over Kontraktova Plosha, the square at the bottom of the steep Andrivskyi Uzviz, and Podil's central street, Sahaydachnoho. Snow walked towards the small green at the north end of the square and, leaning against a bench, pretended to tie up his bootlace. This was again a very open location with several roads intersecting, creating eight immediate escape routes at various places around the square, up the hill behind him, right back the way he had come, left towards Obolon, and down towards the river. Too many routes, he immediately thought.

He checked his watch; it was now almost seven-fifteen and the streets were busy with traffic and more workers. He couldn't stay long as he looked like the only person not in a hurry to get somewhere. Snow surveyed the area, looking for anyone like himself, who looked out of place. Two men stood with plastic coffee cups on the corner of Sahaydachnoho, smoking; a group waited at the bus stop but, apart from that, everyone was moving. Snow turned and walked up Frolivska where it led on to the bottom of Andrivskyi Uzviz. He suddenly remembered something Mitch had once told him. Something that suddenly ruled this branch out of the equation. The residence of the American Ambassador to Ukraine was less than two hundred yards away in Borychiv Street. It was always manned by US marines in addition to having at least two Berkut guards on alert at all times, especially so after the recent threats to US embassies. If anything happened in the square, the Berkut were less than two minutes away. So there it was, the only logical target, the first branch he had been to, on the side street by the botanical gardens. He pulled out his phone and called up Vickers.

'Where are you?' Vickers was irritated.

'Podil. Listen, I know which branch they're going to hit.'

'What? How?'

Snow explained his reasoning. 'The Podil branch is too close to the American residence and the Khreshatik branch is too open. It has to be Ivana Franka.' Snow fought for breath as he half-jogged up the steep hill. On foot he could be there in less than twenty minutes. The start of the rush-hour traffic would make a taxi slower.

'Aidan, the SBU have each branch covered. I'm sure they can stop a bank robbery.'

Snow lost his temper. 'This will be a full-on military assault. Agents with handguns will not stop them.'

Vickers was taken aback but took note. 'I'll tell Blazhevich. Now go directly to the embassy.'

'Yeah, OK.' Snow ended the call. He was minutes from the embassy but had no intention of visiting. It was 7.35, still too early to hit the bank but not too early to take up an OP. He zipped the phone safely away in his pocket and pumped his legs up the rest of the steep hill. At the top he rested momentarily, sweat dripping from his forehead and jeans clammy against his thighs, before heading on a direct route for the target. The streets had grown more congested as Kyiv was now fully awake on this overcast winter's day. Snow stopped at a kiosk and bought a bottle of water and several chocolate bars. He ate one and stuffed the rest into his jacket pockets. This was his first food of the day and he had no idea when he would be able to eat next.

As he neared the bank he slowed and started to focus on his surroundings. Finally reaching the corner of the target address, he looked for somewhere to hide or at least wait as unobtrusively as possible. The buildings on this narrow street were six storeys high and cast shadows, sun permitting, onto the pavement below. In front of each building was a small, grassy area, which, in the case of the restaurant, formed a summer seating area, and for the Siemens office had been removed to provide extra parking. Snow leaned against the corner of the nearest building, cursing silently. There was nowhere on the street itself he could wait; he had to get access to one of the roofs. The buildings directly opposite the bank were residential. Snow tried the first door. Locked with a keypad. Then the next. It opened and in he went as though he were a resident. He climbed the stairs to the very top and was met by a padlocked, mesh-style metal door. *Shit.* This time he swore loudly. He looked around for anything that might be able to prise apart the door. On the floors below, the stairwell had been freshly whitewashed, as befitted an upmarket building, but here at the top, where residents never ventured, the old, flaking paint and rotting windows had been left. Snow grabbed at the nearest windowsill and prised the wood free. It was damp with rot and crumbled in his hand. He kicked the door with frustration and, to his surprise, it gave at the hinge. He kicked again with more force and was now able to lever himself between it and the wall. The hinge was rotten too; lazy maintenance staff had simply painted over the rust and not treated it. Snow was up the final steps within two minutes and had the flimsy wooden roof door open in another three. He paused in the doorway. There had been no sounds from below and he didn't want to risk meeting anyone up top.

Two minutes went by before he edged on to the roof. To his relief it was as solid as the day Lenin's mother had built it. He crouched, keeping himself below the level of the parapet, and scouted the rooftop. Even though they had the same number of floors, he now noticed that all the buildings on this side of the street were slightly higher than those opposite. It had obviously been a drinking day for the architects. To the right he could see the botanical gardens and directly in front of him was the bank. Snow eased himself forward and peered over the edge. People milled about below and the noise of traffic wafted upwards. He looked at the rooftops; those opposite him were empty. He sat back against the parapet. It was impossible to keep a visual on the bank without being exposed to anyone on the other side of the street. He had a decision to make. He would wait for the business day to start and then risk it. He had to risk it.

British Embassy, Kyiv

'We have men at each branch.' Blazhevich had already told his British 'colleague' this twice. 'If they attack we will detain them.'

Vickers had his mobile in his free hand and was again trying to reach Snow. He spoke back into his office handset. 'Snow thinks he knows which one they will hit: the Ivana Franka branch.'

'Yes, that is the most obvious if an attack were to take place, but this is all still only guesswork. Not that I don't think it will happen.' The deployment had been hastily arranged the night before on Snow's 'hunch'. The SBU were doing all in their power to stop any robbery and bring this chain of events to a close. 'Alistair, we have it covered.'

Ivana Franka Street, Kyiv

Snow rolled over and raised his head slowly. It was now almost ten. The Ukrainian banks opened an hour later than those in the UK. Cars were now parked on one side of the road as were two vans. Something stirred in his memory. The vans were parked

278

at either end of the street... In Poznan the street had been sealed by two car bombs, two vans, leaving an escape route for Bull's men. But if this was them, where was the getaway vehicle? Snow looked further past the street to Boulevard Taras Shevchenko. Cars could park on the near side of the road as the pavement was wider. He envisaged several high-powered saloons quietly awaiting the carnage. This was it; it was going to happen here!

SBU Headquarters, Volodymyrska Street, Kyiv

Blazhevich choked on his coffee. '*Motherf—*' He rarely swore and never in the presence of women, and had caught himself just in time. The young female agent was red-faced. He took the phone she held out and spoke to the lead agent in Odessa. Major Bodaretski repeated his news. Armed men were attacking Odessa Bank's head office branch on Deribasovskiy, Odessa's premium boulevard. Varchenko's personal assistant was in the branch and had phoned his master in a state of trouser-wetting panic. Both militia and ALPHA had been despatched.

'Anatoly, get there and give me a live update.' Blazhevich couldn't believe his bad luck; he had barely returned from that very city and this had happened. He felt powerless now he was at arm's length, fighting by remote control without even a live image. He called Varchenko's *dacha* and told the remaining guards to stay vigilant; they might yet be attacked.

Ivana Franka Street, Kyiv

Snow felt his phone vibrate. 'Snow.'
    'Aidan,' Vickers answered. 'They've hit Odessa.'
    'What? Say again?'
    'They've hit the head office in Odessa.'

Snow kept his eyes on the bank below as he tried to take in what the man from the embassy had said. 'When?'

'Half an hour ago. Our Odessa British Council staff saw it on local TV.' Vickers's next call would be to Blazhevich.

Snow thought quickly. 'What are the details?'

'Gunmen entered the bank and shots were fired. Too much of a coincidence to be anyone else.'

On the roof Snow shook his head. 'I don't care what's happening in Odessa. It's going to happen here, I'm telling you. The same MO as Poznan. They have vans at each end to block the road.'

Vickers sighed. 'I think you should be happy we were almost right. They did attack, as you said.' Vickers was somewhat relieved that Kyiv hadn't been targeted, but also annoyed they had been wrong in their target assessment.

'Alistair, I'm on the bloody roof overlooking the bank and I can tell you they're going to attack.' He couldn't be imagining things, could he?

Vickers finally lost his temper. 'Listen. I'll speak to Vitaly and relay your fears. In the meantime, stop buggering about and acting like a sodding pigeon and come down from your perch.'

Odessa Bank, Kyiv

The portly bank clerk was nervous, so nervous in fact that he had spent most of his morning darting to the toilet, which he shared with the other tellers. His manager had suggested he go home, that he had probably eaten something bad, but he had refused. His instructions, from the man who paid him in cash, had been insistent. Stay at your station; it must look normal. The clerk swallowed hard as he popped the second lot of indigestion pills. He wet his face and tried to tidy himself up in the cracked washroom mirror. He subconsciously caressed the new platinum

Rolex that hung snugly on his left wrist, hidden by his shirt cuff. Today was the day. The day that a new client was to 'withdraw' his funds. It was 11 a.m. 'Remain calm and they will never know that you were involved', the man had said, 'then you can resign, blame it on stress, and live a life of luxury.' But he had no way to contact his new master, no way to warn him about the two new security guards who had started work this morning. There were also two more ALPHA officers who had entered before working hours with the bank manager, but neither he nor the other staff had seen this. This had been the same for all three of the Kyiv branches. One more hour and that was it. He returned to his position and nodded once more at the security guards who sat in the banking hall, machine pistols at their sides. He mustn't draw any more attention to himself.

Deribasovskiy Boulevard, Odessa

The boulevard wasn't as wide as those in central Kyiv but looked much more European. The majority of shops and restaurants had a chic boutique feel. The street had now been sealed off at each end and marksmen were placed on roofs and in windows. Major Bodaretski stood behind a militia wagon and assessed the scene. The militia were keeping curious residents and shoppers from entering the area or leaving their apartments. Gribakin, the most senior militia official present, was worried. He had been accustomed to an easy life of petty crime and traffic violations, not gunmen on the streets. In between mopping the cold sweat from his brow with a greying handkerchief, he nodded profusely and gave Bodaretski his full attention and cooperation. One of his juniors, Kiril Kononchuk, had been on duty nearby and actually seen the men entering the bank. Bodaretski had asked questions.

'How many did you see?'

'Four.'

'How were they dressed?'

'Jeans, jackets, and ski masks.'

'What weapons were they carrying?'

'I saw two pistols and two AK-47s.'

'Did you see where they came from?'

'Through the park.'

'So you saw no means of escape? No vehicle?'

'No.'

Bodaretski had then dismissed the young man. Something didn't add up. He spoke to Gribakin. 'How were they planning to escape?'

'I don't know. Is it important?' the militia commander asked, showing his naivety.

Bodaretski gave him a concerned look; it was basic logic and common sense. 'If these men are robbing a bank they expect to leave with the money.'

'Oh, yes, of course.' The militia man reddened with embarrassment.

'Do you know if they were challenged inside?'

Gribakin shook his head. 'Not unless the security guards drew their pistols.'

'Then why draw attention to the raid by letting off rounds?' Bodaretski glanced again at the bank. The gunmen had run from the small park on the opposite side of the boulevard (with masks on and weapons visible), past a busy restaurant complete with customers on the terrace enjoying the mild local climate. Why? To draw attention to themselves! It was a diversion. He picked up a loudhailer and handed it to Gribakin. 'Talk to them. See what they want.'

Gribakin swallowed hard. 'Me?'

'Yes, you. Here.' He handed the officer a Kevlar vest. 'Put this over your shirt and under your jacket. Just in case.'

'Just in case?' The man shook as he took the vest with his free hand.

'I want to know what they want. They didn't come to rob the bank,' continued Bodaretski.

Gribakin was too nervous to see the point his ALPHA colleague was making. 'What shall I say?'

'Try to get them to talk. Empathise with them. Say they won't be harmed if they give themselves up. Surely you've seen enough cop films to know what to say.'

Gribakin smiled weakly, imagining himself as Samuel L Jackson in *The Negotiator*, or his hero, De Niro. 'But isn't it better to use the bank's phone?'

'Get their attention first.' Bodaretski had a plan.

SBU Headquarters, Volodymyrska Street, Kyiv

'That is not good.' Dudka looked at his young agent. 'Any fatalities?'

'None that we can confirm.' Blazhevich had received a sit rep from Odessa. The raiders had entered the bank and fired indiscriminately before demanding the contents of the vaults. They were still inside and had ten known hostages. Major Bodaretski had stated his suspicions about the gunmen's motives and was awaiting the green light from Dudka to storm the building. Both men had been looking at the hastily faxed blueprints and plans. Bodaretski was an experienced Special Forces ALPHA officer. He explained his plans via speakerphone. 'We can go in through the roof and first floor. At that exact time we will send smoke grenades into the ground-floor windows.' It was a classic assault model but nevertheless effective.

'Is it not too soon?' Blazhevich didn't want to endanger any of the hostages. 'What if they intend to blow themselves and the hostages up?'

Bodaretski's tinny voice filled the room. 'We do not believe they possess any explosives. They seem either very amateur or very brazen. As I say, we have not found a means of exfiltration.'

'Which is why they may be about to blow themselves up,' Blazhevich persisted.

Dudka rubbed his chin. He could see the dangers but had to assess the situation quickly. Decision made – he had no alternative. Ukraine could not be seen to be weak; they could not wait as the Russians had with the Moscow Theatre siege. These were criminals and not terrorists. 'Execute your assault plan, Major.' He had potentially just ordered the deaths of innocent members of the public, the very people he was sworn to protect.

Bodaretski closed the phone and returned to Gribakin.

'What have they got to say?'

'So far, nothing.'

'Keep it up.'

'I will.' Gribakin was now almost smiling; he felt he was doing a good job. Bodaretski gave him a nod and walked away. He hadn't told the militia officer of his plans. The pleading voice on the loudhailer would be a diversion in the initial moments of the assault. He entered the neighbouring building and got to the roof. Nine ALPHA assaulters were waiting for him, suited up in flame-retardant dark-blue nomex coveralls. He nodded. As the team adjusted webbing straps and balaclavas, Bodaretski gave the signal to the team on the ground. After a final check of their rubber-soled boots, his team crossed from their roof to the next. The buildings were terraced and had no gaps between them. The group split into two; four men unlooped abseil ropes and secured them on the parapet while Bodaretski's group, in tactical formation, made for the skylight and tried the lock. It opened and the scout dropped slowly, headfirst, through the gap on a rope. He gave a 'thumbs up' and the rest of the team entered the building. At that exact moment, flash-bangs cascaded through the ground-floor windows, immediately followed by the four assailers in teams of two. The loudhailer went quiet as Gribakin dropped it and looked on open-mouthed.

Bodaretski now took the scout position and, with his suppressed HPK5 on semi-automatic, made for the central staircase. The first floor was empty, secure; now the ground floor, with its banking hall, offices and vaults, remained. He heard shots, barks from an AK, followed by almost inaudible whispers from an HPK5. The assaulters' weapons had suppressors fitted; this meant any sounds of gunfire would be coming from the X-rays – the bad guys. He stepped over a dead gunman on the landing and hit the ground floor. Tactically but speedily he led the snake of men along the hall; each member had a specific arc of fire to cover and concentrated on this only. Every office door hid potential gunmen and death; each was opened in turn.

Suddenly bullets impacted all around him; two hit his Kevlar vest, spinning him left and into the wall. He dropped, dazed, as bullets ripped back over his head at the gunman. He was scooped up as the team passed him and entered the banking hall, leaving the third gunman dead. As the smoke cleared, the sole remaining gunman lay facedown on the floor pleading for mercy. His weapon was kicked away as the assault team checked the assumed hostages for any more weapons. Each was plasticuffed and led out through the front doors of the bank before being thrown facedown on to the grass of the nearby park... Several were wounded, two badly needing stretchers. He hoped these hadn't been ALPHA bullets. Bodaretski unclipped his vest and held his side. The Kevlar vest had let him cheat death, but not before allowing the rounds to crack a rib and cause severe bruising. The whole assault had lasted a mere two minutes.

He pulled the striped ski mask off the now cuffed and cowering gunman. 'Your friends are dead. Unless you want to join them, I suggest you talk.'

Eyes reddened by smoke, the man nodded. He was very young and looked beaten. Where his checked shirt had been torn, Bodaretski noticed a tattoo bearing a military insignia.

'Who sent you here and what for?'

'He promised to pay me $20,000 if I could rob this bank.' The smoke had made his voice raspy.

So little? Bodaretski was surprised. 'Who promised?' The suspect coughed. 'Who was this man?'

'I don't know his name. He said he would arrange everything. He said there would be a van waiting by the park and then a boat to take us to Turkey.'

Bodaretski walked away; he had heard enough. He had recognised the tattoo. This boy was a rent-a-thug. One of the ever-growing number of ex-army conscripts who had no work once their time had been served. He retrieved his phone and once again dialled Blazhevich. He had been right.

Chapter 27

Ivana Franka Street, Kyiv

Snow had ignored Vickers's request and stayed put overlooking the bank. He watched the man exit the bank. He noticed that his suit jacket was a size too large, big enough to conceal a Kevlar vest. He had to be one of the SBU men. He lit a cigarette and stood in the sunshine, which was now breaking through the winter sky. *Get back inside, you idiot*, Snow muttered to himself. A second man exited a minute later and bummed a cigarette from the first. They exchanged a joke and smiles, the tension clearly gone. There was a sudden creak from behind him.

The door was opening. Snow ducked and pivoted to face the noise before moving as fast as he could to the blind side of the opening door. With the wood separating them, he saw the point of a Kalashnikov. Snow slammed the door on the unseen figure, causing him to lose his balance and fall. Snow pushed past the flapping door and fell on the newcomer. The intruder tried to roll away but Snow forced his left forearm into his nose with as much force as he could muster. The gunman grunted and dropped the weapon, bringing his arms up to protect himself. *Mistake*, thought Snow, as he slammed his right fist into the man's temple, then again into his nose. Blood and bone burst over his victim's face and his legs kicked wildly. The eyes of the attacker met those of his prey and Snow realised that this was Dmitro, the sentry he had tussled with at the restaurant, the man who had saved Pashinski. Desperately, Dmitro's arms punched and his legs kicked. Snow pressed down again with his forearm but now on the neck. This time he would choke the bastard.

Suddenly, a glint from the corner of his eye. Instinctively Snow rolled left and clear and up to his feet. His opponent was standing quickly, grunting like an animal as blood flew from what used to be his nose, a commando knife in his right hand, and he lunged forward. Snow took a step back and saw the wild look in Dmitro's eyes. He lunged again; this time Snow moved to one side and took a step forward, foreshortening the strike. The knife ripped through his jacket under his left arm but passed clean through. Snow grabbed the arm with his left and the wrist with his right. In a well-practised judo move he twisted the arm backwards and down. Dmitro tried to move away, tried to punch with his free arm, but his own momentum worked against him. Snow's left elbow was on his neck, forcing him down. His face hit the gravel. Snow kept hold of the arm and twisted, hearing the shoulder joint pop. Dmitro let out an animal scream and finally dropped the knife. Changing elbow for left shin, Snow grabbed the knife and plunged it into the side of the man's shoulder.

'Where is Pashinski? Where is Pashinski?' he yelled into the ear no more than six inches from his mouth. Dmitro tried to struggle. Snow applied more pressure and repeated his demand. 'It doesn't have to end like this. Where is Pashinski! Where is Pashinski?'

Cheek pressed against gravel and blood in his mouth, Dmitro replied, 'In bed with your mother!'

Snow now knew he would get nothing out of the soldier and plunged the serrated knife into the man's neck. The entire body bucked and twisted but it was too late. Within seconds Dmitro was dead, blood bubbling out through the wound. Snow looked at his victim. Strangely he felt no remorse for Pashinski's hired killer. He rolled away and caught his breath, wiping his bloodied hands on his jeans. This was the final proof. Still trying to calm his breathing he checked the corpse, undid the knife from its lanyard, and picked up both it and the rifle, which lay ten feet away on the roof. The chamber was full and two magazines were taped together, Chechen-style, to quicken a reload. Snow moved cautiously back into the building and saw a small satchel on the steps. Inside he found several flash-bangs and two more spare magazines. He quickly retook his position at the parapet and looked over. The wind had carried away the sounds of the scuffle so that, six floors below, it had been unheard over the roar of the nearby traffic. The two SBU men still stood outside, winding down; the news of the Odessa raid had obviously been passed on. Snow looked along the small road in an attempt to find the rest of Pashinski's men. He noticed two men in boiler suits exiting the van at the intersection with Bogdan Khmelnitsky Street. It was happening now.

He raised the Kalashnikov and aimed the sights at the van. At this distance he could hit the target, but not with real accuracy. The weapon was for short-range assault and suppression, not precision targeting. He held the target as the figures put packs on their backs. He squinted to get a better view of the target a hundred metres away; now he noticed the black woollen hats. There was movement. A third man exited the bank and excitedly shouted at the other two. They instantly threw away their cigarettes and, eyes scanning the street tactically, retreated into the bank. Snow switched back to the van. The men were approaching. He couldn't yet see a weapon but now one was reaching into the pack for something and the other started to pull down the hat… no balaclava. He had seen enough. Switching the AK to semi-automatic he put first pressure on the trigger, waited until his sights were filled, took second pressure and… 7.62-calibre rounds impacted the pavement around the lead figure. The man grabbed at his legs and fell. The second immediately swung his assault rifle round from under the pack and shot wildly back up the street. Firing one-handed, he dragged his comrade into the shadow of the restaurant. Snow shot again and the first figure went limp as rounds impacted into his chest. Now noise from below. Nearer, at the other end of the road, three armed assaulters exited the second van. Rounds zipped past Snow. Chunks of concrete were kicked up by those that fell short. He threw himself back flat on the roof and changed mags. Five guns against one. He couldn't win if he stayed put. He threw two flash-bangs over the edge, counted, heard them explode, then popped back up and fired the second mag at the street below. He had to move. He ran back into the apartment block and down the stairs as fast as his feet would carry him.

'*Blat,*' Bull swore. This was not the plan. One man down, one compromised, and a team of four left. 'GO, GO.' He wasn't going to stop now. The remaining team members reached the bank to find the heavy security doors shut. Suddenly, from above, there were more shots, this time from the bank. The SBU men inside had regained the advantage. There was no easy way in. Sirens filled the air and he saw flashing lights in front of him. Without hesitation he detonated both vans. Shockwaves spread up the entire street, windows shattered, and car alarms went off. Time seemed to slow as debris fell. They moved, Bull out in front racing for the farthest apartment block. Shooting the door open, Bull raced inside. Back on the street gunfire again came from the bank. A Ukrainian, Taras, went down: clean headshot. Another stumbled – hit in the side. The third assaulter changed course and dived into the restaurant patio.

Snow exited the neighbouring building at the same time. ALPHA troops wearing full BDU – battle dress uniform – entered the street past the burning van. Rounds blew bits of doorframe away. He had no time to think. Snow ran at the next open door and threw himself inside; as he looked up the lift doors closed on a face he recognised.

Bull was suddenly alone. He hit the button for the sixth floor. Weapon trained on the door, he quickly ascended. He pulled out the tactical radio and summoned the helicopter. One to pick up.

Blazhevich was on the line to the bank. Just as Major Bodaretski had warned, Odessa had been a diversion, a feint. He could hear gunfire outside as he sped crazily through the Kyiv lunchtime traffic, sirens blaring and lights blazing. 'Have they been stopped?' he demanded.

'Yes,' came the reply from the agent in the bank.

'Have you got Pashinski?' he asked.

'We don't know,' replied the agent.

Before he had time to analyse the reply he was snarled in a jam caused by the car bomb. Blazhevich left his car in the middle of the road and ran towards the noise. A militia officer shouted at him, Blazhevich waved his shield and pushed him aside. Dark smoke rose from the remains of the van and broken glass crunched underfoot. He squeezed past the wreckage and on to the streets. Shots were being fired in his direction by the ALPHA squad, not at him but towards the restaurant. Two gunmen lay in the doorway. One unmoving on his back, the other crouching behind him trying to line up the sights on an… RPG!

Blazhevich pulled out his government-issue Glock and fired on the move. The first two shots were wide but his third grazed the gunman's shoulder. *Whoompf!* The rocket-propelled grenade left the launcher and flew almost in slow motion down the street until it impacted against the farthest apartment block some three metres above the ALPHA men. Blazhevich continued to run and fire until his clip was empty. The firing stopped as the approaching Special Forces team realised their target was no more. Panting, Blazhevich reached the gunman, only to find him dead, not from his bullet but from a headshot. The street was now secure. He scanned the area. Four bodies lay where they had fallen; each wore a black, three-hole balaclava. He walked towards the bank and, as he did, searched for Pashinski.

Snow leant against the wall to catch his breath and changed magazines on the Kalashnikov. Above him he heard the roof door bang shut. Pashinski. Snow took several deep breaths and moved up the remaining stairs. This was it. He kicked open the door and sprinted across the roof.

A clean shot. Bull stood and emptied the clip on his pursuer. The Kalashnikov spat a deadly shower of lead. Each bullet registered a supersonic crack. On impacting, the bullets traced a neat line up the wall until the last found its target. The round hit Snow mid-stride in the left leg, punching a neat hole through his thigh. Snow let out an inhuman scream and smashed into the gravel-covered roof, gun flying from his hand and over the edge to the street below. As he skidded to a halt, gravel cut deeply into his hands and cheek, ripping the skin. Snow lay crumpled against the parapet. His left leg a bloody mess. He felt no pain, only a cold sensation all over his body. So this was what it felt like to be shot? His vision blurred; he made out a shape approaching.

Bull walked swiftly. In one drilled, fluid movement he swung the empty assault rifle behind his back and unholstered his Glock 9mm. Holding it out in front of him he stopped six feet away, instantly recognising Snow. Snow made a grab for the commando knife and tried to stand. His leg buckling, he fell to his knees. His lungs still fought for oxygen as he raised the knife at the blurry figure. Bull pulled the trigger and a single bullet impacted into the mass of Snow's right shoulder, throwing him flat on his back. The knife now dangled from its lanyard at his side. His vision blurred further and his body started to shake. Even as he sweated he felt cold, so very cold. A boot hit him in the groin and he instinctively tried to ball his body. The knife was ripped away and discarded.

Bull took a step forward, the Glock trained on Snow's skull.

'So, here we are again. We could have worked together, in another life. You are a good soldier, but a very bad hero.'

There was a hint of amusement in his voice.

Snow looked up to meet his executioner's gaze and once more saw the green, snake-like eyes boring into him. Spitting blood he replied, 'And you're a shit villain.'

Bull laughed as his finger exerted more pressure on the trigger. '*Dasvidanya*, Mr—'

A high-velocity shot rang out before Snow had time to react. Bull's head was replaced by a crimson cloud. The body remained erect for a split second before collapsing across Snow's legs. Pinned to the floor, Snow felt a darkness encircle him as he lost consciousness. Fifty metres away the door on another rooftop was delicately closed.

Epilogue

Aurora Hospital, Helsinki, Finland

Vickers pushed open the door. Raising the blinds, the glow of the mid-morning sun warmed the austere walls of the white room. He gave the flowers to the nurse who was tagging along behind him, who promptly put them into a vase. Sensing the patient stir, he sat. Snow slowly opened his eyes. Blurred at first, his vision gradually cleared and a ceiling light swam into focus.

'Good morning, Aidan.'

'Where am I?' Snow's voice was faint.

'Relax, you're in a Finnish hospital bed.'

Turning his head to the right, Snow saw Vickers's familiar face. 'I knew it couldn't be heaven if you were here. What happened?'

Snow tried to sit and felt a dull ache in his shoulder; instinctively he reached for it with his left hand and felt the heavy strapping. Vickers read his mind. 'You're going to make a full recovery apart from a few more scars to add to your collection.'

As Vickers poured him a glass of water he filled Snow in on

294

the events surrounding his shooting. Bull had been killed instantly by a sniper's bullet. Snow had then been collected and lifted by emergency air ambulance operated by Jet Flight Air Ambulance Finland to a hospital in Helsinki that the embassy had an agreement with. For a while it had been touch and go; the artery in Snow's left leg had been partially severed by the AK round, but fortunately for him the flow had been stemmed in time to stop him bleeding out altogether.

'Blazhevich found you and put a tourniquet on your leg. That's what kept you alive.'

Snow smiled. 'Remind me to send him a card.'

'Ah, almost forgot.' Vickers handed Snow a handmade card. 'From the children at school.'

Snow reached for the card, winced, but then broke into a smile as he read it.

Vickers broke his concentration. 'But something doesn't make sense.'

Snow frowned 'What?'

'Pashinski was shot by a sniper but there wasn't an ALPHA sniper present. None of the ballistics match the weapons used either by Pashinski's men or the SBU.'

Snow's mind was still foggy. 'Then who?'

Vickers shrugged. 'No idea, but it was a professional. "One shot one kill", I believe the saying goes.'

Snow closed his eyes and smiled widely. He didn't care. After ten years and the death of a friend, it was finally over: Tauras 'The Bull' Pashinski was no more. The green eyes would never trouble him again, except, he thought coldly, in nightmares. 'What now?' Snow asked, easing himself higher and wincing in doing so.

Vickers took a passport from his jacket pocket. 'Have you ever met a Herr Dietrich Schaeffer?' Snow's mouth smiled but he shook his head. 'Well, he wants the Kyiv militia to press charges against the Russian who mugged him and stole his passport. This passport.' Vickers now genuinely smiled for the first time in weeks, and nodded as he spoke. 'I believe you told me you found this on the train? Didn't you?'

Palace Gardens, Vienna, Austria

'I'm not who you think I am.'

They had walked hand in hand through the palace gardens and had now reached the terrace. Bernadette paused. 'What do you mean?'

'I am not American.' He turned and faced her.

She looked him in the eyes, a strand of hair falling across her face. 'Are you being silly, Mark?'

Gorodetski paused before speaking to her for the first time in her native language. 'Bernadette, I am not American.'

She let go of his hand. 'You speak German?'

'Not as well as English.'

'And your accent is different.'

'I am from Tula; it's a town near Moscow.'

She was bemused. 'You are Russian?'

'*Da.*'

'I don't understand anything. What is your real name? Who are you?' Her cheeks flushed as red as the uniform she wore to work.

'My name is Sergey.'

She was suddenly angry. 'Why did you trick me? To sleep with me? Is that what you wanted? Do you have other girlfriends?'

She continued to speak but he could not hear her words; rather, he imagined he could hear the heart beneath her ample breast breaking. He had thought long and hard about telling her the truth and eventually decided to ignore his training and listen to his own heart. It was the scariest thing he had ever had to do. He looked deeply into her eyes. 'I love you.'

'What?' She stopped mid-sentence. It was the first time in her life that a man had said that to her and meant it.

The statement surprised him. 'I have loved you from the first moment I saw you. I can't stop thinking about you.'

'Then why did you lie to me?' Her arms were now folded.

'My work means that sometimes I have to change who I am, my identity.'

Again she was puzzled. 'Your work? What are you?'

'I used to be in the Russian Army – Special Operations Unit.' He felt relieved; he now had nothing to hide.

Bernadette looked into the eyes of the man she had started to fall in love with. She sensed he was telling the truth but there was something, perhaps a pain behind the eyes. 'Like a spy?'

'*Da*. I had to pretend to be Mark Peters because it wasn't safe for you or anyone else to know who I really was.'

'And now?' What was going to happen to them?

'And now it is safe for you, but not me. I can't be Mark any more. I am Sergey and I am the man who loves you.'

'What about us?' There was a tear in her eye.

'I want to be with you.' He reached out to take her hand...

'Mr Johnson? Mr Johnson...' a voice called in the darkness.

Gorodetski opened his eyes. The fresh face of the American Airlines stewardess smiled. 'Sorry to wake you but you need to fasten your seatbelt. We're about to land at JFK.'

'Oh, thanks.' The passenger now travelling under the name of Mark Johnson sat up, rubbed his eyes, and fastened his seatbelt. Why hadn't he gone back to Vienna and really told her who he was? Why hadn't he said he loved her? He knew the reason. He had a dark stain on his soul that he could never rid himself of: the cold-blooded murders of a father and his son. He shivered as he remembered the shots hitting both targets, the images he would always see when his eyes were closed. He could never be forgiven and he could never forget. Turning to his right he raised the blind and, from his business-class window seat, watched the sun rise over New York. It was a new day.

Dear Reader,

Thank you so much for taking the time to read this book – we hope you enjoyed it! If you did, we'd be so appreciative if you left a review.

Here at HQ Digital we are dedicated to publishing fiction that will keep you turning the pages into the early hours. We publish a variety of genres, from heartwarming romance, to thrilling crime and sweeping historical fiction.

To find out more about our books, enter competitions and discover exclusive content, please join our community of readers by following us at:

🐦 @HQDigitalUK

f facebook.com/HQDigitalUK

Are you a budding writer? We're also looking for authors to join the HQ Digital family! Please submit your manuscript to:

HQDigital@harpercollins.co.uk.

Hope to hear from you soon!

Read on for a sneak peek at *Cold Black*,
the next book in the Aidan Snow
series…

Prologue

Aidan Snow sat on the examination table wearing only a pair of black boxer shorts. Dr Durrani poked Snow's left leg with a gloved index finger, his large, bright eyes focusing intently.

'Hmm. The incision seems to have healed nicely; the reduction in scar tissue is what we would have hoped for.' Turning his attention to the right leg, Durrani continued. 'I'm not as happy with this one, but then you did leave it rather a long time before coming to see me.'

Snow nodded. It hadn't been his idea to visit the doctor, but a direct command from Jack Patchem, his handler at SIS. Patchem's view was that no undercover operative could 'blend in' if he was riddled with scars. Snow saw no reason to complain.

'Now the shoulder. Hmm. If you would just raise your arm for me... that will do fine. Any pain at all? Any discomfort?'

'No.'

'None?'

'None,' Snow lied. He got the occasional twinge from all his old injuries, especially those caused by bullets, but letting the

303

SIS-contracted doctor know that wouldn't help with his operational status.

Snow was fit – above average, even by army standards – but by the ripe old age of thirty-six, he'd had one leg crushed in a car crash and the other punctured with a round from an AK74. This was in addition to a recent bullet to the right shoulder. Ten years separated the first and second set of injuries, but they had been caused by the same ruthless former Spetsnaz member.

The first injury had led to Snow prematurely leaving the SAS and the second set had caused him to be recruited by Her Majesty's Secret Intelligence Service (SIS), or as it was more widely but inaccurately known, 'MI6'. After rehabilitation of his injuries and a refresher course in the Welsh mountains, competing against the newest SAS Selection hopefuls, he had been passed fit for service.

'Medical over. You can get dressed now.' Durrani walked to the sink, removed his gloves, and unnecessarily washed his hands. He straightened his blood-red bow tie. 'How's Jack these days?'

The question took Snow by surprise. 'I'm sorry, Jack who?'

'Good, good, just checking – "Loose lips sink ships" as they used to say.'

'They also make for very bad saxophonists,' Snow replied as he quickly dressed.

'What? Oh, very good. Mind if I use that one?'

'Not at all.'

'Thank you.' Durrani smiled and opened the door. 'Well, all being "well", I'll see you this time next year. Goodbye.'

Snow knew better than to shake the doctor's hand. For a plastic surgeon, Durrani had a strange phobia of 'personal contact'.

Snow exited Durrani's examination room and couldn't help but glance at the pretty receptionist, dressed in her pure white uniform; he could make out the line of a black bra beneath. She smiled at him as he self-consciously looked away and left the building.

Harley Street was busy with lunchtime traffic, business people and a few lost tourists being given directions by a pair of Metropolitan Police officers. Snow headed north towards Regent's Park and the nearest tube station; he had a meeting with Patchem at their Vauxhall Cross headquarters. Snow cared little for London, although living there was a necessity. It was too noisy and too scruffy, especially compared to some other capital cities. But not Paris. Snow remembered his friend, Arnaud, half-French and always defending the homeland of his mother.

Arnaud had argued that Paris was the 'capital of Europe' with its grand architecture. Snow had retorted that the 'grand architecture' didn't make up for the pavements littered with dog shit and the stench of cheap cigarettes. He still blamed himself for what had happened. The events of eighteen months before, in Ukraine, had hit him harder than he had thought possible. Snow's mental scars, too, had been 'cosmetically repaired'. Involuntarily he touched his shoulder and felt for the bullet wound, now almost invisible but still aching. Snow had tried to save the life of a friend and failed.

A noise from behind broke his train of thought. A scream. Snow turned. A figure was standing outside Durrani's building, Middle Eastern or Asian. A voice inside his head tried to tell him something. Snow retraced his steps back towards the doctor's surgery, his eyes on the entrance. Another scream Snow broke into a jog. Two men left the building in a hurry; one had his face obscured by bandages. They joined the first, who had now moved from the building and was holding open the door to a waiting Ford Mondeo. There was an object in the hand of the last man to exit the surgery: a handgun.

The gunman looked directly at Snow, who was still running towards him, and pulled the trigger. There was a 'thud' as a suppressed 9mm round left the weapon and raced towards the SIS operative. Snow instinctively dived left, down the basement steps of the nearest building, crashing into several bins.

305

A car door slammed. Winded, Snow raised his head. The Mondeo was now 'four up' and pulling away south into traffic. Snow sprinted to the surgery, straining his eyes to see the registration number of the Ford. He had a decision to make: follow the X-rays or check the building.

Snow took the steps up, two at a time. The door to the communal hall was open, as was that to the surgery. He hoped beyond hope that he wouldn't find what he did. The receptionist lay sprawled back on her chair, her dress ripped open to expose her breasts. There was a neat bullet hole in her forehead and an explosion of blood on the cream wall behind. Snow swore, fury rising within. He kicked open the doctor's door and found that Durrani had also been executed. Lying at an acute angle across his desk, he had been double-tapped in the chest then shot once through the skull for good measure.

In a flash, Snow was back out on the street, mobile phone to his ear as he waited for the emergency services to connect him. There was a loud honking from further up the street. The Mondeo was still there, caught up at the traffic lights at New Cavendish Street. Snow had to reach it. He ran faster than before, switching his phone to video-capture mode. Snow heard raised voices from behind and turned. The two Metropolitan Police officers. One saw the open door and went up to investigate, the other followed Snow.

'Excuse me, sir… Sir, excuse me,' the officer shouted.

Snow continued to intercept the car, while the policeman quickened his pace, one hand on his helmet in what looked like a scene from the 'Keystone Cops'. Snow drew level with the Mondeo and looked in. Four men, Middle Eastern. The one with the bandages was now removing them; another held a handgun. As Snow aimed his cameraphone at them, a hand grabbed Snow's shoulder. Snow pivoted and flung his unknown attacker to the ground, his phone dangling by its carry cord. The police officer hit the pavement with force, his helmet spinning off into the traffic.

'Security Services,' was all Snow managed to get out, before a round zipped past his face. He fell to the pavement, the lights changed, and the Mondeo moved off. Snow tried to get to his feet but was forcefully pushed flat by the second officer, who had now caught up.

'Secret Intelligent Service. You're stopping the wrong person.' The second officer attempted to place his knee on Snow's chest. 'Stay still!'

'For the love of God…' Snow twisted and, using his right leg, swept the officer's legs out from under him. He sprang to his feet. The first officer, now standing, had extended his folding truncheon and was holding it in his right hand.

'Get down… down!'

'Get out of the bloody way!' Snow lurched forward and ducked inside the officer's advancing arm. He kicked the man in the back of the knee before ripping the truncheon from his hand and hurling it into the street.

Snow sprinted to the end of the road and at the junction reacquired the Mondeo, fifty metres ahead on Wigmore Street, stopped this time by a taxi. He heard sirens now, from Harley Street behind him, an armed response unit arriving on the scene given the sensitive Central London location. As Snow watched, the target vehicle raced off, mounting the pavement and breaking the speed limit. Snow turned and was met with a cloud of CS gas…

'You… sodding… idiots!'

Hands again tried to clamp him. Eyes streaming, Snow fought back, kicking out at the blurred shapes. One officer went down swearing, the other landed a punch. Snow lost control completely and shoulder-barged the second officer before delivering an uppercut to his unprotected jaw. Both officers were down, hurt.

'Listen to me!' Snow yelled. 'There's a kill team out there getting away. We need to call it in!'

'Armed police! Drop your weapon and lie on the floor, facedown.'

307

Snow shut his still-streaming eyes in disbelief. He slowly placed his phone on the pavement and lay down beside it. A black tactical boot kicked the phone into the gutter.

'That's HM Government property. You'll get a bill!'

'Be quiet now, please, sir.'

Gloved hands grabbed Snow's and pulled them behind his back.

His hands secured, Snow was searched before being hoisted to his feet. The tight plasticuffs bit into his wrists. The two 'beat bobbies' were looking none too happy.

'My name is Aidan Snow, I'm an SIS operative. Call Vauxhall Cross – they'll confirm who I am.'

'I'm sure we'll do that at the station,' the CO19 member mocked.

'Come along, please, sir,' a second added.

'An SIS officer is down and the shooter is getting away. Call it in!'

'Move!' The friendly tone evaporated.

Arriving at the secure police station, Snow was led to the front desk for processing. The duty desk officer looked up, unimpressed. The CO19 officer placed a clear plastic bag on the desk. It contained the contents of Snow's pockets, wallet and phone.

'Name?'

'I'm an operative for SIS. Call them.'

'Your name?'

Snow took a deep breath; they were only doing their jobs, all of them, if badly. 'Aidan Snow.'

'Right then, Mr Snow, if you'll just press your fingers there for me, we'll scan your prints.'

There was little point in resisting. Snow put his fingers on the scanner. He wasn't a fan of anyone having his personal information, let alone his fingerprints.

The desk officer looked at the screen and frowned. 'OK, we're going to put you in a holding cell until we can confirm your identity.'

Snow shrugged. He had no idea what had been on the scanner screen or even which database had flagged up, but he knew either way he'd be in for a wait.

'Any chance of a cup of tea?'

'Sure. How do you take it, shaken not stirred?'

If you enjoyed *Cold Blood*, then why not read the next books in the series?

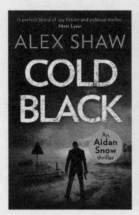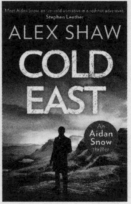